THE TALE OF
BRIAR BANK

THE TALE OF
BRIAR BANK

The Cottage Tales of
BEATRIX POTTER

Susan Wittig Albert

BERKLEY PRIME CRIME, NEW YORK

THE BERKLEY PUBLISHING GROUP
Published by the Penguin Group
Penguin Group (USA) Inc.
375 Hudson Street, New York, New York 10014, USA

Penguin Group (Canada), 90 Eglinton Avenue East, Suite 700, Toronto, Ontario M4P 2Y3, Canada
(a division of Pearson Penguin Canada Inc.)
Penguin Books Ltd., 80 Strand, London WC2R 0RL, England
Penguin Group Ireland, 25 St. Stephen's Green, Dublin 2, Ireland (a division of Penguin Books Ltd.)
Penguin Group (Australia), 250 Camberwell Road, Camberwell, Victoria 3124, Australia
(a division of Pearson Australia Group Pty. Ltd.)
Penguin Books India Pvt. Ltd., 11 Community Centre, Panchsheel Park, New Delhi—110 017, India
Penguin Group (NZ), 67 Apollo Drive, Rosedale, North Shore 0632, New Zealand
(a division of Pearson New Zealand Ltd.)
Penguin Books (South Africa) (Pty.) Ltd., 24 Sturdee Avenue, Rosebank, Johannesburg 2196,
South Africa

SEP 2 5 2008

Penguin Books Ltd., Registered Offices: 80 Strand, London WC2R 0RL, England

This book is an original publication of The Berkley Publishing Group.

This is a work of fiction. Names, characters, places, and incidents either are the product of the author's imagination or are used fictitiously, and any resemblance to actual persons, living or dead, business establishments, events, or locales is entirely coincidental. The publisher does not have any control over and does not assume any responsibility for author or third-party websites or their content.

Frederick Warne & Co Ltd is the sole and exclusive owner of the entire rights titles and interest in and to the copyrights and trade marks of the works of Beatrix Potter, including all names and characters featured therein. No reproduction of these copyrights and trade marks may be made without the prior written consent of Frederick Warne & Co Ltd.

PUBLISHER'S NOTE: The recipes contained in this book are to be followed exactly as written. The publisher is not responsible for your specific health or allergy needs that may require medical supervision. The publisher is not responsible for any adverse reactions to the recipes contained in this book.

First edition: October 2008

Library of Congress Cataloging-in-Publication Data

Albert, Susan Wittig.
    The tale of Briar Bank: the cottage tales of Beatrix Potter / Susan Wittig Albert.—1st ed.
        p.   cm.
    Includes bibliographical references.
    ISBN 978-0-425-22361-1
    1. Potter, Beatrix, 1866–1943—Fiction.   2. Women authors—Fiction.   3. Women artists—Fiction.
4. Human-animal relationships—Fiction.   5. Country life—Fiction.   6. England—Fiction.   I. Title.

    PS3551.L2637T345 2008
    813'.54—dc22

                                                                                            2008023610

For Bill, who knows how to spin a fine story,
with grateful thanks and much love

Fairy tales are more than true; not because they tell us that dragons exist, but because they tell us that dragons can be beaten.

G. K. Chesterton

HOLLY HOW

CUCKOO BROW WOOD

10

6

BRIAR BANK

Moss Eccles Tarn

OATMEAL CRAG

STONY LANE

WILFIN BECK

N

½ mile

NEAR SAWREY

8

7

5

11

3

2

1

4

9

1. Hill Top Farm
2. Tower Bank Arms
3. Courier Cottage
4. Meadowcroft Cottage
5. Anvil Cottage Bakery
6. Post Office
7. Belle Green
8. Briar Bank House
9. Tidmarsh Manor
10. The Brockery
11. Tower Bank House

Cast of Characters

(* indicates an actual historical person or creature)

People of the Land Between the Lakes

Beatrix Potter* is best known for the series of children's books that began with *The Tale of Peter Rabbit*. She lives with her parents, *Helen and Rupert Potter*, at Number Two, Bolton Gardens, in London. She owns Hill Top Farm, in the Lake District village of Near Sawrey. *Mr. and Mrs. Jennings* and their three children live in the Hill Top farmhouse and manage the farm while Miss Potter is in London.

Will Heelis* is a solicitor who lives in the nearby market town of Hawkshead. He is a frequent visitor to Near Sawrey.

Sarah Barwick operates the Anvil Cottage Bakery in Near Sawrey.

Captain Miles Woodcock, Justice of the Peace for Sawrey District, lives in Tower Bank House.

Dimity Woodcock Kittredge, Captain Woodcock's sister, recently married *Major Christopher Kittredge*, the master of Raven Hall. The Kittredges adopted *Flora* (the foundling child whose story is told in *The Tale of Hawthorn House*) and are now expecting a baby.

Mr. and Mrs. Sutton live with their children at Courier Cottage. Desmond Sutton is the local veterinarian. His wife Rose keeps the clinic's books and looks after her family. *Mrs. Pettigrew* cooks and keeps house. *Deirdre Malone*, fifteen, takes care of the Sutton children: *Libby*, twelve; *Jamie*, eleven; *Nan*, ten; and five smaller Suttons.

Mr. Hugh Wickstead (recently deceased) was an eccentric collector of antiquities who lived at Briar Bank Cottage with his sister, *Miss Louisa Wickstead*. The staff at Briar Bank includes *Billie Stoker*, the gardener, and *Mrs. Stoker*, cook-housekeeper.

Sven Knutson, *Nicholas Smythe-Jones*, and *Joseph Adams* are visiting the village. Mr. Knutson and Mr. Smythe-Jones are staying at the Tower Bank Arms, the village inn and pub. Mr. Adams has taken a room with the Crooks at Belle Green.

Mr. and Mrs. Lester Barrow operate the Tower Bank Arms.

George and Mathilda Crook frequently take boarders at Belle Green.

Lydia Dowling runs the village shop in Meadowcroft Cottage—the shop immortalized by Miss Potter in *The Tale of Ginger and Pickles*.

Lucy Skead is the village postmistress. She lives with her husband *Joseph* (the sexton at St. Peter's, in Far Sawrey) at Low Green Gate Cottage.

John Braithwaite is the constable for both Near and Far Sawrey; he and his wife *Hannah* live at Croft End Cottage.

Caroline Longford, fifteen, lives with her grandmother, *Lady Longford*, at Tidmarsh Manor. Also at Tidmarsh Manor: Caroline's governess, *Miss Cecily Burns*.

Creatures of the Land Between the Lakes

Tabitha Twitchet, President of the Village Cat Council, is a calico cat with an orange and white bib. *Crumpet* is a handsome gray tabby cat and Tabitha's rival. *Felicia Frummety* is a ginger cat who lives with the Jennings family at Hill Top Farm. She likes to think that she was the model for Ginger, one of the two unbusinesslike shopkeepers in *The Tale of Ginger and Pickles*.

Rascal, a Jack Russell terrier, lives at Belle Green but spends his time making sure that the daily life of the village goes according to plan. *Pickles* is a fox terrier and Rascal's friend. He lives at Briar Bank House with Mr. Wickstead. Miss Potter cast him as the second shopkeeper in her *The Tale of Ginger and Pickles*.

Thackeray and *Nutmeg* are two guinea pigs intended by Miss Potter as a gift for Caroline Longford. They are meant to join *Tuppenny* and *Thruppence*, Caroline's other two guinea pigs.

Bosworth Badger XVII keeps The Brockery, an animal hostelry on Holly How. *Thorn*, a young badger of much promise, assists Bosworth. *Parsley* serves up fine meals from The Brockery kitchen, while *Primrose* manages the housekeeping.

Bailey Badger lives alone in a largely abandoned badger sett known as Briar Bank. Unknown to him for many years, he has had a tenant: *Thorvaald*, who is occasionally visited by his supervisor, *Yllva*.

Professor Galileo Newton Owl, D.Phil., is a tawny owl who conducts advanced studies in astronomy and applied natural history from his home in a hollow beech at the top of Cuckoo Brow Wood.

Kep* the collie is the Top Dog at Hill Top Farm, assisted by *Mustard*, an old yellow dog. Other barnyard animals include *Winston* the pony; *Aunt Susan** and *Dorcas**, the Berkshire pigs; *Kitchen** the Galway cow and *Blossom**, her calf. The frequent absences of *Jemima Puddle-duck* are the subject of continued speculation.

THE TALE OF
BRIAR BANK

PROLOGUE

Number Two, Bolton Gardens
South Kensington, London

1 DECEMBER, 1909

Come not between the dragon and his wrath.
William Shakespeare, *King Lear*

"I can't quite see," Mrs. Potter said in a complaining tone, "why you feel you *must* go to the Lakes tomorrow—so soon after your last visit there." It was after nine, but Mrs. Potter was not an early riser. "Surely, there is nothing so urgent at that wretched little farm that it can't wait until after our dinner party. And then there's Christmas."

"But the dinner party is almost three weeks away," Beatrix pointed out. "I've already taken care of all the details— the guest list, the place cards, the menu, the shopping list. It's all done." She paused and added quietly, "And of course we never do anything special for Christmas."

Her parents were Unitarians and—to Beatrix's bitter disappointment—Christmas was always just another day at the Potter household. As a child, she would have loved to have a tree with candles and holly and ivy in the hall and mistletoe over the door. Now, grown up, she still longed, childlike, for the magic of the holiday. While everyone else celebrated, she could only watch. That was one of the reasons she desperately wanted to go to the village: to have a little taste of the holiday that the villagers enjoyed so much. The houses would be decorated with green ivy and hollies laden with red berries. There would be carols in the lane, and hopeful children waiting for Father Christmas, and perhaps even snow. Beautiful snow, white and clean and magical, nothing at all like the dirty brown stuff that occasionally fell on London, clogging the streets and creating a catastrophic mix of motor-lorries, horse-drawn hansoms, delivery carts, and struggling foot-travelers. Snow in London was a disaster. One never wished for it.

"It doesn't matter about Christmas," Mrs. Potter said, straightening the pink coverlet over her knees. "It's the dinner party I'm worried about."

"I'll only be gone a fortnight," Beatrix said in a soothing tone. "You will scarcely miss me."

"But I need you *now*," Mrs. Potter complained, her voice rising petulantly. "And I do worry about you, you know, out there in that old farmhouse in that remote village, miles from civilization. Anything could happen." She put her hand to her forehead and shuddered. "After that appalling murder at our lovely old home just last month—Oh, it doesn't bear thinking about!" She closed her eyes.

For once, Beatrix had to agree. She had always loved visiting Gorse Hall, the lovely old family home at Stalybridge, near Manchester, where her mother had grown up. After

Grandmother Leech died, the big old house had sat vacant for a long time. It was finally sold to a local builder and mill owner, who gave it to his son—George Harry Storrs—as a wedding present. Unbelievable as it seemed, Mr. Storrs had been murdered in the house the previous month, stabbed to death by an intruder.

"I know, Mama," Beatrix said with a sigh. "But what happened at Gorse Hall is hardly likely to be repeated in my little village. And in any event, terrible things occur right here in South Kensington. Why, just last week, a woman was—"

"Don't be disagreeable, Beatrix," Mrs. Potter snapped. "You are not to go, and that's my final word. Your father is of the same opinion—he said as much to me last evening." She sighed heavily. "He is so impatient and ill-tempered these days. I must have you here to keep him amused. Now, be a good girl and tell Lucy to bring up my tea and toast straightaway. This odious business has given me a headache, and you know I'm a martyr to migraines. I shan't come down to breakfast."

"Yes, Mama," Beatrix said. She took a deep breath and straightened her shoulders. When her mother got into one of these states, she was a perfect dragon, and there was no point attempting to make her see reason. One simply had to state one's intention, get on with doing whatever one meant to do, and leave her mother to her wrath.

"I am sorry for any inconvenience my absence may cause you, but I shan't be changing my plans. Now I must be on my way, or I shall miss my train." With an effort, she smiled. "Goodbye, Mama. I'll write as soon as I arrive at Hill Top."

"You are the most *obstinate* girl I have ever known!" Mrs. Potter cried, her voice rising on each word. "Why must you always put yourself before others? If you are murdered in your bed, don't blame me, Beatrix! I told you so!"

But she was shouting at the door, for Beatrix had already closed it, quietly, with scrupulous politeness, behind her.

Now, if you are thinking that mothers should not talk to their children (whether little children or grownups) in this disagreeable way, I will tell you that I heartily agree. It is true that many Victorian mamas of Mrs. Potter's social class were in the unfortunate habit of treating their spinster daughters as if they were servants. Beatrix's mother, however, carried the habit to an extreme, expecting her daughter to tend to all the tedious household details as well as make herself available whenever she was wanted.

But no matter how hard Beatrix tried, she could not satisfy her mother, who seems to have been by nature an unhappy woman. In the numerous family photographs taken by Mr. Potter, Mrs. Potter's dark hair is always pulled back into a severe bun and the corners of her mouth are drawn down in an unfailingly disagreeable expression. Perhaps you have known people like this, who are out of sorts even when things are going well, and when things go badly, have a special knack for making everyone around them feel exactly as miserable as they do. I think we may forgive Beatrix—who had the gift (or perhaps it was a curse) of seeing people as they were and not as they tried to seem—for picturing her mother as a perfect dragon.

But that is not how Mrs. Potter saw herself. Not at all! In fact, she quite confidently understood herself to be perfectly superior to everyone else in the world, with the possible exception of Queen Alexandra and the Royal Princesses (and on some days she felt herself superior even to *them*). That was why she had been so utterly, appallingly mortified when her daughter (her only daughter!) received a marriage proposal from Norman Warne, a young man of no special consequence, connections, or fortune. A man employed in the printing trade, who earned his living by making and selling Beatrix's storybooks. Indeed, had not Mrs. Potter warned Mr. Potter from the beginning—the very beginning, when Beatrix began to think of commercializing her hobby—that those foolish little books were bound to cause trouble? Drawing pictures was one thing, and certainly respectable enough, even admirable, as a hobby. Selling them was quite another. Selling was so indisputably *vulgar*.

So the marriage proposal was patently absurd, quite out of the question, and Mrs. Potter (and Mr. Potter, too, of course, for he always agreed with Mrs. Potter) had quite rightly insisted that it be rejected, immediately, firmly, and finally. But Beatrix had an unfortunate obstinate streak (in this, she took after her Potter grandmother) and proved even more perverse than usual. The foolish girl not only refused to reject the proposal, but insisted—*insisted, mind you!*—on accepting it, along with a mean little ring. She could not be persuaded to yield on the matter, only to agree that there would be no immediate public announcement of the engagement.

Mrs. Potter felt this, at least, with a dizzying relief, for if the announcement had appeared in the *Times*, everyone who was anyone would know what an inferior person the Potters' daughter meant to marry. It would have been a social humiliation from which the Potter family could never recover. The appalling business had to be kept secret until Beatrix could be brought to see reason.

There was no telling what might have happened, or how low the Potters might have been brought, socially speaking, by their daughter's wretched insistence on having her own way. But fate intervened, and they escaped the appalling situation by a stroke of great good luck, or at least, that's how Mrs. Potter saw it. Beatrix's suitor (she could not bear to think or speak of him by name) fell ill and died, quite suddenly, only a month after he had caused the up-roar. Very sad for his family, of course, and as a Christian, one had to regret the loss. But as a mother, Mrs. Potter offered thanks and rejoicing to a gracious heaven, only just barely managing not to do this where Beatrix could hear her. The importunate person was dead, the Potters were safe once more, and life in Bolton Gardens could go on with its usual respectable sedateness, under no threat of change or up-heaval.

But only for a little. The fellow was scarcely buried when Beatrix took it into her head to do another unthinkable thing. She had purchased a neglected farm in an unfashion-able village located in an out-of-the-way corner of the Lake District, where there was no Society of any significance what-soever and nothing at all to recommend it but some pretty views of mountains and lakes.

Of course, it would have been one thing if Hill Top Farm had been merely an investment, even a bad investment. Women were not expected to have a very good head where property was concerned, after all, and Beatrix might have been forgiven for making a financial mistake. But it was alto-gether another thing when her daughter, having transferred her affections from an unsuitable person to an unsuitable place, began to behave as though she considered the farm the dearest place in all the world. She announced that she meant to renovate the old house and rebuild the barn and add to the flocks and herds (pouring money down a rat hole, in her mother's opinion) and spend all her spare time there. And then—*and then!*—she bought yet another run-down farm in the neighborhood, and was constantly writing to Jennings, her farm manager, and to the solicitor who had handled the purchase—Heelis, his name was—about the place, which seemed to require a great deal of repair and renovation.

So whenever Beatrix announced her intention to travel to the farm, Mrs. Potter did her best to raise as many objections as possible, as fervently as possible, and insist that Mr. Potter object as well. From her point of view, this was absolutely necessary, to keep Beatrix from shirking her responsibilities and running off to the country every few weeks.

But Beatrix saw it all very differently, of course. Wouldn't you, if you were in her shoes? As far as she was concerned, her mother was simply attempting to assert a dictatorial authority, as she had done throughout the whole of Beatrix's life. The only way to resist was to do as she must, as quietly and as firmly as necessary. Hold fast to her intention, and the unpleasantness would be severe and distressing but short-lived. Give way once, and every future battle would be lost.

So Beatrix (who was truly a dutiful daughter and couldn't help feeling guilty for having replied as she did) went down to the kitchen to ask Mary to take up tea and toast, then climbed back up the stairs to her third-floor bedroom to pack her bag. In earlier years, her animals—the mice, rabbits, hedgehogs, and guinea pigs she used as models for the drawings in her little books—had always gone with her when she traveled. At the moment, she had no pets of her own, only a pair of guinea pigs named Thackeray and Nutmeg, whom she was taking to her young friend Caroline, at Tidmarsh Manor. She popped the little creatures into a wicker traveling cage and fastened the lid. Then she sent the cage and bag downstairs and asked the coachman to drive her to Euston Station, where after only a little delay, the train for the Lake District appeared. Beatrix settled herself and her possessions in the railway carriage, the whistle blew three times, the engine let out a big puff of steam, and they were on their way north.

Beatrix closed her eyes and leaned her head against the

seat back with a smile, feeling as she always did that the train's shrill whistle signaled something magical: another escape, however brief, from dirty, dreary London and the prison of her parents' house. The railway journey would be a long one, and tiring, but every weary moment was worth it. She was riding a magic carpet to a world that was entirely her own, far removed from London and the dragons that dwelt there.

In the cage at Beatrix's feet, the two guinea pigs held conflicting opinions about the business. *"Hidy-ho, here we go, off on another adventure,"* Nutmeg squealed excitedly, as the car jolted from side to side on the bumping, humming rails. *"Where to this time, d'you suppose? And what shall we do when we get there?"*

"Who cares?" grumbled Thackeray, who was already sick to death of Nutmeg's childish chatter. *"Personally, I should prefer to arrive wherever we are going and stay. I do not care for adventures, and I am sick to death of being trundled from pillar to post as if I were a cabbage."*

Nutmeg, who loved adventures, was not darkened by Thackeray's gloom. She had been born in a hutch in Battlesea, then taken from her mother with the rest of her brothers and sisters, and the lot of them bundled off to market. They were sold to a pet shop in the West End of London, which was where she had met Thackeray, whose very long hair (long enough to trail on the floor all round) was black streaked with elegant silver. In fact, his hair covered both ends of him so completely that Nutmeg sometimes found it hard to tell whether Thackeray was coming or going. He was forever combing himself with an ivory comb that he kept in his pocket along with his pipe, tobacco, and gold-rimmed reading glasses. Nutmeg's shaggy fur, in contrast, always looked rumpled and unkempt, as if she'd just got up from a longish nap and hadn't yet found her comb. But she didn't mind. Her hair was a such lovely color—exactly the color of rich, spicy nutmeg—that she felt quite proud of it.

Thackeray (his full name was William Makepeace Thackeray, after the author of *Vanity Fair*) had lived a different sort of life altogether, having spent most of it as a friend and companion to an elderly gentleman named Mr. Travers, a collector of rare books. Thackeray and Mr. Travers had enjoyed many evenings together before the fire, reading and reflecting on fine literature, and Thackeray had from time to time assisted Mr. Travers in the cataloguing of his collection. Upon Mr. Travers' unfortunate death, Thackeray was crated up by Mr. Travers' manservant and taken to the pet shop in South Kensington, where (horror of horrors!) he was put up for sale in the shop window, like a common animal. He had suffered there for nearly a week in the company of an enthusiastic creature with unruly brown hair and the ridiculous name of Nutmeg, at the mercy of unmannerly children who made faces at him through the glass or (worse yet) raced into the shop and poked their grubby fingers into his cage.

But then Miss Potter had chanced to pass by. She noticed the guineas, bought them, and took them to her house in Bolton Gardens, which had been nice and certainly quiet enough, after the commotion of the pet shop and the humiliation of being put on display. Thackeray's only complaint was that Miss Potter neglected to provide any reading matter. For him, a day without reading was an empty day, with no sort of satisfaction at all. He had been driven to read the newspaper in the bottom of his cage, and counted it a good day when there was something beside the classified advertisements: *Flat to let, mod. cons., two flights, no pets* or *Ladies' hats for sale, straw, felt, fancy veils, all colors.* Not much food for thought there.

And now they were on their way again. Nutmeg was light-hearted and gay. But the bouncing made Thackeray even more short-tempered than usual, and he growled deep in his throat every time the train gave a lurch.

Hearing the noise, Miss Potter opened the top of the traveling cage and looked in. "All this to-ing and fro-ing must be a bit uncomfortable," she said, smiling down at them. "But I'm sure you'll like it where you're going. A pretty young girl is waiting for you at Tidmarsh Manor. There'll be a lovely garden, and an outdoor hutch under the trees, and two other guineas, very nice ones. Their names are Tuppenny and Thruppence."

"*Tuppenny and Thruppence!*" Nutmeg exclaimed. "*What clever names!*"

Thackeray rolled his eyes. "*Clever, very clever,*" he muttered darkly. "*Small change. Exactly the sort of clever names a clever lady would give to a clever little pair of guineas.*"

"*Really,*" sniffed Nutmeg, "*it would be nice if you were a little less sarcastic. Life is such an amazing adventure—we should all enjoy every minute of it.*"

"*Sarcasm is in my nature,*" retorted Thackeray. "*And I for one could wish for a little more thoughtful conversation in those around me. I could also wish,*" he added sulkily, "*that the clever lady had thought to bring a newspaper.*" The bottom of the cage was bare. "*I miss the* Times. *Mr. Travers and I used to read it at the breakfast table.*" He sighed regretfully. "*I miss the breakfast table, too. We always had eggs and sausages.*"

"Have some sunflower seeds, my dears," said Miss Potter, taking a small sack from her bag. "Perhaps they'll make you feel better." She put down a piece of folded newsprint in the bottom of the cage and spilled the seeds onto it.

Now, it may seem strange to you that a grown-up lady would bother to talk to a pair of guinea pigs, but Beatrix did not consider this at all unusual. As children, she and her younger brother Bertram had collected animals, observed them, sketched them, held conversations with them, and told stories about them and to them. There had been Benjamin and Peter, fine rabbits both; Punch, the green frog; Judy, the adventurous lizard from Ilfracombe; a very dear hedgehog named Mrs. Tiggy-Winkle; a ring snake and some silly snails and any number of mice. Beatrix had been devoted to her animal friends in those long-ago nursery days, and still cared deeply for them. Not in a sentimental way, though, for she had always taken a scientific interest in her animals, watching closely in order to draw them, and listening intently in order to learn their ways, as any naturalist would do. Now, she took the same sort of interest in the animals who lived on her farm, the Herdwick sheep and the Galway cows, the pigs and chickens and ducks and dogs and cats, each of whom had its own habits, its own special interests and concerns. If she had any talent as a farmer, she often thought, it came from caring enough about the animals to pay them a close and careful attention.

Beatrix closed the cage and looked out the railway-car window at the landscape flashing by. She, too, was growing tired of to-ing and fro-ing. She had always liked to travel—the childhood holidays she and Bertram had spent in Scotland were among the sweetest memories of her life—and she loved getting away to the Lake District, where she could spend happy days at her farm, walk through the moors and fells, and get reacquainted with the villagers. But her pleasure was always shadowed by the knowledge that the days would fly past and soon she would have to go back to Bolton Gardens, where the tall, gloomy house seemed to smolder with her mother's anger and her father's impatience. She sighed. It was too bad, really, that she couldn't escape from her prison without thinking how soon she would have to return, and how gloomy and wretched she would feel when she got there.

But Beatrix was by nature a cheerful and optimistic person, so she put Bolton Gardens firmly out of her mind and began to think ahead to the pleasant chores that awaited her. There was plenty to think about, too, not just at Hill Top but at Castle Farm, which had been sorely neglected. Her new purchase was going to require all sorts of attention before it could be what it once had been.

Nutmeg was also thinking ahead. *"Tuppenny and Thruppence,"* she mused happily. *"Why, that will make four of us, enough for a party or a picnic—even a parade! And there's a garden and an outdoor hutch. Won't that be* fun.*?"*

But Thackeray, who wasn't interested in parties or picnics and detested parades above all other things, did not answer. He had put on his reading glasses and was sitting in the corner, studying the editorial page of the *Times*.

1

Miss Potter Arrives

It was a sunshiny morning when Beatrix began her journey from London to the Lakes, with bright skies and a mild southern breeze that might tempt one to take a longish walk or even a picnic to the park. The calendar declared it to be December, but there had not yet been a hard frost, and the gardens were still green.

But the train had scarcely left the station on its eight-hour journey to the north than the weather took an extraordinary turn. An hour into the trip, the sky turned a dark pewter-gray. Two hours, and a fierce north wind began to blow. Three hours, and it was raining. Five, it was sleeting, and in the next hour the sleet blossomed into fat white flakes of snow. By the time the train puffed into the Windermere Station, the temperatures had tumbled and the mercury had dropped straight into the bottom of the thermometer and huddled there, as if wondering if it could ever get up the courage to rise again.

The Lake District was only some 250 miles north of London, but when Beatrix alighted from the train at Windermere Station, she felt as if she had stepped into a different country. The ground was covered with a thick white snow and swirls of snow filled the air. The December wind had stripped November's leaves right off the trees, so that the poor things stood naked and shivering, with nothing to protect their bare limbs from the blast. The sun, not liking what it saw, went away to hide behind a bank of very thick gray clouds, where it could get on with its business without having to be bothered by the look of things below.

But while the other passengers complained mightily about the unexpected arrival of winter and its interference with their carefully laid plans, Beatrix was not troubled in the least. She loved the crisp, chill air, the clean white blanket that the storm had tossed over the summer-weary grass, and the brisk crackle and crunch of snow underfoot, so different from the ugly sulfurous stuff that fell on London. As she saw her bag and the guinea pigs' cage onto the horse-drawn charabanc, she congratulated herself on having worn a warm woolen coat and sturdy boots and packed a thick hat, muffler, and mittens. She was not surprised when the charabanc reached the ferry across Lake Windermere and several lightly clothed travelers chose not to hazard the crossing, for the waves were a white-capped fury blown straight down the lake by a howling north wind.

But Beatrix was determined to get to Hill Top, and the little steam ferry chugged and puffed so sturdily that they reached the far side without mishap (although Thackeray didn't think so, for he was feeling quite seasick). By the time the horses pulled the charabanc to a stop in front of the Tower Bank Arms in Near Sawrey, the road was drifted hedge-to-wall with knee-deep snow. Dark had already fallen, and Spuggy Pritchard, who came to carry her bag, led the way with a lantern as they climbed the steep, snow-covered path to the farmhouse. But as Beatrix followed, she felt neither cold nor weary, and if she shivered, it was from excitement. The unusual weather had turned the tedious trip into a grand adventure, and she was almost home.

But the very best moment of all came when she stepped inside the Hill Top farmhouse and closed the door on the snowstorm outside. The room was brightened by an oil lamp on the table and warmed by a comfortable fire in the fireplace, laid and lit by Mrs. Jennings, the wife of the farmer who managed the farm in Beatrix's absence. A bubbling pot of lamb stew hung over the fire, a kettle steamed on the hearth, a fresh loaf of crusty bread waited on the table, and chucks of cheese and a fresh apple and a pear lay on a plate. The shadows flickered a welcome against the ceiling, the dishes in the old oak cupboards winked and gleamed happily, and the scent of lemon oil polish brightened the air.

Beatrix took off her coat and hat and hung them on pegs beside the door. Then she picked up the wicker cage and put it by the fire. "First things first," she said with a smile. "I imagine you two must be very tired and hungry." She opened the cage and took out the two guinea pigs, one after the other, setting them in front of the fire. "Are you ready for something to eat?"

"*Oh, yes, please!*" squeaked Nutmeg happily, turning around to warm herself. "*Oh, Miss Potter, is that an apple I smell?*"

"*I suppose I could do with a bit of bread and cheese,*" allowed Thackeray, toasting his frozen toes. He had forgotten all about being sarcastic and seasick, and was only thinking how hungry he was, and that without any trouble at all, he could manage a sandwich or two.

Beatrix glanced at the table, which was covered by a bright

red-and-white-checked cloth. "I think an apple, a bit of bread, and some of Mrs. Jennings' cheese would be just right. I'll fix you a plate."

And in less time than it takes to tell it, she had set a plate on the floor for her friends. For herself, there was a bowl of hot lamb stew, with buttered bread and slices of cheese and a fragrant ripe pear. Then she tucked up her skirts, joined Thackeray and Nutmeg on the blue rug in front of the fire, and they all ate hungrily while the rowdy, raucous north wind howled down the chimney, rattled the door latch, and huffed and puffed at the windows, trying to find a way in. But they were safe and warm. And Beatrix, home at last where her heart belonged, was quietly, ecstatically happy.

Thackeray licked the last bit of cheese from his paw. *"Well,"* he said grudgingly, *"I suppose things have turned out as well as might be expected. For the time being, anyway, although who knows what will happen tomorrow."*

"Tomorrow?" Nutmeg squealed excitedly. She glanced up from the slice of apple she was nibbling. *"Why, all sorts of wonderful things might happen tomorrow! Just look at us now, Thackie, old fellow. We're having a picnic. Tomorrow, there might be a parade!"*

Thackeray growled.

2

A Long Chapter in Which
We Meet the Villagers

Margaret Nash, Joseph Skead,
and Lydia Dowling

The next morning, everyone in the Land Between the
Lakes—that is, that part of northwestern England that lies
between large Lake Windermere on the east and little Esthwaite Water on the west—woke up to a remarkable change
of seasons.

Winter sometimes arrives here with astonishing sudden-
ness, on the breath of a storm that glazes the lanes, freezes
the lakes, and blankets the gardens with snow. In this case,
the winter storm was born from a blizzard somewhere over
Greenland, then gathered itself together and blew all the
way across the Arctic Circle and the gray North Atlantic,
howling like a banshee and whirling like a dervish and in
general finding that it was content to be doing exactly what
it was doing and did not want to stop anytime soon.

And since the temperature had dipped below freezing, the snow happily and quite rightly refused to melt as it fell, so that there was an amazing lot of it, draped and folded and tucked like a wooly white shawl over the rugged fells and moors and across the huddled shoulders of the quaint little village of Near Sawrey. When the snow stopped falling at last, the dark slate roofs of the houses were frosted with white, like so many iced Christmas cakes arranged in a row on either side of the frosted lane. The blue smoke curled from the white-capped village chimneys like the breath of winter. And on the other side of Esthwaite Water, the pretty, snow-belted lake that lay at the foot of the snow-mantled village, the hunched figure of Coniston Old Man—that famous fell—was a dark gray bulk against a pale gray sky.

For the villagers, the snow was a source of both wonder (it was unquestionably beautiful) and irritation (it got very much in the way of things that needed doing). The children, of course, were delighted, for the snow ensured that Father Christmas could not fail to make his rounds on the magical night, and that the Christmas pageant at St. Peter's (to be held the following week) would be wrapped in the all-white wizardry of snow. They hurried to finish their breakfasts and put on their wellies and their mittens and mufflers and run out to make snowmen, for word had gone round the night before that there would be no school today. Even the grownups who had to trudge through the snow to tend to their farm animals or go out to the village shop to buy a necessary something-or-other—even *they* had to stop often, gazing in sheer astonishment at the way the snowfall had transformed their village.

And a surprising number of people—little Nutmeg might have called it a parade—were out and about on this snowy morning, making their way along the Kendal Road and up and down Market Street.

Margaret Nash, headmistress at Sawrey School, set off early for the walk to the school house at Far Sawrey. The villagers knew that school was closed, but Margaret feared that the outlying farms might not have got the message. She planned to unlock the door and fire up the stove so the children could warm themselves before they started back home.

Also on his way to Far Sawrey was Joseph Skead, the sexton at St. Peter's. He needed to check the church for storm damage and to dig Mr. Wickstead's grave—not an easy task, with all this snow. Joseph hated winter burials. It was his opinion that if people had to die, they ought to wait until spring, when the ground had thawed and the digging was easier.

But Hugh Wickstead had not waited. The victim of a tragic accident in the woods the previous week, he had been found, unconscious, under a fallen limb, not far from Moss Eccles Lake. No one knew exactly what had happened, for his only companion on that fateful night had been his fox terrier, Pickles, who had run back to Briar Bank House to fetch help. Mr. Wickstead was carried home, speechless and insensible. He died not long after, and now Joseph had to dig his grave.

Mr. Wickstead was weighing heavily on Joseph's mind as he trudged past Meadowcroft Cottage, at the corner of Market Street and the Kendal Road. He waved when he saw Lydia Dowling sweeping the snow from the path to her shop. A ginger cat sat on the stoop behind her, careful not to get her paws wet.

"A girt surprise, t' snow, wudsta say, Mrs. Dowling?" he called, in the Lakelanders' dialect. "Not too good fer business, I fear."

"Not at all, Mr. Skead," Lydia replied amiably. "I've already

sold two pair o' mittens, a can o' paraffin, a ha' dozen candles, an' a fine sausage for Mr. Llewellyn's dinner. When t'
snow comes, folks wants their comforts."

"That's right, Mr. Skead," said the cat, whose name was
Felicia Frummety. *"We've had several customers this morning."*
Like most of the cats in the village, Felicia had a home (hers
was with the Jennings family at Hill Top Farm). But she
preferred Lydia Dowling's shop, where people came and went
and often spent a moment to admire the gold ribbon Mrs.
Dowling had tied around her neck. Felicia was a cat who appreciated admiration.

Lydia leaned on her broom, regarding Mr. Skead soberly.
"Hast tha dug Mr. Wickstead's grave yet?" The proprietress
of the only shop in the village, she was the nexus of the local
news—she and Mrs. Skead at the post office. Others would
be asking the very same question, and Lydia wanted to have
the right answer.

"Ah, poor Mr. Wickstead," said Felicia sympathetically. She
licked a paw and smoothed the fur of one ear. *"It was a terrible thing."*

"T' grave'll be done by t' evenin'," said Joseph, looking up
at the sky, "unless there's another fall o' snow." He shook his
head gloomily. " 'Tis a sad business, struck down in t' woods
all alone, wi' nobody by." When Joseph died, he hoped that
his family and friends would be gathered around him, seeing
him off with a song, a cheering half-pint, and a plate of cheese
and sausage. "Bit of bad luck, 'twas, that tree comin' down in
a trice, sudden-like."

"Not hardly bad luck," Lydia retorted. "Or if that what
'twas, Mr. Wickstead brought it down on himself. T' curse
of t' treasure trove is what I sez."

"It's what everyone is saying, Mrs. Dowling," put in Felicia,
with a delicious shiver. Cats are superstitious by nature

(which is why witches and wizards find them so congenial, as you probably know). *"Buried treasure is always cursed. Dig it up and die."*

"Oh, aye, Mrs. Dowling," Joseph agreed readily. "'Twas t' curse wot done it, no doubt. But it's still verra sad. And now Lady Longford's hay barn's burnt, too. Hasta heard?"

"Aye," Lydia said. "Dust anybody ken how't happened yet?"

Joseph shook his head grimly. "A girt ball o' fire, they say, like a lightnin' strike, and a loud BANG, like gunpowder. Happened in an instant. Lucky thing 'twas just hay, nae cows nor horses."

"I don't suppose anybody has thought to count the barn cats," said Felicia in an ironic tone.

"Hush, Felicia," Lydia said. "But it couldna been lightnin', not in this weather, Mr. Skead."

"Oh, aye." He nodded. "But it was somethin', tha's for sure. A barn doan't burn by its ownsel, now do it, Mrs. Dowling?"

And having agreed on that score, they parted company. As Joseph waved goodbye and trudged off, Lydia noticed the ginger cat sitting on the doorstep. "Ah, Felicia," she said. "Wudsta like a saucer of milk?"

"I would indeed," Felicia replied. She nodded toward the shop window, decorated with a papier-mâché figure of Father Christmas, a holiday wreath, and three copies of a brand-new children's book called *Ginger and Pickles,* written and illustrated by Miss Beatrix Potter, the village's most famous personage.

"I see that my books are selling quite well," she added smugly. Felicia was never one to be silent about her accomplishments. The week before, there had been seven books in the window, and the week before that, a dozen. Miss Potter insisted that they be sold for a shilling, so that children might

buy them from their pocket-money. And they were quite small, fitted for small hands. Felicia approved.

Lydia smiled, glancing from the cat at her feet to the books in the window. "I suppose tha fancies tha'rt t' model for t' ginger cat in Miss Potter's book," she said indulgently, and bent to pet Felicia.

"Why, of course I'm the model for the ginger cat!" Felicia cried, full of indignation. *"That's why it's selling so well! Everybody wants to see pictures of ME!"*

"Everybody buys t' book to see t' pictures of my shop," Lydia said proudly, straightening. And as it happens, both Felicia and Lydia were right. Every family in the village had wanted a book to read and at least one more to give away for Christmas. The sales had added a gratifying number of shillings to the cash box behind the counter.

But as far as Lydia was concerned, having her shop in the book—a runaway bestseller all over England—was even better than the extra shillings. Miss Potter's shop didn't look exactly the same as hers, of course, for Miss Potter had added a bow window to the shop front, and instead of Lydia serving customers behind the counter, it was Ginger the cat and Pickles the dog. Their story, however, had come to an unhappy end, for they had imprudently allowed their customers too much credit and were finally forced out of business.

Which was exactly what should have happened, in Lydia's opinion. Credit was a very dangerous thing, forever getting people into trouble. Take Mr. Sutton, for instance, the village veterinary. He was having so much trouble collecting the money people owed him that he couldn't pay his own accounts—at least, so said Lucy Skead, the postmistress, through whose hands the bills and invoices inevitably passed. And Lucy ought to know, since she could never resist holding an envelope up to the light to see what was in it.

But taken altogether, Lydia fully approved of the book and was delighted that Miss Potter had chosen the shop as a setting. Her drawings were remarkably accurate, down to the scales and candy jars, the bottles of barley-sugar and boxes of peppermint rock on the counter; the deep-set windows; and the hooks in the ceiling where Lydia hung the sausages. And now her dear little shop was famous—just fancy all those thousands of books in the hands of readers all over the country! As Lydia went inside, closely followed by Felicia Frummety, both of them were basking in the reflected glory of *Ginger and Pickles*. And I daresay that you and I would feel exactly the same way, if Miss Potter had chosen your shop or mine to picture in her book.

Sarah Barwick, Lester Barrow, and Jerry the Coachman

On the other side of Market Street, across from Lydia's shop, stood the Anvil Cottage Bakery, owned and operated and lived in by Sarah Barwick. As Lydia and Felicia went inside and closed the door against the cold, Sarah herself came out of Anvil Cottage, wearing a brown woolen jacket, a green muffler, green knit hat, green mittens, and (surprising to some, but perhaps not to you) a pair of brown corduroy trousers, tucked into the tops of her galoshes. Sarah Barwick, as those trousers tell us, is the village's New Woman. Come rain, snow, or fine weather, she depends on no one but herself to do the things that need to be done. Two canvas bags were slung over her shoulders, one on each hip, and she was about to set off on her daily deliveries. Usually, she rode her green bicycle, but today, the snow made that impossible, so she set out on foot.

Sarah's first stop was at the Tower Bank Arms, the inn and pub on the other side of the Kendal Road. She had just gone round to the kitchen entry to leave three loaves of fresh bread with the cook when a charabanc pulled up and stopped, the four brown horses steaming with exertion. A stout, blond man in a brown caped great-coat climbed down and pulled his bag from the luggage rack.

"Hullo, Mr. Knutson," Lester Barrow said, taking the bag and carrying it to the door. "We're glad to have thi back wi' us." Sven Knutson had stopped at the inn the previous week and had reserved a room for several days this week.

"Glad to be back," Mr. Knutson said, in the accents of a Norwegian. "Lake's bad. Ferry's finished. Wasn't sure we'd make it."

Lester put down the bag. "Mrs. Barrow'll show thi upstairs," he said, and went back out to the charabanc, trailed by a fawn-colored Jack Russell terrier. "Tha'rt late, Jerry," he greeted the driver. "S'pose it's t' snow. A bad mornin', all round. What's this about t' ferry?"

"Shut down. Good thing I'm here at all," said Jerry, hunching his shoulders against the wind. "This'll be t' last trip this week, I fear." He glanced down at the dog. "G'mornin' to thi, Rascal, old chum. Snow up to thi bonny ears, eh?"

"The ferry's shut down, you say?" Rascal asked worriedly. He lived with the Crooks at Belle Green but patrolled the village regularly, even in the worst of weathers, making sure that everything was going the way it should. And if you've ever met a Jack Russell terrier, you know that they take their supervisory responsibilities very seriously. *"That's bad news!"*

Lester Barrow made a face. "Boddersome," he growled. Without the ferry to take them across, the only way people could get from Windermere to Near Sawrey was to go all the way around the top of Lake Windermere to Ambleside, then down the west side of the lake to Hawkshead, and east and south to Sawrey. He stamped his feet, warming them. "What's wrong this time?"

"T' boiler. Henry sez it'll take a week to mend." Henry Stubbs was the ferryman, and his predictions for the length of time it would take to repair the ferry could be counted on as gospel.

Lester Barrow whistled between his teeth. "A week! Nae so good fer bus'ness, I fear." The inn depended on travelers for its income. No ferry meant no customers.

"Think again, Mr. Barrow," objected Rascal. *"The inn might not fare so well, but you'll sell plenty of ale."* With nothing to do but sit by the kitchen fire and talk to their wives, the village men would probably come to the pub in droves. *"In fact,"* he added, *"if the brewer's drayman can't get here through the snow, you'll probably run out."*

"Just listen to t' lit'le dog," said Jerry admiringly. "Quite t' talker, he is. Anyway," he went on, "I wouldn't worry over-much about t' inn business sufferin'. Them that're here are here to stay, if thi takes my meanin'."

Lester brightened, for Jerry was right. In addition to Sven Knutson, the caped Norwegian who had come on the chara-banc, another gentleman had arrived several days before. It would be difficult to get away, so both guests would likely be here for the duration, occupying beds, taking meals, and enjoying a pint or two every evening. In short, spending money. Lester had nothing at all against *that*.

Jerry released the brake, preparing to drive off. "Knowsta awt 'bout auld Hugh Wickstead's inquest? God rest his soul," he added piously.

" 'Tis to be held late this mornin'," Lester replied. "Here at t' pub." Which was also good for the cash box. Drink could not be sold during the proceedings, but it would be sold before and after, and in plenty, for an inquest was thirsty work. He shook his head. "Ill luck, eh?"

"Oh, aye," replied Jerry mournfully, picking up the reins. "Ill luck fer sartain. Although there be plenty that say auld Wickstead brought it on hisself, diggin' up that treasure trove. From that minute on, t' poor fellow was curst."

"Plenty do say that," Lester allowed. For some weeks during the previous spring, the entire village had been alive with talk about the treasure that Hugh Wickstead was said to have found, buried somewhere in the fells. "A girt lot o' gold," it was whispered. "Rings and coins and a gold dagger and buckets o' gemstones."

"Worth a king's ransom, it was," Rascal remarked knowingly. He had the inside story on this, too, for Pickles—the fox terrier who lived with Mr. Wickstead—had been there when that gentleman uncovered the trove.

Mr. Wickstead himself was never asked if the story were true, so he did not have to go to the trouble of denying it, and after a while the rumors died down, as rumors do. But although not much had been heard of the treasure recently, the villagers, being highly superstitious, generally assumed that Mr. Wickstead was bound to encounter some sort of very bad luck, sooner or later.

"Ev'ry fortune buried below ground has got some t'rrible curse on it," they whispered. "Poor Mr. Wickstead is bound for verra bad luck." And when word of his death got out, no one was surprised, for they all understood the facts of the matter.

"Speakin' o' ill luck," Lester said, "t' hay barn at Tidmarsh Manor burnt to t' ground this morning. They say 'twas a lightnin' strike."

"Burnt down by lightnin'!" Jerry exclaimed, dumbfounded. "Nae, nivver! Not in this weather!"

Lester shrugged. "What else could it ha' been, Jerry?

Lanty Snig was milkin' at t' other barn, not fifty paces away. Said he saw a fireball. Barn went up like 'twas gunpowder set it off."

"Maybe 'twas," Jerry said. "Her ladyship's not best liked, tha know'st."

"Aye," Lester said. "But who'd burn her barn?"

Puzzled, Jerry shook his head. "Well, best be off," he said.

Lester raised his hand, Jerry raised the reins, and the charabanc lumbered off in the direction of Hawkshead, the horses pulling hard in the fresh snow.

Sarah Barwick, Mrs. Crook, and Lucy Snead

As Lester Barrow went into the Arms through the front door, Sarah Barwick came out by the back, crossed the road, and made her way up Market Street. Just as she reached Rose Cottage, next up from Lydia's shop, Grace Lythecoe raised the upper window and shook her duster.

Sarah waved and called out a greeting, but too late, for Mrs. Lythecoe had put down the window. Perhaps it was the icy wind. Or perhaps she had seen Agnes Llewellyn, who lives across the street at High Green Gate, peeking out from behind the lace curtain at her front window. It had not escaped the villagers' notice that Vicar Sackett had called upon Mrs. Lythecoe rather frequently of late, and that each visit went on a little longer than the visit before. Things had got to the point where people were beginning to wonder out loud just how much spiritual advice Mrs. Lythecoe (the widow of the former vicar and a devout Christian lady) really required.

Of course, if you know anything about villages and village gossip, I am sure you will not be surprised at Mrs. Llewellyn's peek-a-boo curiosity nor Mrs. Lythecoe's reluctance to linger at her window. Sarah Barwick, however, had lived in the city of Manchester before she came to Sawrey. She knew something of the wider world and was of the opinion that the villagers—whose world was distinctly narrow—were far too interested in other people's business. I daresay Sarah is right, although it is true that she herself likes to pass on the news whenever she feels like it (and never thinks of this as "gossip"). Anyway, neither Sarah's opinion, nor mine, nor yours, for that matter, will keep the villagers from saying and doing anything they please, so we might as well save our breaths.

With a smile and a coy wave at the nosy Agnes Llewellyn, Sarah went on her way up the street. She passed George Crook's smithy, where in fine weather George and his helper, Charlie Hotchkiss, worked out front, shoeing a horse or repairing a wagon wheel. Next came the joinery, where through the window she saw Roger Dowling (husband to Lydia Dowling, who ran the shop), putting the finishing touches on Hugh Wickstead's coffin. Mr. Dowling, the village's only joiner, was always called on when a coffin was required, which was rather infrequently, since the villagers were generally a healthy lot.

Sarah sighed, reminding herself that tomorrow was Mr. Wickstead's funeral and the funeral luncheon at Briar Bank House, to which Miss Wickstead had invited the village. 'Twas a pity that her brother had died so soon after the two of them—separated for many years—had at last been reunited. The villagers blamed his death on a curse, having to do with some treasure he was supposed to have found. But Sarah, an altogether sensible person without a superstitious bone in her body, dismissed such silly talk straight off. The question that bothered her practical brain was how she would manage to get to Briar Bank House, considering all this snow, and especially considering all her bundles and boxes. She was providing baked goods for the lunch.

With a wave at Roger, Sarah went on. Her next stop was Belle Green, at the top of Market Street, where she always left six hot cross buns, with two extra today because the Crooks had a boarder. But in the lane in front of Croft End Cottage, where Constable Braithwaite lived with his wife and children, Sarah met Mathilda Crook, on her way to the post office in Low Green Gate Cottage.

Seizing the opportunity to avoid a few extra snowdrifts, Sarah handed over the buns and took the path to Castle Cottage, her next port of call. But Mathilda Crook has some information that is important to our story, so we shall follow her instead. This is the advantage of being invisible spectators, isn't it? We can follow people without saying hello or bidding goodbye, and without giving any offense at all. Sarah will never know that we have chosen to accompany Mathilda. And Mathilda, that greedy creature, will never know that we watched her gobble down one of those six irresistible buns before she got to the post office, where she has gone to purchase a stamp.

"There," Mathilda said, pasting the stamp on the envelope and handing the envelope to the postmistress. She added the unnecessary instruction, in an officious tone of voice: "See that this gets into t' afternoon post, Lucy."

Lucy Skead, as everyone is aware, has never been able to let a letter pass under her nose without remarking to whom it is sent. She squinted at the address. "Howard Peasmarsh, Queen Anne's Gate, Lon'on," she read aloud. "Why, Tildy, I didn't know tha hast kin in Lon'on."

"Nae, not I," Mathilda replied, and lifted her chin. " 'Tis me gentl'man boarder, Mr. Adams. It's his letter I'm postin'." She leant forward over the counter and lowered her voice, although there's no one else in the room except for you and me, and we're standing behind the penny postcard rack where we're not noticed. "Mr. Adams has just come over from t' King's Crown, in Windermere, y'see, where he was stayin' last week."

"T' King's Crown," Lucy said, raising her eyebrows. "That's a smart hotel, it is. Belle Green 'ud be a bit of a come-down fer him, I'd say. What's he doin' here?"

"He's a famous photographer," Mathilda replied, putting Lucy in her place. Mr. Adams was clearly a cut above her regular boarders, like Charlie Hotchkiss, who worked at the forge with her husband, or the occasional cyclist and fell-walker who came to the Lakes on holiday. "He's here to take pictures."

"Oh, aye," said Lucy, nodding. "Pictures of what?" she added curiously. "S'pose he'll take a picture o' Lady Longford's burnt barn?"

"I doan't know, now, do I?" Mathilda frowned. Tell Lucy a thing, and it'd be around the village twice before teatime— although it wouldn't hurt for folks to know that the Crooks were entertaining a Famous Photographer who sent letters to his London business associates. "Be sure t' letter makes t' post. Mr. Adams was most urgent about it."

Lucy pressed her lips together. "Tell Mr. Adams that t' last post has already went fer t' day. For t' week, likely," she added in a significant tone. "T' ferry's shut down wi' a bad boiler. T' road above Aldgate was took out by a rockslide last night. And t' steam yacht that carries t' mail down Coniston Water is docked fer repairs."

Mathilda's eyes widened at this unexpected news. "Why, we're marooned!" she exclaimed. "As 'twere a desert island."

Mathilda is right, more or less. For if the road through Aldgate is closed, you cannot easily go north to Ambleside, and if the steam yacht isn't sailing, it will be difficult to go south—unless you go by the road, which you won't want to do in bad weather. The great mountains block the way west when the pass is filled with snow, and when the ferry isn't operating, there is no way across Lake Windermere to the east—although I daresay you might hire a sailboat if you are really determined. That is, as long as the lake isn't covered with ice, in which case even a sailboat won't serve you. You shall have to walk the mile across it, and risk the thin ice in the middle.

Lucy nodded agreeably. "Cut off from t' outside world, as 'twere," she said, adding, "I s'pose Mr. Adams'll be stayin' a few more days at Belle Green. Since he can't get away, I mean."

"I s'pose he will," Mathilda agreed, this happy thought having occurred to her at the same moment. Mr. Adams had paid in advance for only three days, but he might be forced to stay for a week or more, depending on the weather. She began to mentally inventory her larder. There was plenty of bacon for breakfast and apples for pie and the hens might be coaxed to lay an egg or two, but she should have to stop in at Lydia's shop and see about a few sausages.

Deirdre Malone and the Young Suttons

Mathilda was still tallying the contents of her cupboard when the door opened.

Lucy looked up. "Deirdre Malone," she said sternly, "tell that gaggle o' young Suttons to stay outside. I doan't need boots trackin' snow on my clean floor. Come in and be sharp about it. Tha'rt lettin' in t' cold."

Deirdre bit her tongue, wanting to say that the three older Suttons were not a "gaggle." She closed the door, handed over her package, and got in return a biggish bundle of post. Deirdre, who had just celebrated her fifteenth birthday, is

Irish, which I am sure you have already guessed from her green eyes, freckles, and tendrils of red hair escaping under her brown knitted cap. She is in the employ of Mr. and Mrs. Sutton, whose many children (eight at last count) require a great deal of looking after.

"'T' letter on top is t' third in three weeks from t' Kendal Bank," Lucy remarked in a meaningful tone. She leaned forward. "Our Mr. Sutton's not in trouble wi' t' bank, is he, Deirdre?" To the villagers, Mr. Sutton was always "*our* Mr. Sutton," quite understandably, too. He was a dedicated veterinarian, and they never hesitated to summon him when their animals were sick or injured, no matter whether it was midnight or broad day. They were not, unfortunately, quite so quick with their payments.

"In trouble wi' t' bank?" Mathilda exclaimed. Her eyes widened. "Folks'll be that sorry to hear it, they will!"

"Mr. Sutton is *not* in trouble!" Deirdre exclaimed tartly. "And it wouldn't matter if he was. His private affairs are nobody's business but his own."

"Mind thi tongue," snapped the postmistress, stung. "Tha's no call to come all over haughty-like, as if tha was a lady."

"And you've no call to go spreadin' rumors," Deirdre retorted, "as if you was a gossip." Her green eyes flashed fire as she turned to Mathilda. "Nor you neither, Mathilda Crook. I'll thank you both to keep your tongues in your mouths."

"Well!" Mathilda exclaimed, trying not to show that she was rattled by Deirdre's reprimand. "This is a pretty business, my girl."

"I am *not* your girl," Deirdre said, and left, closing the door smartly behind her.

Safely hidden behind the penny postcard rack, you and I may smile admiringly, for even though Lucy Skead and Mathilda Crook are reputed to be the worst gossips in the village, they are rarely rebuked for it—let alone by a girl, and Irish at that. But Deirdre Malone is an unusual young person, and often displays a remarkably spirited independence. She is used to fending for herself, and while she knows her place, she is not always known for keeping to it. What's more, she is fiercely protective of the Sutton family, mostly because she loves them, but also because she is very grateful to Mrs. Sutton for choosing her, out of all the other girls in the orphanage, to come to live and work at Courier Cottage.

We shall leave Lydia and Mathilda to speculate about that letter from the bank (and of course they will talk, rebuked or no) and follow Deirdre and the three older Suttons waiting outside the post office door. Barely visible beneath their mufflers and pulled-down hats, they turned out to be Lydia, twelve; Jamie, eleven; and Nan, nine, affectionately known to all as Mouse. They were at loose ends this morning, Miss Nash having dismissed Sawrey School because of the snow and being likely to dismiss it again tomorrow, to the despair of the mothers in the village and the great delight of the children.

Lydia, Jamie, and Nan celebrated their unexpected holiday with a running snowball fight. Deirdre might have joined in (she was, after all, only three years older than her oldest charge), but she was too troubled by the uncomfortable weight of the bank's letter in her coat pocket. For Lucy Skead had hit the mark. The letter was indeed the third in a month, and Deirdre—who had overheard Mr. and Mrs. Sutton discussing the dreadful situation—guessed that it must contain a final ultimatum. She was reluctant to hand it over, for fear of seeing Mrs. Sutton burst into tears again.

The children, unaware of this rising tide of difficulties, were delighting in the magic of the fresh, deep snow. Their noisy, good-natured battle raged from the top of Market Street nearly to the bottom—until Jamie's snowball hit the front window of the joinery, and Roger Dowling, in a fury, jumped up from Mr. Wickstead's coffin and yanked the door open.

"What dost tha young urchins think tha'rt doin', breakin' people's winders?" he roared. "Dost tha want me to tell thi father? He'll warm thi bottoms reet good, I'll warrant."

But thankfully, the snowball had not broken the window, just rattled it a bit. Deirdre made Jamie take off his hat and apologize like a man, then hurried her unruly charges in the direction of Courier Cottage. And while I am as eager as you must be to learn the contents of the letter from the Kendal Bank and to hear what Mrs. Sutton said when she read it, we shall have to leave that scene until later and turn our attention to Miss Potter.

She has just woken up on her first full day at Hill Top, and we don't want to miss a moment of her pleasure.

3

Miss Potter Entertains at Breakfast

At home in London, Beatrix was in the habit of rising an hour before breakfast. There were a great many household matters to supervise, as well as her mother's and father's needs to attend to. She often felt like lingering in bed, but if she didn't get an early start, she would never have time for her own drawing and painting.

At Hill Top Farm, however, Beatrix got not only an early start, but an eager one. She was always out of bed and dressed before the sun peered hopefully over Claife Heights, holding its breath until it saw that the village had survived the long, dark night and was fully prepared to rise to a new day. This morning, however, exhausted after the long railway journey, she slept late, and when she woke at last, she was not quite sure where she was. The light reflected on the beamed ceiling seemed brighter than usual, and the familiar farmyard sounds were strangely muted.

But when she heard Chanticleer greet the sun with a

jubilant crow and Kitchen, the cow, give a tender, chuckling *moo* to her calf, she realized with a shiver of delight that, yes, truly, she was at the farm. The day that lay ahead of her could be filled with all the country pleasures that she loved. She could draw and paint and write letters or bake something sweet or finish the mitten she was knitting, or practice spinning her own Herdwick fleece at the old spinning wheel she'd bought at a farm auction. And of course, there was the letter she'd promised to write to her mother—a chore that had to be finished before the afternoon post went.

But before she did anything else, she had to see the snow. Was it really as deep as it had seemed last night? Was it even deeper? She climbed out of bed, threw a paisley shawl over her flannel nightgown, and hurried to the window that looked out over the garden and the barnyard.

The magical sight made her want to reach straightaway for her paintbrush and watercolors. It was as if an energetic and magical Jack Frost—surely a painter at heart, don't you think?—had transformed the world into a fairyland, just for her. The clean, spare landscape below and beyond was a canvas brushed with a thousand shades of white, smudged with gray-blue shadows, and accented with sketchy charcoal lines of bare black trees and the occasional bright green and red of a holly bush. Snow frosted the branches of all the trees, covered the lane, and drifted over the garden wall. The white blanket across the barnyard was cross-stitched in brown by the narrow path Mr. Jennings had shoveled so he could feed the farm animals—the cows, pigs, and pony, the chickens and ducks—sheltering in the cozy stone barn. Tibbie and Queenie and their lambs, warm and dry in their wooly winter coats, stayed out in the meadows in all kinds of weather. They were Herdwicks, an ancient, hardy breed of sheep whose thick wool was coarse and wiry, perfect for long-wearing garments like the tweed skirt Jane Crossfield had woven for her.

Beatrix put on the skirt now, since it was the warmest thing she owned, and added a white cotton blouse, a green woolen jumper with handy pockets, green woolen stockings, and her serviceable leather clogs—pattens, they were called by the farm wives who wore them. She left her city shoes (leather, with inch-high heels and thin soles) in the closet. They weren't sturdy enough for the country, and besides, they reminded her of London. There, she was Mr. and Mrs. Potter's unstylish and unattractive spinster daughter, who supervised her parents' household and had managed to achieve some small measure of fame with her books for children.

But when she came to Hill Top and put on her tweeds and clogs, she was transformed as if by some mysterious, elemental magic into Miss Potter, countrywoman, farmer, shepherd. This was who she really was. This was where she truly belonged. And someday (how soon or how that might happen, she could not imagine), she dreamed of living here the year around.

Now, if you or I were as old as Beatrix and wanted to live in a house of our own, we wouldn't stand it for a moment, would we? We would pack our things, promise to write, and fly out the door to follow our hearts or seek our fortunes or whatever else we had in mind to do. But in Beatrix's time, an only daughter—especially if she had no suitable prospects for marriage—was expected to stay at home and take care of her parents. When she bought her own farm, Beatrix was attempting something very difficult. She was trying to do what her parents wanted *and* what her heart wanted. I daresay you will agree that this is not an easy task.

Downstairs, Beatrix poked up the fire in the grate, added several lumps of coal to the range, and filled the cast-iron kettle with water. She fed Nutmeg and Thackeray, put some fresh newsprint in the bottom of their cage, and moved it a little closer to the fire. In the chilly dairy-room at the back of the house she found what Mrs. Jennings had put out for her: a half-dozen fresh eggs in an earthenware crock, a bowl of fresh butter, and a pitcher of milk topped with a layer of thick yellow cream. She was measuring coffee into the coffeepot and wondering whether Mrs. Jennings might have some bread and bacon to spare, when she heard a knock at the door and Sarah Barwick's husky voice.

"Yoo-hoo!" Sarah called, and knocked again. "Bea, are you up yet? Spuggy Pritchard told me you'd got here last night, late. I've brought you some breakfast."

Beatrix opened the door and happily greeted Sarah, who was holding a packet of buns and a sausage wrapped in paper. "Well, you're a welcome sight," Beatrix said with a laugh. "I was just wondering what I should have besides eggs, and here you are, sausage and buns in hand. A fairy godmother."

"A fairy godmother with snow all over her boots," Sarah said ruefully, unfastening her galoshes and stepping out of them. She brushed the snow from her corduroy trousers. "It's quite some morning out there, I'll tell you. No bicycle deliveries for me today. The lanes are clogged with snow, and everybody who owns a shovel is using it. Margaret Nash has dismissed school, and the ferry is out and the steam yacht has shut down. Oh, and the roads north and south of Hawkshead are closed." And having delivered all of this information in one breath, she took a fresh one. "We're marooned, or as good as. Not even the post can get through."

"Not even the post!" Beatrix exclaimed, dismayed, thinking that she could not write to her mother.

And then, all of a sudden, she wasn't dismayed at all. If

she could not write to her mother, her mother could not write to *her*. And if the ferry wasn't working and the steam yacht was shut down and the roads were closed, she could not go back to London, no matter how urgently she was wanted. She would have to stay right here until the snow melted and the ferry was repaired, and if luck was with her, that might be a good long time. That knowledge made her feel incredibly light and easy, as if she had suddenly shed a burden she didn't know she carried.

"Right. We're stranded. But it's not too bad, if you like snow." Sarah smoothed her dark hair. Her face was long and narrow, her mouth wide, her nose freckled, and her eyes shone with intelligence and an irrepressible good humor. "I've been out and about for the past two hours, battling the snowdrifts and the cold, and I am hungry enough to eat a horse. You handle the eggs and sausage, Bea, and I'll manage the rest. We'll have breakfast in a jiffy."

Sarah was right. In a very short time, they were sitting down to a nicely laid hot breakfast, with eggs, sausage, buns, marmalade, orange juice, and coffee. Both were famished— Beatrix always felt much hungrier at the farm than she did in London—so they said scarcely a word whilst they ate their breakfast. When they had finished, Beatrix poured them each another cup of coffee with cream, eager to catch up on all the village news.

"What have I missed in the past month or so?" she asked. "I've scarcely heard from anyone. Both you and Dimity have been much too busy to write. Margaret Nash posted a thank-you note for some books I sent to the school, but didn't include any news. Jeremy Crosfield writes that he's doing well at school, but he didn't have any village news. And Mr. Heelis sends me word of the renovations at Castle Farm, but he never sends any gossip."

At the mention of Mr. Heelis, Beatrix noticed that Sarah's cheeks turned pink. She knew that her friend was nurturing a romantic interest in the handsome, well-liked solicitor. She wanted to know more—after all, he had helped her with the purchase of Castle Farm, and was very kind. She hoped for the best for him, and for Sarah, too, of course. Mr. Heelis was very tall and straight, with a shy smile and a look in his eyes that hinted at inward depths; Sarah was lithe and athletic, with an outgoing, friendly directness. It was easy to picture them together, and to think how nicely they complemented one another.

Beatrix gave an unconscious sigh. She was more than a little envious of Sarah, although she explained this to herself by thinking of Norman—it was Norman she missed. It had been four long years since she had lost him so suddenly, so devastatingly, only a month after their engagement. But she was a deeply loyal person. She tended Norman's memory like a hearth fire in her heart, warming herself by it, fueling it by rereading his letters to her, and never letting it die down. She owed that to him, and to herself.

Still, if Beatrix had been able to look just a little deeper into herself at that moment, she might have found someone else in her heart: Mr. Heelis, whom she pictured as one-half of a happy pair, with Sarah Barwick. However, I think it would have been very hard—perhaps impossible—for our Beatrix to acknowledge that what she felt for Mr. Heelis was anything more than friendly affection and gratitude for his help with her property purchase. How could she feel warmly toward another man without being disloyal to Norman, to the good work they had done together, to their hopes and dreams? And how could she feel warmly toward someone her friend Sarah cared for? That, of course, would be equally disloyal. Impossible, on two counts.

Sarah took a sip of her coffee. "As to news," she said, "well, there's Lady Longford's barn. But that's *new* news, since it just burnt this morning, very early."

"My goodness!" Beatrix exclaimed. "Did somebody overturn a lantern?"

"It was the hay barn," Sarah said. "Mr. Snig was milking in the cow barn, which is a little distance away. He said he saw a fireball, and then it just exploded. But other than that—well, let's see. Of course you know that Dimity's expecting." Their friend Dimity Woodcock had married Major Kittredge of Raven Hall the previous year, and the Kittredges had immediately started their family, so that their adopted Flora would have a playmate. "The baby should be here very soon now."

"I'm hoping for a boy," Beatrix said with genuine pleasure. "Flora needs a little brother."

Beatrix was speaking from personal experience, for she remembered her own delight when her brother Bertram was born and she had someone to love and look after. As well, she had a deep personal interest in Flora, the baby who had been left on the Hill Top doorstep. By a stroke of great good luck (or perhaps with the aid of some magic or other—who can tell about such things?), Beatrix had managed to discover the identity of Flora's mother and obtain her permission so that Dimity and Major Kittredge could adopt the baby.

But there. I shan't spoil the story for you. You can read it for yourself in *The Tale of Hawthorn House*, and be as puzzled as I am (I confess to not quite understanding the whole affair) about the intervention of the mysterious Mrs. Overthewall. She always seemed to be at exactly the right place at exactly the right time to make things happen in exactly the right way. You and I should be so clever.

Flora was now walking and babbling in her own little-girl language, and Major and Mrs. Kittredge loved her, and each other, very much, and the three were so happy together that only the birth of their expected baby could make them any happier. And even Captain Woodcock—Dimity's brother, who had at first opposed the match, preferring his friend, Mr. Heelis, as a husband for his sister—had to admit that he had been mistaken when he predicted that Dimity would rue the day she married Major Kittredge.

There it was again, envy! If Norman had lived and they had been able to marry, Beatrix knew that they would have been every bit as happy as Dimity and her major, and very likely happier. They might have had children, too, or perhaps they would have taken a baby or two to raise as their own. Norman found enormous pleasure in making toys and dollhouses for his nieces and playing games with his nephews. He would have been a wonderful father. And Beatrix would have loved to read her own little books aloud to her own little boys and girls, and hear them laugh at Jemima Puddle-duck and Ginger and Pickles and all the rest.

But Beatrix did not like to dwell on what could not happen or fret about things she could not change, so she pushed all these thoughts aside. She was determined to find her own happiness, whatever that was. And just now, sitting in the snug, warm room of her very own farmhouse, with the winter snow and the out-of-service ferry keeping the dragons of the world at bay, Beatrix felt that, while she could not be entirely happy, she was certainly contented.

4

In Which We Look into Sarah Barwick's Heart

Sarah Barwick, sitting on the other side of the table, caught a glimpse of her friend's contentment and was glad. After all Beatrix had been through, she ought to have some happiness. Sarah stole a glance, admiring the way Bea's unruly brown hair curled lightly around her forehead, the high color in her cheeks, and the brilliant blue of her eyes. There was something wistful about her look, though, something sad and far-away.

Well, she would be wistful, wouldn't she? Sarah thought. Rotten luck, her fiancé up and dying the way he had, just a month after they'd got engaged—although from little things Bea had said from time to time, she guessed that it would have been a while, years probably, before they could be free to marry. Proper dragon, that wretched old mother of hers! Mrs. Potter had better not come to Hill Top Farm, or Sarah would give her a piece of her mind. Not that the old lady would come, of course—she was much too toffy to dirty her dainty London shoes on a real farm. A great pity, too. Beatrix had put her whole heart and soul into this place. She'd made it beautiful and perfect, to Sarah's way of thinking, cozy and comfortable and everything looking exactly the way it should. And her mother refused to come and see it, the wretched old lady.

But nothing would be gained by letting on that she was thinking any of this, so Sarah lit a cigarette and crossed her trouser-clad legs. "I see you've brought a pair of pretty little friends with you on this trip." She nodded toward the two guinea pigs in their cage by the fire—one brown, the other with an astonishingly long black coat, streaked with silver.

"Did you hear that, Thackie?" Nutmeg, who had been telling Thackeray all about her mother and her brothers and sisters, interrupted her long story with a giggle. *"A pair of pretty little friends. La-de-da! I like that!"*

"We are not a pair," snorted Thackeray. *"And I am not pretty. Handsome, if you like. Intellectual. A book lover. But not pretty."* He wished crossly that his companion—if he had to have one—were more intellectual than Nutmeg. Failing that, he wished she would not talk so much. He wished she would not talk at all, actually.

"They are promised to Caroline Longford," Beatrix said, getting up to fetch the Queen Victoria ashtray. "I planned to take them to Tidmarsh Manor today, but I doubt that Winston and I could get up the lane." Winston was the Hill Top pony, responsible for pulling the pony cart wherever it was required. "Tomorrow, I think. P'rhaps we'll take the sleigh."

Sarah chuckled to herself, thinking that it was a good thing Winston hadn't heard of the possibility of a trip through the snow. He had his own opinions about where to go and when to get there. She'd wager he wouldn't much like the idea.

Thackeray didn't, either. *"Snow,"* he grumbled. *"All that bouncing and bumping on the train yesterday, and now a sleigh. Will there never be an end to it?"* He glanced down at the fresh newsprint and brightened a little. *"Although I do have something to read, even if it's only Mr. Churchill's latest speech in Parliament. I would rather have a book,"* he added loudly, directing his remark to Miss Potter. *"Gibbon's* The Decline and Fall of the Roman Empire *would be quite acceptable. All six volumes, preferably."* If he had a favorite book, it was this, partly because he enjoyed the footnotes but chiefly because it was so long that he had never quite got to the end of it. Other books seemed always to end just as he had become properly engaged with them.

"But don't you want to meet Tuppenny and Thruppence?" Nutmeg asked. She sincerely hoped that at least one of them would have a positive outlook on life. Thackeray was a dismal fellow. No sense of humor, always going off in a corner to read. What fun was there in a lot of words on paper?

"Two more fellow cell-mates?" Thackeray replied gloomily. *"I think not."* He began looking in his pocket for his reading glasses.

"Funny little creatures," Sarah said, getting up and going to the cage. She put her finger through the wire, scratching Thackeray. "It gets a bit lonely at Anvil Cottage," she said over her shoulder, "and I've been wanting a pet. I'm allergic to cats, but I've never been around guinea pigs. Maybe they'd be better for me than—OW!" She jerked her finger back. "It bit me!"

"I'm sorry, Sarah," Beatrix said contritely. "I hope he didn't hurt you."

"I thought I was scratching his rear end," Sarah muttered. "I had no idea I was anywhere near his teeth."

Beatrix chuckled. "It's a bit hard to tell which end is which, I'm afraid. And Thackeray is rather antisocial."

"I am NOT antisocial," Thackeray retorted loudly, retreating behind a large cabbage leaf. *"I prefer not to be scratched on the nose, that's all."* He sniffed. *"And I'd rather my fur not be singed, thank you very much."* (Before you blame Thackeray, you might try to understand his point of view. I daresay you wouldn't like it if a giant stranger, some fifteen or twenty feet tall, bent over and scratched you on the nose while you were looking in your pocket for something—especially if she were waving a burning stick that might catch your fur on fire.)

"It's just a nip," Sarah said, nursing her finger. She sat back down at the table. "Not to worry—although perhaps I shan't have a guinea pig, after all. A fish, maybe. Or a bird. I admire Grace Lythecoe's canary. Such a cheerful creature, Caruso, always warbling in the window when I walk past." She picked up her coffee cup, frowning at Thackeray. "Guinea pigs aren't good for much, I don't suppose."

Thackeray rolled his eyes. *"What does she expect us to do?"* he groused. *"Sing? Fly? Dance on our toes? Pull rabbits out of hats?"* He found his glasses, put them on, and retired with Mr. Churchill's speech, which to his pleasure proved just as full of bombastic language and unintelligible asides as *The Rise and Fall of the Roman Empire.*

"Speaking of Grace Lythecoe, I hope she's feeling better," Beatrix said. "When I was here last, she wasn't very well."

"She's better," Sarah replied. "I'm not much for gossip, you know." She paused, considered the truth of that claim, and added, "Unless it's really important, that is, in which case it's not really gossip, in my opinion." She pulled on her cigarette. "It appears that Grace and the vicar have struck up a special friendship. A romantic one, it's said. There are a great many opinions on the subject, as you can well imagine." She shook her head. "It's rubbish, of course. I wish people wouldn't be so small-minded. But quite a few don't approve."

"Whyever not?" Beatrix asked, puzzled. She tucked a lock of loose hair behind her ear, thinking that perhaps, next time, she would ask Sarah not to smoke in the house. "I shouldn't think a romantic friendship would trouble anyone, especially when it's between two such likable people."

"I don't understand it myself," Sarah confessed. "Grace is probably the most respected lady in the village, and Vicar Sackett, of course, is beyond reproach. It's Agnes Llewellyn who seems to have the most against it. She stands at her front window for hours on end, peering across the street, making notes on the vicar's comings and goings." She made a face. "You know Agnes. She's a terrible busybody. But they all are. The whole village. Give them the hint of a romance and they will speculate. Endlessly."

As of course they were speculating about herself and Mr. Heelis, Sarah thought with a half-ironic amusement. What a pity there wasn't anything worth speculating about.

Which was not Sarah's fault. Until she met Will Heelis, she was determined not to marry, being of the opinion (and saying so, too, repeatedly) that men on the whole weren't worth the turmoil and trouble they caused in one's otherwise well-ordered life. But Mr. Heelis had turned that determination on its ear. Sarah had lost her heart to him months and months ago at a dinner party at Tower Bank House, on the very night that Dimity and Major Kittredge had surprised everybody, especially Dimity's brother, by announcing their engagement. Mr. Heelis had been quite friendly and attentive, and she had decided on the spot that he would make a perfect husband (which I should have to say is probably pretty accurate, although the perfect husband for *whom* is the question).

Sarah always said of herself that she was not one to let the grass grow under her feet. So in this case, she had taken the initiative. She stopped in at the Heelis and Heelis Law Offices to say hello whenever she was in Hawkshead and attended events when she knew he'd be present, like the fairs and country dances. Mr. Heelis was an enthusiastic Morris dancer, quite handsome kitted out in his gay vest, his tie, his sash, and his hat. She loved to stand at the front of the crowd and applaud his performance.

And Mr. Heelis was interested in her, or so it seemed to our Sarah. He had asked her to be his partner when they had "happened" to meet at one of the dances Sarah had "happened" to attend. When she met him in the village (he was there quite frequently on business, or visiting his friend, Captain Woodcock), she would ask him to step into the bakery and would give him a sticky bun or a scone. Twice, she had encountered him when she was setting out on her delivery rounds, and it was the easiest, most natural thing in the world to invite him, and easy (or so it seemed) for him to say yes.

And not long ago, Mr. Heelis had even brought her a lovely bunch of wildflowers he'd picked, Michaelmas daisies and buttercups and fall asters. Wouldn't you think that was an open declaration of a romantic intention? Sarah certainly did, and had displayed his wildflowers in the bakery window until they wilted, after which she had dried and pasted them in a scrapbook, on a page hopefully encircled with little red hearts, with his initials and hers, intertwined.

But still he said nothing.

Sarah, however, was not the kind of person who gave up easily. Mr. Heelis was certainly very shy with women, although he got on quite comfortably with men. And as long as he remained friendly—and hadn't lost his heart to somebody else—there was hope. The villagers certainly seemed to think so, anyway. Every time Agnes Llewellyn came into the bakery, she'd ask if Mr. Heelis had stopped in lately and give Sarah a look, as if to say, "You don't fool me for one minute, Sarah Barwick! I know what you're up to with that good-looking fellow!"

And of course, Sarah always looked straight back at her, dead in the eye, daring her to come out and say it, right out loud. Which she never did. Agnes Llewellyn always said what she said behind people's backs, not to their faces. She probably thought that Sarah and Mr. Heelis were definitely up to something, and went straightaway to Elsa Grape or Bertha Stubbs and told them so.

Beatrix stirred her coffee. "I imagine the villagers are speculating about Castle Farm, too," she said quietly.

"Oh, absolutely," Sarah replied without thinking. "They're afraid that you're about to buy up the whole of the village and put everybody right out in the lane, bag and baggage." The minute the words were out of her mouth, she saw the hurt look on her friend's face and desperately wished them back.

"I'm sorry to hear that," Beatrix said with a sigh, but she was not terribly surprised. The villagers had never made a secret of their feelings about off-comers. They hated it when she first bought Hill Top Farm, partly because she was a woman (women should *not* own farms!) but also because she was from London and had no experience with farming. She'd hoped things would change when people got to know her. But whilst the Crooks and the Dowlings and the Stubbses might respect and even like her a little, she knew now that they would never feel as friendly and affectionate toward her as they did toward the other villagers. She would never quite belong, not in the way they did.

She didn't blame them, though, for she shared their

feelings about the land. She resented it when she saw people buying up Lake District farms, selling off the sheep and cows, and tearing down a lovely, centuries-old house in order to build a new and huge and ugly house in its place. If she had the money, she would buy every bit of property that came up for sale, just to keep the farms and houses from being destroyed. To her, even one farm lost was a tragedy.

In fact, she had hoped the villagers might even be glad that she had bought Castle Farm. She had likely saved it from falling into the hands of some greedy real-estate speculator from Liverpool or Manchester who would build a row of ugly cottages in the place of the lovely old house and its gardens and sell them off to people from the cities who would insist on "modernizing" the village and making things "convenient" and changing everything to suit their "up-to-date tastes." Which wouldn't do at all, for Beatrix loved the little village (in spite of itself) and wanted it to stay just as it was forever and ever.

"It's quite rotten of them to think such a thing, of course," Sarah said apologetically, wishing she hadn't been so blunt. Sometimes her tongue had no tact at all. "They have nothing whatsoever to base it on. But that's how they are. And they do worry about the village, about who's selling this or that and what's to become of it once it's sold. They weren't very happy, if you remember, that Miss Tolliver died and left Anvil Cottage to an off-coming female who turned it into a bakery and rides her bicycle down the street. In trousers," she added wryly.

"I know," Beatrix said, and chuckled. Perhaps that was why she and Sarah had become such fast friends. They were both off-comers, and even though Beatrix did not smoke or wear trousers or ride a bicycle, the villagers viewed them both with the same suspicion.

Sarah put out her cigarette and changed the subject. "Not to be a nosey parker, Bea, but what's your plan? For Castle Farm, I mean. If you don't mind my asking, that is." She shook her head, frowning. "Blast. Now I've gone and done the same thing I fault Agnes Llewellyn and Lucy Skead for. Poking my long nose into somebody else's business."

Beatrix's chuckle became a laugh. One of the things she liked best about Sarah was her straightforwardness. She could be brusque and blunt, but she always spoke her mind. And Beatrix was glad to have someone to talk to about her plans. She certainly couldn't discuss them back in London, where her mother detested the idea of her owning one farm, much less *two*.

"I mean to do just what I've done with Hill Top," she replied. "I'll repair the barns and the outbuildings and fences. And continue to let the farmhouse to Mr. and Mrs. Wilson, as long as they want it. They've lived there since the Crabbe sisters moved away, and they're reliable tenants." (If you haven't heard the story of the three Crabbe sisters and why they left Castle Cottage, you can read it in *The Tale of Hill Top Farm.* If you've already read it, you might be interested to know that although Miss Myrtle Crabbe has died, Miss Pansy and Miss Viola continue to live happily in Bournemouth, where their musical and dramatic contributions to Bournemouth Cultural Association are much appreciated, and where they keep a very fine garden.)

"What about the farmland?" Sarah asked. "Will you keep it?"

"Why, of course," Beatrix said, surprised at the question. "Mr. Jennings is going to manage the Castle fields, as well as Hill Top. In the spring, we'll put sheep in the pastures and lay on some new drains. And as far as Hill Top itself is concerned," she added, looking around proudly, "both the house and the land are to stay just as they are—forever, if I can manage it. I want it never to change, not in the slightest." Her blue eyes twinkled. "So there. If people ask, that's what you may tell them. Everything here is to stay just as it is, forever. Do you suppose that will be enough to satisfy everyone's curiosity?"

"I very much doubt it," Sarah said, with an answering smile. "But on the whole I imagine it will have to do." A few of the villagers had never given up hope that Miss Potter would marry Captain Woodcock and turn over the running of her farms to him, so they could be properly managed, which of course was impossible for a woman. She sobered, thinking of something. "I don't suppose Castle Farm includes the land around Moss Eccles, does it?"

Beatrix shook her head regretfully. Moss Eccles was the small tarn lake above the village, home to some quite remarkable brown trout and some equally remarkable frogs. She loved the lake. There was something mysterious about it, as if secrets lurked in the depths of the dark water or whispered with the breeze that blew through the surrounding trees. She went there as often as she could and stayed as long as she dared, often well past sundown.

"I wish it were a part of the farm," she replied. "It's lovely up there, and I'm always afraid that someone is going to come along and do something to spoil the lake." She sipped her coffee. "Why do you ask?"

"Because that's where Mr. Wickstead died. Injured somewhere near Moss Eccles, one evening last week."

"Mr. Wickstead is dead?" Beatrix set down her coffee cup with a clatter. "Good heavens! I was hoping to see him during this visit. Oh, dear, oh, dear, I'm so sorry to hear that he's died!" She frowned. "Near the lake, you say? It was an accident?"

"So I've heard. The inquest is scheduled for this morning. Of course, it may be postponed because of the snow. And Mr. Skead is already complaining about having to dig the grave. Can't say I blame him, but it has to be done, of course." Sarah raised both eyebrows. "You knew Mr. Wickstead, then?"

Beatrix nodded. "My father and he became acquainted some years ago, when we were on holiday at Lakeside. Father heard that Mr. Wickstead had a fine collection of Roman antiquities, and we were invited to Briar Bank House to see them. Father photographed the collection and I sketched a few of the pieces—rather nice ones, I must say." She chuckled. "Oh, and just last year, I used his fox terrier, Pickles, as a model for the drawings in *Ginger and Pickles*."

"Mr. Wickstead was an eccentric old fellow, I've heard," Sarah said reflectively.

"I didn't find him eccentric at all," Beatrix replied, "although he certainly held some decided views. And he isn't—wasn't—all that old, certainly not so old as my father. I thought him rather nice, and very expert in his field." She frowned. "How did he die, Sarah? When?"

"Seems a tree fell on him. Just a few nights ago, actually—although what he was doing out in the woods at night, I'm sure I don't know. Roger Dowling was at work on his coffin as I came past the joiner's shop this morning." Sarah shook her head. "Always seems so final, doesn't it? The coffin, I mean."

"A tree fell on him!" Beatrix exclaimed, her eyes widening. "How horrible!"

"Well, the top part of the tree. That's what I heard, anyway. He's to be buried tomorrow. A private ceremony, which is just as well, with all this snow." Sarah leaned forward. "Well, then, since you knew Mr. Wickstead, perhaps you can tell me whether it's true about his treasure. The village is all agog, of course. They say it's worth a king's ransom. Some are speculating that he was killed for it. The rest are saying it must have been the curse."

"Treasure?" Beatrix asked blankly. "What treasure? What curse?"

"So you don't know, then," Sarah replied with a disappointed sigh. She settled back in her chair. "Well, it seems that Mr. Wickstead discovered a treasure trove last spring. Nobody knows much about it because he kept it a deep, dark secret, but of course everybody has an opinion. They all think that anybody who digs up a treasure is—" She lowered her voice with ominous exaggeration. "Cursed."

"A *real* treasure?" Beatrix said doubtfully. "Gold and silver, you mean?"

"That's what people are saying," Sarah replied. "Billie Stoker—he works for Mr. Wickstead—said it was a Viking treasure. And according to his sister, it—"

"His sister?" Beatrix blinked. "Why, for heaven's sake! I didn't know Mr. Wickstead had a sister." She frowned. "In fact, I distinctly remember his telling me that he was an only child. He was bundled off to an orphanage when his parents died. Near Manchester, it was. I remember, because my mother's family is from the area."

"I'm from Manchester, too," Sarah reminded her. "And Mr. Wickstead didn't know he had a sister, either. I'm not quite sure how she managed to locate him—it happened in the middle of last summer, July or August, or thereabouts. At any rate, when he found out who she was, he invited her for a visit and they got along so famously that he invited her to stay. I know about this," she added, "because Mr. Wickstead had got quite fond of my sticky buns—couldn't do without them, he said. He asked his sister—Louisa Wickstead, quite a nice lady, she seems—to order them from me. But that was before he died," she added. "I don't know if Miss Wickstead will continue the order. I somehow don't picture her as the sticky-bun sort."

"I had better send Miss Wickstead a note of condolence," Beatrix said thoughtfully. "Is there to be an arval dinner?" The arval was the traditional funeral feast celebrated throughout the Land Between the Lakes. It was customary to invite all who had known the deceased.

"Miss Wickstead has invited everyone to Briar Bank House after the private burial, which is tomorrow morning. So there's to be a luncheon. Rather like an arval, only at midday, instead of evening, since it's winter. I'm sure you'd be welcome."

"Do you mean to go?" Beatrix asked. She was shy in large groups, but she felt it would be important to pay her sympathies to Miss Wickstead. It was sad to think that her brother had died, and under such circumstances, too—alone and lonely, in the woods beside the lake.

Sarah nodded. "I'm baking some tea cakes and the arval bread." These were sweet loaves spiced with cinnamon and nutmeg and filled with raisins that were given to people to take home. She paused. "If you're going, Bea, maybe you'd give me a lift. I'll have boxes and baskets and things, and I've been wondering how I'm going to get it all there."

"Of course," Beatrix said promptly. She nodded at the guinea pigs. "Since Tidmarsh Manor is on the way, we could stop there and leave those little fellows with Caroline."

"*How wonderful!*" cried Nutmeg excitedly. "*Did you hear that, Thackeray? Tomorrow we get to meet Thruppence and Tuppenny!*"

"*Maybe it will snow again,*" Thackeray said grumpily. "*Maybe it will snow and snow and keep on snowing. In fact, I think I should like that very much."* He turned around so that his back was to her and raised his scrap of newspaper. *"I can sit right here and read."*

"Well!" Nutmeg sniffed. *"I'm glad you're not in charge of the weather, then. Really, Thackeray, you simply must learn to accept what you cannot change. If not, you are going to be unhappy your whole life long."*

"What I cannot accept is this constant chatter," Thackeray said darkly. *"Pray be quiet, and let me read."*

"On second thought, we'll take the sleigh," Beatrix said. "It's larger than the pony cart, and Briar Bank Lane is rather steep. Of course, if there's more snow, the luncheon will probably be postponed."

"We'll know by tomorrow morning." Sarah pushed her chair back. "I'd better be on my way. Today's baking is extra large. If I don't get started, I'll be up until midnight."

"Thank you for coming," Beatrix said, getting up. "And for bringing breakfast. You've got my day off to a good start."

After Sarah had gone, Beatrix gathered up the breakfast things. She still felt saddened at the thought of Mr. Wickstead's dying in the woods all alone, but she put it aside and, as she did the washing up, made a mental list of all she wanted to do that day. She would check to see how the animals were faring, and walk up to Castle Farm to have a look at the barn repairs. Oh, and she had better ask Mr. Jennings to hitch Winston to the sleigh early tomorrow afternoon, so she and Sarah could go out. With a wry smile, she thought of her mother, who was no doubt still in bed, with another dull London day ahead of her. Here at the farm, there were no dull days.

Now, since we have listened in on the conversation between Miss Potter and Sarah Barwick and learnt about

Sarah's feelings for Mr. Heelis and the plan for tomorrow's visit to Briar Bank House, perhaps you are thinking that it is time we went over to Courier Cottage to find out about the letter that the Kendal Bank has sent to Mr. Sutton, the village's beloved veterinarian.

But we shall have to put off that visit for just a little while longer. Our attention is required elsewhere at the moment, in the snowy fells beyond the village, across the narrow valley of Wilfin Beck and beyond Tidmarsh Manor, at the very edge of Cuckoo Brow Wood. (It is a good thing that we don't require the services of Winston the pony, for I fear he would find the journey rather hard, with snow to his withers and the lane frozen and cold.) Our destination is the rocky rise called Holly How (*how* is the Lakelanders' word for *hill*), the home of a certain worthy badger of our acquaintance. A substantial fellow with gleaming white stripes on his handsome black head, he has come out onto his front porch to have a look at the drifted snow and make a note of exactly how deep it is, for the record.

5

Bosworth Badger Is Surprised

"*How extraordinary!*" exclaimed Bosworth Badger, looking out westward across the snow-covered meadow to the white fells beyond, then turning to look to the east, where the snow-covered trees of Cuckoo Brow Wood rose to the top of Claife Heights. "*Why, bless my stripes, what a snowstorm we've had!*"

He took three steps to the right to peer at a measuring stick, only an inch or two of which could be glimpsed above the snow. "*And not one of those namby-pamby sparkly sprinklings, gone in five minutes when the sun shines on it.*" He brushed the snow away from the top mark on the stick. "*Thirty-three inches. A record-breaker, I don't doubt. I must make a note of it.*"

Now, a badger who was younger and more adventurous than Bosworth—young Thorn, for example, who loved nothing better than a ramble over the wild fells—might have packed up some sandwiches and gingerbread, strapped on snowshoes, and taken himself off to explore the silver-threaded valley of Wilfin Beck and the snow-drifted hills beyond. In fact, young Thorn had done just that early this morning, leaving behind him a trail of snowshoe tracks that descended from the porch, zigzagged down the steep side of Holly How, and disappeared into the snowy distance, in the direction of Moss Eccles Lake.

But Bosworth Badger XVII was by nature an armchair adventurer who preferred to read about the wide world in books, settled in safety and security well underground, in front of a cozy fire. As well, he had in recent years attained a rather sizable girth, which made him even more reluctant to indulge in strenuous exercise—and of course, the less exercise he took, the more sizable became his girth.

As a consequence, unless he had some specific business that required him to be out and about, Bosworth was fully content to remain indoors and underground, where the weather was always perfectly perfect day in, day out, the full year round. He fully agreed with a cousin, Badger of the Wild Wood, who asserted that underground life was the very best life imaginable: *"No builders, no tradesmen, no remarks passed on you by fellows looking over your wall, and, above all, no weather."*

So this morning, having completed his scientific measurement of the depth of the snowfall, Bosworth turned away from the vast white chilliness of the out-of-doors to go inside. (It is unfortunate that he didn't linger a little longer, or look to the south, over the edge of the hill. If he had, he might have seen Lady Longford's barn blazing merrily away, having been struck by an unidentified flaming object that plunged out of the sky an hour or so earlier.) But he didn't, and hence will not be informed about the barn until later. He merely turned and stepped back into the grateful warmth and comfort of The Brockery Inn, of which he was the proud proprietor.

I am sure that you must have heard of this inn, for it is among the best known of all the animal hostelries in England, its reputation extending from the northern reaches of Scotland to the Great Wild Wood in the South. The Brockery (its name is derived from the Celtic word *broc*, or badger) is located in what is reputed to be the oldest continually occupied badger sett—or badger burrow, or badger earth, or even badger den—in all of northwestern England. (As we shall see as our story unfolds, however, this may not be an accurate description.)

Through decades and even centuries, this sett was excavated by generations of badgers, who dug out their burrows and chambers inch by tedious inch, piling the dirt teacup by tiresome teacup on large mounds outside the door. (Outside, that is, of the *nearest* door. A badger sett has a great many doors, for in the event of an invasion, an exit is a great convenience.) The Brockery is made up of at least a mile, perhaps more, of tunnels and chambers and corridors and passageways, all offering seclusion and security underground, safe from the terrors of wide fields, empty horizons, open skies, and men with guns and dogs.

At the time of our story, five badgers made The Brockery their home: Primrose, her daughter Hyacinth, and her son Thorn; Parsley, the cook-housekeeper; and Bosworth himself. In permanent residence with them were Flotsam and Jetsam, the twin rabbits who helped with the cooking and cleaning, and old Felix, a blind ferret who served as odd-jobs animal. Frequent visitors were a pair of young hedgehogs who lived nearby and were especially partial to Parsley's mushroom pie, and Tuppence, a guinea pig who lived with Miss Caroline Longford at Tidmarsh Manor, not far away and visible from The Brockery's front porch. (Tuppence had devised a clever means of escaping from his cage and climbed the hill every once in a while, just to say hello.)

In addition, The Brockery offered a refuge to travelers passing through on their way to somewhere else, or those seeking refuge from a storm, as in the case of the trio of circus rats who had arrived the previous afternoon, wet through and in danger of losing their tails to frostbite. Most guests paid for their lodging in kind, with services or food or even entertainment, like the juggling act that the rats had put on after dinner. But Bosworth understood the obligations of a host, and offered refuge and comfort even to animals whose pockets were empty. In this, he was observing the Third Badger Rule of Thumb (generally thought of as the Aiding and Abetting Rule): *One must be as helpful to others as one can, for one never knows when one might require help oneself.*

Bosworth had inherited the proprietorship of the inn from his father, Bosworth Badger XVI, along with the important responsibility of maintaining the official *History of the Badgers of the Land Between the Lakes* and its companion work, the *Holly How Badger Genealogy*, contained in several dozen leather-bound volumes in The Brockery's library. Because earlier badger historians had recorded not only their own clan's activities but those of a great many other animals as well (including the humans who lived in the village and on the nearby farms), the *History* was regarded as a reliable record of everything that went on in the Land Between the Lakes. When animals got into arguments about this or that, they consulted Bosworth, who would go to The Brockery's library and look up the answer in the *History.*

It was to the library that Bosworth had gone just now, with the intention of recording the extraordinary snowfall.

This was the room the badger loved best, loved the cheerful fire (especially welcome on such a chilly day as today), the portraits of distinguished ancestral badgers on the walls, the comfortable leather chairs beside the fireplace, and the oil lamp casting its golden light over the heavy oak table he used as a desk. He was fond of the Badger Coat of Arms that hung over the fireplace, commemorating the family habit of diligent, dutiful industry. It pictured twin badgers rampant on an azure field and bore the Latin inscription:

De parbis, grandis acerbus erit

In English, this reads *From small things, there will grow a mighty heap*, or (as the Lakelanders are fond of saying) *Many a little make a mickle, Many a mickle makes a mile.* It was a sentiment with which Bosworth heartily agreed.

From the shelf, he pulled down the current volume of the *History* and sat down with it at the table. Arrayed in front of him on the blotter were his father's heavy glass inkpot, an engraved silver letter opener that had been in his mother's family for generations, and a silver cup containing his goose-quill pens, extra pencils, and a penknife for sharpening both—all very convenient and comfortable for a badger who enjoys his work as an historian. It was with considerable pleasure that Bosworth opened the book and found his place, directly under the entry he had made two days before: *Mr. Hugh Wickstead killed by a falling tree.*

Bosworth sighed when he saw the entry. It was always sad to record a death, whether it was the death of a hedgehog under the wheels of the drayman's lorry or Mr. Wickstead, under a falling tree. But animals understand (better than humans, I fear) that this earth and the blue sky and the white clouds and the four seasons are all perfectly capable of going along on their cheerful, everyday way without the dear departed. So he dipped his quill into the silver inkpot and began to write, in a neat, careful script, beside the date: *Heavy snowfall last night. 33 inches on the measuring stick beside the*

But "beside the—" was as far as he got, for out in the corridor there was a terrific clatter, the crash of breaking china, and a cry so loud that it startled Bosworth into dropping a large inkblot right in the center of the page.

"*Bother!*" he muttered. "*Blast.*" Hurriedly, he blotted the ink to keep it from spreading. "*What's all that noise?*" he called, irritated.

The door opened and young Thorn came in, his nose rosy from the cold.

"*My fault, sir,*" he said apologetically. "*Flotsam was here with your tea and I bumped into her in the passageway. I'm afraid there's a bit of a mess, but we'll soon have it cleaned up.*"

Bosworth brightened at the thought of tea, and the scones that would go with it. Anyway, he found it difficult to be out of sorts with Thorn, his favorite young badger. The boy had a good heart and an excellent head, the two major characteristics of leadership. Bosworth hoped that someday he might pass on to him the Badger Badge of Authority, entitling him to manage The Brockery and record events in the *History* and *Genealogy*.

"*That's all right, then,*" he said. "*I didn't expect you back quite so soon, Thorn. Did you have a nice ramble in the snow?*"

"*Not exactly.*" Thorn's face became serious. "*I've brought Mr. Bailey Badger back with me.*"

"*Bailey!*" Bosworth exclaimed, surprised. "*Why, I haven't seen the fellow in months. He's not the sort of creature who goes about dropping in on his friends. He doesn't exactly encourage callers, either.*"

A distant relative (second cousin, twice removed), Bailey Badger lived near Moss Eccles Lake, in a very large and very old and mostly abandoned sett (in a sad state of disrepair, in Bosworth's opinion) on the western side of Briar Bank. A bookish badger, Bailey almost never ventured far afield. He devoted his days to deep thought, reflection, and serious reading in the quite remarkable library that he had inherited from his father, grandfather, and great-grandfather, and to which he had himself added substantially over the years. A sardonic and unsociable animal, he preferred to live alone in his spartan bachelor digs, without any of the creature comforts that Bosworth himself enjoyed so immensely. In fact, Bosworth tried to plan his infrequent visits to his cousin so that he did not arrive at teatime, for Bailey's menu was apt to consist of whatever happened to be in the larder at the moment: what was left of day-before-yesterday's pork-pie, say, along with a slice of dry bread, a bit of cheese, and a swallow of dandelion wine.

"*But of course I'm always happy to see him,*" Bosworth added, fearing that he might have sounded ungracious. "*Bailey may not be the jolliest of animals, but he knows a great deal about a great many things, and what he doesn't know, he can always look up in that library of his. Well, well. You say he's dropped in for a visit? Where is he?*"

"Not '*dropped in for a visit,*' exactly." Thorn frowned. "*I've left him in the kitchen, getting a bit of hot soup down him. He's not in very good shape, I'm afraid.*"

"Oh, dear! Whatever is wrong with the poor old chap?" Bosworth asked. But by that time, he was making for the door, and in less time than it takes to tell it, he was in the kitchen at the end of the corridor. There, he found the badger, his fur deplorably damp, huddled in a rocking chair by the fire crackling in the open hearth. Parsley's knitted shawl was draped over his head and shoulders, Bosworth's winter plaid was spread across his knees, and a tray sat on his lap. A fresh white bandage was wound around his right paw. With his left, he was clumsily dipping a spoon into a bowl of hot chicken broth.

"Well, for pity's sake, if it isn't Bailey!" Bosworth said warmly. *"Welcome, old chap, welcome! I'm delighted to see you!"* He said nothing for the moment about that bandaged paw, for the Badgers' Thirteenth Rule of Thumb states very clearly that it is impolite to inquire about a colleague's ragged ear or missing tail or other injuries. Humans are regrettably fond of setting traps and snares. Poor old Bailey, whose eyesight was not the best, must have stumbled upon one of them.

"Well, to be perfectly frank, I've had a devil of a time." Bailey's voice was gruff and he wore a scowl. But his expression lightened when he glanced at Thorn, who was pouring out fresh cups of tea for all of them, whilst Parsley bustled about, piling fresh scones on a plate and getting out pots of marmalade and strawberry jam. *"If it hadn't been for your boy here, I'd be a gone goose, I'll tell you."*

"A gone goose?" Bosworth exclaimed, staring. *"Why, whatever do you mean, Bailey?"*

"I mean that he fished me out of Moss Eccles." Bailey slid a glance at Thorn, grudgingly admiring. *"Brave, I'd call it. Excessively brave."*

"Not at all," said Thorn, his ears pinking at the edges. *"I only ventured out on the ice a bit and extended a branch. Any other animal would have done just as well."* He began handing the teacups round. *"It's a good thing you're a strong swimmer, Mr. Bailey. You were able to stay afloat until help arrived."*

Bosworth pulled up a chair and sat down. *"But Moss Eccles!"* He shook his head in wonderment. *"Why, my dear fellow, however did you come to fall into the lake?"*

"I *didn't 'fall,'*" Bailey said defensively. "*That isn't how it happened.*"

"*It was the ice, sir,*" Thorn said, taking a scone and sprawling on the floor in front of the hearth. "*From the shore, it looks perfectly strong, but in places it just isn't quite thick enough. A mouse or a rabbit might have made it all the way across, but a badger—*"

"*It's a good thing that ice was thin, I'll tell you,*" Bailey interrupted. He was shivering again, uncontrollably, and his teeth began to chatter. "*If I hadn't dived into that lake, I'd be a dead duck.*"

Bosworth frowned, confused. "*But I don't understand, dear fellow. Why should you want to dive into the water at this time of year? I can understand the attraction of a cooling swim in July or August—I've done the same myself. But December?*"

Bailey took a gulp of hot tea. "*You won't believe me,*" he said gruffly. "*So why should I go to the bother of telling you?*"

"*Of course we'll believe you,*" Bosworth assured him, in the sort of humoring tone you might use if you are talking to someone who has been recently ill and needs an extra bit of coddling. "*Whyever wouldn't we?*"

Bailey looked into his teacup. "*Because,*" he muttered.

"*Don't be a foolish animal,*" Bosworth said affectionately. "*We want to hear the whole thing, from beginning to end. Don't we, Thorn?*"

"*Indeed we do,*" said Thorn, and settled himself to listen.

But Bailey's tale is rather a long one, and he has a way of taking a while to get to the point. I'm afraid we can't stop to listen right now, because it's time that we learned what is in that letter that the Kendal Bank sent to Mr. and Mrs. Sutton. I promise you, though, that we will make a special attempt to catch up to Bailey Badger's story as quickly as we can, and that you won't miss a single word.

6

Deirdre Makes a
Frightening Discovery

As you have probably suspected, Deirdre was right to dread Mrs. Sutton's response to the letter from the Kendal Bank. When she returned from the post office, she took off her coat and boots and sent Libby and Jamie and Mouse out to play with their sleds on the hill behind Courier Cottage. The youngest Suttons were taking their morning naps, except for Lillian, who was helping Mrs. Pettigrew, the Suttons' cook-housekeeper, by peeling potatoes. Deirdre stopped to admire her work, then took the envelope and made for the dispensary at the back of the house.

Tabitha Twitchit, an elderly but still-spry calico cat, tagged along to see if her recent discussion with the mice who lived behind the baseboard in the dispensary had had the desired effect. Tabitha had been invited to take the post of Chief Mouser at Belle Green when Miss Tolliver died and Miss Barwick inherited Anvil Cottage. When the Belle Green barn was cleared of mice, Tabitha had packed her bags and moved down the hill to Courier Cottage, where she set up house-keeping in the attic. She was most welcome, too, for there had been no cats at Courier for several years, and the mice had rather made themselves at home. Tabitha was the senior village cat, and other cats could be heard to say that her age was slowing her down. But her years had given her a great deal of experience when it came to mouse-management, and it took only a few days to make it very clear to the Courier Cottage mice that a new Chief Mouser was in charge and they had better make themselves scarce or *else*. (Tabitha had been at the business long enough to know that a good bargain tasted much better than a mouthful of mouse.)

The dispensary was lined with floor-to-ceiling shelves of gleaming glass bottles with carefully hand-printed labels that always fascinated Deirdre: Tincture of Camphor, Sugar of Lead, Perchloride of Mercury, Gentian Violet, Castor Oil. On the floor were wooden bins filled with empty medicine bottles, variously sized corks, pill boxes, and powder papers. Against another wall stood a white-painted glass-fronted cabinet, in which porcelain trays held hypodermic syringes, forceps, probes, and tweezers with oddly shaped tips. The door in that wall led into the surgery, but Mr. Sutton wasn't there. He had left the morning before to treat a sick horse on the other side of Esthwaite Water, and planned to go on to visit several other patients. With the snow, it was likely that he wouldn't be back for two or three days.

Against one wall of the dispensary, in front of a window, stood a scarred wooden desk and a chair with a green cor-duroy cushion, where Mrs. Sutton worked on the veterinary accounts. When Deirdre and Tabitha came into the room, they found her seated at the desk with a heap of papers and customers' bills in front of her. A slim, pretty woman with bright hazel eyes and an unruly mop of brown hair that tore itself loose from its moorings five minutes after it was pinned up, Mrs. Sutton did not look nearly old enough to be the mother of eight children. At the moment, in fact, she looked very young indeed, and on the edge of tears, pushing the papers away impatiently, as if she could not bear the sight of them for another minute. But she brightened when Deirdre came in.

"Oh, good, it's the post," she said, with an artificial cheeriness, "come to rescue me from these utterly boring accounts. Thank you, Deirdre, my dear. You've brought me a book, I hope." Mrs. Sutton (who would much rather be reading a romantic novel than working at the desk or darning heels on socks) subscribed to a lending library that dispatched books through the post.

"No book today, I'm afraid," Deirdre said apologetically. She put the bundle of post on the desk, the bank's letter on top. Mrs. Sutton's eyes widened when she saw it, and her face grew pale. She gave a little cry, shrinking away from it as if it were a bomb that might go off in her face.

"Oh, no," she whispered in a frightened voice. "Not that. Oh, please, not *that*. I really can't bear it. I'm sure I can't bear it at all! Especially now, with dear Mr. Sutton away."

"Why?" Deirdre asked. "What does the bank want?"

Now, this may seem to you to be a rather impertinent question, coming from a mere household servant. But Deirdre had lived with the Suttons for over three years now, and was a member of the family. More than that, she was an *important* member of the family. Mrs. Sutton relied on her for so much where the children were concerned. And not just the daily work, either, baths and hair ribbons and shoelaces and tea and that sort of thing. Mrs. Sutton always asked Deirdre what should be done when the children were ill or out-of-sorts, or when they needed new clothes or shoes. She also asked her advice when it came to running the household and dealing with things that needed to be repaired, or bought, or thrown away.

Of course, Mrs. Sutton might have asked the cook-housekeeper. But whilst Mrs. Pettigrew was quite good at putting a dinner together out of practically nothing (if necessary) and dealing with the laundry and the cleaning, she wasn't at all good at management, and since she was really rather deaf, there was no point in asking her advice about anything at all. And it was no good asking Mr. Sutton, either, for he was dreadfully busy with his veterinary practice and inclined to become vague when asked his opinion about family matters. So Mrs. Sutton had got into the habit of depending on Deirdre, who, when you get right down to it, was a very dependable young person indeed.

But I shouldn't like you to think that Mrs. Sutton lacks the skill or the temperament to manage the children and the household, or that she is avoiding her responsibilities as a mother and wife. It is true that she is inclined to be excitable and that she occasionally flees into the garden with a book, just to get away from the children's noise and the household hurly-burly. And it has to be admitted (as Mr. Sutton is wont to remind her when things get into a muddle) that sums are not her strong point, to which she usually retorts that, yes indeed, she is an awful muff at keeping accounts and wouldn't it be better if Mr. Sutton would arrange for someone else—someone with a better head than hers—to step in and straighten everything out? Her husband is just as vague about the accounts as he is about family matters, however, so Mrs. Sutton is left to get along by herself as best she can.

But Mrs. Sutton's chief difficulty is that she is terribly overworked. Eight children are rather a lot for one mother to manage, as I daresay you will agree. And she is often required in Mr. Sutton's surgery, for although a village boy comes in to help, he isn't always available when he is most needed. And there are the accounts, and bills, and the medicines and surgical supplies to deal with, together with the many things that are required to keep a veterinarian's business operating.

All in all, whilst Mrs. Sutton always tried her very best, she often had the feeling that things were quite out of control, which was in fact true. And so she often turned to Deirdre, whom she knew to have a good head on her shoulders, not to mention a stiff spine, a strong pair of arms, and a great willingness to help.

Which is why Deirdre felt able to ask again, very gently, "What does the bank want now, Mrs. Sutton?"

"*Ah, it's the bank, is it?*" Tabitha Twitchit said. She wound herself around Mrs. Sutton's ankles in a comforting sort of way. "*Banks are a world of trouble.*"

"What do banks always want?" Mrs. Sutton wailed despairingly. "Money, of course! The mortgage-money payment on this house, which is overdue by three months."

"But shouldn't you open the envelope and see what the letter says?" Deirdre asked reasonably.

Mrs. Sutton picked up the envelope in one hand and the letter opener in the other, and slit the envelope. Then she dropped both. "I can't bear to look at it!" she exclaimed, putting her hands over her eyes as if to close out the sight. "We have no money to pay the mortgage, whatever it is. We have no money because nobody pays *us!*"

"*It's what comes of giving credit,*" Tabitha Twitchit said darkly. "*If you allow it, people will only take advantage.*" Tabitha had long been of this opinion, and was gratified when Miss Potter pictured her in *Ginger and Pickles* as a shopkeeper who refused to give credit. Very right, she thought.

Mrs. Sutton opened her eyes wide and pounded her small fist on the papers in front of her. "Just look at all these unpaid accounts!" she cried. "Dozens of them. People just won't pay!" But Deirdre couldn't have looked, even if she had wanted to, for Mrs. Sutton had swept her arm wildly across the desk, sending all the papers flying.

Deirdre bit her lip. She wished she could say something to comfort Mrs. Sutton, who was a loving person at heart, even if she was a bit harum-scarum when it came to accounts. At last she managed, "If there's anything I can do—"

"Do? Do?" Mrs. Sutton cried, tearing at her hair so that all the pins popped out and fell onto the floor. "Why, bless you, dear, dear Deirdre, what in the world can you do? What can *anyone* do, if people won't pay what they owe? Dear Mr. Sutton works so hard taking care of everyone's animals—he's almost never home for meals, you know, and gets up in the middle of the night or at the weekend and goes wherever he is summoned, no matter the weather or the state of his health. I worry about him out there in the rain and snow and fog, I really do."

And with that, she stopped tearing at her hair, which was by now quite loose and disheveled, and began to weep as though her heart would break.

"I should have thought," Tabitha remarked sadly, *"that Mr. Sutton would be making quite a lot of money. There are always so many patients lined up outside the surgery door."* This was true, too. He never failed to treat every sick and injured animal carefully and compassionately, and people left giving grateful thanks for the doctor's expert attention.

The trouble was, though, that they almost always left

without paying their bills. Instead, Mrs. Sutton wrote down the amount that they owed in the large black leather account book that she kept on the desk. At the end of every month, she sent them a very nice letter with the bill enclosed, politely requesting payment. Sometimes people sent a little money in reply, sometimes they sent a little more, but almost never did they send *all* they owed.

"It's not a matter of their not having money, you know," Mrs. Sutton said bitterly, gulping back the tears. "The men have money to go to the pub, and the women have money for new hats or teakettles or whatever else they want to buy. And there are people—Lady Longford and Major Kittredge, for instance—who have *plenty* of money. They could pay, if only they would." She took out a pocket handkerchief and blew her nose. "If only they would," she added hopelessly.

Not knowing what to say, Deirdre got down on her hands and knees and began picking up the scattered papers. She stood, put them on the desk, and said, "These have got all muddled, I'm afraid. Why don't you let Mrs. Pettigrew fix you a nice cup of tea whilst I sort them out? I could make a list of the accounts that are owing, if you like. That way, we can see where we are."

"I don't understand how seeing where we are will pay the bank its mortgage-money," Mrs. Sutton said gloomily. "But a cup of tea would be nice." She wiped her eyes and began pinning up her hair. "I'm sorry about scattering the papers. You're sure you won't mind sorting them, dear?"

"Not at all," Deirdre said with a smile. "I'll have it all done by the time you've finished your tea." She could say this with confidence because she knew that Mrs. Sutton always dawdled over her tea, taking time to help Libby turn the heel in the stocking she was knitting or read a story to one of the smaller Suttons.

Of course, as I'm sure you've already guessed, Deirdre had a reason for making the offer, for it had occurred to her that perhaps there might be a way to collect the money. But first she had to see how much was owed and by whom.

Tabitha Twitchit jumped up on the desk. *"I'll be glad to help,"* she offered. *"Miss Tolliver always let me lend a paw with her accounts."*

Deirdre chuckled. Cats had a way of getting right under your nose when you were working—especially this one, who always seemed to have an opinion about how things should be done. But Tabitha was such an old dear—and a great mouser—that Deirdre didn't mind.

"I'll tell you what, Tabitha," she said, taking the cushion off the chair and putting it on the far corner of the desk. "Why don't you just curl up on this cushion? That way, you can supervise what I'm doing, and if you get tired, you can take a little catnap."

"That's a very good idea," said Tabitha, and jumped onto the cushion, where she curled herself into a ball. *"I must say again, however, that giving credit is simply bad business. When I was mousing at Belle Green, I often heard Mr. and Mrs. Crook discussing the matter. Mr. Crook refuses to give credit at his smithy. And so does Mr. Dowling, at the joinery, and Mrs. Dowling, at the village shop. I simply do not see why Mr. Sutton should—"*

"Hush, Tabitha," Deirdre said sternly. "I can't work with you meowing."

Tabitha yawned, showing pointed white teeth and a pink tongue. *"It's time for my nap, anyway,"* she said. She tucked her nose under her tail, closed her eyes, and fell fast asleep.

For the next half hour, Deirdre worked at sorting the bills into various piles, depending on how long the account had been overdue: some just a month or two, others for several months, some for a year or longer. Then she put everything into one large pile, the oldest accounts on top, and made a list of who owed how much, for how long. And then she went from the top to the bottom, adding the amounts.

When she was finished, she stared at the total with stunned disbelief. Twenty-one people owed Mr. Sutton the grand total of twenty-five pounds, three shillings, tuppence.

Twenty-five pounds! Deirdre swallowed, hard. It was an enormous amount of money, a vast amount of money, more money than she could possibly imagine. Why, twenty-five pounds would pay the salary of a day-laborer for six whole months. Twenty-five pounds would buy a whole lorry-load of books, or boots, or enough food to feed a family for a year.

It might even be enough to pay the Suttons' mortgage payment and satisfy the Kendal Bank.

Then Deirdre did something she knew was wrong—but she felt she had a very good reason, so she did it anyway. (As you may have already guessed, Deirdre is the sort of person who lives by her own personal rules, although I have to say that her rules, by and large, are as fair and reasonable as we might wish, and she tries not to take advantage.) She picked up the envelope that Mrs. Sutton had already opened, took out the typewritten letter from the bank, unfolded it, and began to read.

Dear Mr. Sutton,

We regret to inform you that no further delay can be permitted in the matter of the repayment of the mortgage on Courier Cottage, in the village of Near Sawrey, which is held by this bank. Pursuant to the terms of the contract, the full amount owing must be paid, which is, to wit, twenty-six pounds, seven shillings, and fourpence. If this debt is not fully discharged within fifteen days, we shall be required to foreclose on this property.

Yours with great regret, etc. etc.

Mr. Franklin Ferrit

President, The Kendal Bank

Deirdre sucked in a long, shaky breath and leaned back in the chair, feeling utterly defeated. Twenty-six pounds! No wonder Mrs. Sutton hadn't wanted to open the envelope, since she already knew the amount. And even if all the people who owed Mr. Sutton money paid what they owed—which was not at all likely—it still would not be enough. The bank would foreclose.

Deirdre clenched her fists and closed her eyes, a wave of bleak despair sweeping over her. *Foreclosure.* The word roared like a dragon. It threatened to swallow up Courier Cottage and spit it out into someone else's hands. It warned that she would be out of a place and so would Mrs. Pettigrew, and that Mr. Sutton would have nowhere to carry on his veterinary practice. But worst of all, it promised that Mrs. Sutton and the eight little Suttons would have no beds to sleep in, no kitchen to cook in, and no fire to keep them warm. They would have to throw themselves on the mercy of the parish. They would be sent to the workhouse at Ulverston. The entire family would face ruin, disaster, calamity!

Now, it may seem to you that our Deirdre is making a mountain out of a molehill. Surely (you may be thinking) there is someone with money to whom Mr. and Mrs. Sutton could appeal for help—a well-off family member, say, who (out of pity for the eight homeless little Suttons, if nothing else) would be willing to proffer twenty-six pounds, seven shillings, and fourpence. Or perhaps Mr. Sutton could prevail upon Mr. Ferrit of Kendal Bank (who was surely not so heartless as to turn them out just at Christmas) to relent and extend the mortgage.

But please bear in mind that Deirdre is only fifteen, and though she is remarkably mature and dependable for her age, she certainly does not have as much experience of the wide world as you do. And if you remember that she is an orphan, and that she was once homeless herself and recalls living in the orphanage as vividly as if it were yesterday, I think you will understand why she fears that when the fiendish Mr. Ferrit forecloses on Courier Cottage, Mrs. Sutton and all of the little Suttons will be driven to the workhouse. And if you further consider that Deirdre loves these children as if they were her very own brothers and sisters and that she feels every bit as tenderly responsible for them as a mother would feel, I am sure you will understand why, if the little Suttons must go the workhouse, she will have to go there, too.

Deirdre will do anything in the world to keep that from happening.

Anything.

7

Breakfast at Tower Bank House

If you consult the map of Near Sawrey at the front of this book, you will see that Tower Bank House is on the opposite side of the Kendal Road from the Tower Bank Arms and from Courier Cottage. Built against the side of the hill, it is a largish house and somewhat grand, for it was once the home of the village squire. This gentleman also owned the pub, which was, at the time, called The Blue Pig. Feeling that "The Blue Pig" lacked a certain *je ne sais quoi*, he re-named it the Tower Bank Arms. The villagers snickered and snorted at this personal conceit (they were perfectly content with The Blue Pig), and everyone else was terribly confused. People who wanted to stay at the Tower Bank Arms found themselves pulling the squire's bellrope, whilst people who had business at Tower Bank House found themselves having a pint at the pub, which is a good deal easier to find.

But at the time of our story (and for quite some time before that), Tower Bank House has been the home of Captain

Miles Woodcock, who—in addition to being retired from His Majesty's Army—serves as the Justice of the Peace for the Land Between the Lakes. Captain Woodcock is a fine-looking gentleman of just above forty years, a lover of fine food, fine wine, and fox hunting, and (ordinarily) a man of a mild and even disposition.

On this snowy morning, however, Captain Woodcock was not in the best of tempers. In the previous year, his sister Dimity had married Christopher Kittredge and gone to live at Raven Hall. For a while, the captain had fancied—indeed, he had even hoped (which is to say planned)—that Miss Potter might become his wife. The villagers agreed that this was a Very Good Idea, for various reasons. The women thought that the captain wanted looking after, and that it was quite right for Miss Potter to take on that task. The men thought that Hill Top Farm wanted looking after, and that it was quite right for Miss Potter to hand over its management to a man. In fact, if the villagers had had their way, the captain and Miss Potter would likely be married by now. But the lady was utterly devoted to the memory of her deceased fiancé, and whilst the captain certainly had his regrets (the longer he knew Miss Potter, the more he admired her), he was a practical man. There was nothing he could do to move her, so there was no point in trying.

Of course, Captain Woodcock had to admit that there were certain advantages to being a bachelor. He did not have to adjust his habits to another. He could read until dawn, if he chose, without anyone bidding him to bed. He could hunt and fish and play cards and go on holiday whenever he liked. And his ordinary comforts of meals and laundry were competently seen to by Elsa Grape, who had managed his household since Dimity's marriage. Elsa was dedicated and reliable, but she had fallen on the ice the previous week and suffered such a serious injury to her knee that Dr. Butters had ordered her to bed. Florence, the girl who usually helped Elsa in the kitchen, now had temporary charge of it. As a consequence of this unfortunate change in household management, the captain's breakfast had been (to put it bluntly) nothing less than disagreeable.

To begin with, it was late. And when it arrived, the coffee was bitter, the bacon was burnt, the eggs were leathery, the toast was charred. The blame for all of these misadventures the captain laid squarely upon Florence. All this, on a morning when the captain (in his capacity as the Justice of the Peace) was to convene an inquest into the death of his friend, Mr. Hugh Wickstead. Perhaps, he thought morosely, turning from the window, he ought to call it off. Dr. Butters had to drive over from Hawkshead, and with the depth of the drifted snow and the difficulty in travel, the captain doubted that he would be able to make it.

Given these annoyances, perhaps Captain Woodcock may be excused for frowning mightily when Florence set the second plate of burnt toast on the table, just as the front doorbell rang. "I'll get it myself," the captain said to Florence. He handed the plate back to her. "Try again. More coffee, too, please. A fresh pot. And do *not* boil it."

The caller, to Captain Woodcock's happy surprise, turned out to be the intrepid Dr. Butters, bundled up against the cold.

"Good morning, Woodcock," said the doctor, pulling off his gloves. "I hope I'm not too early."

"Not at all," the captain said, as the doctor took off his overshoes, hat, and coat, and began to unwrap the various mufflers wound round his neck. "I didn't expect you to make it. Snow looks devilish deep out there."

"It is. The roads are completely shut down north and south of Hawkshead," the doctor replied.

"And the ferry and the steam yacht aren't operating, I'm told," the captain said, leading the way to the breakfast room. Mr. Llewellyn had delivered that word just a short while ago, along with the morning's milk and the news about the mysterious burning of Lady Longford's barn. "We are effectively isolated from the rest of the civilized world."

"Not an altogether unhappy proposition," said the doctor. He was a tall, thin man with a narrow, intelligent face, ginger-gray moustache and hair, and a rather cynical disposition. "There are times when I should much prefer isolation. The rest of the world isn't always as civilized as one might like." He went to stand close to the fire, rubbing his hands together.

The captain acknowledged his friend's characteristically gloomy remark with a smile. "Breakfast?" He indicated the table. "Barely palatable, I'm afraid, but it's all that's on offer this morning. As you know, Elsa is flat on her back, which leaves Florence to manage the kitchen."

At that moment, the unfortunate Florence appeared with a new pot of coffee and a plate of fresh toast, happily unburnt.

The doctor took a chair at the table. "I've eaten, but I'll have something to warm me. Anything will do, as long as it's hot." He pulled down his mouth. "If it weren't for wanting to get this wretched business out of the way, I would've stayed at home, close to the fire—until I was called out on an emergency, that is. People have a way of waiting until the weather turns foul before they get sick."

"I'm not looking forward to the inquest much, myself," the captain said, pouring coffee. "Wickstead didn't allow himself many friends. I'm glad to say I was one—which only makes my task that much harder."

"Indeed," Dr. Butters said, and began to spread marmalade on toast. "I didn't know him as well as you, but I, too, counted him a friend." He sighed. "I just wish I had answers to all the questions. It's a mystery. A girt mezzlement, as the villagers say."

The captain looked up sharply. "A mystery? Where's the mystery? I thought Hugh's death was fairly straightforward."

"It was," said the doctor. "I gather that you haven't seen the photographs yet."

"What photographs?" The captain picked up his coffee, took a sip, and made a face. The toast might be improved, but there was no change in the coffee. "I hope you're not suggesting foul play," he added grimly, setting down the cup.

The doctor shook his head. "No, not at all. Wickstead died when the top portion of a tree—a yew, I understand—snapped off and struck him on the head, out there in the woods above Moss Eccles Lake. Might've lain out there for a week, if the dog hadn't gone for help. A case of being at the wrong place at the wrong time, I'm afraid—although what he was doing out there at night, I haven't a clue. Still, it was an accident. I'm comfortable with that."

Now, if there was anything the captain hated, it was not knowing all that he needed in order to draw a logical conclusion. He was one of those people—you've met them, I'm sure—who firmly believes that a logical conclusion can always be drawn from a set of facts, no matter how mezzling the facts might be. And having drawn a conclusion, he firmly believed that it was correct. Given the facts, how could it be otherwise?

"Well, then, what's this about photographs?" he demanded.

The doctor spoke slowly. "It seems that your constable—good man, John Braithwaite—saw something at the accident scene that piqued his curiosity. So he brought his camera and took pictures of the tree that broke at the top and fell on Wickstead. He had them with him yesterday when I chanced to encounter him in Hawkshead. I expect he hasn't had time yet to show them to you—given the storm, that is."

"And?" the captain inquired cautiously, not sure where this was going.

"Well, it's very peculiar," the doctor said, chewing his toast. "Braithwaite's photographs distinctly reveal claw marks on the tree, as if an animal had climbed it. Quite a large animal, I'd say. Bigger than a badger, by far. The constable—he examined the tree itself, I only saw the photographs—was under the impression that the claw marks were fresh, made quite recently. Perhaps as recently as the night the tree fell." He shook his head. "I must confess that I am mystified."

"Bigger than a badger?" The captain chuckled. "A bear, perhaps? Or a panther, escaped from a circus?" (As I'm sure you know, there are no native bears or panthers in England. And the wolves have been gone for centuries.) He chuckled again, ironically. "Or maybe the monster has left Loch Ness and come to live in Moss Eccles Lake. I've heard that it's rather deep out there in the middle. Perhaps the marks should be analyzed from that point of view."

"That's right, Woodcock, have your fun." The doctor gave him a frowning look.

"Sorry, old chap," the captain said. "I just meant—" He chuckled. "I suppose we could put the marks on the tree into the same category as the flaming fireball that struck Lady Longford's barn this morning. Burnt it to the ground, Llewellyn said, when he brought the morning's milk."

"A fireball, eh?" the doctor said, with interest. "A meteorite, do you suppose?"

The captain grinned. "Divine retribution, according to Llewellyn. He claims her ladyship cheated him when she sold him a cow."

"No doubt Llewellyn would put the marks on the tree into the same category," the doctor said. "However, I am not attempting to analyze them, merely to report them. I thought they might be of some interest to you, since you are convening the inquest. You intend to call Constable Braithwaite to testify, I suppose. For the sake of completeness, you might wish to enter his photographs into evidence."

"I'm not inclined to do so unless the photographs have a bearing on the way Wickstead died. Likely, they'd only fuel the gossip. You've heard what the villagers are saying, I suppose."

"Ah, yes. They love nothing better than a good curse, don't they?" The doctor finished his toast and put his napkin to his lips. "I shouldn't worry, Woodcock. Talk is the villagers' cheapest entertainment. Gossip, speculation, rumor, scandal. It'll keep everyone busy until after Christmas, I'm sure." He shrugged his shoulders. "And p'rhaps it's better for them to be talking about claw marks on a tree than a secret treasure trove, mythical or not."

"I don't know about the claw marks, but the treasure is no myth," the captain said quietly. "Wickstead really did discover something up there in the woods. Something he found quite . . . intriguing."

The doctor gave him a questioning look. "He told you about it, then? Or perhaps showed it to you?"

"Neither," the captain said. "He only hinted, but he was quite excited. And I certainly got the general picture. I felt that he was not more specific because of the Treasure Trove Act."

"I wondered about that," said the doctor with a wry smile. "I suppose the old fellow was trying to avoid surrendering his loot to the Crown." He frowned. "Although why I persist in calling him 'old,' I don't know. Wickstead was no more than five years older than I. And I am by no means ancient."

"You're right," the captain said ruefully. "His hair was gray, which made him seem older than he was. In fact, I rather think he cultivated the appearance. Wickstead was, after all, an antiquarian. Thought he ought to look the part, perhaps." He leaned back in his chair. "Anyway, had he come straight out and told me he'd found a treasure trove, I should have had to direct him to hand it over to the Home Office, straightaway. Frankly, I thought it better not to inquire."

Both the captain and the doctor know exactly what they are talking about here, but I suspect that you have not a clue—nor did I, until I took the trouble of looking it up. You see, in England, at the time of our story, the law required that anyone who found any sort of treasure had to give it over to the king, to be disposed of as His Majesty wished. Here, word for word, is what the law said:

When any gold or silver, in coin, plate or bullion hath been of ancient time hidden, wheresoever it be found, whereof no person can prove any property, it doth belong to the King, or to some Lord or other by the King's grant, or prescription.

Well, now. To me, this sounds as if there is no getting around it. If the deceased Mr. Wickstead had indeed found some sort of treasure (as the doctor and the captain and the villagers seem to think), he was supposed to have turned it in.

"Personally, I doubt it was much of a treasure," the captain went on. "A few gold coins, a dagger, a piece of jewelry or two. The villagers have blown it up into a magnificent trove, worth a king's ransom, but Wickstead gave me the impression that it wasn't worth bothering the Home Office about."

"Don't tell the Crown that," the doctor remarked. "It's always been the position that *every* treasure uncovered, no matter how insignificant, belongs to the king. And some people have got into serious trouble for concealing what they found. I read recently about a Yorkshire chap who dug up a hoard of coins on his property—on his own property, mind! He tried to keep it dark, but of course word got out. Before long, people were swarming all over the place, digging here and there, hoping to find their own cache of coins. And the next thing he knew, the agents from the Home Office were on to him, demanding that he turn it over. He paid a hefty fine for concealment." He grunted. "Great lot of nonsense, if you ask me. A man digs up something valuable on his property, it ought to belong to him. Crown's got no right to it."

"I agree," the captain said. "Perhaps Wickstead intended to dispose of his find quickly, before anybody from the Home Office got on to him." The doorbell pealed. "Florence!" the captain shouted. "Answer that, would you?"

"And did he in fact dispose of it?" Dr. Butters asked curiously. "The fellow was well known among antiquarians. If he wanted to sell his treasure quickly—large or small—I'm sure he could find a buyer."

"Dispose of it? I haven't the foggiest," the captain confessed. "If the treasure was still in Wickstead's possession when he died, I should think it will go to his sister. And then it will be her problem."

"Ah, his sister." The doctor brightened. "The fair Louisa. A handsome woman, indeed, and quite charming."

The captain cocked his head and raised one eyebrow. "Interested, are you, Butters?"

"Well, I suppose, a little," said the doctor offhandedly. "Bit of luck, wasn't it, though? Her turning up the way she did. Cheered Wickstead's last days, I'll warrant, just having her around. A very pleasant lady."

Florence opened the door. "Mr. Heelis," she murmured, blushing (Florence always blushed in the presence of single gentlemen), and ushered in a tall, good-looking man in a brown coat and brown bowler.

"Well, Heelis," the captain said heartily. "So you've made it, after all." Will Heelis, Mr. Wickstead's solicitor and the captain's best friend, was expected to be at the inquest. But when the snow began, the captain had doubted that he would come.

"I drove my sleigh." Mr. Heelis rubbed his hands together. "The Kendal Road's been plowed, so people are beginning to get about. Hullo, Butters. Good to see you—although I'm sorry for the occasion that brings us together. Wickstead was an odd bird, but he was all right, at heart. At least, I always found him so."

This did not surprise the captain, for Mr. Heelis was the sort of person who found that everyone was all right, at heart. Perhaps that's why he was so well liked. "We were just discussing Wickstead's sister," said the captain, with a teasing glance at the doctor. "Butters here admits to being an admirer of hers."

The doctor colored and ducked his head.

"Well, I for one wish you luck, Butters," Will Heelis said, for he was a generous man and did not want the doctor to feel that he was being tormented, or take offense. "Miss Wickstead is handsome and agreeable, and about to be rather wealthy. Not that her circumstance should make any difference," he added hastily. "If you find her amiable in other ways."

"Wealthy?" the captain asked, raising his eyebrows. "So she is to inherit Wickstead's fortune, then?"

"Yes, indeed," Heelis replied. "Her brother left Briar Bank Farm to her, and all of his personal property, including his collection of antiquities, which is quite extensive."

"Including, I suppose," the captain said, "that treasure trove he dug up last spring. Have you seen it, Will?"

"Not I," Heelis said, shaking his head. "And if you want the truth, I wasn't keen to hear about it. If he had found something valuable and intended to keep it from the government, that was his business, not mine." He paused. "His last will and testament won't be officially read out for another few days, but I have already informed Miss Wickstead that she is to inherit. She'll be at the inquest, no doubt." He eyed the doctor. "If you want to speak to her about this matter, that is."

"Oh, I see no reason for that," said the doctor, rather flustered. "Although I shall of course pay my respects."

"And you, Heelis?" the captain asked. "What's the state of your courtship these days?"

"Your courtship?" asked Dr. Butters, raising his eyebrow. "Who's the lucky lady?"

"Why, Miss Sarah Barwick," the captain said with a grin. "Haven't you heard, Butters? It's all over the village. We expect an announcement at any time."

Will Heelis frowned. "The village has it wrong." It wasn't the first time people had linked his name with that of a local young lady. As a solicitor active in various business affairs throughout the district, he met quite a few unmarried women, and as a confirmed bachelor, he was vaguely aware of their occasional efforts to interest him. But he was a shy man, and did not find it easy to talk to the ladies.

"I think," said the captain, consulting his watch, "that we had better be on our way to the pub. I hope our jurors will be able to get there. It would be a pity to convene the inquest and find ourselves two or three jurors short."

"It will take more than a three-foot snowfall to keep people away from this morning's inquest," the doctor said. "If nothing else, they'll be hoping to hear something about the treasure—or the curse."

"And Lester Barrow will be celebrating afterward," Will Heelis added with a grin, "when everyone requires a half-pint of his best to wash down the jury's finding." To the captain, he said, "I've stabled my horse in your barn. Hope you don't object."

"Not at all," said the captain, showing his guests into the hall. "You're welcome to stay the night, you know, should you decide not to go back home." Over his shoulder, he added, to the doctor: "I shan't be requiring Braithwaite to enter those photographs into evidence, Butters. There's no need to fire up the villagers' imaginations—they're quite lively enough already." He shook his head disgustedly. "All this talk about a curse. Nonsense."

"What photographs?" Will Heelis asked the doctor as they followed their host down the hallway.

"The photographs of the tree that killed poor Wickstead," the doctor replied. "Taken by the constable. You haven't seen them, then?"

"Not I," Heelis said. "Are they important? Do they reveal anything that's not already known?"

"Yes," said the doctor.

"No," said the captain firmly, taking down his guests' coats from their pegs and handing them out.

"How the devil do you know, Woodcock?" the doctor challenged. "You haven't seen them." To Will Heelis, he added, "The tree bears fresh claw marks. *Large* claw marks, made by an animal of substantial size. Larger than a badger, I'd say, perhaps three or four times as large." He frowned. "And of course, badgers don't climb trees. At least not to the top."

"An animal of substantial size?" asked Heelis in surprise. "What could it have been?"

"Two badgers, perhaps," said the captain, with a sarcastic chuckle. "Escaped from a traveling circus. In the company of a panther. Or a panther and a bear, as the case may be." At Will Heelis' raised eyebrow, he added, "Or perhaps a Loch Ness monster, out for a nocturnal jaunt. Who knows? In any event, the villagers do not need any additional fuel for their fancies. Arboreal animals!" He snorted. "Next thing you know, they'll be saying that Wickstead was killed by the same agency that fired the Longford barn."

"Lady Longford's barn burned?" Will asked, concerned.

"This morning," the captain said, pulling on his galoshes.

"I don't think we ought to be so quick to dismiss the photographs," the doctor remarked cautiously.

"I'm not dismissing them," Captain Woodcock replied. He straightened and reached for his coat. "I'm just keeping them out of my inquest—and out of the villagers' rumor mill. It's already been concluded that poor Wickstead was doomed the minute he dug up that treasure. So the constable can keep those photographs in his pocket. Or burn them—that would be far better."

The doctor shrugged into his coat. "And what makes you think you can quash those photos? I'll wager a quid they've already been seen and discussed by every male in the village."

The captain put on his hat. "I'm sure you're right, blast it," he muttered. "But at least I can keep them out of the inquest. Come along, gentlemen. We don't want to be late."

"Claw marks," Will Heelis said to himself, as they went out the door. "I wonder what *that's* all about." He made a mental note to ask Constable Braithwaite to show him the photographs. And to find out what had happened to Lady Longford's barn.

8

Bailey's Story: Episode One
What Mr. Wickstead Found in Briar Bank

At the end of Chapter Five, we left Bailey Badger telling his story in front of the fire in The Brockery kitchen. It was rather rude of me to take you away just as the badger was getting started, and I apologize, although as I pointed out at the time, urgent matters commanded our attention. But whilst Captain Woodcock and his friends are making their way through the snow to the Tower Bank Arms, we shall hurry back to The Brockery and rejoin Bailey, Bosworth, and young Thorn, at the point at which we left off listening. (This is a special privilege of writers and readers of books, who are not regulated by the rules of Real Time or Chronological Order, which, when you get right down to it, are very boring indeed.)

We find the three badgers gathered around the kitchen fire, just as we left them, Bosworth and Thorn listening as Bailey, still damp from his plunge into icy Moss Eccles Lake, tells his tale. The first part, however, like the first chapter of many stories, was made up mostly of Bailey's personal history, which Bosworth already knew, so it was hard to keep his mind from wandering. He would have liked to say, *"Get on with it, won't you?"* but he had in mind the Eighth Badger Rule of Thumb: *It is rude to criticize another animal's story, no matter how wanting in art it might be, for one's stories are as important to one's self-esteem as are one's fur and whiskers and ought to be admired in much the same way.*

Thorn, however, was paying close attention. Sprawled on the floor in front of the fire, he listened with genuine interest, for Bailey's personal history was news to him. And since Thorn occasionally interrupted the story with a question or two, and because Bailey himself was in no special hurry, it took a rather long time to relate. I hope you will pardon me if I take the liberty of summarizing it for you.

Bailey grew up where he lived now, in a large and mostly abandoned sett near Moss Eccles Lake. He lived alone, having elected to remain a bachelor. (None of the nearby lady badgers had ever suited his rather finicky requirements, and he was not a badger to be content with a second choice.) However, it is a settled truth that no badger ever lives completely alone, for many other animals—foxes, rabbits, mice, hedgehogs, spiders, and the like—often make free of the unused rooms and chambers in the sett. The Fifth Badger Rule of Thumb acknowledges this fact and directs that all badgers should practice the art of hospitality, gladly accommodating any animal who finds himself temporarily without bed, board, or a roof, and turning away only those who would be a danger to their neighbors.

But it takes all sorts of animals to make up this big, wide, wonderful world of ours, and Bailey was not of an hospitable turn of mind. He had no intention to let lodgings. He took no pleasure in the company of others, and was repulsed by the idea of hosting a community kitchen where anybody could wander in, raid the pantry, eat his fill, and leave without doing the washing-up. Bailey was a recluse and a hermit, a misanthrope who had chosen to live a solitary life, free of the encumbrances and distractions of family and society. To avoid the bother of turning other animals away, he had simply walled off a section at the south end of the Briar Bank badger sett for himself, and in these private apartments, made himself comfortably at home. And to make sure that he would be comfortably at home by *himself*, he put up a notice-board at the end of the path, painted in large red letters.

WARNING!
No day-trippers,
fell-walkers, moor-ramblers,
or marsh-rovers
allowed.
KEEP OUT!!
THIS MEANS YOU!!!

Anyone who disregarded this notice and wandered down Bailey's path was warned again by a smaller sign that was posted beside the door. (There was no bell-pull to post it under, because bell-pulling guests were not anticipated.) This sign read, more simply:

Badger Digs
Go away

Inside, Bailey's lodging was simple but spartan. (Bosworth, who braved Bailey's displeasure and visited from time to time, described it as "bare.") The sitting room featured a fireplace, a drinks cupboard, a chair for Bailey, and a footstool upon which the occasional (*very* occasional) guest might be seated. The pantry kitchen was tidily equipped, with a range, a washing-up sink, and a table and one chair. The sleeping room had a pallet of clean straw stuffed into a bed-tick, an oaken dresser for clothes and boots, and a mirror on the wall, with a shelf beneath for Bailey's combs and hairbrushes. (Badgers are noted for their good grooming habits.) There was a smaller room that had been Bailey's when he was a boy, and a larger chamber that had belonged to his grandparents, but these were closed off now.

But whilst Bailey lived in three simple rooms (spartan or bare, depending on your point of view), his library enjoyed a much larger space than he did. It occupied six commodious chambers, each room filled floor to ceiling with bookshelves containing works of history, biography, science, philosophy, and literature. These works had been collected, through numerous generations, by badgers who believed that "Reader" was the most rewarding vocation to which a virtuous badger might be called, and who gauged their week's anticipated pleasure by the height of their to-be-read piles.

In consequence of this belief, an additional library area had been nicely fitted out as a reading room, with a fire, a comfortably upholstered chair (a knitted shawl folded handily over the back in case of chilly evenings), and a pair of fleece-lined slippers, since Bailey suffered from chronically cold feet. There was a lamp, of course, and a small table for such chair-side necessities as pipe and tobacco and a small glass of something. Stacks of books yet to be read—some stacks head high, some as high as the ceiling—were ranged against the walls. Pursuing a well-organized personal reading program, Bailey spent long, leisurely days in the library, and long, leisurely nights, too, for when you are deep underground (and to a badger, deep underground is the very best place in the world to be), it makes no matter whether the sun is riding across the sky or the moon, or whether the weather is fair or foul.

If there was anything lacking about this arrangement, Bailey would not have been in a hurry to admit it. However, if he were to be completely honest with himself—that is, utterly and entirely candid, without reservation (which is of course not possible for anyone, not you, not I, and certainly not Bailey)—he might have owned up to feeling lonely on occasion. Granted, there is nothing better in the whole, wide world than books and the leisure time to read them, but lately Bailey had begun to fancy, deep down in the secret spaces of his badger heart, that it might be rather nice to have another animal around, one with whom he might hold a serious conversation about books and reading, over a cress sandwich, say, or a raisin scone and a cup of hot tea. Of course, it went without saying that the animal, whoever he was, should have a wide variety of interests and reading experiences, as well as being a clever conversationalist, accustomed to expressing his opinions confidently and without hesitation. A good argument now and then would do wonders to clear the cobwebs from his brain, Bailey felt.

But since such an animal was not in the offing (Bailey suspected that none existed—other than himself, of course), the badger was content to go on just as he was, eating and sleeping in his three small rooms and spending the bulk of his days in his library.

There was a great deal more to the Briar Bank sett than the section occupied by Bailey and his library. Bailey himself had no idea how old it was, only a vague sense that it dated back to the Very First Days when badgers came to live in the Land Between the Lakes, before the Bronze Age people built their sacred stone circles, before the methodical

Romans sent their army to construct roads and forts and a Wall, before the Norsemen swept down on the north wind from the wintry lands at the top of the world. The sett's tunnels and corridors and passageways made up an extensive underground network that went right the way through from one side of Briar Bank to the other and all across the middle, so that the whole of the hill that stretched along the western side of Moss Eccles Lake was honeycombed with badger burrows, now abandoned, unexplored, and empty.

Even as a boy, Bailey had been busy with his books and had never gone to the trouble of exploring the whole sett— nor had his father nor his grandfather nor his great-grandfather. In fact, from things these badger forebears had said (or seemed to say, or had not said), he'd got the vague sort of sense that there might be an occupant—uncouth, unpleasant, or merely bad-mannered—living in some far, distant corner of the sett. Whatever or whoever it was didn't bear looking into, and hence it was better to leave well enough alone. *"Let sleeping dogs lie,"* was the phrase that Bailey remembered, accompanied by a careless toss of the head and a nervous laugh.

So, because Bailey was a bookish badger with no interest in stirring up sleeping creatures of any species, he confined himself to the small area in which he lived. That is, until the day some eight or nine months ago when he became aware that someone was attempting to dig into Briar Bank.

Now, if you have read *The Tale of Holly How*, you know that digging into badger setts is a sadly common affair. Badger baiting—the appalling sport of pitting badgers against fierce dogs and letting them fight to the death—had been outlawed some years before the era of our *Tales*, and badger baiters were prosecuted whenever they could be caught. (In fact, as is related in *Holly How*, Bosworth Badger and young Thorn were largely responsible for the capture and arrest of a notorious badger baiter who had kidnapped Primrose and her daughter.)

However, the law, in its usual contradictory way, continued to permit badger digging, which in the Land Between the Lakes, as elsewhere in England, was a favorite local sport. Farmers and gardeners and gamekeepers blamed badgers for killing chickens and eating strawberries and apples and garden vegetables, when they might better have blamed themselves for not fencing the badgers out and the chickens and garden in. And when they had nothing better to do, they set off with their terriers and their tongs and their shovels to dig their badger neighbors out of their dens and slaughter them.

So you can understand why Bailey was alarmed when he discovered, one afternoon some months before our story, that someone was digging at the far end of Briar Bank. The badger had taken a recess from his reading and gone out with his basket to pick some salad burnet near the top of Briar Bank. It was a brilliant spring afternoon and the sun warmed his dark fur in an agreeable way, so that that he was feeling less grumpy than usual and had even begun to whistle a little tune to himself. But his pleasant mood was broken when, turning away from the salad burnet patch to go back home, he heard the sound that every badger dreads. It was the unmistakable metallic clang of shovel against stone.

Suddenly apprehensive, Bailey dropped his basket and the fur rose on his shoulders. Digging! Who? Why? To his knowledge, this end of the sett had not been occupied for a very, very long time—centuries, in fact. But he made no effort to keep in touch with local affairs. A family of itinerant badgers could certainly have moved in without his knowing. If so, they were in serious danger. Besides, it was the principle of the thing. Digging could simply not be permitted at Briar Bank. He wasn't sure what he could do to stop it—Bailey was a reader, not a warrior—but surely he could do *something.*

The clanking sound was coming from the west end of Briar Bank. Keeping low to the ground, behind a scrim of bracken, Bailey crept to the edge of a rocky outcrop and looked down. From this vantage point, he had a clear view of what was going on below. Yes, there was a man with a shovel, and he was digging.

But to his great surprise, the man wasn't a farmer or a gardener or even a gamekeeper. It was Mr. Wickstead, the fine gentleman who owned Briar Bank Farm and lived in Briar Bank House, which was just visible down the hill and through the trees. Judging from his dress—tweed shooting jacket, tweed knickers, woolen socks, leather boots—and from the game bag leaning against a nearby tree, Mr. Wickstead had been out for an afternoon's shooting, although why he should have brought a shovel instead of a gun, Bailey couldn't guess. He was digging near an ancient entry to the sett that had been abandoned long, long ago—so long ago that a large yew had grown up over it, hiding the opening amongst its tangled roots. Lying on the ground beside him, nose on his paws, was a brown and black and white fox terrier named Pickles, with whom Bailey had a slight acquaintance.

The dog, a boisterous young terrier who was somewhat overenthusiastic about life, belonged to Mr. Wickstead but was usually left in the care of Billie Stoker, Mr. Wickstead's gardener. The terrier was called Pickles because he was always getting into trouble, not paying the proper attention or frolicking off to pursue his own pleasures. Bailey had met him some while before, on an evening when the badger took himself down to the garden behind Briar Bank House in search of ripe gooseberries. Pickles ought to have been on patrol, of course—that was his job. This evening, however, the terrier didn't appear until after Bailey had topped off his leisurely repast of gooseberries with a bit of fresh cheese from the dairy and was about to take his leave under the fence.

"You must be Badger!" barked Pickles, bouncing up and down with all the exuberant impertinence of a friendly puppy. *"I've been hearing a great deal about you. Nice to finally meet you at last, old fellow."*

Bailey took a step backward. Dogs made him nervous. *"You live here, I take it, then."*

"Oh, yes." Pickles bounced away, then back again. *"I would've been round earlier, but I was delayed."*

"Ah," said Bailey. *"And what did you say your name was?"*

"I'm Pickles." Bounce, bounce.

"I should say," remarked Bailey ironically, beginning to feel that he had nothing to fear from this particular terrier. *"Pity about the gooseberries. It seems they're all gone. I hope you don't mind."* He scowled. *"I do so wish you would sit. It is excessively difficult to have a conversation with a bouncing ball."*

Pickles stopped bouncing and sat down on his haunches, his tongue lolling out. *"I don't mind about the gooseberries. I heard Cook say she hoped she'd never see another one, so it's just as well you finished them off."* He tilted his head, one terrier ear flopped up, the other down, and smiled gaily. *"I was delayed because of an engagement this evening. I was sitting for my portrait."*

"Do tell," Bailey said, rolling his eyes. The dog was obviously full of himself—thought he was top dog when he was clearly no more than an unruly pup.

"It was Miss Potter," Pickles barked blithely. *"She came to draw my picture. She's putting me into one of her books, you see. I'm*

to be a shopkeeper. The book will have my name on the cover!" He did a lively little dance, stiff-legged. "The Tale of Ginger and Pickles, *it's called."*

(As I'm sure you know, Pickles was telling the absolute truth. If you have Miss Potter's book handy, you might turn to page thirteen, where you will see a drawing of Pickles standing behind the counter of his shop. Or page eighteen, where Pickles is writing down the amount Mrs. Tiggy-Winkle—a hedgehog who works as a laundress—owes for the bar of soap she is putting into her reticule.)

"The Tale of Ginger and Pickles." Bailey chuckled sarcastically. *"Why, fancy that!"* He had never heard of Miss Potter. Some figment of this terrier's overactive imagination, no doubt. The badger did not for one single moment believe that anyone would put this silly puppy into a book. Why, the idea was absurd! Books were the most important things in the whole wide world. There was nothing better than books (unless it might be gooseberries), and certainly no place in them for impudent, self-important animals with not a brain in their empty heads.

Pickles sobered. *"I do so wish you would believe me,"* he said plaintively, looking as if he were about to cry. *"Nobody ever believes me about* anything."

"Try telling the truth and they might," Bailey said, very rudely. *"I shan't keep you, as you no doubt want to go off and admire yourself in the mirror. Convey my compliments to Cook and tell her that the gooseberries were excellent. Goodbye."*

And off he went, just in time, too, for as he departed by the usual exit, he saw Billie Stoker, the gardener, running toward them. He was waving a rake and shouting angrily.

"What's wrong with you, dog? That big auld badger has been raidin' t' gooseberries again. Get after him, blast it! He's goin' under t' fence!"

But of course, Bailey was already gone, laughing up his sleeve. And since that evening, the badger had made a good many trips back to the Briar Bank garden and orchard, where he helped himself to everything from ripe apples to lettuce and strawberries and the delicious earthworms that thrived in the decaying layers of Billie Stoker's compost heap, which Bailey delighted in rummaging through. Whenever he had seen Pickles, they had exchanged pleasant greetings. Whatever else could be said of the terrier, he was not much of a watchdog.

Now, Bailey parted the bracken and poked his head over the ledge to get a better look. He saw a torn, dirty sack of some sort—was it leather? he couldn't quite tell from this distance—lying beside the dog, its contents spilled on the ground. Bailey guessed that Mr. Wickstead had dispatched the terrier into the hole after a badger or a mole or a rabbit. Pickles had, instead, encountered the sack and dragged it out.

Bailey sat back, now less concerned, since Mr. Wickstead did not appear to be digging for badgers. Perhaps he himself had hidden the sack in the burrow and had come back to retrieve it. Or perhaps someone else had hidden whatever-it-was and gone home to tea and then got busy with the post and forgot about it. One way or another, a hole in the ground, whether man-made or badger-made, would make a convenient hiding place for any number of things, valuable or valueless and anywhere in between.

But when Bailey peered more closely at what had spilt out of the sack, it seemed to him that he was looking at something . . . well, valuable. On the ground lay several handfuls of coins, a slim dagger, what appeared to be a brooch or a buckle, a heavy chain, and a sizable goblet. And in spite of the fact that the sack itself appeared to be very old, its contents sparkled in the sunlight as if they had been just recently polished.

Bailey stared at the bright heap, astonished. Why, it looked like—

At that moment, Mr. Wickstead stopped digging, threw down his shovel, and cried, "In with you, Pickles! Go, boy!" The terrier scrambled to his feet, ran to the burrow, and wriggled eagerly inside. After only a few minutes, he was backing out, his tail wagging frantically. He was pulling something with him—another leather sack, it looked like, whilst the eccentric Mr. Wickstead danced from one foot to another, waving his arms and crying out such things as, "Oh, my goodness gracious!" and "Dear me, dear me, dear me!" and "Just look what you've found, you clever fellow! Another bag of treasure!"

For that's what it was, or what it seemed to be. It was a small leather sack, as full of glittering gold—coins, jewelry, a chain, another dagger—as the first one had been. Mr. Wickstead squatted down, poured everything on the ground in front of him, and began pawing through it, exclaiming excitedly as he did so.

"My, this ring is a beauty!" he cried. And, "Oh, here we have something truly unique! Never seen anything like it, never!" And finally, "Topping, I'd say! Simply topping! Pickles, old chap, my hat's off to you!" And with that, he jumped up, doffed his hat, and bowed neatly from his waist to the dog. "If you hadn't carried that dagger home, m'boy, I would never have known this treasure was here. I owe it all to you, you clever little fellow, you."

Ah, Bailey thought. So that was what had happened. Pickles had been prospecting on his own, and had struck gold.

"It was nothing, really, sir," Pickles barked modestly. *"It just seemed like something you should know about, given the kinds*

of antiquities you like to collect." He sat back on his haunches, tilted his head, and grinned from ear to ear in the cocky way of fox terriers.

Mr. Wickstead fetched his game bag and put the treasure carefully inside, along with the two leather sacks. Then he went back to the hole and began scooping up dirt and leaves to disguise his digging. Straightening, he looked down at what he had done and began to speak, as if to himself. "No one must know," he said, so low that Bailey had to strain to hear. "The law about treasure trove is very clear. If word of this gets out, I'll be forced to hand it over to the Crown. All of it. All these remarkable golden beauties."

Pickles looked concerned. *"I didn't see any crowns in those bags,"* he barked, *"but you can certainly depend on me not to say a word."*

"Not a word, not a word, not a single, solitary word," Mr. Wickstead repeated to himself, picking up the bag and shouldering the shovel. "I must be as silent as the grave. As tightlipped as a tomb. As quiet as a mouse. As—"

"I swear," said Pickles. *"You can count on me. Wild horses couldn't drag the story out of me."*

"Harrumph," Bailey said disgustedly, under his breath. Pickles would undoubtedly dash straight down to the village and tell all the other dogs about his find. And he would be sure to exaggerate it. When the terrier was finished with the story, it would be known in the farthest corners of the Land Between the Lakes, and the treasure—if that's what it was—would be worth a king's ransom.

I am sorry to tell you that the badger was at least partially right in his prediction, although he did not learn this until some months later. Pickles had no sooner finished his tea that evening than he romped right off to Belle Green, where his friend Rascal lived. He didn't *intend* to tell Rascal the story, of course. He was just so exuberantly full and bubbling over with what had happened that he simply couldn't hold it in. The story erupted and exploded and burst and poured out of him as if it were hot molten lava and he were a volcano, and before he realized what he was doing, he had told the whole thing, every bit, down to the part where he promised Mr. Wickstead he'd never ever say a word, not a single, solitary word to anyone. At which point he was abysmally ashamed and embarrassed—for all of fifteen seconds, after which he was his usual bouncy, irrepressible puppy-self again and quite proud of finding the treasure.

Now, Rascal, a fawn-colored Jack Russell terrier who kept himself informed about all village affairs, was very much impressed by Pickles' story. He was so impressed, in fact, that he repeated it to Max the Manx when he encountered him later that same evening, out behind the Llewellyns' barn. It is not clear whether Rascal failed to get the facts right or whether Max somehow got the facts wrong, but either way, the result was an increase in the number of bags dragged out of the badger hole, from two bags to three.

Which is what Max reported to his friends at the Village Cat Council, when it convened later that night. And since the village cats all believe that when a cat knows a thing, she has to tell it to three more cats before sundown the next day or she will turn into a fat orange pumpkin—well, I think you can understand why the tale of Pickles' treasure made at least two circuits around the entire village within the next week, gaining in size as it went, like a snowball that gets bigger and bigger as it careens down the hill. By the end of the week, Mr. Wickstead was twice as rich as Croesus and the twelve mammoth bags of treasure that Pickles had pulled out of the badger burrow were worth a king's ransom.

But Pickles isn't responsible for the fact that the Big Folk in the village also got the story, for it was Billie Stoker who saw to *that*. He stopped in at the pub and whispered to his good friend Lester Barrow that his employer had come home from somewhere with two small sacks of a very valuable— not to say priceless—treasure trove.

"Treasure!" Lester Barrow exclaimed. "Treasure?"

"Aye, that's reet, Mr. Barrow," said Billie Stoker confidentially. "Treasure trove is what it was an' treasure trove is what it is. Viking treasure. Priceless Viking treasure, buried fer hunderts an' hunderts o'years, an' tha's no lie."

Not that Billie Stoker would say exactly what this treasure was, of course, or where it had been found, or what Mr. Wickstead intended to do with it now that he had it. Billie Stoker was sworn to secrecy. Billie Stoker's lips were sealed. Nothing in the world could make him tell.

That wasn't the end of it, of course. After Billie Stoker left the pub that night, Lester Barrow told Mr. Llewellyn all about the Viking treasure Mr. Wickstead had dug up, and Mr. Llewellyn told George Crook, who told Roger Dowling, who told Joseph Skead. And then they all went home and told their wives—Agnes Llewellyn and Mathilda Crook and Lydia Dowling and Lucy Skead—who told their sisters and their cousins and their aunts, who told their husbands, and so on and so forth.

And somewhere along the line, someone (it might have been old Dolly Dorking, Lucy Skead's mother, who is reputed to be a witch) pointed out that anyone who found a treasure trove and took it home with him was curst, and they could all expect Mr. Wickstead to die, sooner rather than later. All agreed with Dolly Dorking's prediction, and not one was in the least surprised when Mr. Wickstead turned up dead.

But as I said, Bailey was not to know any of this for quite some time. When Mr. Wickstead and Pickles had disappeared down the hill toward Briar Bank House, the badger picked up his basket and made his way back home, where he made himself a sandwich of watercress and salad burnet leaves and poured a glass of elderberry wine. Having eaten, he put on his smoking jacket and slippers (his feet were feeling very cold) and shuffled to his library, where he searched the shelves until he found what he was looking for. It was a slim leather-bound book with an ornately engraved title:

English Law As It Pertains to the Discovery & Declaration of Treasure Trove

Perusing this volume, the badger by and by came upon the paragraph that you and I noticed earlier: "When any gold or silver, in coin, plate or bullion hath been of ancient time hidden, wheresoever it be found, whereof no person can prove any property, it doth belong to the King, or to some Lord or other by the King's grant, or prescription."

Bailey closed the book, satisfied. What Mr. Wickstead had found had clearly been gold coin and gold plate that appeared to have been "of ancient time hidden," by whom, Bailey could not even guess. Consequently, the treasure did not belong to Mr. Wickstead, but to the king, who at this time (as Bailey well knew, for he read the *Times* whenever he a copy fell into his paws) was King Edward VII. It behooved Mr. Wickstead to hand it over at once.

But of course, what Mr. Wickstead did was none of Bailey's business. As he returned the book to its place on the shelf, he briefly wished that he might have been the one to find the treasure—a logical wish, since Mr. Wickstead had found it in *his* burrow. But Bailey was basically a law-abiding badger. Had he found the treasure, he would have had the great nuisance of traveling all the way to London, locating King Edward (what a bother that would be), and turning it over.

And then another thought struck the badger, with the force of a bolt of lightning. He had better hope—no, he had better *pray*—that Mr. Wickstead told no one where he had found the treasure. No one! Not the Crown, not anyone in his household or the village, not anyone at all!

Because once it got about that there was gold in Briar Bank, there would be a Gold Rush that would rival the one at Sutter's Mill in California in 1849, of which Bailey had read only last month and which he now thought of with horror. From the moment people knew where the treasure had been found, he would not have a single moment's peace, not one. They would come with their picks and their shovels and their buckets and their bags and dig from morning to night, clanking and crying and swearing and disturbing the peace. Intruders would investigate every one of the dozens of entries to the Briar Bank sett, including his own. They would badger the life out of him.

So as he went off to spend the evening in his reading room, Bailey sent a fervent plea in Mr. Wickstead's direction, imploring him to hold firm. Then he poked up the fire, poured his port, filled his pipe, pulled a shawl around his chilly shoulders, and sat in his chair, toasting his cold toes by the hearth. He congratulated himself on being done with the business and reached for the next book. He had a great many more books to read, and if he didn't hurry, he would quickly fall behind.

But was he?

Done with the business, I mean.

No, of course he wasn't. If he were done with the business, there wouldn't be any more story, would there? In fact, if you want to know the truth, it has only just begun. There are a great many adventures yet to be had, some of them downright thrilling, at least for a badger who is a reader, not a warrior.

But this much of the story has taken a rather long time to tell, and Bailey is not even half finished. Since this is a good point at which to leave him, we shall do just that, for things are happening in the village that require our attention. Contain your soul in patience, and we shall return to Bailey's tale when we have the chance.

In the meanwhile . . .

9

Miss Potter Does Business

Beatrix spent a quiet hour tidying up and getting reacquainted with her house, the place she loved more than anything else in the world. Outside, the sky was gray, the world was covered with snow, and the wind was blustery, but inside, all was delightfully warm and cozy. The guinea pigs napped by the fire, the kettle sang, and Beatrix settled happily into her day.

Taking out her feather duster, she dusted the collection of blue-and-white ware in the handsome oak dresser, and the blue willow Staffordshire earthenware and the portrait bowls of George III and Queen Charlotte. She wiped the pretty painted face of the tall oak long-case clock, which was over 120 years old, and stood on her tiptoes to dust the top. She flicked her duster over the mantelshelf as well, admiring the Doulton stoneware jugs and the pair of wooden Peter Rabbits she had found in a toy store, as well as the row of shining brasses beneath.

The wooden rabbits were unauthorized, of course, but she had learnt that it was simply impossible to keep people from copying Peter. When it came to pirating, the Americans were by far the worst. But it was hard to blame them, for her publisher had foolishly failed to register the copyright to *The Tale of Peter Rabbit* in America. Which meant that Americans could legally purchase picture books and toy bunnies that looked rather like Peter (at least to Americans), but were not *hers*, and that a substantial amount of money had been lost to literary pirates.

Beatrix, who had inherited a good head for business from her Lancashire calico-manufacturing grandfather, was quite aware of this loss. In fact, she kept the rabbits on the shelf to remind her that creativity was all very well and good, but it was also necessary to keep an eye on one's business interests. She knew that her books had a great deal of commercial potential—people wanted to buy toy rabbits and Peter Rabbit games and Mrs. Tiggy-Winkle puzzles and dishes and even wallpaper. The difficulty was that even though she had plenty of ideas along these lines, Harold Warne (who had taken over her books after Norman died) had not much interest in hearing them. And when he did take an interest, he got things all muddled.

That wasn't the only bothersome thing about dealing with Harold these days. He was forever raising silly objections to this or that trivial bit in a book, and she had to write several letters to straighten things out. Much more worrying, her royalty account was always months overdue, and she was put in the unfortunate position of having to ask him for the payments that should have been sent automatically. This was deeply mortifying, of course, and to her mind, a simply appalling way to do business. If one owed money, one paid it when it was due, and that's all there was to that.

She opened the door on the other side of the room and stepped into what had once been an ordinary bedroom, now transformed into a fine parlor. She had made the small room seem very grand by installing an imposing marble chimney-piece and adding French-style chairs, a small table, and a rather ornate rug. But it was her personal treasures that gave the room its real richness: the red Italian lacquer box on the worktable, the oriental cabinet decorated with parquetry and copper mounts, even the Potter coat of arms, in an ornate gilt frame. If her mother ever came to visit Hill Top, this is where they would have tea, poured from her most splendid teapot into her best porcelain cups and served with Sarah Barwick's finest scones. (Beatrix knew, of course, that this would never happen, but still, it was a nice dream.)

The parlor dusted and tidied, she went back into the hall (the name Lakelanders gave to the main room of the house), stirred the fire, and brewed a pot of tea. She took out the notebook in which she was writing and drawing a new story, *The Tale of Mrs. Tittlemouse*, which she planned to give as a New Year's present to Nellie Warne, Norman's little niece. After that, she would turn the colored drawings into more carefully painted pictures for the book, which was scheduled for publication next June. Beatrix liked Mrs. Tittlemouse very much, and fancied that there was something of herself in the little creature—something, at least, of her contentment at Hill Top.

Mrs. Tittlemouse was a wood-mouse who lived in a sandy bank under a leafy green hedge. Her house had long, lovely winding passages, convenient cupboards, and a snugly curtained bed for the mouse of the house to sleep in (a bed that had green curtains, like those on Beatrix's own bed upstairs). Her store-rooms were full, the nut-cellars and seed-cellars satisfactorily stocked with cherry-stones and thistle-down and acorns, and everything was exceptionally clean and tidy and arranged just as Mrs. Tittlemouse liked. Indeed, her life would be perfect if she weren't always being interrupted. Beetles wandered in without invitation, and humblebees and spiders and the toadish Mr. Jackson, who came looking for honey and left a mess behind. "I am not in the habit of letting lodgings," snapped Mrs. Tittlemouse, brandishing her broom. "This is an intrusion!" But still the trespassers came, for a wood-mouse's house is a perfect place for a smallish creature to take shelter from the rain.

Beatrix was just getting out her watercolors to work on the picture of Mrs. Tittlemouse confronting the humblebees (I am looking at the picture just now, and so can you, for it is in the very front of *The Tale of Mrs. Tittlemouse*) when she herself was interrupted. Hearing a knock at the door and wondering who might be out on such a snowy day, she hurried to the door to open it.

"Why, Deirdre Malone!" she exclaimed happily, drawing the mittened and muffled girl inside out of the wind. "How good of you to come out in all this snow and wind! And just in time for tea, too! Come and have a cup with me."

As Deirdre took off her things and hung them up, Beatrix thought what a pretty girl she had become—nearly a young woman now, fifteen and growing fast. Gone was the awkward lankiness of her early teens, when Beatrix had first met her and shared an adventure at Cuckoo Brow Wood. But with her unruly red hair, dancing green eyes, and the freckles scattered across her stubby nose, Deirdre was still unmistakably Irish. She had an Irish practicality, too, and a loving but firm hand with the little Suttons that Beatrix particularly admired.

"Oh, look, Miss Potter!" Deirdre exclaimed. "Guinea pigs! Are these for Caroline?" Deirdre and Caroline Longford were fast friends, although since both had finished at the village school, they weren't together as often as they liked. Caroline was continuing her studies with a governess and Deirdre had her hands full with the little Suttons.

"Yes, they are," Beatrix said, moving her artwork out of the way. "Their names are Nutmeg and Thackeray."

"Such sweet little creatures," Deirdre said admiringly.

"*Thank you,*" Nutmeg said, preening. She had just been telling Thackeray about her elder sister Hazel, really the prettiest of her family, who had been bought by a nanny and a little girl in a lovely pink pinafore with ruffles and lace and gone to live in a big house where they had strawberries and cream for tea every day.

"*I am neither sweet nor little,*" Thackeray growled. He was entirely out of patience with Nutmeg, who had been going on and on for hours. "*I am a fully grown adult guinea pig, who prefers to be left alone. Left alone, do you hear?*"

"*I really think it would be better, miss,*" Nutmeg said hastily, "*if you did not put your finger in the cage. Thackeray might—*"

"Ow!" Deirdre exclaimed, and jerked her hand back.

"He didn't hurt you, did he?" Beatrix asked, concerned.

"Not much," Deirdre said, putting her finger in her mouth. "Bit unfriendly, isn't he?"

Thackeray narrowed his eyes. "*I don't like being poked in the face,*" he muttered. "*And I am sick to death of female chatter!*"

Beatrix sighed and began to slice a lemon. "Actually, I'm beginning to question the wisdom of taking him to Caroline. I was planning to go there tomorrow, and—"

"Tomorrow!" Deirdre brightened. "Why, tomorrow is my holiday. Do you suppose I could go along? I should love to see Caroline. It's been a very long time."

"I don't see why not," Beatrix replied. "Miss Barwick is going with me, but we're taking the sleigh, so there's plenty

of room. We plan to drive up to Briar Bank House for the
funeral luncheon, and can stop for you on the way home.
But do wrap up well. It may be a chilly ride."

"I don't suppose anyone cares about it being a chilly ride for me,"
remarked Thackeray with a dark sarcasm, retiring to reread
Mr. Churchill's speech for the fifth or sixth time.

Beatrix poured the tea, set out sugar and lemon, and put
several biscuits on a plate. "What brings you out on such a
morning, my dear?"

Deirdre sat down at the table and took a folded paper
out of her pocket. "I feel simply wretched about this, Miss
Potter."

Beatrix looked at her in surprise. The girl was pale and
tense, nothing like her usual exuberant self. "About what?
Is something wrong?"

"Yes," Deirdre said simply. "Very wrong." She unfolded
the paper and put it on the table. "If someone doesn't do
something quickly, the Suttons will be forced to leave Courier
Cottage."

Beatrix stared. Of all the things she might have expected
Deirdre to say, this was the very last. "Leave Courier Cottage?"
she managed finally. "Oh, dear! But . . . but how? Why?"

"Because the Kendal Bank is going to foreclose on the
mortgage," Deirdre said quietly.

"Foreclose!" Beatrix was horrified.

"People aren't settling their accounts, you see," Deirdre
said. "Almost all of Mr. Sutton's clients are on credit.
Which means that the Suttons have no money to pay the
bank." She pushed the paper across the table. "If everybody
paid their bills, it still wouldn't be quite enough for the
mortgage payment. But maybe if Mr. Sutton gave the bank
something—" She broke off, nodding at the paper. "That's
the bill for Hill Top Farm, Miss Potter. Mr. Jennings hasn't

paid it. It's one and eight. I thought . . . well, I was hoping you might be able to settle it up today."

"Oh, dear," Beatrix said, and looked down at the paper. One pound and eight shillings for the vet's visit and some medicine for Kitchen, the cow, who had had a badly infected foot several months ago. She pushed her chair back, shaking her head. She remembered now when Mr. Jennings had sent her the bill, along with several others. Mr. Jennings had asked for the money, but she had put him off because of not having received her royalties. ("This is what comes," she thought crossly to herself, "of people not doing business properly.") She had finally sent a cheque, but apparently Mr. Jennings hadn't yet paid Mr. Sutton.

"I had no idea that the account wasn't settled," she said. "I'll take care of this immediately."

Deirdre closed her eyes, and let out her breath. "Thank you, Miss Potter," she said, in a voice that was close to tears. "Oh, thank you!"

"You don't need to thank me," Beatrix said firmly, getting her purse out of the dresser. "It should have been paid before this." She counted out one pound and eight shillings onto the table.

Deirdre took out a pencil and carefully wrote PAID and the date on the bill. "Thank you," she said again, and put the money into a leather purse. "You've given me courage. I just hope that the rest of the people feel as you do."

"The rest?" Beatrix sat down, frowning. "Do you have many more accounts to collect?"

"Twenty," Deirdre said, and looked out the window. She gave a shaky laugh. "The snow complicates things. I'm afraid it's going to take a little while."

Beatrix gave her a long look. "I must ask you, Deirdre. Do Mr. and Mrs. Sutton know you're doing this?"

Mutely, Deirdre shook her head. "I didn't—I couldn't—" Her eyes suddenly filled with tears, and Beatrix thought she looked close to despair. "Mr. Sutton is out in the country-side somewhere, and may not be back for several days. Mrs. Sutton was too upset even to read the letter from the bank. She's lying down right now with a sick headache. I told her I was coming to see you. But I didn't tell her why."

"I see," Beatrix said.

Deirdre swallowed, trying to smile. "It's not their faults, really. Mr. Sutton is a considerate man and a good doctor who thinks of nothing else but his work. And Mrs. Sutton does the very best she can. She has sent out several very kind letters. But I have the idea that she thinks asking for money is common, and perhaps her letters aren't strong enough. People just don't pay!"

Beatrix understood. Mr. Sutton was a very fine veterinary surgeon. She would give over any of her animals to his care without question. But when his work was done, he did not always leave a bill—and when he did, one could not be sure that he had included all the things that should be paid for. And Mrs. Sutton, who managed the accounts, had always struck her as being . . . well, disorganized, to put it kindly. Neither of them was a very good businessperson.

Allowing people to go on credit was obliging but un-wise, in Beatrix's view. In fact, one of the housemaids at Bolton Gardens had gotten into a very awkward fix over boots and bonnets on credit, which was where the idea for the plot of *Ginger and Pickles* had come from. In the book, the dog and cat who ran the village shop extended so much credit to their customers that they were ruined. And now the Suttons! It seemed like an ironic coincidence, but per-haps this sort of thing happened more often than she guessed.

"You have a brave idea, Deirdre," Beatrix said at last. "And you are a splendid, stout-hearted girl to think of it." Deirdre was like St. George, always ready to confront the dragon. "But money is such a . . . a delicate matter. When Mr. Sutton learns that you have gone round the village, asking people to—"

"Asking people for what?" Deirdre exclaimed heatedly. She put her hand into her pinafore pocket and took out a piece of folded paper. "Here's the list I made of people who are owing. Is it so awf'lly wrong to ask them to pay what they owe?"

Beatrix frowned. "No, of course not. They ought to pay. They *must* pay. But Mr. Sutton may be very annoyed when he finds out that you—"

"Yes, I'm sure he will," Deirdre said stoutly. "He will say I shouldn't have done this, and he may even turn me out of my place." Her voice rose. "But don't you see, Miss Potter? If I *don't* do this, the cottage will be foreclosed. Mrs. Sutton and the children will be sent to the workhouse at Ulverston, and then I'll be out of a place anyway."

"I really don't think it will come to that," Beatrix began, and then stopped. How could she be sure? Banks were enormously powerful, and they didn't worry about whether collecting money was "common" or not. If money was owed, it was owed, and that was that. What's more, they had solicitors and judges on their side, and the police. They could do almost anything they pleased, and there was almost no way to stop them.

Beatrix took a deep breath. She hated asking for money. It seemed such a mean, *vulgar* thing. But even as she thought the word, she remembered her mother using it to describe what Norman did for a living, which was really only good, honest work. And she remembered how hard it was for her when she didn't receive her royalty checks on time, and how very difficult it was to ask for the money that was owed her. She could understand the Suttons' dilemma. Mr. Sutton had done honest work and should be paid and that was that.

"Perhaps I can help, Deirdre," she said. "But only on condition that you postpone talking to others until we see what I am able to do." Beatrix knew the villagers well enough to know that they would never listen to the pleas of a young person, especially one they knew as well as they knew Deirdre and whom they considered nothing more than a servant in the Sutton household.

"Postpone it?" Deirdre looked uncertain. "Well, if you think—" She stopped. And then, frank and straightforward as always, she said, scowling, "It's because I'm not a grownup, isn't it? And because it looks like begging."

Matching honesty with honesty, Beatrix said, "Yes to both, Deirdre. But please don't take it to heart, my dear. You've already done the hardest part—making the list. If you wouldn't mind my giving you a hand, I'd be glad to see what I can do. I'm not sure what that will be," she added hastily, not wanting Deirdre to get her hopes up. "But I'm willing to try."

"Of course I'd be glad if you'd help," Deirdre said promptly.

"Then let me see the list."

Deirdre put it on the table. "We can mark off your name," she said. She drew a line through it.

Beatrix's eyes widened as she scanned the list. She recognized every name on it—most of the villagers, actually—and knew that all but one or two could pay what they owed. It might be a squeeze, with Christmas coming up and every shilling spoken for. But once they understood the importance, they would do it.

"I can help by starting here," she said, and put a mark

beside one of the names. "If this person pays up, I think the rest will follow suit."

Deirdre frowned. "You're starting at the hardest place," she said. " 'A perfect dragon of parsimony' is what Mrs. Sutton calls her."

" 'A perfect dragon of parsimony.' " Beatrix smiled, a very small smile. "I think that's exactly the right description, Deirdre."

The name Beatrix had marked was that of Lady Longford.

10

The Inquest: Act One

Captain Woodcock's fear that the jurors would not be able to make it through the snow was unfounded. It was exactly as the doctor had said: this was simply too interesting an event to miss, no matter how deep the snow or how biting the wind. And it wasn't just the jurors who came, either. The pub was packed so full that not another spectator could have found a place, and the room reeked with the powerful scents of tobacco, onions, garlic, wet wool, and unwashed bodies. In fact, if you and I had been there, I am sure we would have opened a window to bring in a breath of fresher air.

Most of the men were villagers whose names and faces are familiar to us: George Crook, Roger Dowling, Mr. Llewellyn, Mr. Wilson from Castle Cottage, and Joseph Skead, the St. Peter's sexton, among many others. Several strangers had joined the crowd, as well, probably wondering what this was all about. Sven Knutson, the stout blond gentleman who had arrived at the Arms that morning, stood with his shoulder against the wall, smoking a fat cigar and watching the group attentively. Another inn guest, an elegant man in green tweeds with a long pointed nose and reddish moustache—Nicholas Smythe-Jones was his name—was pressed into a far corner, holding a white linen handkerchief to his mouth as if the odor was overwhelming (it probably was). Mr. Joseph Adams, the photographer who had taken a room with the Crooks at Belle Green, could be identified by the camera he carried. A very tall, very thin man with gray side-whiskers, he seemed to think the interior of the pub and the gathering itself was picturesque, a nice bit of local color. He walked around the room, taking the occasional photo, until everyone grew so accustomed to his camera that they scarcely noticed it.

There was a noticeable buzz when the deceased's sister, veiled in black, entered the room through the kitchen door on the arm of Dr. Butters, who had waited outside until she arrived. She took a seat behind the bar, where she was hidden from the gaze of the curious—except for the photographer, for whom she reluctantly removed her veil, managing a small smile. There was an even louder buzz when the captain came in and took a seat in front of the fireplace.

Constable Braithwaite, serving as bailiff, raised his voice over the general hubbub. "Oyez, oyez, oyez! Ye good men of this district are summoned to appear here this day to inquire for His Sovereign Majesty the King when, how, and by what means Hugh Wickstead, of Briar Bank Farm, came to his death."

By the time he finished, the room had fallen so still that the boards of the floor could be heard creaking as the audience shifted from one foot to the other. The jurors were solemnly sworn and took their seats in front of the dart board. Everyone watched expectantly as Captain Woodcock, in his capacity as Justice of the Peace, called the inquest to order and summoned the first witness.

This proved to be Mr. Wickstead's gardener, Billie Stoker, a short, wiry man with a full black beard, who gave the camera a gap-toothed smile as the constable swore him in. He testified that he and his brother Gerald had found their employer lying under the fallen tree, a large yew that had snapped completely off. Asked how they had managed to find him, he replied simply, "T' dog fetched us. 'Twas black night. Wi'out t' dog, we'd nivver 'uv found 'im. Smart 'un, he is. Verra smart."

"The dog," the captain said. "That would be—"

"That'ud be Pickles," Billie Stoker replied. He looked around. "Where's Pickles? Anybody seen Pickles?"

"Here!" cried Pickles, lost amid a forest of legs.

"Here's Pickles," said Lester Barrow. He bent over, picked up the brown-and-white fox terrier, and put him up on the bar.

"Aye, that's Pickles," Billie Stoker said authoritatively. "Mr. Wickstead allus took 'im when he went out. This time, t' dog come back alone, wi' Mr. Wickstead's wool cap in his mouth, and we had t' idea that somethin' was wrong."

"Wrong!" Pickles barked affirmatively. *"Of course it was wrong!"*

The captain raised his voice. "So the dog took you to the place where Mr. Wickstead was injured?"

"Aye, he did, pitch black though it were." Billie Stoker grinned. "Real smart dog, that 'un. You can ask him if you doan't believe me."

Pickles bounced up and down on the bar, stiff-legged. *"I'd be glad to testify. I have something very important to say."*

"I believe I shall forgo questioning the dog," the captain said in a dry tone. "Now, Mr. Stoker, you say that you and your brother—"

"Wait!" Pickles cried desperately. *"If you don't ask me to testify, you'll never find out what really happened! You see, I was there! I was the ONLY one there. I saw it with my very own eyes!"*

"Hey, Cap'n!" called Henry Stubbs, who should have been minding the ferry, except that it was out of commission. "T' pup's got sommat to say, he does. Better hear 'im out!"

"That's right!" cried Pickles, now standing up on his hind legs and lifting one front leg high in the air, like an eager scholar who wants to be called on. *"I'm the only one who—!"*

"Put that dog out, Lester," the captain commanded. "There's enough commotion in here already." He glared at Henry Stubbs. "This is a court of law. Be quiet, Henry, or I'll hold you in contempt."

"No, no!" Pickles shouted. *"You have to listen!"* He tried to avoid Lester Barrow by jumping off the bar. Unfortunately, he landed with a CRASH! on a stack of china crockery, knocking it to the floor.

"Come 'ere, dog," growled the innkeeper. Capturing Pickles, he put him out the back door, while the crowd laughed, the captain shouted for order, and Henry Stubbs hung his head.

When quiet had been restored, the captain resumed his questioning. "Now, Mr. Stoker. You say that you and your brother carried Mr. Wickstead home. He was alive at the time?"

"Aye, that he was, but barely. He had no chance, I'm sorry to say. He died in his bed, like a proper gentl'man."

"Did he say anything before he died? Give any indication how the accident happened?"

"No, sir. None, sir." Billie Stoker was emphatic. "Didn't say a single, solitary word, sir." He frowned. " 'Tis a girt puzzle, sir, if thi doan't mind me sayin'. There was no wind that night, see, sir? 'Twas calm as calm could be. T' tree had no call to break off and come down on poor Mr. Wickstead's head."

"I see," the captain said, frowning. "And where, exactly, did this event take place, Mr. Stoker?"

"On t' end o' Briar Bank, sir. Just west o' t' lake. Moss Eccles, that be."

"And what was Mr. Wickstead doing at the spot, if you know?"

Billie Stoker scratched his head. "Diggin' out a badger, was what I guessed," he replied, but doubtfully. "He had a shovel."

"You're not sure that he was digging out a badger?" the captain pressed.

Billie pursed his lips. "Well, he weren't eggsactly t' badger-diggin' sort, now, was he? And it was dark night, pure dark, wi'out a moon. Folk 'oo dig badgers gen'rally dig 'em in t' day, so they can see what they're doin'." He shook his head. "Diggin' badgers at night. Doan't seem right, not at all."

As the captain dismissed Billie Stoker, he also had to admit, but privately, to being deeply puzzled as to what Hugh Wickstead had been doing at Briar Bank on a dark, cold night. Many men in the village dug badgers for fun and profit, but Wickstead had never been among them. And Billie was right: badgers were dug in the daytime. It was odd.

Next to testify was Billie Stoker's brother, Gerald, who confirmed everything that Billie had said, adding only that they conveyed Mr. Wickstead home in a wagon, poor chap, pulled by Gerald's pony Rupert. Then Miss Wickstead had sent Gerald to fetch the constable from the village and the doctor from Hawkshead, so it had been nearly dawn by the time Gerald returned to his own fireside and had a bowl of porridge. After that—

"Thank you, Mr. Stoker," the captain said, and called Constable Braithwaite.

The constable testified that he had been summoned to investigate the scene. He had done so, and now gave his opinion that Mr. Wickstead had been killed when the top thirty feet of a fifty-foot yew had snapped off and fallen on him. As to how the tree came to fall on a calm night, he could not hazard a guess.

Constable Braithwaite was uncomfortably aware of the three photographs in his pocket and was relieved when the captain excused him without asking to see them. The claw marks on the tree could have nothing to do with Mr. Wickstead's accident, and were better left out of the legal business. Which did not mean that he himself wasn't interested. He *was*. He had gone back up to the scene of the accident twice, trying to figure out just what it was that had left those marks—and the odd scorch, which looked rather like the mark of a lightning bolt. As soon as the snow permitted, he hoped to get Captain Woodcock to go up there with him and have a look. Odd thing, too: the second time he went back, he found another man at the scene, also taking photographs. In fact, the man himself was in the pub—that is, the courtroom—at this very moment, taking pictures. Joseph Adams, he was, some kind of famous photographer, lodging with the Crooks at Belle Green. Said he was out taking photos of Moss Eccles Lake, which was quite beautiful, frozen right the way across now, and deep with snow. Made for good photographs, the constable had no doubt.

The final witness was Dr. Butters, who testified to the nature of the injury to the victim's head ("a fracture of the skull," he said), which was so severe that it was unlikely that any man, no matter how young or how old, might have survived. The doctor also expressed the opinion that this injury was the sole cause of death, inflicted by no other weapon than the tree (if the tree could be called a weapon). The doctor did not mention the photographs, either, since the captain was in charge of the inquest, and if Woodcock didn't want to see them introduced, why, that was the end of it—although the doctor, like the constable, confessed to being abominably curious about those marks.

At the captain's instruction, the jurors retired to the pub's kitchen to discuss the testimony and the evidence and drink a cup of tea. They returned in fifteen minutes to render their verdict. It was their unanimous opinion that the unlucky Mr. Hugh Wickstead had died by accident, having been struck down and crushed by a falling tree.

The captain thanked the jurors for their service.

Mr. Wickstead's sister tearfully thanked the captain for his conduct of the inquest and departed by the kitchen door.

Lester Barrow opened the bar, and the whole thirsty audience thankfully crowded round for their half-pints—a gratifying conclusion to an entirely satisfactory event.

Scarcely anyone noticed Mr. Joseph Adams taking a photograph or two as the men reached for their mugs, and then venturing outside to take one or two more of the departing Miss Wickstead.

11

The Inquest: Act Two

Rascal, George Crook's fawn-colored terrier, crept out from under the kitchen table where he had been listening to the jurors discuss their verdict. He followed Miss Wickstead through the kitchen door and watched while Mr. Knutson—the stoutish blond gentleman who had arrived that morning in Jerry's charabanc—strode up and said something to her. (Personally, I am rather sorry that Rascal was not curious enough about this conversational exchange to eavesdrop. Had he gone just a little closer and listened a little harder, you and I might have learned something rather important to our story. But he wasn't and he didn't, so we shall have to wait a while longer to find out whether the gentleman was offering his condolences, or flirting with a pretty woman, or something else altogether.)

When the bereaved sister had climbed into a sleigh and was driven off by Billie Stoker, Rascal trotted out to the small

stone-built storage shed, where the other animals were waiting to hear the news.

"*Is the inquest over?*" Tabitha Twitchit cried eagerly, jumping down from the large overturned flower pot where she'd
been sitting. "*What was the verdict?*"

"*Accidental death,*" Rascal reported. "*Struck down by a
falling tree. No surprise there, I suppose.*"

"*If the jury had heard my story, their ruling might have been
different,*" Pickles muttered darkly. "*Captain Woodcock should
have called me as a witness.*"

"*Your story?*" Tabitha laughed scornfully. "*You wanted to
tell them* your *story?*"

"*As if they cared,*" Crumpet added.

"*You silly puppy,*" Rascal said, with affectionate indul-
gence. He liked Pickles. A bit excitable, perhaps, but always up for a romp and good times. "*The Big Folks can't hear
you. Oh, they can hear you barking, of course. They find it rather
annoying, unless they're following you and you are following a fox.
But not even the smartest of them knows that you've anything important to say. Except about foxes,*" he added, for it was well
known that huntsmen could tell by the sound of the dogs'
voices whether and where they had found the fox.

Crumpet snorted. "*That's because they don't listen. They
don't pay the proper attention. They're careless.*" She was a sleek,
handsome gray tabby cat with a red collar and gold bell of
which she was excessively proud, as she was proud of her
reasoning capacity. Crumpet considered herself to be extraordinarily gifted with intelligence.

"*But it's really not their fault,*" Tabitha Twitchit pointed
out. "*Their ears just don't work as well as ours, or their brains.
They don't have our superior sense of smell. They can't see in the
dark, either.*" She licked her paw and rubbed it over her face.

"As everyone knows, they are regrettably deficient—compared to cats, that is."

Pickles shook his head sadly. *"But I could have told them the whole story. Everything that happened up there at Briar Bank that awful day—although they probably wouldn't have believed me."* He gave a discouraged sigh. *"So I suppose it wouldn't have been any good telling them. P'rhaps it's just as well I wasn't called as a witness."*

"If they didn't believe you," put in Crumpet disapprovingly, *"it was because of that wild story you told about the treasure. Everybody knows you're not a credible witness, Pickles. You exaggerate."*

"But I didn't *exaggerate!"* Pickles protested, much offended. *"I said that Mr. Wickstead and I found two small sacks of treasure. It's not my fault that the story got blown out of all proportion. I told the* truth!*"*

"Two small sacks!" Crumpet exclaimed, her green eyes going wide. *"Why, that's not what you said at all. You said there were four sacks."*

"Four!" cried Tabitha. *"It was six, and the sacks were so large they had to be carried home in the wagon!"*

"I did NOT say it was four sacks," Pickles barked crossly. *"And certainly not six! I said that Mr. Wickstead put everything that we found in his game bag, and carried it home himself."*

"Nonsense!" hissed Tabitha, flicking her tail. *"That's not what I heard."*

"Absurd!" spit Crumpet, arching her back. *"That's not what happened at all! What happened was—"*

"There, there, girls," said Rascal soothingly. *"What matters is that we now know the truth."*

Of course, *you* know the truth, too, because you and I heard the story from an eyewitness who had no reason to exaggerate the size of the treasure—in fact, every reason *not* to.

That would be Bailey Badger, who watched as Mr. Wickstead and Pickles retrieved the two small bags of gold treasure from Briar Bank. And we saw how quickly the truth got exaggerated, as truth has a way of doing when it flies around a village, and how Auld Dolly Dorking, Lucy Skead's mother, reminded everyone that anyone who found a treasure was curst, so that no one was in any degree surprised when Mr. Wickstead was felled by a falling tree and carried home to die in his bed. (It had not escaped anyone, either, that the tree in question was a yew, the Tree of Death, which was always planted in cemeteries.)

As far as the villagers were concerned, it was the curse, and that's all there was to that.

"*Well,*" soothed Tabitha. "*Whether you said two bags, or four, or six, it doesn't matter, Pickles. It's the value that counts, not the quantity.*" She licked the tip of her tail. "*The Wickstead treasure is priceless, we understand. Worth a king's ransom.*"

"*What counts is my reputation,*" retorted Pickles indignantly. "*You've destroyed it with your own exaggerations. Now, when I tell what really happened at Briar Bank, nobody will believe me.*" I'm afraid that what Pickles is saying is true, although there's nothing he can do about it. It is a sad fact that once one's credibility has been destroyed, it's all but impossible to redeem oneself.

"*Well, then, what* did *happen at Briar Bank?*" Crumpet demanded. "*Come, come, Pickles. We should like to know how Mr. Wickstead died. Was he really killed by the tree?*" She snickered. "*Or p'rhaps some sly evil doer did him in?*"

"*We should very much like to know,*" Tabitha repeated, in a tone more kindly than Crumpet's. "*It's a pity that Captain Woodcock wouldn't allow you to enter your testimony in evidence, but we shall be glad to hear it.*"

"*Of course we shall!*" exclaimed Crumpet, who had just had

a very bright idea. *"And we shall do it right! We'll have another inquest. Rascal can be bailiff and swear you in, Pickles. I'll be the Justice of the Peace and ask the questions. Tabitha can be the jury."*

"No, no, Crumpet," Tabitha objected. *"I should be the Justice of the Peace. After all, I am the president of the Village Cat Council. I am Senior Cat."*

"Oh, you certainly are," Crumpet said cattily. *"You are very senior, Tabitha. In fact, you are so senior that you can barely get around. You ought to think of retiring and letting someone younger do the job. And who is best suited to the task? Moi, of course."* She lifted her chin and raised her voice. "MOI!"

"You?" Tabitha was shrill. *"You are nothing but a silly puss who thinks too well of herself. You need to learn humility. And I'm just the one to teach—"*

"Tabitha!" Rascal barked authoritatively. *"Crumpet! Let's not quarrel! I'll be the bailiff and the Justice of the Peace. You two can be the jury and render a verdict. Now, go sit on that shelf over there—that's your jury box. Pickles, sit on that wooden box and hold up your paw to be sworn."*

"He can't be sworn," Crumpet objected sourly. She still thought she ought to be the Justice of the Peace. *"We don't have a Bible."*

Rascal looked around. The storage shed was full of cast-offs from the inn, including a broken lamp, several discarded jugs and pots, and a box of books. *"We have this,"* he said, picking up the first book he laid his paw on. *"We'll pretend it's a Bible."*

Pickles squinted at the book. *"I don't think—"* he began.

"It's not quite the same thing as—" Tabitha remonstrated.

"Personally," said Crumpet, *"I am of the opinion that—"*

"Oyez!" barked Rascal loudly, overriding their objections. *"Oyez, Oyez! This court is in session!"*

And with due solemnity, Pickles was sworn to tell the

truth, the whole truth, and nothing but the truth, so help him God—on a leather-bound copy of Charles Darwin's *The Origin of Species.*

Rascal sat on his haunches behind the overturned flower-pot, using it as the judge's bench. He picked up a broken-handled hammer to serve as a gavel and began. *"Now, then, Pickles,"* said he sternly, *"You will confine yourself to the facts, please. You accompanied Mr. Wickstead on the afternoon of his death?"*

"Yes," Pickles said. *"That's a fact,"* he added.

"What time was that?"

"We left about nine in the evening. Another fact. We had a lantern. Also a fact."

"And where were you going?" Rascal asked, adding in an admonitory tone, *"You don't need to restate the thing about it being a fact. We'll stipulate it."*

"I just want to be sure they know it's true," Pickles said, eyeing the jury.

Rascal nodded. *"Well, then. Where were you going?"*

"To Briar Bank."

"And your purpose?"

"This is so boring," one of the jurors meowed, sotto voce, to the other. *"When are we going to get to the good part?"*

"Your purpose?" Rascal repeated, glaring at the cats.

Pickles cocked his head, perplexed. *"Why, to go with Mr. Wickstead. What other purpose would I have?"*

The jury giggled.

Rascal gave a long-suffering sigh. *"And what was Mr. Wickstead's purpose?"*

"Oh, that." Pickles' expression cleared. *"He was putting the treasure back."*

"What?" Rascal cried, astonished. *"He was putting it back? You mean, back in the place where he first found it?"*

Pickles nodded.

"*Why in the world was he doing that?*"

"*He didn't say, but I assumed*—" Pickles looked at Rascal, frowning. "*Can I say what I assumed? I mean, it's not exactly a fact, it's more like a guess, based on . . . well, on some things he said to me. But it's a pretty good guess, if I do*—"

"*For pity's sake, just SAY it!*" cried the jury in one voice, leaning forward impatiently.

Rascal banged the flowerpot with his gavel. "*The jury will be silent,*" he barked. To the witness, he added, "*You may state your assumption.*"

"*Wonderful,*" muttered Crumpet.

"*He was putting it back to keep someone else from finding it,*" Pickles said. "*And maybe taking it,*" he added.

"*Someone else?*" Tabitha cried. "*Who?*"

"I'll *ask the questions,*" Rascal said, feeling that he was losing control of the situation. "*Who?*" he asked, addressing the witness.

Pickles shifted position. "*His sister.*"

"*His sister?*" Rascal asked in surprise. "*You're referring to Miss Wickstead?*"

"*That's right. You see, he found her taking photographs of the treasure, which seemed to disturb him.*" Pickles smiled sadly. "*Mr. Wickstead talked to himself sometimes, and sometimes he talked to me. In this case, I overheard him saying to himself that he didn't trust her. Miss Wickstead, I mean. So when he took the treasure back to Briar Bank, I assumed he wanted to hide it from her.*"

"*All six bags of it?*" Crumpet interrupted.

"*Four,*" disputed Tabitha.

"*Two,*" Pickles corrected, with a hard look at the jury. "*Two small leather bags. No more, no less.*"

"*So,*" Rascal said firmly. "*Mr. Wickstead carried the two leather bags full of treasure to Briar Bank. And then what?*"

Pickles scratched his nose with his paw. *"Then he told me to put them back where they came from in the first place."*

"Which was?"

"An open badger burrow." He cocked his head. *"Well, not exactly open. There's a big yew tree there, and the roots rather cover up the hole, as tree roots do. And there are rocks and twigs. And bracken. The usual sort of things."*

The jury fidgeted.

"So you put the bags back into the badger burrow?"

"Yes."

"How far into the burrow?"

"Well," said the dog, *"I—"*

The jury sighed impatiently.

"Never mind about that," Rascal said. *"What happened next?"*

"I'm not . . . exactly sure," Pickles said doubtfully. *"I mean, whatever-it-was happened while I was in the burrow, you see. I had just put the second bag back where I found it and was turning around to come out, when I heard—"* He stopped, biting his lip. *"I heard—"*

The jury leaned forward.

"You heard?" Rascal prompted.

Pickles closed his eyes as if to help him remember the scene. *"I heard a loud cracking and splintering,"* he said, in a very low voice. *"Like a tree . . . snapping off. Then there was a tremendous crash, you see, and the ground shook, like an earthquake. Some rocks began to fall around me, and there was a lot of dust. I was afraid the ceiling was going to come down."* He took a deep breath. *"When I crawled out, I saw poor Mr. Wickstead lying on the ground. He . . . he wasn't moving. The top part of the yew tree was lying on him. I knew right away he was badly hurt."* A tear trickled down his furry cheek. *"Mr. Wickstead was always good to me, you know. I miss him. I miss him very much."*

"Yes, of course you do," murmured Tabitha softly. She had

had a soft heart and had never quite got over Miss Tolliver's sudden death. She also understood that Pickles was probably uncertain about his future. Billie Stoker might keep him. But would Miss Wickstead want him around Briar Bank House, as a reminder of the tragic way her brother had died?

"The yew tree." Rascal frowned, trying to picture the scene. *"You mean, it came down, just like that? Snap, crackle, splinter, and the top popped off? All by itself?"*

"All by itself?" echoed Crumpet skeptically.

Pickles bit his lip. *"Well, not exactly,"* he said. *"That is, it—"*

"What do you mean, 'not exactly'?" Rascal demanded. *"Did the wind push it over?"* He stopped, remembering. *"No, it couldn't have been the wind. Mr. Stoker, in his sworn testimony, said it was calm as calm could be the night Mr. Wickstead died."* He frowned sternly. *"Unless you wish to contradict Mr. Stoker, in which case we shall have to consider bringing charges of perjury against somebody."*

Pickles shook his head. *"It wasn't the wind. It was—"* He swallowed.

"It was WHAT?" cried Crumpet, now completely out of patience.

"You are under oath, Pickles," Rascal reminded him gravely. *"How did the tree come down?"*

Pickles was looking quite miserable. *"There was . . . there was something in the top of the tree. Something very . . . large."*

"Something IN the tree?" chuckled Tabitha. *"Really, now, Pickles."*

Crumpet snickered. *"Something large? An eagle, maybe?"* She cackled. *"An ostrich? A moa? A gyrfalcon?"* By this time, she was howling with laughter.

"A phoenix!" cried Tabitha, and both cats were convulsed.

"The jury will be silent!" Rascal roared, and they subsided, putting their paws over their mouths to stifle the giggles. *"Well, what was it?"* he asked the witness. *"This large thing in the tree. Did you see it?"*

"I saw it as it flew away," Pickles said, and gulped.

"So it was a bird, then," Rascal said, glad to have that settled.

But Pickles shook his head. *"No, not a bird. It was . . . it was . . ."*

"A duck," derided Tabitha.

"A goose," mocked Crumpet, rolling her eyes.

Rascal banged with his gavel. *"Order! We will have order in this court! I direct the witness to answer."* Out of the side of his mouth, he added, in an urgent whisper, *"Come on, old chap. Out with it!"*

Pickles covered his eyes with his paw. *"It was a . . . dragon."*

"A dragon?" echoed Rascal incredulously.

"A DRAGON!" cried the jurors in one outraged voice. *"There ARE no dragons!"*

"A dragon," whispered Pickles. *"Not a huge dragon. Actually, a rather small dragon, as dragons go. Not that I've actually seen any,"* he amended hastily. *"Only pictures in Mr. Wickstead's books. But this dragon was large enough,"* he added hastily. *"A little larger than Kep the collie. Oh, and he had wings, leathery wings. And green scales and a tail."* He closed his eyes, concentrating. *"Yes, a tail. I'm sure of it. Which made him look larger, of course."*

"Wings and scales and a tail," Crumpet repeated cynically. *"The next thing you know, Pickles will be telling us that his miniature dragon breathed smoke and fire."*

"He did!" cried Pickles, opening his eyes wide. *"Yes, that's right, Crumpet. There was smoke. And fire! That's how I could see*

him. It was dark, you see, and Mr. Wickstead dropped the lantern when he fell. But the dragon gave enough light to—"

"Impeach this witness!" Tabitha hissed angrily. *"We can't believe a word he says. First he lied about the size of the treasure, and now he's making up a ridiculous story about a dragon."*

Pickles gave a disconsolate wail. *"Why would I make up something like this?"*

Tabitha shrugged. *"So we'll think you're important, I suppose."*

"When you're nothing but a foolish little puppy who hasn't a brain in his head," Crumpet added.

At this, Pickles was reduced to tears. *"But it's true,"* he sobbed. *"I swear it! The dragon was big enough so that when he was perched in the top of the tree, he snapped it right off. And the tree came down, and the dragon, and—"*

"So you're saying that this miniature dragon murdered Mr. Wickstead," Rascal said, trying his best to piece the scene together.

"Well, I don't know about 'murdered,' " said Pickles, wiping his eyes on the back of his paw. *"That is, I don't know whether he was deliberately trying to hit Mr. Wickstead with the tree, or—"*

"Stuff and nonsense," muttered Tabitha.

"I have better things to do than listen to this ridiculous story," Crumpet growled. *"Adjourn the inquest, Rascal. We're not getting anywhere."*

"But we can't adjourn without a verdict," Rascal reminded them hastily. *"What say you, jurors? Death by accident? Death by misadventure? Death by—"*

"Death by dragon!" chorused the cats. *"Court's adjourned!"* And with that, they jumped off the shelf and scampered out into the snow, shouting with wild laughter.

"But it's true," Pickles said sadly, after they had gone. *"I'm not lying, Rascal. Every word I've said is the truth."*

"You shall have to prove it, then," said Rascal, with a dis-

couraging shake of the head. *"The witness is dismissed. You may step down."*

"But how in the world am I to prove a dragon?" Pickles cried in despair.

I am sure you must understand his feelings. For while most of us are called upon to prove quite a few things in the course of our lives—geometry theorems, or last wills and testaments, or a claim we have staked, or a bowl of yeast dough, or our strength, or whether we truly love someone, or where we actually were when we were alleged to have committed some youthful indiscretion—I think we must admit that the difficulty of proving a dragon is almost as great as that of proving God or heaven or hell or any of the other things we may believe in but have not actually seen.

"Prove a dragon? I'm afraid that's your problem." Rascal tossed his gavel aside. *"Court's adjourned. You can go home now, Pickles."*

"Go home?" Pickles asked mournfully. *"I have the feeling that Briar Bank House won't be my home much longer. Billie Stoker wants me to stay on, but Miss Wickstead's opposed."* He made a low growling noise in his throat. *"She isn't what she seems to be, Rascal, and that's a fact. Mr. Wickstead was just getting on to her when he died."*

"Not what she seems to be?" Rascal asked. *"Why, what do you mean?"*

"Well, take that gentleman who saw her out, for instance. The stout fellow with the whiskers."

"Mr. Knutson, his name is," Rascal said. *"Arrived here just this morning."*

Pickles snorted. *"He may have come back just this morning. But he was here earlier, for he visited Miss Wickstead just a day or two before her brother died. When Mr. Wickstead had gone to Kendal."*

"So they're friends. So what do you make of that?"

"Miss Wickstead gave all the servants a half-holiday that

afternoon—even Billie Stoker, who had already had his half-holiday the week before. She was alone when Mr. Knutson arrived."

Rascal raised his eyebrows. *"Ah-ha!"* he said, in a knowing tone. *"It sounds as if they are a little more than friends. Perhaps they just wanted some time alone."* And he gave a broad wink.

"I don't believe it's what you're thinking," Pickles replied, shaking his head. *"I didn't see any kissing or hand-holding or any of that—at least, not while I was in the house. Unfortunately, Miss Wickstead put me out not long after her gentleman caller arrived. They—"*

"Scat, you dogs, get out of here!" cried Mrs. Barrow, who had come out to the shed to get some lamp oil, which was stored there. "This ain't yer place! Go home where you belong!"

And since Mrs. Barrow obviously meant business, the two dogs ran, Rascal in one direction and Pickles in the other. I am afraid that we shall have to wait until later to find out what Miss Wickstead and Mr. Knutson were up to when they spent the afternoon alone.

12

Bailey's Story: Episode Two

Did not learned men, too, hold, till within the last twenty-five years, that a flying dragon was an impossible monster? And do we not now know that there are hundreds of them found fossil up and down the world? People call them Pterodactyls: but that is only because they are ashamed to call them flying dragons, after denying so long that flying dragons could not exist.

Charles Kingsley, *The Water Babies*

Mr. Heelis had more than one reason for coming to Sawrey that day. After the inquest, he planned to drop in at Hill Top Farm to discuss a few business matters with Miss Potter, matters having to do with her recent purchase of Castle Farm and some repairs she had commissioned there. In fact, he had been quite pleased when she wrote to tell him that she would be at the farm and would like the opportunity of a conversation.

I am sorry to tell you, however, that Mr. Heelis was not entirely aware of just how pleased he was at the prospect of seeing Miss Potter again. Indeed, it is fair to say that he, like so many other British men of his time, is not at all conscious of his feelings, especially those that lurk deep at the very bottom of his heart. If we were to peer inside that marvelous organ, we would be likely to find that something is going on of which our Will has only a vague understanding. Yes, he is becoming more aware of the distinct warmth and pleasure he feels when he thinks about Miss Potter—an awareness that has seemed to be growing of late, rather than dwindling. Yes, he finds himself looking forward to her letters and their meetings with an increasing eagerness that surely has little to do with the property business they are transacting. Still, perhaps you will agree with me that it is a pity that he is not more mindful of all that is in his heart.

Actually, Mr. Heelis has recently had occasion to think rather more often of Miss Potter, for he had helped her purchase Castle Farm—a jolly good thing, in his opinion, since this kept a nice old farm from going to some off-comer who could never appreciate its uniqueness. In Will's estimation, Miss Potter is a thoughtful, forthright, and very sensible young lady—and quite attractive, too, with those brilliant blue eyes and unruly brown hair. She seems totally indifferent to fashion and prefers country tweeds to city silks. But there is a certain soft charm and old-fashioned shyness about her that he finds unusually appealing, especially in comparison to some of the brasher ladies of his acquaintance. Miss Barwick, for example, with whom the villagers have apparently linked him. Will himself is a very shy man, and when a lady pursues him, he wants to turn and flee in the opposite direction as fast as two feet or a good horse will carry him.

Miss Potter, of course, is anything but brash, although, beneath her seeming softness, Will has already encountered a shrewd business sense and a determination about as unyielding as a stone wall. Watching her bargain for property and livestock, he has come to suspect that when Miss Potter knows what Miss Potter wants, she does not hesitate to pursue it.

He smiles when he thinks this, but his smile fades as he remembers (still without any conscious awareness) that Miss Potter gave her heart to the fiancé she lost a few years before, and there is not much chance that she will ever take it back. In addition to her many other fine qualities, she is an extraordinarily loyal person, a quality which he admires but in this case (also quite unconsciously) has every reason to regret.

Still, as I said, Will Heelis has business with the lady, whatever the state of her heart or his. So the minute the captain dismisses the jurors, Will makes for the door, aiming to take the path to Hill Top Farm, which (as you know if you have visited the village of Near Sawrey) is only a short way up the hill from the Tower Bank Arms. He has just wound his muffler around his neck and is putting his hat on his head when he is accosted by a very serious Constable Braithwaite.

"I wonder if I might have a word," the constable says in a low voice. " 'Tis about some photographs I took at t' place where auld man Wickstead met his unfortunate fate. I'd like thi opinion on 'em, Mr. Heelis, sir. I would indeed."

"Of course," Will replies, glad to be reminded of something he had meant to do, anyway. At that moment, the clock strikes, and he is reminded of something else. "Ah, lunchtime, Constable Braithwaite. Will you join me?" And setting aside for the moment his errand at Hill Top Farm (but not forgetting it), Will unwinds his muffler, takes off his hat, and finds a seat at the nearest vacant table.

This discussion of photographs is likely to occupy Mr. Heelis and Constable Braithwaite for the better part of an hour, for I see that they are ordering a substantial lunch— a hot mutton pie, a half of bitters, and a dish of bread pudding—from Mrs. Lester Barrow. So you and I shall not stand idly by and wait whilst Will examines the photographs and eats his lunch. Instead, we shall take ourselves up to The Brockery, where we may hear something to help us make sense of the puzzling and (dare I say?) incredible dragon tale that Pickles has just offered in sworn testimony at the inquest held by Rascal and the two cats. (I certainly shan't blame you if you question the veracity of a testimony that is sworn on *The Origin of Species.* However, you might want to suspend your disbelief until you have heard what Bailey has to say.)

At the end of Chapter Eight, we left Bailey Badger telling his tale in front of the kitchen fire at The Brockery, with Thorn sprawled on the hearth, Bosworth dozing in his chair, and Parsley pottering about the kitchen. In our absence, however, Bailey's audience has grown, for Professor Galileo Newton Owl, D.Phil., has dropped in to see how his friends at The Brockery have weathered the winter storm, and whether they might need anything he can fetch for them.

The professor, a large tawny owl of great age and even greater reputation, lives in a great hollow beech tree at the top of Cuckoo Brow Wood, where it spreads out across Claife Heights before tumbling down the steep eastern slope to Lake Windermere. The owl's beech may be distinguished from all the other beeches in the woods by a painted notice board posted beside a low wooden door that opens onto a circular stairs within the tree:

G. N. OWL, D. PHIL.
OBSREVER AT LARJE
MIND YR HED!

The door and the stairs, of course, are designed for the convenience of the professor's earthbound guests, for the owl flies both to his apartments and to his treetop observatory, where he has installed a powerful telescope. Over the years, he has earned international recognition for his extensive scholarship in celestial mechanics, with particular emphasis on navigating by the stars (although as you can see, he's not much for spelling).

Now, equipped with a fresh cup of tea, the owl was seated beside Bosworth at the fire. *"Whooom,"* he said, peering intently at Bailey, *"have we here?"* He blinked, turning the flat disc of his face from one side to the other for a better look. *"Oooh, I see. It is Bailey Badger, of Briar Bank."* He frowned. *"What has happened tooo your paw, Bailey?"*

Please do not take this remark as revealing a kindly solicitude. The professor, who spends a great deal of time on the wing above the Land Between the Lakes, prides himself on knowing everything that happens in the village or on farms and fell. He is vexed when he discovers that an event (such as Bailey's injury) has dared to occur without his knowledge or consent.

Knowing this, Bosworth hastened to tell how he had come into his kitchen to see Bailey, damp and miserable, sitting beside the fire with his newly bandaged paw. Thorn immediately went on to relate tell how he had found the poor badger struggling to stay afloat in the icy waters of Moss Eccles Lake. And Bailey himself repeated, for the Professor's edification, a summary of Mr. Wickstead's discovery of the treasure trove.

"*A quite extraooordinary stooory,*" said the owl, much offended at the thought that all this has gone on without his permission. "*I dooon't think I've ever heard a stooory quite like it.*"

"*I really wish, Bailey,*" Bosworth put in, "*that you had told me about this remarkable find of Mr. Wickstead's when it occurred. I should have liked to enter it into the* History."

"*We did hear a rumor,*" Thorn reminded him, "*from that vole who was passing through.*" He glanced at the owl. "*He was on his way to his cousin's house at the top of Cuckoo Brow Wood.*"

"*Ah, that one,*" the professor said thoughtfully. "*Quite a tasty fellooow, albeit a trifle small.*"

While Bosworth and Thorn might not have liked the idea that a recent guest had become a friend's dinner, they said nothing, remembering the Ninth Rule of Thumb: *Animals have different tastes. A respectful badger does not inquire into his friends' dietary preferences.*

"*Voles and rabbits exaggerate to the point where it's impossible to know whether one is telling the truth,*" Bosworth explained to Bailey. "*And of course the* History *is not to be used as a repository of rumor. Had I understood that you were an eyewitness to the discovery of the treasure and could tell me, for the record, exactly where it was found—*"

"*But I didn't* want *it recorded,*" Bailey protested. "*I knew that if word got around, people would come with their shovels, and before long, they'd have dug up the whole of Briar Bank.*" He buried his face in his paws. "*I'd have to find someplace else to live,*" he said in a very low voice. "*And I am likely to have to do that soon, now that people know where Mr. Wickstead died. They will put two and two together, and come looking for the treasure.*" He shuddered.

If you know anything about badgers, you know how they hate the idea of moving house. Once they are settled, they are *settled.* And of course this particular badger faces an especially daunting challenge, for what can he do with all those books—chamber after chamber of them, shelved from floor to ceiling? The very thought of moving them made him feel quite faint. (Humans share Bailey's predicament, for it must be confessed that some of us have too many books altogether and wonder how we are going to find good homes for them when we are no longer able to keep a roof over their heads.)

"*We will dooo all we can,*" the professor said gently, "*tooo ensure that the Big Folk dooo not find out.*"

Thorn leaned forward. "*But now that we know about the treasure, we must know all the rest,*" he said urgently. "*Please tell us! We promise not to tell a soul.*"

And Bosworth added, "*Yes, tell us, Bailey, old chap. What happened next, after the discovery of the treasure?*"

Bailey dropped his paws and settled back in his chair, seemingly reassured. "*Nothing happened next,*" he replied in a retrospective tone. "*At least, not for quite a few months. I was very busy, of course, with a project having to do with the library, and then with—well, I'll tell you. And of course Mr. Wickstead was killed—*"

"*Yes,*" the owl said gloomily. "*Hit by a falling tree, I was tooold.*"

"*A sad event,*" Bosworth added. "*Very sad.*"

"*So you know about that,*" Bailey remarked with a sidewise glance. "*I thought perhaps you hadn't heard.*"

"*My mother learnt about it when she went to visit my aunt, who lives in the sheep meadow at Hill Top Farm,*" said Thorn. He glanced up at the clock. "*The inquest was to be held this morning. I wonder if the jury has rendered its verdict yet.*" He chuckled wryly. "*Everyone in the village seems to blame it on what they call the 'curse.'*"

"*How irrational,*" grumped the owl. "*One never ceases tooo be amazed at the foooolishness of the Big Fooolk.*"

Bailey looked away for a moment, as if he might be trying to decide how much to tell them. At last he said, half under his breath, *"I don't need a jury to tell me how Mr. Wickstead died. I know."*

"You know?" his audience chorused, in surprised unison.

"Yes, I know," Bailey replied matter-of-factly. *"But you won't believe me."*

Bosworth gave an affectionate laugh. *"Of course we'll believe you, my dear fellow,"* he said, in the sort of humoring tone animals use when they are talking to someone who has been recently ill and needs an extra bit of coddling. *"Whyever wouldn't we?"*

Bailey looked into his teacup, as if he were trying to read the scattering of tea leaves at the bottom. There was a long silence. *"Because it was a dragon,"* he muttered at last.

"A dragon!" Bosworth and Thorn exclaimed in unison.

"Dooo tell!" the owl hooted derisively.

And Parsley (taking a fresh batch of scones out of the oven) stifled a nervous sound that was half-gasp, half-giggle.

Bailey glared at the four of them. *"There. I said you wouldn't believe me, and you don't."*

Uncomfortably, Bosworth cleared his throat. His guest was clearly delusional—quite understandable, really, given all he had been through. *"It's not that we don't believe you, old chap. Certainly, we believe you, yes, yes, indeed we do. It's just that—"* He coughed. *"It's just that—"*

"It's just that we are not accustomed tooo dragons," the owl put in helpfully.

"The thing is, you see," Thorn added, *"that none of us have ever actually met one."*

"And since you haven't met one, my young hero, ergo they do not exist." Bailey got up from his chair and began to pace back and forth, his paws clasped behind his back. *"Now, I call that*

logic, I do. How about thunder, eh? Has anyone ever seen a thunder? Or a North Pole, or an equator, or—"

"There's no record of a dragon in this area," Bosworth said, recovering himself. *"If there were, it would be in the* History. *But it isn't,"* he added, just to make things perfectly clear.

Bailey chuckled bitterly. *"Oh, it's there. You just haven't happened across it. Which is understandable, I suppose, since there are—"* He stopped in front of Bosworth. *"How many volumes? How far back do they go?"*

"Of the History, *two dozen,"* Bosworth replied proudly. The devoted industry of the previous keepers of the *History* was really quite remarkable. All was noted, nothing omitted. He was confident that if there had been dragons in the Land Between the Lakes, there would be dragons in the *History*. *"They go back quite a very, very long time, to the days of the Bonnie Prince. That's when our branch of the badger clan came from Scotland to settle here."* (If you know your British history, you will remember that Bonnie Prince Charlie came to England, with the idea of seizing the throne, in 1745.)

"Only two dozen volumes?" Bailey gave a short, sardonic laugh. *"And they go back only as far as the Young Pretender? If you're looking for dragons, that's not nearly far enough."* He took another turn. *"But still—two dozen volumes, with hundreds of pages in each volume. I don't suppose you should like to claim that you've read every paragraph on every page and can therefore declare with absolute certainty that there is no mention of a dragon, living or dead. Or fossilized,"* he added. *"Don't forget about fossils."*

"Well, no, I shouldn't," Bosworth confessed. To read the great badger chronicle from the beginning to end, he should have had to give over the greater part of every day to reading, and Bosworth wasn't that sort of badger. He had other things to look after, such as the running of The Brockery and the well-being of the creatures who depended on him.

"But a dragon*?"* Bosworth took a deep breath. *"Really, Bailey, old chap, I very much doubt that—"*

" 'There are more things in heaven and earth, Horatio,' " growled Bailey, *" 'than are dreamt of in your philosophy.' "*

Thorn glanced around, puzzled, as if he were looking for someone. *"Horatio?"*

"A character in a Shakespeare play," the owl explained professorially. *"It's a quooootation."*

Bosworth tried again. *"Look here, old fellow. I'm not saying there hasn't been a dragon or two in the area at some point in the past, and you're undoubtedly right about fossils. People are always turning up fossilized thises and thats—I don't see why they shouldn't be finding fossilized dragons."*

"If they are there tooo find, that is," remarked the owl wisely. *"There may be nooone."*

Bailey gave a sardonic chuckle and stumped back and forth in front of the fire again.

"But we live in modern times," Bosworth hurried on. *"And there are railways and steamships and telegraphs and telephones and electricity—although not here, necessarily,"* he amended. One read about such innovations in newspapers, but they were slow to reach the Land Between the Lakes, where there were as yet no telephones or electricity, although Captain Woodcock did have a motor car, and there were electric lights at Windermere, on the other side of the lake.

"The thing about dragons—if there were *dragons—is that they lived so very long ago. In fact,"* he went on, warming to his subject, *"I have often heard Great-grandfather Basil Badger say that the Norse folk who settled this area in the ninth and tenth centuries were very well acquainted with dragons. Mythical dragons, that is. They wrote about them in their sagas and pictured them on their jewelry and shields and—"*

"And put them on the prows of their ships," said Bailey impa-

tiently, stopping for a moment. *"Yes, yes, of course, the Vikings were well acquainted with dragons. They understood them. They lived with them. But the dragons are not entirely mythical. And not fossilized, either."* He gave Bosworth a meaningful look, as if he had just made an important point, and resumed his pacing.

Bosworth frowned, sensing that he had somehow missed the significance. *"But the Vikings have been dead for centuries,"* he protested. *"All that's left of them are the old stone crosses and the names they gave to places. Any dragons they might have brought with them are dead, too."*

He concluded with a "so there" flourish, feeling much an expert on the topic. His great-grandfather had been a serious student of Viking history and lore, and Bosworth was well aware that the human language and dialects of the Lake District were heavily influenced by the Norsemen who landed on the western coast and moved inland during the tenth and eleventh centuries. If you should be so fortunate as to visit there, please watch for the evidence of their long-ago occupation, which you may see all around: their sheep (the ancestors of the hardy Herdwicks who still live on the fells), their stone-built farmsteads, their customs, along with words that both describe the landscape and evoke it: *tarn* for lake and *fell* for hill and *beck* and *ghyll* for stream. And when you look at a map of the Lake District, be on the lookout for the many Norse place names, some of which may make you smile. Bassenthwaite and Newbiggen and Skiddaw Dodd, and Hardknott, for instance.

But Bailey wasn't smiling at Bosworth's glib defense. *"So the dragons have all died, have they?"* He rolled his eyes and sat back down in the rocking chair. *"And just how long do you think a dragon lives?"*

The professor, who knew a great deal about a great many

things, let out a long, slow breath. *"A very looong time, nooo doubt."* His tone suggested that this was not something to which he had given a great deal of thought.

Bosworth thought for a moment, then hazarded a guess. *"A hundred years, perhaps? Two hundred?"*

Bailey snorted.

Bosworth, of course, was thinking of the professor's "very long time" in terms of badger generations. And since a badger life span is just fifteen years, a century is a very long time. Now feeling himself at a distinct disadvantage, he said, *"Well, then, how long do they live?"*

"Hundreds of years," Bailey said. *"Thousands."* He paused, so as to give more weight to what he said next. *"A dragon the Vikings brought with them—a real one, that is, not just the ones on their shields or their boats—might easily be alive still. In fact,"* he added grimly, *"one of them is very much alive, as I can attest."*

Thorn was staring at the visitor, wide-eyed, with an indescribable astonishment. *"You're telling us,"* he said incredulously, *"that a dragon has lived here—in the Land Between the Lakes—since the time of the* Vikings?*"*

The professor did a quick calculation. *"That would be,"* he said definitively, *"ten centuries. Mooore ooor less."*

"That's what I'm telling you." Bailey held up his bandaged paw. *"In witness whereof, I offer you this."* He extended it shakily.

Oh, if only Pickles could have seen and heard this testimony, the very proof that Rascal had asked him for! Or perhaps it isn't, since Bailey has not yet told us exactly how his paw came to be burnt. I suppose he might be making up the story to account for his quite unaccountable swim in the freezing waters of Moss Eccles Lake. But still, it does seem as though we are getting closer to the truth.

Thorn leaned toward Bosworth. *"It's a burn, all right,"* he said, in a low voice. *"The paw is badly singed, all the way to the elbow. I noticed it when I pulled him out of the water."*

"And a very nasty burn it is, too," Parsley put in, stepping forward with another plate of scones, fresh from the oven. *"But I think it will heal right away, Mr. Bailey, sir,"* she added reassuringly. *"I applied plenty of old Mrs. Prickle-Pin's comfrey salve. 'Tis the very best thing for a burn."*

Glad for the distraction, Bosworth took a scone. *"Let me see if I understand this correctly, Bailey. You had a close encounter with a dragon that resulted in a singed paw—"*

"Barbequed badger, if I hadn't dived into the water," Bailey said, in a dark tone. *"The lake was the only safe place. Of course, it was the other dragon, Yllva. Not my friend."*

"Your friend?" the owl hooted in a disbelieving tone. *"Yooou are talking about a dragon?"* He helped himself as Parsley handed round the tray. *"Thank yooou, Parsley. Yooor scoooones are delicious."*

"Yes," Bailey repeated firmly. *"My friend would never have done such a thing, even if he did bring that yew tree down on Mr. Wickstead's head. That was an accident."*

"A dragon brought down the tree?" Bosworth asked, startled.

Bailey nodded. *"The thing is that he's a rather young dragon, and he's been cooped up in close quarters for seven or eight centuries. He doesn't have a very good sense of how big he is—although he's certainly not very large, compared to Yllva."* He shuddered. *"I had to get away from her fire-burner. That's why I went into the lake."*

"Fire-burner?" Thorn repeated, as if he weren't sure that he had heard correctly.

"Fire-burner, flame-thrower, furnace, incinerator, chimneypot. Whatever you like to call the part of a dragon that makes the fire," said Bailey.

"*Incinerator, chimneypot,*" said Bosworth, under his breath. "*Oh, dear.*" He settled back into his chair and began to eat his scone, feeling in need of sustenance. "*I think that we had better hear the story. The* whole *story, I beg you, Bailey. From beginning to end.*"

"*And dooo not leave anything out,*" instructed the professor.

"*Not even the smallest detail,*" said Thorn, picking up the teapot to pour tea into Bosworth's cup.

The owl scowled. "*This sooo-called dragon, the one who killed Mr. Wickstead. What's his name?*"

"*Thorvaald,*" said Bailey.

"*Excuse me.*" The owl leaned forward. "*I didn't quite get that.*"

"*T-h-o-r-v-a-a-l-d,*" Bailey said. "*Double a. And he didn't kill Mr. Wickstead. Not on purpose, anyway. I was there. I saw it all.*"

Thorn raised his head, his eyes widening. "*You were there?*"

"*Well—*"

"*Thorn!*" Bosworth exclaimed as tea spilled over the rim of his cup and onto the floor. "*Mind what you're about, young fellow!*"

"*Ah, sorry, sir,*" Thorn muttered, and went to fetch a mop-up cloth.

At that moment, the clock began to chime. The owl looked up regretfully. "*Oooh, dear,*" he said, and gobbled the rest of his scone, scattering crumbs all around him. "*Is it really sooo late? I'm afraid I shan't be able tooo stay for the story. I must fly.*"

"*Not in here, please,*" said Bosworth hurriedly, for the professor (whilst he was a very intelligent owl when it came to such things as calculating the position of Mars or the phase of the moon) was apt to be absentminded about takeoffs and landings. To Bailey, he added, *"I'll be back in a moment. Don't go on with your story until I've returned."*

"*I shan't,*" said Bailey, and yawned widely.

Bosworth saw the professor to the front door and waved goodbye as he flew off, then turned and hurried back to the fire to hear the rest of the story. But Bailey's chin had dropped to his chest and he had fallen fast asleep. And since there is no telling how long the badger will nap, we shall take this opportunity to hurry back down the hill to Sawrey Village to see whether Mr. Heelis has as yet found his way to Hill Top Farm.

13

In Which Mr. Heelis and Miss Potter
Make a Surprising Discovery

After Deirdre left, Beatrix got out her watercolors and began coloring the drawing she had made of Mrs. Tittlemouse and the humblebees. She was troubled, though, wishing she had not been so quick to agree to help Deirdre with her scheme to collect the money owed to Mr. Sutton. Money was always such a troubling subject—as she very well knew from her own experience with Harold Warne. But she had agreed, and she would honor her promise, no matter how awkward she felt about the business.

After a while, she put down her brush and put on her blue coat and her favorite floppy-brimmed felt hat and went out to the barn to say an affectionate hello to the farmyard creatures: Kitchen and Blossom, the Galloway cow and her calf; Aunt Susan and Dorcas, the pigs; and Kep the collie. She still occasionally kept pets at Bolton Gardens, for the times when she needed models for her drawings. But her latest books had been about the farm animals and the village dogs and cats, and she was beginning to feel very close to them. They had more freedom than caged pets, and their lives seemed more mysterious, somehow—fuller, richer, more various, more *real*. And what's more, they were part of the farm life she was learning to love. So as she said hello, she gave each of them a careful looking-over, to make sure that they were all in good health and seemed happy. She lingered to collect a few eggs from Bonnet and Boots—only a few of the older and more experienced hens went on laying through the winter—and exchange greetings with the Puddle-ducks, noting that Jemima was nowhere around.

"That preposterous duCK has flown off with that QUACK ridiculous fox again," said Jemima's sister-in-law, Rebecca. *"An unnatural union. Heaven only knows what they see in each other."*

"Our Jemima hasn't been QUACK right in the head since she hatched that nestful of QUACK tortoises," said Rachel Puddle-duck in a tone that mixed sympathy with disapproval—rather more of the latter.

"She wasn't right before then, either," retorted Rebecca snappishly. *"Always wanting to go off on her own, instead of staying in the barnyard, tending to QUACK business."*

Beatrix shook her head. Jemima seemed to come and go as she chose, although no one could quite think how she got out of the various coops into which she was put. One almost suspected magic. (You'll find the full story of Jemima, the fox, and the tortoises, in *The Tale of Hawthorn House.*)

In his stall, Winston, the shaggy brown pony, lifted his head with a pleasant whinny. *"Mornin', Miss Potter. Up from London again, are we?"*

"Good morning, Winston," she said, scratching his ears. "I've given you a holiday today, but tomorrow, you and I are taking the sleigh up to Briar Bank House, with a stop at Tidmarsh Manor."

"*Nay!*" Winston tossed his head obstinately. "*You need a horse for that sleigh! I'm a mere pony. It's too heavy for me.*"

"Don't worry," Beatrix said, smoothing his mane. "The lane will be well traveled by that time, and we'll breeze right along."

"*Don't worry,*" Winston muttered in a sepulchral voice. "*It's not herself that's doin' the pullin', now is it?*" Sulkily, he shook off her hand and retired to the rear of his stall. "*City ladies have no idea how hard a farm pony has to work.*"

"*Don't pay him any mind, Miss Potter,*" barked Kep, the farm collie and one of Beatrix's favorites. "*He'll do as he's bid, I'll see to that. And a fine job he'll make of it, too.*" Kep, whose task it was to keep the barnyard animals in line, slipped into the stall and nipped sharply at Winston's hoof. "*Won't you, Winston?*"

"But I do wonder," Beatrix said, "whether I've made a mistake." She frowned at the pony. He did a fine job pulling the pony cart, but he really wasn't very large. "The sleigh might be too heavy for you, Winston. Perhaps I'll ask Mr. Llewellyn if I might borrow one of his horses."

"*There, y'see, Kep?*" Winston gave a triumphant flick of his brown tail. "*We'll make a farmer out of this city lady yet!*"

"*If she says go, you'll go,*" Kep growled. "*Stay, you'll stay. She's the boss.*"

Beatrix smiled, thinking (not for the first time) how clever animals were, and how it was almost possible to know what they were saying. She left the barn and was just going back to the house with her basket of eggs when someone called her name. She turned.

"Why, Mr. Heelis!" she exclaimed, discovering that she was suddenly quite flustered. "How . . . how very nice to see you!"

"Delighted to see you, Miss Potter," Mr. Heelis said, doffing his brown bowler hat. "Mr. Llewellyn has just finished plowing a path up Market Street. I thought perhaps you might like to walk up to Castle Farm and inspect the repairs to the barn. The job was finished last week—before the snow-fall, I'm glad to say."

"What a very good idea," Beatrix said. "But I've been outside for a bit. I should like to warm up first. Would you care for a cup of tea? Or perhaps lunch?" She held out her basket. "The hens produced only four eggs this morning, but there are enough for an omelet. I should be glad to make it for you. I don't do much cooking, but I'm happy to say I'm rather good with omelets."

"Thank you, no," Mr. Heelis said, as he followed Beatrix into the house. "The constable and I have just had a hot mutton pie and some of Mrs. Barrow's bread pudding. But I could certainly do with a cup of tea, if you're making one for yourself. I've been at the Wickstead inquest all morning," he added, as if in explanation. "It's dry work."

"Poor Mr. Wickstead," Beatrix said, hanging up her coat and shawl on the pegs behind the door. "He was struck down by a tree, Miss Barwick told me."

"Yes," Heelis said. He frowned as he took off his brown overcoat and hung it beside Miss Potter's blue woolen coat—a handsome coat, he thought in passing, nearly the same color as her eyes. "An unlucky accident. I must say, it is rather curious, though."

"Curious?" Miss Potter asked, putting the kettle on. "How so?"

Will came close to the fire, holding out his hands to warm them. "I've just seen some photographs," he said, pulling him-self back to the subject. "Constable Braithwaite took them, of the yew tree that came down on poor Wickstead. There are what appear to be claw marks on it. The marks of quite a large animal. At the top of the tree."

"My goodness," Miss Potter said, turning to face him,

quite surprised. "But that is very odd, isn't it? The largest wild animal in this area is the badger. I've often seen their claw marks on trees, but only near the bottom, where they've scratched off the bark, looking for grubs."

"Oh, it was larger than a badger," Will said, and sat down at the table. "Three or four times as large, easily." He looked around, admiring the way the firelight winked from the brass and china and thinking that Miss Potter had made the old farmhouse—which had been dirty and uncared for when she bought it—into something quite beautiful and very comfortable. Furnished it with antiques, too, like that oak dresser and that old clock with the painted face. And the spinning wheel, with a basket of fleece and spindle full of spun yarn. Real treasures that made him think of his grandmother's home, where he had spent happy days as a child.

"Twice as large as a badger." Miss Potter tilted her head to one side. "If I might make a suggestion," she said, "perhaps the photographs could be sent to Professor Trevor Hall, at Carlisle. I met him at the museum there. He is quite expert on the natural history of this area—he may be able to venture an opinion about the marks."

"Jolly good idea, Miss Potter!" Will exclaimed, wondering why he hadn't thought of it. "I shall obtain copies of the photographs and take care of the matter myself."

"So it is settled that Mr. Wickstead was killed by the tree," Miss Potter said quietly, as she measured tea into a pretty china teapot.

"That's the jury's verdict," Will said. "Dr. Butters' opinion, as well. Accidental death. No foul play involved." He tilted his head and gave her a teasing smile. "No mysteries to solve, I'm afraid, Miss Potter. Unless, that is, you'd like to tackle the mystery of the claw marks. Or Lady Longford's burnt barn."

When they were first acquainted, Will remembered, Miss Potter had used her knowledge of painting to put an end to a ring of art thieves, and not long after—through powers of observation that still seemed to him quite remarkable—had identified the man who shoved old Ben Hornby off the cliff. Reflecting on this now, Will thought he had never met anyone with Miss Potter's astonishing knack for seeing *through* things, past the surface features, with all their distractions, to the essential reality beneath. Perhaps it was her artist's eye, or her attention to small details, he thought. Whatever it was, it seemed to him quite uncanny.

But Miss Potter did not apparently take his remark as expressing admiration. She turned away, flushing. "I hope I have not seemed very forward," she said, in a low voice. "Or intrusive. Meddling in situations that are none of my business, I mean. I should not like you to think—"

"Oh, no, not at all!" Mr. Heelis exclaimed, very warmly. "I am sorry—really, I am!—if I seemed to be teasing you. That was not my intention." And quite without knowing what he was doing, he found himself taking her hand.

She turned and looked at him quite directly, saying nothing. The color had flooded her cheeks and her eyes were very blue. And shining, yes, they were shining, as if lit by some inner light, and he saw that they were wet with tears.

"I hope I haven't offended you," he said, feeling like an awkward schoolboy who has said exactly the opposite from what he meant and has hurt someone whose good opinion he valued. "Please forgive me, Miss Potter." He looked down at the small hand he was holding, and knew that he should let it go. He tried, and found that he couldn't. "I mean—"

"No," she said, very softly. "You haven't offended me. Thank you, Mr. Heelis. It's quite all right. Truly." She smiled, if a little crookedly. "I shall try not to mind if you think of me as a female Sherlock Holmes."

And with that, her fingers tightened on his, or seemed to. It was almost imperceptible, this tightening. Had he really felt it? Or only imagined it?

Outside, a rooster crowed, breaking the silence. On the range, the kettle began to hiss.

Miss Potter repossessed her hand. "The kettle," she said, and turned quickly to fetch it.

And since we have already taken the liberty of looking into Will's heart, perhaps we shall have another look, for what has just happened has had rather a surprising effect on him. Will is not in the habit of holding ladies' hands. In fact, he has done so only twice in his entire adult life, and one of those hands belonged to his cousin. That he has done so now—quite without intending to, or consciously willing it—utterly astounds him. He feels as if he has been turned to stone. Or perhaps he feels rather that he *was* stone, and now he has been turned to life. Actually, he doesn't know how he feels, for there is such a confused, incoherent chaos of feelings whirling around inside him that he can scarcely pick out any. He has to sit there and pretend that nothing at all has happened, other than his impulsively taking Miss Potter's hand for five or ten seconds or an hour and her fingers tightening on his—or did they?—before she pulled her hand away.

Beatrix, for her part, feels a similar confusion. Did Mr. Heelis really intend to take her hand, or was it only a thoughtless, impulsive gesture? She blinks the tears away. And why are her eyes wet? Is it because no other man but Norman has ever taken her hand, and that so very long ago that she remembers it only in the way we remember dreams? And then, in a guilty flash, she remembers returning the pressure of Mr. Heelis' fingers. She presses her lips together, the color flooding her face and neck. How could she have done such a thing? She'd been disloyal—and not just to her beloved Norman, but to Sarah Barwick, who hopes for happiness with Mr. Heelis.

And if it seems to you that these two people are making far too much of a simple, innocent gesture, and that things would be so much easier and quicker if they would just fling their arms around each other and kiss and get on with the business of falling in love (that *is* what they're about, isn't it?), please remember that this is impossible. Miss Potter and Mr. Heelis live in a time and place and belong to a social class in which the expression of feeling is much more limited than it is in our own. There is nothing in their experience that gives them permission to do what you and I would certainly find quite natural and uncomplicated, and everything that teaches them that passionate emotional exhibits are not only wrong but very likely immoral, if not downright sinful. And if you think that's sad, well, so do I. But it *is* their time and their place, and they live and breathe within it just as we live and breathe within ours, and if we want to know them, we shall have to allow them to be as they are, and not as we would like.

And there may be something positive to be said for the social conventions that keep them from the quick and easy. The longer they postpone the mutual acknowledgment of what they have just discovered, the richer and deeper and more intense it is likely to be. And enduring, too, I daresay. How many times have you impulsively flung your arms around someone, only to discover the next day or the next week that you never wanted to see him or her again? The longer the delay, the more likely it is that whatever happens, when it happens, will be lasting.

When it happens? I hear you saying, with an ironic laugh.

More likely, if it happens. And look what occurred when Beatrix gave in to her parents and agreed to delay her marriage to Norman. He died.

Sadly, I shall have to agree. When we seize time by the forelock, we have at least the forelock in our hands, however briefly. Well, there are things to be said on both sides of the argument.

Miss Potter and Mr. Heelis, however, did not seize anything. There was an awkward silence in which the ticking of the clock could be distinctly heard. To cover her feelings, Beatrix paid a great deal of attention to pouring hot water from the kettle into the teapot—and a good thing, too, for her hand was shaking. Mr. Heelis, trying to act as if nothing at all out of the ordinary had happened (or if it had, that he had not noticed), got up from the table, and ambled nonchalantly to the guinea pigs' cage.

"I see you've brought your friends," he remarked casually, bending over and putting out a finger.

"Be careful!" Beatrix warned. "Thackeray—"

"Ouch!" Mr. Heelis jumped back.

"—bites," Beatrix said, with a helpless laugh. She set the kettle back on the range. "Oh, dear. I'm so sorry."

"Just startled me," Mr. Heelis said, nursing his knuckle. "No damage done." He laughed wryly. "A fierce guinea pig, no less."

"Fiercer and fiercer," Thackeray muttered. *"If I could, I would leave this place and—"*

"Do hush, Thackeray!" Nutmeg shrilled. *"If you don't behave yourself, Miss Potter is going to decide that we're not suitable for Miss Longford. We'll have to go back to London. There'll be no Tuppence and Thruppenny, no afternoons in the garden—"*

"Nag, nag, nag," growled Thackeray. *"How I'm to put up with you for the rest of my life, I don't know."*

"I'm taking them to Caroline tomorrow," Beatrix said. "On my way up to Briar Bank House. At least, that was my intention. But now I'm not sure I ought to leave Thackeray with Caroline. He's becoming very ill-tempered."

"It has nothing to do with temper, ill or otherwise," Thackeray retorted. *"It simply has to do with preferences. I do not prefer fingers in my face. Nor would you, I daresay, Miss Potter."*

"Ah, yes," said Mr. Heelis, coming back to the table. "Briar Bank. You're going to the luncheon, then?"

Beatrix nodded, relieved to be back in a more neutral conversational territory. "I want to pay my respects to Miss Wickstead." She set out sugar on a tray and, remembering that Mr. Heelis took lemon, added several slices. "It's odd, I must say. I didn't know Mr. Wickstead had a sister."

"Neither did I," Mr. Heelis said. "He told me that she found him by tracing the records of the orphanage near Manchester, where he grew up. A lucky reunion for him. Lucky for her, too, in the circumstance. She's to have a tidy little inheritance."

Beatrix put the tray on the table. "Speaking of money, there's something I should like to ask you about. It has to do with the Suttons."

Mr. Heelis raised his eyebrows. "That mortgage business, p'rhaps?"

She felt relieved at not having to explain. "You know, then?"

"I know they're in rather a difficult patch." He tilted his head to one side. "Mr. Sutton spoke to you about it?"

"No, Deirdre Malone told me." Beatrix related their discussion and Deirdre's scheme. "I volunteered," she added, "and now I'm not sure it was the right thing to do. I said I would discuss the situation with Lady Longford. She owes the largest amount—almost a third of the total. If she pays what she owes, the rest are likely to follow suit." She cast a quick glance at Mr. Heelis' face, to see whether he was disapproving. As Lady Longford's solicitor, he would know whether this was a good plan or a bad one. "It won't be quite enough to cover the mortgage," she added, "but perhaps something can be worked out with the bank."

"I don't see that there's anything wrong with that scheme at all," Mr. Heelis said thoughtfully. "If the village wants to have a veterinary—and surely that's a good idea—he ought to be supported. Lady Longford is perfectly capable of paying what she owes, and ought to have done before now. Probably just overlooked it, or enjoys being supplicated." He grinned. "I have no doubt that you'll help her see her duty, Miss Potter. Do you remember when you talked her around to providing Jeremy Crosfield's school tuition? Good job, that."

Beatrix had to return the smile. "Well, I rather think you played a role in it. Jeremy writes that he is enjoying his studies and doing well, and asks to be remembered to you." She picked up the china teapot and began to pour.

"He's a good boy," Mr. Heelis said. "I'm glad he's doing well." He paused. "I've just thought of something, Miss Potter. The snow is deep, and it's likely to be a bit difficult getting up to Briar Bank House tomorrow. I have my sleigh here—it seats four easily, with room to spare—and a horse, and was thinking of staying the night here in the village. How would it be if I took you to Briar Bank? We could stop at Tidmarsh Manor and get Lady Longford to handle that business."

Beatrix found it necessary to take a deep breath. Her first answer—an impulsive yes, oh, yes!—was just barely restrained by common sense and the thought of her friend. "Miss Barwick asked for a lift," she said. "She's taking baked goods. And I've promised Deirdre that she can ride as far as

Tidmarsh Manor, to visit Caroline. I'm sure there won't be room—"

"Of course there's room," Mr. Heelis interrupted eagerly. "Room for all four of us, as well as all Miss Barwick's bakery stuff." He glanced at the guinea pigs. "And your friends, too." He looked at her, his brown eyes smiling. "We shall be quite a gay party, in spite of the sad occasion. Say you will, Miss Potter."

Beatrix looked down and picked up her cup. "I'm sure that Miss Barwick will be glad of the extra room," she said, in a voice that sounded prim even to her ears. "Yes. I think it is a good idea if we all go together."

"Well, then," Mr. Heelis said heartily. "It's settled. I shall come for you at—shall we say, ten? That will give us time to do our business with Lady Longford and get up to Briar Bank House in time for the luncheon."

"Ten it is, Mr. Heelis," Beatrix said, trying very hard to ignore the pleasure she felt bubbling up inside her. "I shall let Deirdre know. And I am sure that Miss Barwick will be quite delighted. Thank you for your offer."

If Mr. Heelis heard the unusual emphasis that Miss Potter placed on the words *Miss Barwick*, he did not let on.

"You're very welcome," he said, and drank his tea. "Now, are we ready for our visit to Castle Farm?"

"Quite ready, I should think," Beatrix said, and went to get her coat.

14

Bailey's Story: Episode Three

It does not do to leave a live dragon out of your calculations, if you live near him.

J.R.R. Tolkien, *The Hobbit*

It took quite some time for Bailey to awaken from his nap and prepare to go on with his story. But only about as much time, I am glad to say, as it took for Mr. Heelis and Miss Potter to mutually discover their attraction for each other, although neither of them has any idea what to do with the discovery. And since their inspection of the barn at Castle Farm has nothing in particular to do with our story, we shall leave them to it, while we return to the badgers to see what we have missed.

In fact, we find things just about where we left them, except that the storytelling has removed to the library, where a fine fire is blazing merrily, Bosworth and Bailey are installed in comfortable leather chairs in front of it, and Thorn has just opened a bottle of Bosworth's nettle beer, which he brewed himself in The Brockery kitchen.

"I say, Bosworth, old chap," said Bailey, holding up his mug of beer to the light. *"This is a bit of all right."* He wouldn't have admitted it, but it did feel rather fine to be in company, with such a nice glass of something. It felt good to have his toes warm, too.

"I should be glad to send you home with a bottle or two," said Bosworth amiably. *"Well, then. Shall we begin?"*

"We had got to the part about the incinerator," Thorn said, and shivered. *"Or fire-pot or flame-thrower or whatever it is that makes a dragon breathe fire."*

"You had just mentioned the dragon's name," Bosworth added. *"And were about to tell us how you met him."* He reached for a pen and pad. *"I think I shall take notes, if you don't mind."*

"Be my guest," Bailey said, wiggling his toes.

And so, with Bosworth scribbling madly, Bailey related the story of his encounter with the dragon, whose name, as he has reported, was Thorvaald. Or rather, I should say that the dragon's name *is* Thorvaald, for according to all the eminent authorities on dragons, they live for a very long time. In fact, for all I know, Thorvaald is living there still, in the Land Between the Lakes, and will go on living there long after you and I are dead—a thought I find rather more comforting than not. I must confess to being happy to live in a world in which dragons are at least a possibility, and I should be glad to adjust my calculations if I found one residing in my vicinity.

However that may be and whatever your opinion about dragons, what follows is the story Bailey told and Bosworth recorded—an interesting tale, and entertaining, and perhaps even thrilling. Or perhaps not, measured against the car crashes and gunfights and murder noir of our own age—but there it is. It is also, or so Bailey says, entirely true. That, I cannot guarantee, I'm afraid.

The Tale of Bailey the Badger and the Dragon of Briar Bank

Nothing very much out of the ordinary happened for some time after Bailey watched Mr. Wickstead carry off the treasure he had found hidden in Briar Bank. And as the days and weeks went along and no one from the village arrived with shovels, eager to dig for buried treasure, the badger felt much less apprehensive. He stopped looking over his shoulder when he was out gathering mushrooms and acorns and crabapples, and the episode began to fade into the background of memory, as a forbidding mountain diminishes in size the farther we go away from it, becoming much less threatening than when we are nearby.

Bailey's thoughts were full of a great many other things, anyway, for he had made up his mind to begin a project that he had really meant to undertake the previous year, and indeed, the year before that and the year before that—an enormous venture that his father (and before his father, his grandfather and great-grandfather) had always meant to undertake but had somehow never quite got around to, either. This was the cataloguing of the Briar Bank library.

To prepare for this monumental task, Bailey had laid in a large supply of small white cards, as well as a case of clever wooden drawers with brass drawer-pulls within which the cards might be arranged in alphabetical order, ingeniously threaded (through holes in the bottom of the cards) on brass rods, so that if a drawer was accidentally overturned, the cards would not fall out. He also acquired the necessary pen-holders and nibs and bottles of ink and sheets of blotting paper and flannel pen wipes and extra candles—all the things a badger is likely to need in order to catalogue a very large collection of books. He planned to write the title of each book at the top of a card, along with the name of the author, the date of publication, the name and location of the publisher, and the condition and approximate value of the book, as well as anything else he knew about it, such as how it had come to be in the collection, to whom it had previously belonged, and so forth.

Being a thoughtful and methodical badger, Bailey began his work in the very farthest section of the library, in the chamber that was most distant from his living quarters. Here were shelved the very oldest books, those collected by his forebears in the dim, distant reaches of Briar Bank's history, when the library was first begun. Bailey had never spent a great deal of time in this chamber, for the books were written in languages he could not read—nor, as far as he knew, could his father or his grandfather before him. These books, not having been consulted for a very long time, were about as dusty as books can be. As a consequence, they had all to be removed from their shelves and stacked on the floor in order that the shelves, as well as the books themselves, might be thoroughly dusted. So Bailey tied on an apron, got his feather duster and a supply of clean flannel cloths, and set to work.

It was while he was engaged in this tedious and somewhat sneezy task that he became aware of a strange sound: a low sort of grumbling, rumbling growl, like continuous thunder in the very far distance, or the noise a railway train makes underground, or the snoring of one of Mr. Llewellyn's large draught horses, asleep in the barn on a winter's night. For a time, Bailey barely heard the noise, for it hovered around him like the ghost of a sound, at a level just below his conscious awareness. Then, having become aware of it, he heard it but managed to ignore it (I am sure you understand how this is accomplished), because he was busy with dusting and examining a great many fine old books he had never before examined and pondering the very many strange words that were printed in them and wondering if it would be worth his while to learn the language so that he could read them.

But at last Bailey became so aware of the noise that he could hear nothing *but* the noise, which he now seemed to feel grumbling in his bones, and he began to be very curious about what was causing this rumble—as well as a little apprehensive. He put his duster down and, holding his candle high in the air, walked all around the chamber, clockwise, one thoughtful step at a time. He stopped, listened a little more, then walked slowly around it again, counterclockwise. Finally, finding that the noise was decidedly louder at the back of the room than it was at the front, he set his candle on a shelf and began an inch-by-inch examination of the back wall.

And that was when he found the door, concealed behind a section of tall shelves and exactly the same color as the wall into which it was tightly fitted. Indeed, Bailey would not have noticed the door at all, had he not already pulled the books from the shelf to dust them, thus revealing the bare wall. Seeing the door, he was greatly surprised, since he had always been of the impression (indeed, he could swear that his father had actually *told* him) that this particular room lay at the end of the corridor of library rooms and that there was nothing at all beyond it except the unpenetrated innards of Briar Bank.

When Bailey put his paw to the door, his surprise turned to apprehension, for he could feel it faintly vibrate, as if whatever was making the grumbling, rumbling, growling noise was just on the other side of his back wall. And what was more, the door felt rather warm to the touch—inexplicably warm, since the climate in a badger burrow deep underground is always temperate and (at least as far as Bailey was concerned) even a bit on the chilly side, so that a fire is usually quite welcome. A warm door, underground, while not of itself threatening, is difficult to explain.

Now, boldness is not among our badger's many fine qualities. He pulled his paw back quickly from this warm, throbbing door, as I'm sure I would have done, and took quite a large step backward, happening to bump into a tall stack of books and tumbling them all across the floor, completely out of order. In the circumstance, he thought it was best to ignore the door, in the same way he had ignored the noise. So he stacked up the books again, being careful to get them in the correct order, and busied himself with dusting, first one stack and then another, pausing now and then to turn a few pages and humming carelessly under his breath to help with the ignoring.

But the more he ignored the door, the larger and more mysterious it grew, looming behind him until it seemed to take up the whole of the entire wall with its strange rumble, its pulsing vibration, its weird warmth. I know that I could not have ignored that door, and I daresay you couldn't, either. And—finally—neither could Bailey. He turned and regarded it for a very long moment with a deep foreboding. And then, reluctantly, he surrendered. Feeling that he was doing something he would be sorry for later, but completely unable to resist doing it, he fetched a hammer and took down the shelves and stood face to face with the door.

Now, you may remember that even as a boy, Bailey had never put himself to the trouble of exploring the whole of

Briar Bank. He had, in fact, rather come to understand that there was some reason (which was never made very clear) that he shouldn't bother exploring, and had developed the vague sort of sense that there might be something not quite worth the trouble (or the difficulty or the danger) of looking into, something ill-mannered and rather uncivilized, or perhaps merely unpleasant, living in some distant corner of Briar Bank, as a great hairy spider and her brood of small hairy spiders might take up residence in a dark corner of your basement, so that you avoided all commerce with that corner unless it was absolutely necessary.

It was therefore possible that a very strange creature was sharing Briar Bank with Bailey. As I have said, all sorts of animals come and go in the distant, unused parts of a badger sett, some staying for a short time, others for a longer. Not only that, but from time unremembered, the Land Between the Lakes has been the home of fairies (such as Mrs. Overthewall, whom we met in *The Tale of Hawthorn House*) and dwarves and trolls and other magical creatures, some who are courteous and helpful and others whom one might not wish to encounter in a dark, dead-end, underground corridor. For all Bailey knew, he might be sharing Briar Bank with a troll.

But as he contemplated the door, other, more attractive possibilities came into the badger's mind. What if this were actually a door into a secret part of the library, into a part that his father and his grandfather had never known? What if there were more and rarer books—or perhaps even *banned* books!—on the other side of the door, deposited there by ancient badger book collectors and then walled off and forgotten? What if the rumbling noise and the vibration and the warmth were created by some sort of ingenious ventilation system that had been installed in the burrow and completely forgotten? This made a certain sense, for dampness was a persistent problem in the library and Bailey (and his forebears) had gone to great lengths to combat it with vents and ducts and suchlike.

Having glimpsed this possibility and by now willing to admit that there was at least a chance that it would be be better to know what was on the other side of that door, Bailey became bolder. There was no doorknob (which might have been a signal, if he had stopped to think about it), so taking down the shelves and opening the door required a bit of doing. But at last, confronted with the right tool (a pry bar) wielded with the right force, it was done. Taking a deep breath and holding his candle high, Bailey stepped through. He was still wearing his apron, which you might think a rather incongruous costume for an intrepid explorer. But apron or no, he was nonetheless an explorer, and I think should duly be recognized as such.

I suppose that you have encountered, a time or two in your life, a door like this one—a door through which you might step, or might not. Perhaps it was just an ordinary door, a door that looked like any other, and you went right through it and surprised yourself by tumbling down a steep flight of stairs. (I hope you weren't badly hurt.) Perhaps it was a door that seemed somehow different from other doors, and you hesitated for a time before you found it convenient to turn the knob, push it open, and step through. Or perhaps it wasn't a real door at all, but an opening, a chance, an opportunity to move from one place or situation in life or even from one kind of self to another.

Well, Bailey's door was of these latter two sorts. It was a different door, in a place where a door was completely unexpected, and he was understandably apprehensive about what he might find on the other side. In another sense, it wasn't a door at all—or rather, it was more than a door. It was a portal into the unimaginable, and the Bailey that stepped so bravely through it, wearing his apron and carrying his candle high over his head, would never be the same again.

If the badger had expected a room filled with books like the one he had just left, he would have been disappointed, and indeed, rather frightened, for the door opened onto a long, dark corridor. The air was warm but with a distinctly disagreeable odor, rather like wet woolen socks hung before the fire to dry, and left an oddly sulfurous taste, like burnt matches, on the tongue. The sound—the grumbling and rumbling that had first attracted his attention—was louder now. It seemed to pulse and wheeze, rising and falling, in and out, like a creaky leather bellows. And in the dark distance, a faint reddish glow, like that of a banked fire, was just visible. A fireplace, beside which a badger might warm his chilly paws? Or a furnace, designed to dry the air?

But as he went closer, Bailey realized that what lay ahead of him was not as convenient and comfortable as a fireplace or a furnace with a hot-air system. By this time, his knees were knocking. His breath was puffing harder and faster, and his eyes were round as guineas with astonishment and fear, as he crept closer and closer.

Was this—?

No, of course it couldn't be.

Bailey gulped. Well, yes, it was.

A dragon.

You couldn't say that this was a large dragon, however. Compared with the pictures of dragons Bailey had happened across in books, it was very much on the smallish side, perhaps three times as large as himself, although its tail (which was wrapped around itself and tucked under its nose, like the tail of a sleeping cat) was as long as its greenish body, and its membranous bat-like wings, now folded against its scaly sides, when they were stretched out were likely to be as wide as its tail was long. Unfolded and unfurled, even a smallish dragon was a formidable beast, even when he was having a nap.

And Bailey could not help but recall one of the Badger Rules of Thumb that his father and grandfather had taught him—the eleventh, if he remembered right: *Never wake a sleeping dragon, for badger flesh is firm and fat and tastes better grilled.* (Nervously, he recalled the corollary: *If you come upon the carcass of a dragon, do not linger, for whatever killed it may still be in the neighborhood.*)

And this creature, small as it might be, was nevertheless and unmistakably a dragon. The grumbling, growling noise was coming from within him as his breath rose and fell, the translucent scales of his belly glowing with the banked fire that burned inside. And even though Bailey was some yards away, he could feel the heat emanating from the dragon. The chamber within which the beast was sleeping was a good deal more pleasant (temperature-wise) than the badger's chilly apartments.

And then, as Bailey watched, transfixed and trembling, the dragon, eyes still closed, sleepily straightened one long foreleg, clenching and unclenching his scimitar-like claws, and then the other foreleg, as a cat does, stretching. Eyes still shut, he rolled over on his belly, then arched his back and opened his jaws in a magnificent jaw-splitting yawn that showed gleaming fiery tonsils. Tendrils of gray smoke curled out of his nose. Finally, reluctantly, he opened one large ruby-colored dragon eye.

"Iszs it time to get up?" He spoke in a sleepy voice, exactly like the voice of a boy who does not want to get out of bed

and be on his way to school, but with an occasional steamy sibilant hiss. His gaze fell upon Bailey, and both eyes popped open.

"*I szsay!*" he said, quite surprised. "*What are you?*"

Bailey was offended. "*I am a badger, of course,*" he said huffily. "*My name is Bailey. I live here. Who are you? And what are you doing in my house?*"

"*Your houszse?*" The dragon rolled over onto his back. "*Excuse me. I thought it was mine. That is—*" He stopped. "*Excuse me,*" he said, and put one claw under his nose. "*A-a-a-choo!*"

Bailey barely had time to duck. Streamers of fire and smoke shot out of the dragon's nostrils and ignited the dust in a five-yard radius, so that it sparked like tiny coals, glowed briefly, and then sputtered out.

"*Sorry about that,*" apologized the dragon cheerfully. "*I hope you're not badly szsinged.*"

Bailey felt the fur on the top of his head. "*Just a little,*" he said. "*Who did you say you are?*"

"*Thorvaald,*" said the dragon. "*Son of Thunnor, son of Snurrt, son of—*" He yawned again. "*Excuse me, but I rather looszse track. Take my word for it. There have been quite a lot of us, over the centuries.*"

Bailey looked around nervously. "*Quite a lot?*" he squeaked, wondering where they all were at the moment.

"*Oh, not here,*" said the dragon. "*I was speaking figuratively.*" He stretched, his scaly green hide rippling from his nose to his tail. "*Thanks for dropping in, Bailey. Rather nice to have company for a change. This has been quite a lonely watch. Boring, very. I find myself napping moszst of the time.*"

Thanks for dropping in? This rather annoyed Bailey, who considered that the dragon was the one who had "dropped in."

"*What are you doing here?*" he demanded. "*What sort of watch are you talking about?*" Bailey was beginning to recover his equanimity. This conversational dragon—quite a small one, at that—was nothing at all like the ferocious dragons that appeared from time to time in the pages of his books, and reappeared in his nightmares. That is often the way of it, you know. What terrifies us in dreams in the darkest of nights turns out to be much less frightening in the light of day.

"*Well, let's szsee,*" said the dragon. "*I was assigned to thizs duty by Yllva, who said I should—*" He stopped and sat up straight on his haunches, exactly like a very, very large dog. "*Oh, bother,*" he said, frowning. "*What was it she said? Which duty was I szsupposzsed to—*" He stopped again, and began to look around him, curiously at first, and then with a frantic haste.

"*Where iszs it?*" he hissed. "*Where is my treaszsure? I've been burgled! Szsomeone haszs taken my treaszsure!*" He whirled on Bailey. "*Did you take it, Badger? What have you done with my treaszsure?*" He stood on his hind legs, flapped his membranous wings like a gigantic bat, and opened his mouth to roar, wide, wide, and wider. Inside, Bailey could see the fiery tonsils glowing, and flames flickering at the back of his throat. White smoke laced with burning sparks poured from the wide nostrils.

"*NO!*" Bailey shouted as loud as he could. "*It wasn't me! You've got the wrong animal!*" He held up his paws. "*You see? I don't have it.*" He flapped his apron frantically. "*Not here, either.*"

By this time, of course, Bailey realized what had happened. He knew who had taken the treasure and where it was. He did not, however, think he wanted to be the one to give Thorvaald the bad news, as I imagine you can understand.

The dragon's mouth snapped shut, his wings drooped, and he sat back on his haunches. *"Not you?"* he asked, perplexed. *"But if it wasn't you, who waszs it? Has someone else been here, messzsing about while I've been aszsleep?"* His ruby eyes grew very wide, his tail lashed from side to side. *"Oh, dear,"* he cried plaintively, pulling one wing over his face, as if to hide behind it. *"Oh, bleszs my scaleszs! The treasure's gone! Yllva will be so angry with me!"* He shuddered. *"And when she's angry, Yllva is ferocious. She has a fiery temper."*

"Oh, come now, really," began Bailey sternly, somewhat embarrassed by all this passion. Badgers, as you may know, are rather even-tempered animals, not given to emotional display. *"Pull yourself together. Be a man."*

But Thorvaald was paying no attention. He was holding both wings to his eyes now, sobbing wildly. The smoke curling out of his nostrils was thick and tarry like smoke from a damp coal fire, and had a sooty smell. His words seemed to hiss and steam with self-pity. *"And on my firszst asszsignment, too! I szshall certainly be demoted. I szshall never receive another asszsignment! My mother will be ashamed of me, and my father—"* Great tears, like football-sized blobs of glycerin, squeezed out of his eyes and ran down the scales of his face and neck. *"It doeszsn't bear thinking of."*

Sternness having failed, Bailey changed tactics. *"There, there, now,"* he said, approaching the weeping dragon and stroking his scaly foreleg with one paw. (I shouldn't like you to think that Bailey did this easily. Touching those scales took a great deal more courage than he knew he possessed. You can understand this, I daresay. How would you feel if someone asked you to pet a hippopotamus?) *"I say, old boy,"* he muttered uneasily. *"It can't be as bad as all that."*

"Oh, yeszs, it can," cried the dragon. *"You juszst don't know Yllva! Her name means 'she-wolf,' if that tells you anything. She*

is merciless. She's a stickler for the ruleszs, and if you break them, she'll roast you."

But as the badger petted and stroked and soothed, the dragon's sobs gradually quieted. After a moment, Thorvaald hiccupped—at least, Bailey guessed it was a hiccup. He had never heard a dragon hiccup before, and none of his books suggested that hiccupping was something that dragons were capable of. It produced a little burp of white smoke.

"Thank you," Thorvaald said, a little more calmly now. He glanced down at the badger's paw, sniffling. *"That'szs very nice. I've never been petted before."*

Bailey, seeing that his paw was not about to be bitten or burnt off, continued to stroke, until in a moment, he became aware that Thorvaald was purring.

"Very nice, indeed," said the dragon in a soft, dreamy voice, and lay down on his belly like a cat. With one claw, he pulled the badger close against him. *"Would you mind? Juszst a bit of a cuddle? It takes some of the sting out the losszs."*

"I'm glad you're feeling better," said Bailey, trying to relax into the curve of the dragon's large claw. If you want to know the truth, he felt rather flattered by this whole thing. It's not every badger who is given the opportunity to be embraced by a dragon—in a nonthreatening way, of course.

Thorvaald sighed, and the dark smoke curled smudgily around his head. *"But feeling better doeszsn't change anything, I'm afraid. Yllva will be furious. She insists on following the ruleszs, and of course, she will have to file a report."* He gave a long, shuddery hiss. *"You've never seen anything until you've szseen Yllva angry. She's fierce beyond description."*

"It seems a little strange that your supervisor is a female," Bailey mused. Badgers are open-minded animals and value the contributions of both sexes to the community welfare. In fact, the Tenth Badger Rule of Thumb states that all

badgers, regardless of sex, age, and state of health, are important to the well-being of the badger clan and must be honored for the roles they play in maintaining a stable and productive family life. The females, however, are generally occupied with the children and with housekeeping arrangements, and leave the administrative business to the males. Bailey had assumed that dragons operated in the same way, although now it appeared that he was wrong.

"*Of course she's a female,*" said Thorvaald, and frowned. "*And a very exacting taskmistresszs, too. You'd better stay away from her, Bailey. She's extremely territorial. And when she stokeszs those fireszs of herszs—*" He shook his head. "*She's the kind of dragon that gives the rest of us a bad name. Can't control her temper in the slightest. Flies off the handle at nothing at all. Temper is rather a liability, you know, when one has fire in the belly. Thingszs have a tendency to get scorched.*"

"I see," said the badger, although he didn't quite. "*Yllva pops in now and again, then?*"

The dragon nodded. "*This cave iszs an outpost in her territory.*"

"*It is NOT a cave!*" Badger corrected him firmly. "*It is a badger burrow. A sett. An earth. Badgers dug it, at great expense and effort.*"

"*Well, then, somebody made a mistake,*" Thorvaald said. "*It was clearly marked CAVE on the map. Anyway, Yllva haszs a dozen dragons in her cadre, scattered here and there in caveszs among the fells, guarding treaszsure. We're all junior dragons. Young. Learning the trade, aszs it were.*"

"Ah," said Bailey. "*Just how young are you?*"

"*Oh, very young,*" the dragon said proudly. "*When I got my asszsignment, I was the youngest dragon ever in this job.*" His face clouded. "*Which is why they'll make such a fusszs about my losing track of the treaszsure. Higher up, I mean.*"

"Higher up?"

"In the Grand Asszsembly of Dragons." Thorvaald launched a giant, smoky sigh that nearly blew Bailey away. *"They'll take it as an opportunity to szsay that young dragonszs should be kept at home for another century or so before they're allowed employment."*

"Oh," said Bailey, coughing. *"I see."*

"Yllva will be livid. And it doesn't matter that the treaszsure was a little one, only two small bags. She'szs very possessive. Obsessive, you might say. Anyway, it was a test, you see. If I guarded it successfully, I would be promoted to bigger treaszsures. And now thiszs. Oh, it's hopelesszs, hopelesszs!" And Thorvaald gave another despondent sigh, a sulfurous, sibilant hiss, laced with gray-blue smoke.

Bailey turned his head away, trying not to breathe until the smoke had dissipated. *"Well,"* he said, finally, *"I don't see that there's much that can be done about it now. I'm sure Mr. Wickstead didn't realize what he was doing. He—"*

"Mr. Wickstead?" the dragon interrupted. *"Who iszs Mr. Wickstead?"*

"The man who took it," Bailey said. *"I saw the whole thing, actually—although of course I had no way of knowing that the treasure belonged to you. Mr. Wickstead was looking for rabbits or badgers or something, you see. He sent Pickles into the burrow."*

"Pickleszs?" the dragon hissed darkly *"What iszs thiszs Pickleszs?"*

"He's a dog," the badger explained. *"A fox terrier."*

"A dog?" cried the dragon, and shuddered. *"I hate dogszs. I'm deathly afraid of dogszs. Just to think of them makes me ill."*

Bailey had to smile at the idea that a dragon—even a rather small one—could be afraid of a dog. *"Pickles isn't very big,"* he said. *"I don't suppose he woke you."*

"I've always been a hard sleeper," the dragon muttered. *"My mother used to say that it would cause me trouble."*

"*I suppose it might,*" agreed Bailey. "*Anyway, the dog pulled out two sacks, and Mr. Wickstead took them away.*"

"*Yes, two sacks,*" Thorvaald said. "*I have the inventory right here.*" He flipped up a scale and fished with one claw in a pocket, pulling out a piece of ragged parchment. "*One golden chalice,*" he read. "*Two belt buckles, three brooches, two decorative chains, a dozen coins—*" He stopped and looked at Bailey, suddenly eager. "*If you know who has the bagszs, Bailey, you must know where they are. Tell me, and I shall go and get them before Yllva comes round again.*"

Bailey shuddered as he tried to imagine the havoc that a visit from the dragon would wreak at Briar Bank House. "*I really don't think that would be a good idea,*" he said cautiously.

"*Well, then, could you go and get them?*" The dragon's tone became a wheedle. "*Pleaszse?*"

"*No,*" Bailey said firmly. "*I could not.*" He thought for a moment. "*When are you expecting Yllva to come back and check on you?*"

Thorvaald puckered his brow. "*What year is thiszs?*"

"*Nineteen-oh-nine,*" Bailey said. "*It's—*"

"*Nineteen-oh-nine!*" the dragon roared, rising onto his haunches. "*Nineteen-oh-nine? It can't be!*"

Bailey scrambled out of his way. "*Well, it is,*" he replied. "*Why? What's the matter with that?*"

"*What'szs the matter? What'szs the MATTER? The matter is that Yllva should have been back three hundred yearszs ago! I've been abandoned! I've been forgotten! I've been deszserted!*" And with that, he broke into fresh sobs.

"*This isn't solving anything,*" Bailey said at last. "*Do you have any way of getting in touch with her? Some way to post a message? Say, a carrier pigeon or some such? Or do you just have to wait until—*"

"*I just have to wait,*" said the dragon disconsolately. "*That'szs*

her method, you see, for keeping us on our toeszs. Her visits are im-
promptu. She just pops in, that's all. Sometimes she comes once a
year, sometimes, once a decade. But she'szs never before let three cen-
turies passzs without stopping by." He began searching for
something and found it at last, his pocket handkerchief, under his right flank. He wiped his eyes.

"*Well,*" Bailey said, in a reasonable tone, "*since she's three*
hundred years late already, I hardly think she'll be round today.
Tomorrow, either." He suspected that Thorvaald's supervisor
wasn't coming back at all, ever, but there was no point in
adding to the dragon's misery. "*Perhaps we'll be able to think of*
a way to get your treasure back before she pops in again."

The dragon brightened. "*Well, yes. I imagine you're right.*
What do you propose to do?"

"*I propose that we have some tea and think about it,*" said Bailey.

"*Tea?*" The dragon was perplexed.

"*Oh, dear,*" Bailey said, sighing. "*Well, then, what do drag-*
ons eat?"

The dragon grinned. "*I'm rather fond of fricasseed knights,*"
he said carelessly. "*Lightly toasted damselszs are nice. And of*
course cows and horses and—" He closed his eyes, licked his
chops, and whispered, "*Badgerszs.*"

Bailey felt himself turning pale.

Thorvaald's ruby eyes popped open. "*Just joking,*" he said
reassuringly. "*I've only tasted one knight—he was tough as toe-*
nails and just about as tasty. It wasn't an easy job getting him out
of that tin, either. As to damselszs—"

"*How about mushrooms?*" interrupted the badger, making
a mental inventory of his pantry. "*I have some very nice apples*
from Miss Potter's orchard, and some eggs from Mrs. Crook's hens."
As far as Bailey was concerned, the entire village was his
storehouse. But since the Crooks and the Llewelleyns were
closest and their gardens and hen houses were quite large,

they were always the first stop. *"Mr. Llewellyn has potatoes in his root cellar,"* he added. *"Can you think of anything else you might like?"*

"Actually, I'm an omnivore. I'll eat whatever's handy. All things being equal, I'd prefer a live chicken or two, or a duck. But I can manage on browse—young shoots and twigs." The dragon frowned down at himself. *"Actually, I haven't had anything to eat for, oh, several centuries. It's probably time for a snack."*

"I hope you won't mind waiting until nightfall," Bailey said. *"It wouldn't do to attract attention, you know."*

The dragon looked down at himself in a puzzled way. *"Attract attention?"*

"Just take my word for it," Bailey said.

Bailey had got this far with his tale when he was interrupted by a rap on the door. A rabbit put her head in. It was Flotsam, one of the twins (her sister's name was Jetsam) who helped with the housekeeping.

"Parsley said to tell you that dinner is served, Mr. Badger, sir," she said.

Bosworth put down his pen and pad and rubbed his aching shoulder. Being a scribe required muscle. *"I hope our dinner is as tasty as what you and your dragon found that night,"* he said to Bailey.

"We turned up some fresh cheeses in the Castle Farm dairy," the badger replied. *"And on the way home, Thorvaald found a pheasant. Quite an elegant little supper."*

"Ah," said Bosworth appreciatively. *"Well, what's on our menu this evening, Flotsam? What are we having?"*

"Some fine Cumberland sausage, sir, with fried potatoes and red cabbage."

"*That'll do,*" said the badger happily. "*It'll do very nicely, in fact.*"

As they left the library, Thorn said to Bailey, "*Excuse me, but may I ask, sir, what's become of the dragon?*"

"*I think,*" Bailey said in a grave voice, "*that we had better leave that until later. After dinner, perhaps.*"

But as it happened, the tale had to be postponed, for The Brockery's dining table was crowded with company. The weather being so cold and snowy, quite a few animals had popped in to get warm, and since there was plenty of sausage and potatoes and cabbage, Parsley just kept ladling it out until all the appetites were satisfied. Everyone was so tired that after a round of songs in front of the fire whilst the little ones played at noughts and crosses, it was an early bed for all.

Bosworth himself lingered in the library after everyone had taken their candles and gone. He pulled out the current volume of the *History* and opened it to the page where, this morning, he had written: *Tremendous snowfall last night. 33 inches on the measuring stick beside the*

He completed the unfinished sentence with the words *front door,* added a period, and began a new paragraph.

Thorn pulled Bailey Badger out of Moss Eccles Lake and Bailey spent the rest of the day telling us about the dragon who has been living at Briar Bank. The dragon, by the name of Thorvaald, was guarding the treasure Mr. Wickstead took. Bosworth thought for a moment, then added, *I don't suppose it does to leave a dragon out of one's calculations, if he happens to be living in one's spare bedroom.*

Then he wrote a little note to himself to search the *History* for any mention of dragons living in the Land Between the Lakes, stoppered his ink bottle, banked the fire, and went early to bed.

And so shall we, I think, for tomorrow promises to be a long and eventful day.

15

Miss Potter Receives Another Caller and Dimity Kittredge Has a Very Good Idea

Beatrix spent a very chilly but warm-spirited afternoon in the company of Mr. Heelis, as the two of them surveyed the repairs that had been made to the barn at Castle Farm and talked about some of the improvements that needed to be made in the fields.

One of the things Beatrix liked about Mr. Heelis was his practical understanding of farming matters. The youngest of eleven children, he had grown up near Appleby, some thirty miles to the north, where his father had been the rector of Kirkby Thore. He was an avid hunter and fisherman and knew a great deal about the land between Appleby and Sawrey. What's more, he had been involved in quite a few farm sales, and seemed to have the same feelings about the old farms that she did—that is, that the land and the way of life it offered should be somehow preserved. She thought it would be good if he could meet Canon Rawnsley, a friend of her family, who a few years before had begun an organization called the National Trust. If what Mr. Heelis knew about Lake District property could be put together with Canon Rawnsley's unquenchable energy for preservation, the land— some of it, at least—might be kept for grazing and small-holding, rather than sold off for cottage development.

What with one thing and another, the afternoon wore on, and even though the air was cold and the snow was deep, the conversation was so lively and spirited that neither Beatrix nor Will noted the passage of time. If Agnes Llewellyn (or you or I) had been eavesdropping in the hope of hearing a romantic exchange, however, we would have been disap-pointed, for amidst all the brisk back-and-forth between Mr. Heelis and Miss Potter, there was not a single word that might be considered personal. Lake District land and what ought to be done with it was undoubtedly a safe topic for them, and interesting, and if other feelings were already be-ginning to flourish under the umbrella of that opportune subject—well, things will just have to develop at their own natural pace, won't they? I can tell you, however, that it will take several years and require more than a few very unhappy conflicts before the story of Beatrix and Will is resolved. I rather think that both of them would have preferred to face real dragons than those that were lying in wait for them, but it is unfortunately true that we do not get to choose our dragons: they choose us.

And while Sarah Barwick is not quite a dragon (at least I don't think so), it is true that Beatrix happened to see her rearranging the display in the Anvil Cottage window just as she and Mr. Heelis walked past, coming down the hill from Castle Farm. He and Beatrix had been laughing at some-thing or another just at the moment that Sarah looked up and saw them. Sarah's expression, in which Beatrix read first surprise, then shock, and then distress, reminded her that her friend had a special interest in the gentleman, and that she might blame Beatrix for intruding. But there was nothing to do but smile and wave and wish that she had had the foresight to part company from Mr. Heelis at the farm, instead of parading past Anvil Cottage as if they were a couple. It was an unhappy reminder (as if she needed one) that life was very complicated indeed.

One other thing happened on the walk that is of some significance, although Beatrix did not know this until later. As she and Mr. Heelis passed in front of the Tower Bank Arms, they met a gentleman coming out, with Rascal, the village dog, at his heels. A stranger, quite tall and thin, the man wore heavy side-whiskers and carried a camera. Beatrix noticed it, and the man, because his camera was the very same model that her father had recently purchased, and rather expensive. He tipped his hat and smiled and went on his way.

"His name is Joseph Adams," Mr. Heelis said, in answer to Beatrix's question. "A photographer of some note, according to Constable Braithwaite, going all about the countryside with his camera. He was at the inquest this morning, taking pictures." He smiled wryly. "Mr. Adams seemed to feel that the scene inside the pub was picturesque. As it was," he added with a chuckle. "Especially when Hugh Wickstead's fox terrier was hoisted onto the bar so he could tell his side of the story. The dog was with Wickstead when he died."

"I'm sure Pickles had a story to tell, then," Beatrix said, remembering that she had used the terrier as a model. "It's too bad we can't understand the animals. Or perhaps it isn't. Perhaps we wouldn't like to know what they think of us—or what they know about us."

There was an hour left before teatime when Beatrix got back to Hill Top. She warmed her hands by the fire and then settled down for the rest of the afternoon, contentedly alone with her paints and brushes and Mrs. Thomasina Tittlemouse, who proved to be a comfortable companion.

But not alone for long, as it happened. Dimity Kittredge stopped in unexpectedly just at teatime, having driven to the village with her major, who had business at the Arms. "I was just tired of staying indoors," she said, as she took off her things. "It's so beautiful out there—a fairyland. I wanted a drive in the snow, and I heard you'd come and thought it would be grand to see you. How are you, Bea?"

"Oh, not another one," muttered Thackeray. He began counting on his toes. *"This makes four, by my count. How many callers can one person reasonably entertain in one day? There's such a thing as being too popular, you know."*

"Now, be nice," cautioned Nutmeg.

"Not if that one pokes her finger in my face," Thackeray growled. *"This time, I'll bite it off. We'll see how she likes being a knuckle short."*

"I'm very glad to be here," Beatrix said, putting away her work and setting out the tea things. "Getting away from Bolton Gardens was even more of a struggle than usual this time. And now with the snow—"

Dimity clapped her hands happily. "With the snow, you won't be able to get back to London," she said, laughing. "The ferry shut down, the road to Ambleside closed—you'll just have to tell Mama that you were marooned. Serves her right," she added wickedly. Dimity was not afraid to voice her opinion about Mrs. Potter, who she felt was selfish and self-centered. She glanced at the guinea pigs. "Oh, how sweet!" she exclaimed. "They're lovely, Beatrix! I wonder if Flora wouldn't like to have a little pet."

"I am not sweet!" Thackeray said, puffing up his long, silky

fur so that he looked twice his size. *"There's nothing lovely about me. I'm grumpy, growly, and I BITE."*

"I shouldn't try to pet them," Beatrix said hastily. "The male, the one with the long hair, hasn't been very friendly today. If he can't get along with Caroline Longford's other two guineas, I'm afraid he'll have to go back to London with me."

"There! You see?" said Nutmeg. *"That's what you get for being so bad tempered. Personally, I'm looking forward to friends and new surroundings and—"*

"Oh, shut up!" said Thackeray, and retired behind the cabbage leaf to reread Mr. Churchill's speech.

"I'm not sure that a guinea pig would be right for Flora," Beatrix went on. "But what would you say to a bunny? I could find one easily in London."

"Oh, yes," Dimity said. "Emily can take care of it until Flora is big enough to do it herself."

"Emily is still with you, then?" Beatrix thought rather highly of Emily, who had made some difficult choices where it came to Baby Flora. (That's part of the story of *The Tale of Hawthorn House*, which I hope you will read.)

Dimity nodded. "Emily does a wonderful job, and I think she's happy. I thought of bringing Flora to see you today, but she has a bit of a cold, so I decided against it."

"Well, I'm grateful for small favors, anyway," grumped Thackeray, over his bit of newspaper. *"Children's fingers aren't very tasty."*

"You are so wicked, Thackeray," snapped Nutmeg.

"You are so right, Nutmeg," retorted Thackeray, and went back to Mr. Churchill.

"I have something for you," Beatrix said, and gave her a copy of *Ginger and Pickles* for Flora and a wool cap she had knitted for the coming baby. It was white with yellow ribbons, because of course they could not know whether it would be a boy or a girl.

"A boy for Christopher," Dimity said firmly. She smiled. "Or a sister for Flora. Of course, we'll be happy, either way." She tilted her head to one side. "It's wonderful, Bea, how Miles has come around in the end." Captain Woodcock had been entirely opposed to her marriage, but as time had gone on, he could not deny that Christopher Kittredge had succeeded in making his sister very happy. "I only wish my brother could find someone who would make him as contented as I am," she said with a sigh. She gave Beatrix a significant glance.

Beatrix colored. She was aware that Dimity believed her suited to her brother. Captain Woodcock had seemed to think so, too. He had on several occasions asked her to motor to Ambleside with him or drive out into the fells, and once she had gone with him. They'd enjoyed an agreeable drive on a lovely day, stopping at a quaint little tea shop in Hawkshead on the way back. Unfortunately, they were seen together there, by Mrs. Stubbs' niece, and word had got back to the village. Lucy Skead, at the post office, had asked her the next day if she and the captain had set a date for the wedding.

But although Captain Woodcock was a fine-looking gentleman and a lively conversationalist, intelligent and informed, Beatrix found him a little too—well, perhaps "intolerant" would be the right word. Of course, he dealt all the time in legal affairs, but it seemed to her that he was too entirely inspired by the letter of the law, rather than by its spirit. Beatrix had quite enough of that at home in London.

And there was the matter of her work, for the captain was occasionally condescending about her children's books and hinted that perhaps she would have more time for other worthwhile things if she were not quite so busy producing two books a year. He was not specific about what he thought those "other worthwhile things" might be, but she suspected that he might have it in mind that she would marry him and manage the Tower Bank household, a role in which she had absolutely no interest. So when he asked her to accompany him again, this time to a fair at Appleby, she declined. Once more after that (to an ice cream social at St. Peter's), and he apparently understood. He had not asked her again.

"Well, I *did* wish it might be you," Dimity said delicately. Impulsively, she put her hand on Beatrix's. "I am so happy, you see, that I wish I could share it with all my dears, as if happiness were a great basket of ripe apples. And especially with you, Bea. I'm sorry that Miles isn't the man to make you happy, but I'm sure you'll find someone equally nice and—"

"I *am* happy, Dimity," Beatrix protested testily, and then felt a little ashamed of her tart reply. She softened her tone. "At least, I'm happy when I am here at Hill Top, away from London. And I don't see why my happiness has to depend on having a husband. I have my farm and my work, and—"

"Yes, of course you are." Dimity looked away. "Happy, I mean. I'm sorry, Beatrix. Having your work does make a difference, I'm sure."

Her tone implied that whatever happiness Beatrix's writing might contribute to her general well-being couldn't measure up to the happiness she would find in a husband, an implication that Beatrix found rather annoying, especially since Dimity had completely changed her own position on the subject over the four years Beatrix had known her.

But there was no point in being argumentative about it. Beatrix had made her choice and she didn't find it necessary to defend it to Dimity. But there was something she had to ask about, even though she didn't want to. "I wonder—"

She hesitated, feeling terribly awkward. If it was this hard to talk to Dimity, it might be even harder to bring up the subject with Lady Longford. "I was asked by—"

She stopped. Surely this was not the way to go about it. There must be a way to get Dimity's cooperation without revealing the Suttons' dire straits. She thought quickly, then took an entirely different tack, diving straight into the problem, without preamble.

"We may be about to lose our veterinarian."

Dimity's eyes widened. "Lose our veterinarian!" she cried anxiously. "Oh, dear heavens! That's appalling, Beatrix! It can't be allowed to happen. The only other vet is in Hawkshead, and he's overworked—he'd never come over here to doctor animals. All the farmers depend on Mr. Sutton. And not just the farmers, either. Mr. Sutton saved poor Snapper when we'd given him up for lost." Snapper was the major's English bulldog.

"I knew you'd feel that way," Beatrix said warmly. "On all counts, it would be a great shame to lose him, not only for the village, but for the whole district. Mr. Sutton almost seems to work miracles, and he is very conscientious." She paused, then added the essential piece of her strategy. "And of course he is kind enough to extend credit to anyone in need."

"He extends credit to *everyone*," Dimity replied promptly. "Without regard to need. In fact, I believe that Christopher still owes him a pound or two for taking that fishhook out of Snapper's throat." She sighed. "I'm sure that Mr. Sutton has many opportunities, some of them much more lucrative than Sawrey. He could go almost anywhere." Her voice became firm. "So it's up to us to do whatever is required to keep him here."

Beatrix felt immediately relieved. Dimity had taken the bait, as it were. Now, on to the next step. "Perhaps you have an idea how this might be done," she said. "You know, I was thinking that Christmas is just around the corner. I believe that almost everyone in the village owes Mr. Sutton a little something. If they would all pay—"

Dimity snapped her fingers. "What do you think of this, Beatrix? All the villagers could be asked to enclose a little note with their bill payment, saying how much they appreciate Mr. Sutton's good work. Don't you think that might tip the balance? If he knew how sincerely he is valued, he might decide to stay."

"What a very good idea, Dimity!" Beatrix replied. "I've just paid what Mr. Jennings and I owed for treating Kitchen. I'll write a note this evening. And I'll speak to Lady Longford about it, as well. I'm sure she owes something."

"Oh, brave you!" Dimity said with a little laugh. "She's a perfect dragon when it comes to money. But if she will pay up, that will encourage others. I'll ask Christopher to stop by Courier Cottage and leave the money—and a note—before we go home this afternoon." She paused. "Oh, and I'll speak to my brother about this, too, Beatrix. He had Mr. Sutton for that little filly of his, Topaz, and he may not have yet paid his bill. And he can put out the word, as well. If he speaks to the farmers and the local gentry, I'm sure they'll come through."

Beatrix smiled. If his sister asked, Captain Woodcock would be sure to pay. And putting out the word was just the sort of thing the captain would be glad to do. He'd probably order everyone to pay up, or else!

"I knew you would come up with a scheme for keeping Mr. Sutton here," Beatrix said, feeling not in the least dishonest. After all, it *had* been Dimity's idea. "Thank you."

"And I'll mention it to the vicar, as well," Dimity went on. "But really, Beatrix, it is I who should thank you. It's wonderful to be able to think about something else for a change, other than this baby." She patted the bulge under her dress. "I'm afraid I've become a little single-minded. Why, I haven't even asked how your work is coming along!"

"I have a new book, about a wood-mouse who has to cope with unwelcome visitors—beetles and spiders and a toad. Would you like to see the drawings?"

Dimity hurriedly finished her tea. "Thank you, but I think I hadn't better. Christopher is probably ready to leave and I do so hate to keep him waiting." She put on her coat and hat and gloves, promising to be sure that Major Kittredge stopped at Courier Cottage before they drove back to Raven Hall. She cast a last glance at the guinea pigs.

"It's too bad that the male is so ill-tempered," she said. "He's beautiful, with that long, silky fur. I'm sure Flora would love him."

"She'd probably pull my hair," Thackeray growled, and for once, Nutmeg had to agree with him.

"Next time, I'll bring a bunny for Flora," Beatrix said, and saw her friend to the door.

Dimity paused, her hand on the latch. "I do wish you could find it in your heart to like Miles a little," she said wistfully. "I should love for both of you to be happy—together."

Beatrix did not know what to say, so she only smiled and gave a small shrug. And if she felt a little forlorn when Dimity left, who could blame her? For much as she liked Dimity and was glad to have her as a friend, it seemed to her that there was now a gulf between the two of them—the kind of gulf that exists between women who think that marriage is the best, indeed the *only* way to happiness and fulfillment and women who believe that they can be happy and live full, independent, self-sustaining lives centered around work they have chosen. She sighed. There was a gulf between herself and Sarah, too, for she could not forget the expression on Sarah's face when she had looked up and seen her walking with Mr. Heelis.

But Beatrix was not one to give in to forlorn feelings. Mrs. Tittlemouse was waiting, in her cozy, tidy, deeply satisfying mouse house. Determined to do her justice, Beatrix picked up her brush, and began painting pink stripes on the little white mouse sleeves.

"Well, my dear," she said to the little mouse in her drawing. "You and I shall be perfectly happy, even if we don't have husbands. Shan't we?"

But Mrs. Tittlemouse was very busy turning out several humblebees who had built a nest in her acorn storeroom. *"I am not in the habit of letting lodgings,"* she muttered. *"This is an intrusion!"*

To Beatrix's question about husbands, she had no answer.

16

Bailey's Story: Episode Four

The Brockery breakfast table was a bit crowded, since a few more animals—mostly small ones who were able to get around by skating over the hardened surface of the snow—had dropped in to get warm and stayed for eggs, oat biscuits with clover honey syrup, and a rasher of bacon. On such a cold day, the hot food was very welcome, and Parsley, Flotsam, and Jetsam were kept busy frying bacon and boiling eggs and passing pitchers of syrup.

Bosworth Badger sat at the head of the table, beaming. He was never happier than when the table was lined with guests and the meal ended with a satisfied smile on every guest's face. To his left sat Thorn, who was busy helping the smaller creatures cut their bacon. To his right sat Bailey Badger, who was not accustomed to having a meal in the company of so many strangers and squirmed through the whole affair. As soon as breakfast was over, Bosworth suggested that they have their morning coffee in the library, where Bailey could finish his story—and of course, Thorn had to come along.

"If I recall correctly," Thorn said, when they were settled, *"you left off telling just as you and the dragon went out for something to eat. And then I asked—"*

"You asked what had become of the dragon," said Bailey gravely. *"Well, I will tell you what I know, although it does not make me happy."* He sighed. *"Yes, Thorvaald and I went down to the village after it was very dark and had something to eat. He was delighted to be out and about—I expect I should have been, too, if I had been cooped up in a cave for hundreds of years. So he did quite a bit of stretching and wing-flapping and some flying—"*

"Flying!" exclaimed Bosworth.

"Well, yes. That's what dragons do, you know. I discouraged him from making too much of a show, of course—didn't want the rest of the world in on our little secret, did I?" Bailey rolled his eyes. *"If they knew a dragon was living at Briar Bank . . . well, it would have been almost as powerful an attraction to the Big Folk as buried treasure."*

"I see," said Thorn thoughtfully. *"So the dragon has been living with you, then?"*

Bailey nodded. *"I put him up in the chamber next to mine, where my parents slept. It a bit cramped, and if he'd been any larger, we couldn't have done it. As it is, he was forever flicking things off shelves with his tail."* Bailey chuckled wryly. *"I rather think, you know, that he wanted a place to hide out, just in case that supervisor of his—Yllva—should come back and find the treasure gone. This way, both dragon and treasure would be gone, so she wouldn't know who to blame."*

"It surprises me a little," said Bosworth, *"that you were willing to take in a lodger. I thought you rather liked your solitude. No offense meant, old chap,"* he added hastily. *"It's just something I was wondering."*

"No offense taken," Bailey replied. *"You're right, of course. I have been a rather solitary badger in my time. Nothing like you, Bosworth, with that throng of friends and relations around the breakfast table."* He shuddered. *"Perfectly fine and normal here at The Brockery, although I shouldn't like it myself much, at least on a daily basis."*

Bosworth nodded. Sometimes the crowd did seem a bit excessive, even to him, and it was good to retreat to the library for a bit of a read, or find a chore in a remote corner of the burrow. *"All the more interesting that you were able to tolerate a guest,"* he said.

"Ah, yes," sighed Bailey. *"I have to say, while Thorvaald was with me, I learnt that company can be rather a good thing. He wasn't much of a reader, which was a disappointment, for we couldn't share books. But he loved to tell stories—great, rip-roaring dragon adventures that had been handed down in his family for eons. You've no idea what a great number of adventures dragons have had in this world."* He grinned ruefully. *"And of course, it was very nice, having that fire-burner around. Rather like central heating. Cut down on carrying coal and wood for the fireplace. And good for a bit of grilled beef-steak, as well."*

Thorn, always the perceptive one, had been listening closely. *"You've been speaking of Thorvaald in the past tense,"* he remarked. *"The dragon is no longer with you?"*

Bailey shook his head sadly.

"Why, where's he gone?" Bosworth asked, trying to imagine where a dragon might fly off to, in this modern day and age. Surely he would be seen and shot down, like a dirigible. Or perhaps he could hire himself out to the British army, in place of one of their aeroplanes. Instead of torpedoes or whatever it was that they thought of firing out of aeroplanes, he could just aim his fire-burner. He sat for a moment, bemused

at the idea of the Foreign Office employing a dragon to guard the new dreadnoughts they were building.

"Where's he gone?" Bailey repeated in a somber tone, as Bosworth picked up his pad and dipped his pen in the inkwell. *"I'm sorry to say I don't know. But you will want to know what happened, so I had better get on with my story."*

The Tale of Bailey the Badger and the Dragon of Briar Bank (Conclusion)

To his great surprise, Bailey discovered that he and Thorvaald got on surprisingly well together. In the beginning, the badger left the door open between the library and the dragon's lair (as he was calling Thorvaald's chamber), and the two of them came and went as neighbors do, with Thorvaald gradually spending more time with Bailey until finally he began sleeping over. Bailey got on with the task of cataloguing his library. Thorvaald napped a good deal, and was quite content to doze in a corner of the library chamber in which Bailey was working, providing both a welcome warmth (he was very handy as a portable stove) and a bit of useful additional lighting.

In the evenings, Bailey often read aloud from his books. He began with a volume he had always enjoyed called *A Natural History of Dragons and Other Mythic Beasts*, but had to leave off after the third paragraph of the first chapter, in which the author stated that all of the dragons had either been killed by brave knights with magical swords or had never existed in the first place.

Thorvaald snorted derisively at this, commenting sarcastically that he would be glad to allow the author to interview him. He much preferred another of Bailey's books, *On the Habits of English Dragons,* which gave numerous examples of treasure-guarding dragons in Shropshire, at Old Field Barrows; in Herfordshire, at Wormelow Tump; and in Northumberland, on Gunnarton Fell, where a dragon was said to guard a cave deep under Money Hill.

"Gunnarton Fell!" the dragon cried, when Bailey read him that bit. *"Why, that's where my cousin Thorwinn was assigned."* His belly glowed with a fiery excitement. *"Where is that, do you know?"*

"East of Carlisle," said the badger, edging away. It wasn't comfortable, sitting close to the dragon when he was stoking up. *"Some sixty miles from here, I suppose, as the owl flies. Or the dragon,"* he amended.

"Old Thorwinn," Thorvaald said with a musing affection. *"Wonder if he's still at his post."* His fire died down a bit, his color ebbed, and he sounded gloomy. *"Or whether someone has thieved his treaszsure, too. All these humans finding things. What's a dragon to do? We'll all be out of a job."* He thought for a moment. *"Which might not be a bad thing. Treaszsure-guarding is about as exciting as doing the washing-up."*

Other evenings, Thorvaald would regale Bailey with thrilling stories of dragon derring-do, in which the dragon turned out to be the hero, slaying the knight with his own sword, or breathing on a drove of dwarves until they were toasted to a crisp. These were Yllva's tales, Thorvaald said. *"Every time she came, she had a new story. Tended to be rather sensational, all larded with fire and brimstone and the like, but that's the kind of dragon she is. There's nothing she likes better than seeing something go up in flames. Actually, I was glad to have the news. It gave me something to think about, between naps."*

On evenings when it was particularly dark and discovery unlikely, they went out foraging, Bailey for mushrooms and

grubs and earthworms, Thorvaald for—well, we shan't inquire too closely into what the dragon found to eat. We shall
just have to hope that Jemima Puddle-duck was not out and
about on those evenings, and that all of the Hill Top hens
were safe in the barn. (I can tell you, however, that no
damsels were reported missing. As for knights—well, there
weren't any at this time in the Land Between the Lakes,
tinned or otherwise, which is certainly a lucky thing for
them.)

But since Bailey was now cooking for two, it was sometimes a challenge to keep food in the house. The foraging
expeditions began to occur more frequently, to the point
where Bailey and Thorvaald were out and about almost
every night. This concerned Bailey greatly, since the more
often the dragon took to the air to look for something to eat,
the more likely he was to be spotted. The badger made
Thorvaald promise to keep to the ground and try to be as
inconspicuous as possible—which was unfortunately not all
that inconspicuous, given the unmistakable color, shape,
and size of even a smallish dragon.

It was on the most recent of these foraging expeditions
that the very unfortunate incident involving Mr. Wickstead
occurred. Bailey and Thorvaald, who was browsing on
bracken (lightly toasted), were at the western end of Briar
Bank, which as you know is the place where Pickles and Mr.
Wickstead had originally discovered the treasure. It was a
cold night, and dark, the snow was just beginning to fall,
and Bailey did not expect anyone to be out and about. But
to his surprise, he saw a lantern bobbing up the dark hill-
side. Since lanterns don't bob by themselves, he knew that
someone had to be carrying it. But who? Why? Somewhat
alarmed, he lay down on his belly and peered over the ledge.

The lantern was being carried by Mr. Wickstead, who

had a shovel in the other hand and a canvas knapsack over his shoulder. With him was Pickles the fox terrier. When they reached the entrance to the badger sett, Mr. Wickstead set the lantern on the ground and took the knapsack off his shoulders. Opening it, he pulled out two leather bags.

Bailey blinked. Those bags looked like the very same ones that Pickles had pulled from the burrow months before—and full, from the look of them. Full of Thorvaald's treasure? What was going on here? Bailey looked around for the dragon, to see if he had noticed, but he was nowhere in sight.

"Come here, Pickles," said Mr. Wickstead. "I want you to put these bags back in the sett."

"Are you sure about this?" Pickles asked doubtfully. *"I mean, it does seem rather an odd thing to—"*

"Let's not argue about it," Mr. Wickstead said, kneeling down and stroking Pickles' ears. "Put those bags back where you got them, and then I'll shovel in some dirt and stones. The treasure will be safer here than it is at the house. She'll never in the world think to look here. Why, she doesn't even know this place exists. When the man from the Home Office gets here, we'll dig it up again and hand it over. It'll be better off at the British Museum."

"She?" Bailey muttered to himself. *"Who is this* she *he's talking about?"*

Mr. Wickstead sighed. "I had such hopes," he said, with sad resignation. "Don't know what's gone wrong. Don't know what she has in mind. Not sure I care, now. All over. It's all over." He straightened up. "Do it, old chum. Back where they came from, now. That's a good lad."

"Yessir, if you say so, sir," Pickles said, *"although I still don't—"*

"Just do it," Mr. Wickstead said firmly.

The dog obediently took the first sack in his teeth, dragged it to the dark, cavernous entrance, and was gone, while Mr. Wickstead stood waiting, his hands in his pockets. Some minutes later the dog emerged, seized the other sack, and disappeared again.

Just at that moment, Bailey heard a rustling sound in the yew tree overhead and looked up to see the tree swaying. His eyes widened. It was Thorvaald, high in the branches and scrambling higher. Higher, higher. What was he doing up there? Bailey wondered, and narrowed his eyes. He had cautioned the dragon against flying, for fear of attracting attention, but he had not thought to tell him to stay out of the trees. What was he—

CRACK! There was a sharp, splintering sound, almost like a gunshot, and the top of the yew tree snapped off. Thorvaald gave a startled shriek that sounded like all the hounds of hell let loose. And with the dragon riding the tree like a witch clinging to a runaway broomstick, the trunk came down, hard, very hard. There was a heart-stopping thud as it struck Mr. Wickstead on the head and shoulders. Dropping the lantern, he fell facedown to the ground without a sound. The light went out and everything was dark, except for the throbbing, ruby-colored glow that was Thorvaald.

"What happened?" Bailey cried.

"I don't know," Thorvaald replied, sounding dazed. He picked himself up and tried his wings. *"I don't think I'm hurt but—"* He looked down at Mr. Wickstead. *"Oh, no!"* he exclaimed. *"Did I do thiszs?"*

"Your tree did," the badger answered grimly. *"What were you doing up there, anyway?"*

"Trying to get a better view," replied Thorvaald. *"You told me not to fly, but I had to see what he was doing, didn't I? After all, that's my treaszsure in those sacks."*

"Yes, I know, but—"

"Anyway, I don't WANT it back," Thorvaald said petulantly. *"I'll have to guard it, and I'm sick to death of guarding it. I'd rather—"*

"What's going on?" Pickles barked, emerging from the badger sett. He looked around, bewildered. *"Who's out there? What's happened?"*

"Uh-oh," said Thorvaald. *"It'szs a dog! I'm leaving!"* He flapped his wings, lashed his tail, and took to the air.

Pickles stared up at the retreating figure. *"A dragon?"* he whispered incredulously. And then he saw Mr. Wickstead, lying facedown on the ground under the tree. He ran to the still figure and frantically licked his cheek. *"Wake up!"* he barked. *"Wake up, Mr. Wickstead, wake up!"*

But Mr. Wickstead didn't wake up. He didn't move, didn't make a sound. Pickles trotted around the fallen man, grabbing first a sleeve in his teeth and tugging, then a trouser leg, trying to pull Mr. Wickstead out from under the tree. When that didn't work, he gripped a limb in his teeth and tried to drag the tree off Mr. Wickstead. But that attempt was unsuccessful, as well. Panting, he sat down on his haunches, his head cocked to one side.

"Got to get help," he muttered to himself. *"But Billie Stoker will never understand what's needed."* He looked around, spied Mr. Wickstead's wool cap lying on the ground where it had been knocked off, and picked it up in his teeth. *"Don't worry, Mr. Wickstead,"* he said, around a mouthful of wool. *"You just lie right there. I'll bring help."* And with that, he was off, racing down the hill.

The badger waited until the dog was gone. Then he stood up and called, into the dark heavens. *"Thorvaald? Thorvaald, you can come down now. The dog's gone."*

At first, Bailey called hopefully, feeling that the dragon had just gone around the corner and would be along just any minute, hanging his head and very sorry for what he had done. But no dragon appeared out of the sky. Bailey called and called while the night got darker (or so it seemed) and colder (most definitely) and the snow began to fall. All the while, Mr. Wickstead lay silent and unmoving on the ground, under Thorvaald's tree, and Bailey knew that if the poor man were not dead already, he would be, very soon. And it was the dragon's fault.

"Wretched dragon," Bailey muttered under his breath. *"The least you could do was to stay and keep watch with me. And what's this business about not wanting the treasure back?"*

But of course, the badger knew the answer to that. When Mr. Wickstead took the treasure, he had released Thorvaald from what was essentially a prison sentence—the tedious, mind-numbing business of being a treasure guardian, whose only relief came in the form of an occasional visit from Yllva. Now that the treasure was returned, the dragon would have to go back to the dull, boring job of guarding it, and he didn't want to. It wasn't just the dog he had flown from, but the prospect of having to return to work.

After a while, Pickles came with Billie Stoker and his brother and the pony and wagon. The two men lifted the tree off Mr. Wickstead and put him into the wagon, shaking their heads and muttering about what an unfortunate accident it was, and how it didn't look good at all for the poor old gentleman, and who ought to be sent to fetch Dr. Butters, and things of that sort. And then they trundled off down the hill and all was silent again.

"Thorvaald!" Bailey shouted, hoping that now that everyone had gone, including the dog, the dragon would come back. By this time, his concern had given way to frustration and then to irritation and finally to anger with Thorvaald's adolescent behavior. But although the badger stayed until

his nose and his toes felt entirely frozen, his shouts echoed hollowly across the snowy land and the empty sky. At last he gave it up as a bad job and trudged home alone, thinking dark thoughts about dragons who climbed trees, killed people, and then flew off, leaving others to clean up the mess they had made.

When he finally reached Briar Bank and unlatched his door and went inside, the place felt strangely empty. Bailey had always loved coming in out of the cold and dark on a snowy evening, being greeted warmly by this or that little thing, by the rug on the floor, the kettle on the fire, the lamp's golden glow. But tonight, his house seemed musty and dark and everything seemed to whisper accusingly, *"Where's Thorvaald? Where's our dragon? What have you done with him?"*

And it was chilly—yes, very chilly indeed, for the badger had become so accustomed to the dragon's delightfully warm company that he had scarcely bothered to lay a fire in weeks. Worst of all, the fire in the kitchen range had gone out, and Bailey was too tired and despondent and angry— yes, angry at Thorvaald, for being such an irresponsible dragon—to fire it up again just to brew a cup of tea. The badger went to bed that night with cold feet. He never quite got warmed up, which as you undoubtedly know from your own experience does not make for a good night's sleep.

The next morning, Bailey got up, put on his slippers, and not stopping to wash his face or comb his ears, made straight for the door to the dragon's lair. He had convinced himself along about four A.M. that Thorvaald had been detained by a tasty young lamb or (perish the thought) a damsel, and had returned very late. Not wanting to wake his friend, the dragon had decided to sleep in his old spot, where he could also keep an eye on his treasure. For surely

Thorvaald would not be so immature as to fly away forever, abandoning his post, his treasure, and his friend. Surely he had returned.

But sadly, this was not the case. There was no familiar red glow, all was dark and chilly, and the two bags of treasure lay, unguarded, in the middle of the chamber. Not knowing what to do with them, Bailey left them where they were and went back to his apartments. Somberly, silently, he rebuilt the fires and ate a lonely breakfast. The irritation and anger he had felt last night had now turned to miserable, unmitigated worry. Where had the dragon flown off to? What could he be doing, out there in broad daylight? Where could he be hiding himself? Or perhaps something had happened to him. Dragons lived to very great ages, but they weren't indestructible.

These were the kinds of thoughts that filled Bailey's head as he puttered around all the rest of that day, pretending to work on his cataloguing project but really keeping both ears cocked for the sound of a returning dragon. He heard nothing, however, no welcoming slam of the door, no cheerful dragon calling out, *"I'm home!"* He felt more anxious and desolate with each passing hour, until finally he was so totally, entirely wretched that he gave up every pretense of working altogether. He didn't feel like eating or drinking or even smoking his pipe, and he couldn't keep his mind on a book. Finally, even though it was not nearly bedtime, he went to bed and pulled the covers over his head.

When he got up the following morning (badgers get up very early, so it was still quite dark), Bailey's spirits were still very low and he viewed the coming day with a notable lack of enthusiasm. But at least he was feeling hungry, which is always a good sign. Life must go on, even when someone you care about has flown off somewhere and hasn't sent so much as a postcard to let you know when he might be flying back. He got out of bed, splashed water into his eyes, combed his face and ears, and (just in case) opened the door to Thorvaald's dragon lair and peered inside. He told himself that he wasn't disappointed to see that it was empty. How could he be disappointed, since he had not expected to see anything but the sacks of treasure, waiting there in the chilly dark? But of course he was. His heart sank down to his badger toes and his spirits fell even lower.

So he stumped back to the kitchen to make some breakfast, thinking that he would feel better once he had eaten a bowl of hot porridge with brown sugar and a splash of condensed milk. But he had been cooking for two for the past several weeks, and when he opened the cupboard door, he found that the shelves were bare. No porridge, no tins of condensed milk, not even a slice of bread for toast or a bit of butter to spread on it. There was nothing in the pantry, either, except for a shriveled potato and a moldy onion, hardly appetizing breakfast fare.

"*Bother*," the badger muttered, with a bitter scowl. "*Blast and bother.*" That's what came of having house guests. No matter how interesting they were, or what good listeners, or how nicely they warmed the room, they *ate*. And what's more, they distracted one from one's proper housekeeping duties, such as supplying the larder. He should have to go down to Mrs. Crook's garden this morning and look out some of the carrots and parsnips she had not yet pulled—there were bound to be quite a few, and potatoes, as well. He would take a burlap sack and bring back enough to tide him over for a good while. If there were a few mutton bones in the refuse tip behind High Green Gate, he would have mutton stew with his winter vegetables. And perhaps Miss Barwick had carelessly left a tray of sticky buns cooling on the back stoop, as she had the previous fortnight.

Now, a food-foraging expedition was actually a very good plan, for it would take Bailey's mind off the dragon. And on a normal morning, such an outing would not have been at all difficult—only just nip around the lake, scamper down the hill, and you're there, in the Crooks' back garden. But on this particular morning, there was a problem, which Bailey discovered when he opened his front door and found the doorstep waist-high with snow, and the path so covered over that all he could see was the top of his WARNING sign, most of which was buried in the snow. The gray clouds scudded across the gray sky, in a tearing hurry to get somewhere else. The wind was licking the snow from the drifts and spitting it into new drifts, and the trees had wrapped their limbs around their trunks in an effort to ward off the chill. Not a good day for man nor beast.

Now, a prudent badger, looking out at the vast, bleak whiteness beyond his stoop, might have shut the door, selected a good book, and retired to his bed for the day, where he could be at least warm, dry, and well read, if not well fed. By this time, however, Bailey had worked himself into a proper state (I'm sure you know how easily this can happen when you have already begun your day in a Very Bad Mood). And since feeling out of sorts only added to his hunger pangs, there was nothing for it but to go out and let the wind blow his ill feelings away. He pulled on his boots and his thickest jacket and hat and muffler and strapped on his willow-twig snowshoes. With his walking stick in one hand and the empty burlap bag slung over his shoulder, he set off.

The path from Briar Bank to Near Sawrey skirted the marshy western end of Moss Eccles Lake, skipped to the left along its steeper southern shore, made a sharp right turn at the large, leafless willow, hopped a stone fence, and dashed off down the hill to the south, arriving at the village in a matter of twenty minutes, thirty at the most. The badger took this path so often that he knew every stone, every hollow, every tree root and overhanging shrub along the way, and (being a sure-footed animal with a strong sense of direction) could follow it on even the darkest night. But in the pearly gray light of this very early morning, he saw that the wind had pushed the snow over the path, completely obliterating it and making it impossible to tell when one might flounder through the snow's crust into a wet patch of marsh or slide down a steep bit of shore. Getting to the village by the usual route wasn't impossible, but it was certainly not the easiest way.

On the other hand (on Bailey's left hand, actually), there was the lake, and the badger could see that its surface was frozen right the way across to the other shore. It would take no more than ten minutes to cross the ice. And it was certainly cold enough (his badger nose ached with cold and his badger paws were already numb) so that the ice would be solid and safe—perhaps not thick enough yet for one of the weightier Big Folk, but certainly for a badger. It had even been swept clean by the helpful wind, so he could see where there might be a tricky place, not quite frozen through, and give it a wide berth.

But while snowshoes were convenient on the crusted snow, they were not exactly the thing for crossing the ice. Ice skates would have better served, but Bailey had not thought to bring them. So he sat down on a rock, took off his snowshoes, and stowed them in his empty burlap sack. Slinging it over his shoulder once more, he tested the ice with his walking stick before trusting his full weight to it. Finding it solid, he made his way across the lake for the willow. Looking ahead, he saw what appeared to be a mushy patch, off to the right. Thin ice! Just to be safe, he veered to the left to stay away from it.

I think you will agree that being all by oneself in the middle of a frozen lake is a much different thing than standing securely on the bank, thinking about it. On the bank, with good terra firma under the badger's feet, all seemed safe enough, and the prospect of walking across the ice only an amusing adventure. In the middle of the lake, however, with the merest thickness of ice between himself and a very cold and dangerous, possibly even a life-threatening swim, nothing seemed at all safe. What's more, the badger was beginning to worry that the ice might be thinner in the direction he was going, for the water on the southern side of the lake was warmed by an underground spring. Why he hadn't thought of this sooner, he couldn't imagine, but there it was. Supposing there was a long, wide ribbon of spongy, squishy ice all along the shore! How would he ever cross it? Perhaps he had better go back. Perhaps—

But by this time, the badger had reached the point of no return. It had begun to snow again, and the bank from which he had so confidently departed was hidden behind a white scrim of swirling, whirling flakes. Worse, the hardworking wind had industriously swept his footprints from the ice so he could not simply turn and backtrack. The only thing he could do was go forward, although by this time he could just barely glimpse the faint, blurred motion of the smaller trees swaying like dancers along the shore and the taller outline of the waiting willow, its limbs outstretched eagerly, welcoming him to the safety and shelter of the bank.

I am sure you can imagine how vulnerable and defenseless Bailey felt, a very small and insecure badger in the middle of a largish lake, enveloped in a cold cloud of blowing snow. He was so intent on reaching the willow that he was oblivious to everything but the delicate business of putting one foot in front of the other, at the same time trying to keep an eye on the tree that beckoned him forward but now perversely seemed to retreat two steps away for every step he took toward it.

Concentrating so intently on his destination, Bailey failed to notice an ominous rusty-red winged shadow that emerged out of the low, blowing clouds and circled silently over the badger, eyeing the burlap sack slung over his shoulder. Nor did he see it turning to fly in for a closer look, nor the angry, ruby-red incandescence of its eye, nor the pulsing throb of the fire in its belly. It was only when he heard the unmistakable FLAP-FLAP-FLAP of dragon wings, exactly like the snapping of sheets on a clothesline in a high wind, that he looked up. And just at that moment, the dragon opened its mouth and gave a triumphant ear-splitting shriek, like the shrill cries of a thousand locomotives, all sounding in chorus. Snorting fire, it swooped down on him, narrowly missing him, its flame turning a large patch of ice to steam and water in an instant.

Stricken with horror, the badger tried to run, but fear held him fast and he could not move. There was no refuge, anyway, no rock, no tree to shelter him, only flat, empty, open ice. As the dragon wheeled on one wing and whirled back for him, he could only crouch and cover his head with his arms as, with one huge, horny claw, the beast, belching flame, snatched the burlap sack from his shoulder. With a blazing pain, his right sleeve and the fur on his paw caught fire.

"Thorvaald!" he cried frantically, clutching his burnt forearm. *"Don't you know me, Thorvaald? It's me, Bailey! Your friend!"*

But even as the wind plucked the words from his lips and tossed them like fragile snowflakes into the cold, gray air, the badger understood. This wasn't Thorvaald. This was a larger, heavier dragon, a malicious, merciless, murderous dragon. It could only be Yllva. Yllva, the she-wolf, Thorvaald's stern taskmistress. The dragon who could not control her fiery temper.

And he also knew why she had attacked him. She thought there was something else in the sack he was carrying—not a simple pair of willow-twig snowshoes, but the treasure that had been stolen from Thorvaald once and was now (she thought) being stolen again! She thought he was a thief. And now she was circling again, turning in a spiraling inward gyre, whistling shrilly, her mighty wings stroking the air. She was coming back to punish him for his audacity. She was coming in for the kill.

"No, Yllva!" he cried. *"No! It's not the treasure! It's only my snowshoes!"*

But his terrified protest was as a whisper against the furious screeching of the dragon. She had circled for the strike, turning on her flame-thrower full blast. Fire flashed from her nostrils, smoke billowed out of her mouth, her tail lashed. She was plunging straight for him like a flaming arrow. If he somehow managed to escape incineration (unlikely!), that tail would knock him into tomorrow.

So Bailey sought the only refuge that was available on that wide, frozen lake. He took a dozen running steps to his right, heading straight for the patch of ice that Yllva had turned to steam and water with her blast of fire. Without a second's thought, he dove straight in, plunging down, down, down into the inky blackness, preferring death by drowning to death by incineration. And as he sank like a heavy stone to the muddy bottom, the badger had only two regrets. He was very sorry that he had not finished cataloguing his library. And he was very, very sorry that he would never again see his dear friend Thorvaald.

But death was not to come so quickly, for (while this is not a widely known fact) badgers can swim. They definitely do not enjoy swimming. In fact, they will avoid it whenever possible. But they will swim—an ungainly kind of doggie-paddle—when it is a matter of life and death. And since animals, unlike humans, are rarely inclined to give up, even in the most desperate of situations, Bailey had no sooner sunk to the bottom than he kicked off his boots, struggled out of his thick jacket and muffler, and rose, amid a froth of bubbles, to the top of the water. He surfaced, coughing and sputtering and flailing, sank briefly, then surfaced again, gasping for air.

He shook the water out of his eyes and peered anxiously around for the dragon. Where was she? Was she coming back? But she was nowhere in sight. She probably thought the world had seen the last of the badger when he dove into the lake, and for a moment he felt a sharp sense of relief. He had escaped being burnt to a cinder. But now, he realized, he faced a different fate. The ice had been melted by the dragon's breath, yes, and the water had been turned to steam. But that was only a temporary situation. The lake was incredibly, unspeakably cold, and the chill penetrated into the badger's very bones. His teeth were chattering and he was shivering uncontrollably. He had to get out of this icy water before he froze to death.

But that was easier said than done. He paddled awkwardly to the nearest edge of ice, grasped it, and tried to pull himself out. But his paw—burnt very badly when he had flung his arm over his head to ward off the dragon's hot breath—was useless. And worse, the ice was so brittle that it broke off in his grasp. With a despairing cry, he tumbled backward and sank down into the black water. There was no way to pull himself out!

But Bailey was not a badger who gave up easily. Trying again, breaking the edge of the ice again, sinking again—he repeated his effort so many times that he lost all track, so that finally, all he could do was cling, spent and breathless, to the crumbling edge of the ice. He was so cold now that his arms and legs were numb and he could scarcely breathe. He knew he would be dead in only a few more minutes.

"And that was when I found you!" Thorn exclaimed, getting up to poke the fire. *"I was coming along the shore of the lake, admiring the way the snow lay along the bare branches, and there you were, out there in the lake, thrashing about. Not that far from shore, luckily. Close enough that I could crawl out and reach you with a dead willow branch."*

"Sounds like you took a chance," Bosworth said. *"It was a very brave thing to do, Thorn. I shall record this rescue in the His*tory." He stifled a shiver, not wanting to think what would have happened if the ice had given way under Thorn and both badgers had ended up in the water. They wouldn't be here now, telling the story.

"Not brave at all," Thorn replied modestly, ducking his head. *"Mr. Bailey was the brave one, diving into that water."*

"But you were the one who fished me out," retorted Bailey. *"Just in time, too. I doubt if I could have hung on much longer."*

"It was a lucky thing that the dragon flew away." Thorn managed a small smile. *"If she'd stayed around, there might have been two roasted badgers. I hope she's gone for good."*

Bailey harrumphed. *"She might be back when she finds out what was in that sack,"* he said. *"In fact, it's quite possible that she's checked the dragon's lair, found the treasure, and carried it off. I hope so, actually. That stuff has brought nothing but unhappiness.*

The villagers may be right when they talk about a curse—although it's not what they think."

"And what about Thorvaald?" Bosworth inquired. *"What do you think happened to him?"*

"I think he flew off because he couldn't bear the thought of returning to guard that treasure," Bailey replied sadly. *"And I can't say that I blame him, can you? Just think of all the centuries he's wasted, guarding that gold. And why? To what good end? He probably flew as fast as he could, as far as he could. Heaven only knows where he's got to by now."*

The clock chimed.

"Why, bless my stripes, look at the hour," Bosworth exclaimed. *"It's almost time for luncheon."*

The words were no more out of his mouth than there was a rap at the door and Thorn's mother, Primrose, opened it and came in.

"Parsley says she's about to put lunch on the table," she said. *"It's just soup and sandwiches, and the soup is in the pot over the fire, so you can come whenever you like. Oh, and we have a new pair of guests."* She smiled at Bosworth. *"One of your favorite little animals has dropped in."*

"Oh?" Bosworth asked, wondering which of his favorites had come calling on such a snowy day. *"And who is that?"*

"Tuppenny, the guinea pig from Tidmarsh Manor," said Primrose happily, for Tuppenny (who had helped to save her and her two cubs from the horrible badger baiter) was a special favorite of hers, too.

"Tuppenny!" Thorn exclaimed. *"Tidmarsh Manor isn't that far away, but it must have been hard going for a small creature to get up to the top of Holly How through such deep snow."*

"Actually, I think not," said Bailey. *"Mice and voles and the like have an easier time of it than we badgers, especially when the snow is crusted. They simply scamper over the top."*

"*Well, however he got here, I'll be very glad to see him,*" said Bosworth, pushing himself up out of his comfortable leather chair. "*And you say he's brought a friend? That other guinea pig who comes with him sometimes—what's her name? Thruppence?*"

"*No, not Thruppence,*" Primrose replied. "*This is an animal we've never met before. Says his name is Thackeray.*" She hesitated. "*I rather think he must be running away from something. He doesn't look very happy.*"

"*Another runaway, eh?*" said Bosworth. It wasn't unusual for animals who had got lost or had left unhappy situations to find their way to The Brockery, where they could spend all the time they liked, resting and recuperating. "*Well, I daresay we can find room for one more, can't we, Primrose?*"

"*Oh, I think so,*" Primrose said with a warm smile, adding, "*The soup is potato, if anyone is interested.*"

Are you as surprised as I am to hear that Thackeray has somehow made his way to The Brockery? Why, the last time we saw him, it was the previous afternoon, just at teatime, and he and Nutmeg were safely fastened in their cage at Miss Potter's Hill Top Farm.

How in the world did he get all the way to the top of Holly How?

I think we shall have to find out.

17

In Which Miss Potter Makes a Deposit, Accepts a Payment, and Arranges Lessons

It turned out that Mr. Heelis had been overly optimistic about the number of persons who could fit comfortably into his sleigh, along with all their bundles and boxes. So it was actually a good thing that, at the last minute, Deirdre Malone was not able to go. Mrs. Sutton had developed a migraine—small wonder, Beatrix thought sympathetically, given all that poor lady had to cope with. Deirdre was required to stay behind and manage the children.

Deirdre conveyed this information in a note she sent to Hill Top Farm by way of the oldest Sutton boy, Jamie. The note ended with this: "Thought you would like to know that Major Kittredge stopped by last evening and paid his bill in full. And not long after, here came Captain Woodcock, and paid *his*! They made a point of saying they hoped Mr. Sutton would never leave Sawrey. Mrs. Sutton is greatly cheered (in spite of her headache). Thank you, Miss Potter!" Beatrix had to smile, although she thought that Deirdre should thank Dimity Kittredge, who had no doubt told her husband and her brother what to do. Still, it did sound as if the project was moving along, with all due speed.

But even without Deirdre, getting everyone and everything into the sleigh was a challenge, for Miss Barwick's boxes and bags of baked goods occupied the whole of the rear seat, and the cage containing Miss Potter's guinea pigs had to go on the floor. Beatrix offered to sit in the back and hold some of the boxes on her lap, but Mr. Heelis wouldn't hear of it. And so, quite without meaning it to happen, she found herself tightly wedged into the front seat between Mr. Heelis and Miss Barwick. In one sense this was a very uncomfortable place to be (considering her friend's feelings about Mr. Heelis) and in another sense it felt very comfortable indeed. Beatrix promised herself that on the return trip, Miss Barwick would sit beside Mr. Heelis and she would sit in the back.

And then she simply relaxed and enjoyed herself as Mr. Heelis' handsome gray horse pulled the sleigh swiftly along the lane. They seemed to fly, barely touching the earth between snow-frosted stone walls, under trees glossed with ice, and beside Wilfin Beck, its sparkling surface frozen and still. It was a magical scene, a winter fairyland, and under its enchanting spell the lingering worries about London vanished, Beatrix's heart lightened, and her spirits soared. The three of them were very gay, as Mr. Heelis had promised, and there was a great deal of lighthearted banter and joking and laughing and even a snatch or two of song, until Beatrix thought that she had never had quite so much *fun* in her life—an irony, she felt with some guilt, since they were on their way to a funeral luncheon.

In the rear, however, things were not going so well. The wind was cold, the sleigh bounced, and the guinea pigs were tossed from one corner of their cage to the other.

"*Enough!*" Thackeray burst out, trying desperately to hold on. "*I've had enough! I simply cannot take being bandied about from pillar to post any longer! I have absolutely no desire to share a cage with three other guinea pigs at this place where we are going. And I am willing to wager as much as you like that if I stay there, I will never see a page of another book.*" He gave a gloomy cry. "*I must find a better place to live. I simply must! A life without reading is not worth living.*"

"*There is nothing at all you can do about it,*" Nutmeg replied crossly, bounced about and quite out of temper herself. "*A guinea pig's destiny is in the hands of the Big Folk.*"

But as it turned out, this was not true. There *was* something that Thackeray could do about it, and he set about doing it just as soon as they arrived at Tidmarsh Manor. Miss Potter took the guinea pigs upstairs and deposited them into a commodious cage in Miss Caroline's school room. Caroline held Nutmeg and petted her, but Thackeray went into a corner and sulked.

"You'll need to be careful around him for a few days," Beatrix cautioned. "I'm afraid he's developing a few bad habits. If he doesn't behave himself, please let me know and I'll take him back to London."

Then she and Caroline and Miss Burns, Caroline's governess, went downstairs so Caroline could play the piano piece she had been practicing for the past month. On the way, Caroline confided that there was nothing in the world she loved more than playing the piano.

"I'm glad you've found something you enjoy," Beatrix said. "That's what makes life worth living."

The minute Miss Potter left them, Thackeray went to talk to Tuppenny (who has rather grown up since we met him in *The Tale of Holly How*). It took Thackeray only fifteen minutes' conversation to convey the earnestness of his desire to find another place to live, where he could get off by himself with a good book.

"*Well, I don't know about books,*" said Tuppenny doubtfully. He had once belonged to Miss Potter and served as a model for some of her drawings, but had not had an opportunity to learn to read. "*I do know where you can find lodgings, however— if you're serious about not stopping here, that is.*" He frowned thoughtfully. "*Although I must say, old chap, I really think you should reconsider. It's awf'lly nice here. Good food, plenty of room, a garden to run in when the weather's fine, even an outdoor hutch. And Miss Caroline plays the piano, so we do enjoy a bit of culture.*"

"*Oh, I'm serious, all right,*" Thackeray replied grimly. "*Nothing against you, of course, Tuppenny. You seem like a very fine animal, and I'm glad to know you. But frankly, it's the females I have an aversion to.*" He nodded at Nutmeg and Thruppence, who had put their heads together and were chattering nineteen to the dozen, like old friends instead of brand-new acquaintances. "*One was bad enough—talk, talk, talk, all day and half the night. But two are utterly unendurable. If I stay here, their constant prittle-prattle will surely drive me out of my mind.*"

Tuppenny chuckled ruefully. "*The girls are a bit clattery, I will admit, and if you don't like that sort of thing, well, you don't, that's all. I've learnt to put up with Thruppence, but every now and then things get on my nerves and I have to get away myself. Since you're determined, I'll show you where I go for a bit of a rest. It'll be a challenge, given the snow, but I'm sure we'll make it.*"

And with that, Tuppenny outlined the plan of action that, in less than an hour, brought Tuppenny and Thackeray to The Brockery, just in time for a sandwich and a bowl of Parsley's delicious potato soup. During lunch, Thackeray sat next to Bailey Badger, and the two struck up a conversation over a passing mention of a book. Within two minutes they were fast friends, and in another hour—

But we must save this part of the story until later, for other things are happening—important things—that we need to observe.

While this hastily plotted escape was taking place upstairs in Caroline's school room, Beatrix and Mr. Heelis, in the company of Lady Longford and Miss Burns, were seated in the drawing room, listening to Caroline—who was now nearly fifteen, and quite the young lady—play Mozart's "Fantasy in C-minor" on the piano. She played very well, Beatrix thought, and was glad to whisper a compliment to Miss Burns, whose employment as Caroline's governess she had recommended.

"Caroline has a very real talent," Miss Burns replied, in a whisper, "and she is quickly moving beyond my ability to teach her. She would love to have lessons with a real teacher—she's begged again and again. It's a pity she can't."

"And why can't she?" Beatrix asked. "The last time I was here, I heard Mrs. Rachel King play, at St. Michael's in Hawkshead. She is a fine performer and is said to be an excellent teacher. I understand that she is taking a few students. With Caroline's talent—"

Miss Burns slid a meaningful glance in the direction of Lady Longford, who was listening to her granddaughter's playing with closed eyes, lightly tapping her walking stick in time to the music.

Beatrix understood. Caroline, the only daughter of her ladyship's estranged son, was orphaned at eleven, when both her father and her mother died in her native New Zealand. Lady Longford had at first refused to take the girl, but when Will Heelis pointed out that her ladyship was Caroline's closest relative and Vicar Sackett implored her to do her

Christian duty, she had at last agreed. But Lady Longford hated to spend a shilling she didn't have to. She hadn't been eager to hire a governess to continue Caroline's education, and no doubt she viewed piano lessons as an unnecessary extravagance.

Miss Burns sighed. "I've even suggested that we plan a recital—nothing elaborate, just a short performance for the vicar and Major and Mrs. Kittredge and Captain Woodcock. It would be good for Caroline to have something to work toward. But her ladyship is . . . opposed." She sighed again.

Beatrix frowned thoughtfully. Something would have to be done, but what?

When the performance was over, everyone clapped approvingly. Beatrix clapped long and hard, and Mr. Heelis, quirking his eyebrow at her, followed suit, to the point where Caroline was called back for a short encore. Then Miss Burns took the girl off to say hello to Miss Barwick, who was having tea in the kitchen with Mrs. Beever, the Tidmarsh Manor cook. Beatrix and Mr. Heelis were left alone with Lady Longford, Caroline's grandmother.

Her ladyship was a tall, strong-looking person with graying hair severely drawn back, formidable dark brows, a perpetual frown, and a thin mouth. She dressed in black, even though her husband had been dead for some fifteen years. She was not well liked in the village, where she had a reputation for meddling in things that were not her concern—such as the business with Sawrey School, a few years before. To tell the truth, most people thought she was rather an old dragon.

But Beatrix felt very strongly that she had right on her side—or rather, on the side of Mr. Sutton. So she began by saying that the village might be at risk of losing its veterinarian (without saying why), and related Dimity Kittredge's idea—that is, the idea that Beatrix herself had encouraged Dimity to form. While her ladyship was digesting this, Beatrix added in an offhand way that Major Kittredge and Captain Woodcock had both paid their bills in full and had conveyed their hopes that the Suttons would continue to live and work in Sawrey, thereby setting an example for others. The Longfords and the Kittredges, the two major landowners in the district, had always been competitive, and Beatrix knew full well that Lady Longford always hated it when Major Kittredge made some sort of generous gesture, for she felt obliged to top it.

"I see." Lady Longford put on a dour look. "All these good-doing people—one wonders whether it is quite necessary."

"Oh, I should think so," Mr. Heelis said firmly. "It would be a great pity if the village lost its veterinarian."

"Mrs. Kittredge hopes," Beatrix added, "that everyone in the district who has used Mr. Sutton's services will write a Christmas note, thanking him. And that they will pay whatever they owe, as well, as a special token of appreciation. As Major Kittredge has done," she added significantly.

Mr. Heelis cleared his throat. "I rather think you might have an outstanding balance with Mr. Sutton, Lady Longford. I seem to recall that he visited here frequently some months ago, to treat one of your coach horses. Isn't that right?"

"I suppose it is." Lady Longford gave an elaborate, long-suffering sigh. "I believe that Mrs. Sutton has written to me about it. Well, since the amount is owing, I may as well pay it and be done with it. Mr. Heelis, fetch my cheque-book, if you please. And the bill. Both are in the right-hand desk drawer." She scowled. "Although I shouldn't be spending the money. I've suffered a great calamity, as you've no doubt heard. An expensive calamity. My hay barn burnt yesterday morning. To the ground."

"Yes, I've heard," Mr. Heelis said. "Has the cause been determined?"

Lady Longford pulled down her mouth. "Mr. Snig was in the cowbarn, milking. He said he saw a fireball descend from the heavens, strike the barn, and explode."

"A fireball!" Beatrix exclaimed. "A meteorite?" A fiery meteorite had fallen not long before in Yorkshire, causing a great deal of local consternation. A farmer had found the object—a ball of some fifteen pounds, with the appearance of burnt iron—half-buried in his newly plowed field.

Lady Longford shrugged. "Perhaps. This morning, Mr. Snig and Mr. Beever were to sift through the embers to see if they could learn anything about the cause. If they have, I haven't been told." She wrote out the cheque and put it in an envelope and sealed it, writing Mr. Sutton's name on the outside, along with the words "Thank you and Merry Christmas."

"Be so good as to give this to Mr. Sutton," she said, handing the envelope to Beatrix. "It will serve as a Christmas card. And your delivery will save me a postage stamp."

The corners of Mr. Heelis' mouth quirked almost uncontrollably, and it was all Beatrix could do to keep a straight face. But she only said, "I shall," and tucked the envelope into her purse. Now that Lady Longford had joined the ranks, the rest of the villagers would be sure to follow suit. But they weren't finished just yet.

"I must congratulate you on Caroline's playing," Beatrix said. "She is talented."

"Indeed." Mr. Heelis joined in warmly. "I was quite astonished."

"She does well enough," her ladyship acknowledged. "For a beginner."

"Oh, much better than that," Beatrix said firmly. "I wonder if you have thought of having a teacher for her."

Her ladyship frowned. "Miss Burns is perfectly capable of instructing the child in piano. I see no need to go to the expense of employing another teacher."

"I only bring it up," Beatrix said, "because I understand that Mrs. Rachel King has agreed to take a few students. Only a *very* few, though." She raised one eyebrow. "No doubt you've heard of Mrs. King."

Lady Longford, who hated to admit that she didn't know everyone there was to know, especially anyone important, inclined her head in what might have been an assent.

"Mrs. King!" Mr. Heelis exclaimed. "Ah, yes! I heard her play not long ago. An exceptional talent. Exceptional!"

"She is recently down from London," Beatrix said, "and living in Hawkshead. Everyone speaks very highly of her performance. I understand that she is a superb teacher, as well."

Lady Longford waved her hand in a dismissive gesture. "No doubt. But Miss Burns is perfectly competent."

"That's to the good, I suppose," Beatrix said to Mr. Heelis, confidentially. "It's not very likely that Mrs. King would accept Caroline."

Just catching Beatrix's remark, Lady Longford hesitated, her eyes narrowing. Then, as if she couldn't quite help herself, she leaned forward. "She wouldn't accept Caroline? And why not, may I ask?"

"Well, as you point out, the girl *is* just a beginner," Beatrix said in an apologetic tone. "And Mrs. King does come from London. She will have her pick of students."

"But Caroline is off to a very good beginning," Mr. Heelis said warmly. "I can tell you that."

"Exactly." Her ladyship sniffed, offended. "Londoners have got a nerve, always thinking that they are superior to those who live in the country. As if we have no refinement. No appreciation of the arts." She glanced up at the oil portrait of her dead husband. "Lord Longford always made the opening speech at the annual Ladies' Lecture Series. He felt it was important to broaden people's cultural understanding."

"And of course there is the matter of the expense," Beatrix went on. "I am sure that Mrs. King can command—"

"I daresay that whatever Mrs. King can command, her ladyship can afford," Mr. Heelis interrupted soothingly. He smiled at Beatrix. "We do value the arts, you know, Miss Potter. Even here in the Lakes."

Lady Longford's lips thinned. "Londoners," she muttered darkly, shaking her head. "Always imagining that those who live in the country are nothing but barbarians."

"They are very mistaken, indeed." Mr. Heelis was grave. "But I am sure that your ladyship will be glad to show Mrs. King how uninformed a viewpoint that is."

"I certainly shall!" Lady Longford exclaimed, and rapped her walking stick on the floor. "Very well, Miss Potter. Since you seem to be acquainted with this Mrs. King, I should like you to make arrangements for her to hear Caroline play. And if all goes well, and Caroline continues to improve under her tutelage, we shall arrange a small recital. What do you say to that?"

"Well done, Lady Longford," Beatrix replied enthusiastically. It could not be said that her ladyship's heart was in the right place, but after a certain amount of prodding (and with a poke or two), she could be moved in the right direction.

The clock struck, and Lady Longford stood, leaning on her stick, her dark silk skirt rustling. "Now, if you will excuse me, I must dress. Mr. Beever is driving me to Briar Bank House to express my condolences to dear Miss Wickstead."

"You know Miss Wickstead, then?" Beatrix asked, standing as well.

"I do. Her brother brought her here to introduce us, and

she later came to call. It was a lucky thing, you know—her finding her brother, after all those years. She felt very fortunate." Lady Longford glanced at Mr. Heelis. "She is to inherit, I suppose."

"Yes," Mr. Heelis said, "although the will has not yet been read out."

"Do you know how it happened that she and Mr. Wickstead were reunited?" Beatrix asked curiously, walking with Lady Longford to the drawing room door.

"Miss Wickstead didn't say. Only that the family came from Manchester."

"Ah," Beatrix said thoughtfully. "My mother came from the Manchester area. Perhaps we shall discover a connection." Of course, Manchester was a large city, and her mother's family had lived in Stalybridge, a few miles away. The chance of shared acquaintance was slim.

Beatrix and Mr. Heelis bade her ladyship goodbye. Mr. Heelis went outside to see to the horse and Beatrix went to the kitchen to fetch Sarah Barwick. Her report to Caroline and Miss Burns that Mrs. King was to be invited to listen to Caroline play was greeted with an incredulous delight.

"I don't know how you manage it, Miss Potter," Mr. Heelis said, handing her into the sleigh. He handed her in first, Beatrix noticed with some consternation, ensuring that she would be in the middle. "I do believe that you would be able to persuade Lady Longford to do almost anything."

"I'll agree to that," Miss Barwick said. "Miss Burns was telling us how unfortunate it was that her ladyship refused to allow Caroline to have lessons—and now she's gone and reversed herself. Well done, Bea!"

"Thank you," Beatrix said, settling herself. "But I haven't done anything special, only just noticed that her ladyship does not like to be bested, which gives her a certain vulnerability. If one feels that one has to be at the very top all the time, one is likely to do whatever is necessary to stay there."

"Even if it costs money," Mr. Heelis said, picking up the reins. And then they were on their way again, more soberly now that the funeral luncheon lay directly ahead.

18

At the Funeral Luncheon

Briar Bank House was built in the symmetrical Georgian style of local stone and roofed with blue slate from a nearby quarry. It had a great many tall, narrow windows and the front was draped with wisteria vines and climbing roses. On a bright summer's day, when the sun was shining and the roses were blooming, the old house wore a cheerful, expectant look, as if hoping for good things. But its native optimism was dampened by today's wintry weather and the somber occasion, and the snow hanging over the eaves gave the place a frowning look. The sky had become overcast and the gray clouds, low and gloomy against the gray-blue fells, seemed to promise more snow.

As they pulled up in front and Mr. Stoker's boy took Mr. Heelis' horse, Beatrix saw that the circular drive had been trampled to a mushy mess by people and their horses and conveyances. Inside, she knew, the guests would be dressed in dark colors, wear sober expressions, and speak in muted tones, as befitted a funeral luncheon. The gathering would include both villagers and gentry—Mr. Wickstead had lived long enough in the area to be acquainted with a great many people—and the house would be full. Everyone of consequence in the district would want to say a sentimental farewell to him and meet his sister, the new mistress of Briar Bank.

Mr. Heelis carried Miss Barwick's boxes and bags into the kitchen at the rear of the house, and Miss Barwick went along to help Mrs. Stoker organize the baked goods. Beatrix rang the bell beside the crepe-draped front door and was greeted by a pretty young maid wearing a black lace apron and black cap who took her coat. The butler showed her to the drawing room, where she hesitated just inside the door. Beatrix had never been an eager partygoer, and large groups made her feel shy. She preferred to find a quiet corner where she could observe the other guests without being noticed. She liked to study people's faces and their mannerisms, to try to guess what sort of person was concealed behind the social façade of most men and women.

Briar Bank's new mistress, Miss Louisa Wickstead, was standing before an array of green ferns and white hothouse carnations, decorated with a large black crepe wreath. Beatrix would have introduced herself and offered condolences, but Miss Wickstead was surrounded by others at the moment, and Beatrix held back, watching. Perhaps five or six years younger than her brother, Miss Wickstead was a lady in her middle forties. She wore black, of course, as befitted the bereaved: a simple black bombazine, its severity accented, rather than relieved, by a ruching of black lace and a small black lace kerchief pinned over her light blond hair. She had once been beautiful and was still quite pretty, with a pliant softness of figure. But her delicate face, very pale, was shadowed, and her blue eyes seemed almost wary, like a rabbit startled among the lettuces, skittishly looking over its shoulder.

Well, I should be wary, too, Beatrix thought sympathetically, if I were surrounded by a houseful of people, most of whom were total strangers, and if the only person I knew I could trust—my poor brother—was dead and buried. Miss Wickstead must feel very lonely. It didn't help, either, Beatrix supposed, that everyone in the room knew that she was an heiress with a substantial property. There might be some who would have an eye on her fortune.

Or on herself, Beatrix thought with an inward smile, seeing Dr. Butters leaning solicitously toward her, saying something in her ear. Miss Wickstead glanced up at him with obvious admiration. As well she might. Dr. Butters was a fine man, Beatrix thought, kind and thoughtful and much loved throughout the district. If Miss Wickstead was inclined to take a husband—after a suitable period of mourning, of course—and chose Dr. Butters, everyone would no doubt applaud her choice.

There were two other gentlemen in the group, both very attentive to Miss Wickstead. One had a long, pointed nose, a red moustache, and reddish hair worn long and swept back from his forehead, rather like a fox, Beatrix thought with amusement. But a dapper fox, for he was elegantly dressed and held a white handkerchief in his hand, putting it often to his nose, as if it were perfumed. Beatrix heard him say that his name was Smythe-Jones, and that he was a fellow antiquarian who had been long acquainted with Mr. Wickstead and deeply admired his collections. He did not say, Beatrix noticed, why he happened to be in the vicinity at this particular time, or what it was he wanted.

The other gentleman was stout and blond, with shrewd blue eyes and a cheery waistcoat the color of a robin's breast.

Beatrix didn't recognize him, but he seemed to be an acquaintance of Miss Wickstead. Mr. Knutson, she called him, and indeed, he seemed to speak with a Scandinavian accent. He regarded the lady, Beatrix thought, with something of a proprietary interest, and she rather guessed that there might be some competition between him and Dr. Butters for Miss Wickstead's favor. Or was it something else? Mr. Knutson looked at the lady with what seemed to be a disapproval, and she avoided his glance by turning her head away, biting her lip. She did not seem entirely comfortable in his presence.

Of course, Miss Potter might have observed this pair with a greater interest if she'd had our advantage, for we know that there is a prior acquaintance between them and are likely to be just a little suspicious. I'm sure you remember what Pickles told Rascal after the inquest: that Mr. Knutson had visited Miss Wickstead at Briar Bank House whilst her brother was away at Kendal and all the servants were off on an unusual half-holiday. I wonder what went on that afternoon, and perhaps you are wondering, too. How is it that these two are acquainted? What is the nature of their connection with each other?

But Beatrix—who has no reason to suppose that anything unseemly might be going on—reminded herself that she had no business poking her nose into people's private affairs. What Dr. Butters and Mr. Knutson felt toward Miss Wickstead, or she toward either or both of them, might be of interest to someone like Sherlock Holmes or Dr. Watson, who were in the habit of finding mysteries everywhere. But it was no business of hers, especially on such a funereal occasion.

Beatrix turned away. She had been at Briar Bank House before, when she and her father had come to see Mr. Wickstead's collections, and knew how the ground floor was laid out. The double doors at one end of the large drawing room opened into a smaller dining room, where a substantial meal was laid on a damask cloth. A half-dozen tall black candles in silver holders were arranged in the center, surrounded by loops of green smilax and black ribbon. There was a great quantity of cold boiled fowl, a large pickled tongue sliced and ornamented with cloves and a splendid parsley ruff, several raised chicken pies, a ham sliced in paper-thin curls and embellished with scallions and radishes cut into the shapes of flowers. There were several plates of sausages and meat rolls, a tray of sandwiches, a tier of fresh fruits, and sweets and baked goods of all kinds, including Sarah Barwick's Queen cakes, light and airy. It was the sort of elaborate display that might be expected of a ball supper, Beatrix thought, but would likely be criticized (by some) as a little too ostentatious for this occasion.

Since there were far too many people to be seated, the food was to be taken on china plates and eaten standing. Wine was being poured by the butler and a man-servant. Those of the villagers who were not accustomed to drinking wine at luncheon regarded it doubtfully, while the gentry accepted without remark and were obviously pleased at the fine array laid out for them. Beatrix suspected that Miss Wickstead's social standing in the district would be elevated by the way she had celebrated this occasion, and briefly wondered if that was her object. (Of course, you and I, having a little more reason to be suspicious of Miss Wickstead, might be inclined to think that it was.)

The gathering in the drawing room included many people Beatrix recognized. In the corner, Mrs. Llewellyn, Mrs. Crook, and Mrs. Braithwaite, wearing their best winter hats, were surreptitiously discussing the furnishings and draperies, some of which appeared to Beatrix to be quite new. (The draperies and chair backs were swagged with black crepe in the approved fashion.) Mr. Llewellyn, Mr. Crook, and Constable Braithwaite, plates in their hands, were peering eagerly around the room as if they hoped that Mr. Wickstead's treasure might be on display somewhere.

Mr. Barrow, the owner of the Tower Bank Arms, had taken his plate to the window for a better light and was carefully examining the pickled tongue, perhaps comparing it to the same dish as it was prepared by Mrs. Barrow and served to diners at the pub.

Bertha and Henry Stubbs stood in another corner, with Lucy and Joseph Skead. Mr. Stubbs, the ferryman, was looking extremely cheerful, no doubt because he was having a holiday (the ferry still wasn't operating) and enjoying free food. Mr. Skead, however, wore a mournful expression, befitting the man who had dug Mr. Wickstead's grave and seen him lowered into it at the private burial that had taken place that morning.

The fireplace mantel was heavily draped in black, with green ferns, white carnations, and a large black bow perfectly centered. In front of it stood Miss Nash, headmistress of Sawrey School, chatting quietly with Grace Lythecoe. Beside Mrs. Lythecoe stood Vicar Samuel Sackett. The vicar was glancing toward Mrs. Llewellyn with a half-defiant look, Beatrix thought, remembering what Sarah Barwick had said about that lady's disapproval of the vicar's frequent visits to Mrs. Lythecoe. (She herself felt it would be a very good thing if Vicar Sackett were to marry Mrs. Lythecoe, if that's what the two of them planned to do. Not only would the vicar benefit, but the whole parish would be the better for it.)

And in another grouping, Beatrix saw Captain Woodcock, Major Kittredge, and Dimity. Dimity was wearing a pretty dark gray maternity dress that made her look like a plump gray dove. She was seated on a sofa with Lady Long-ford. Dimity caught her eye and waved and smiled, and Beatrix smiled back, shaking her head just a little. She would have been glad to join her friend, but one session with Lady Longford would do for the entire day.

And then something puzzling happened. As Beatrix watched, the gentleman she had seen in the village the after-noon before—the tall, thin, dark-whiskered man with the camera—came up to Captain Woodcock and introduced him-self. Beatrix couldn't hear, but Mr. Heelis had told her the man's name. He was Joseph Adams, the photographer who was staying with the Crooks and was going around with his camera, taking photographs of various picturesque scenes. He did not have his camera with him now, of course, and Beatrix wondered why he was here. Had he been acquainted with Mr. Wickstead? Perhaps he had photographed the collections, as had her father. Or perhaps he had simply come with the Crooks—but in that case, what was his business with Captain Woodcock?

After a moment, Mr. Adams and Captain Woodcock stepped to one side and continued talking, the captain frowning intently, Mr. Adams' face grave. Another moment, and Captain Woodcock was beckoning to Mr. Heelis, who had just come into the drawing room. Mr. Heelis was intro-duced to Mr. Adams, and then the three of them carried on what was obviously a serious conversation, putting their heads together and speaking in low voices. At one point, all three men glanced in the direction of the group around Miss Wickstead, as if they were discussing someone there. The skittish Miss Wickstead? Mr. Knutson, of the robin red-breast waistcoat? Or perhaps the fox-like gentleman?

It was all very curious, Beatrix thought. Something was

afoot—what was it? But she was not likely to find out at the moment, so unless she wanted to join Dimity and Lady Longford, she should have to find something else to occupy herself. That was the bother of gatherings. One had to be sociable whether one wanted to or not, or feel oneself a fifth wheel, if not totally outcast.

But there was another alternative. At the opposite end of the drawing room were the double doors that opened into the oak-paneled library where Mr. Wickstead had kept his antiquities. Beatrix went through them and into the library, which was happily empty of people, and spent several moments looking at the locked, glass-fronted cases in which were displayed the ancient coins and bowls and jewelry and works of art that Mr. Wickstead had collected, all uniquely contrived and (to Beatrix's eye) extraordinarily beautiful. Several pieces were so cleverly detailed that her fingers itched for a pencil so that she could sketch them. What would Miss Wickstead do with all these lovely things, now that they were hers? Did she admire them as much as her brother had? Or perhaps she had no interest in them. Such rare and valuable items belonged in a museum, of course, but other collectors would certainly be willing to pay a great deal to acquire them. Would she sell?

"Pardon me," said a voice, cultured and supercilious. "Are you acquainted with Mr. Wickstead's collections?"

Beatrix turned. It was the elegant gentleman with the fox-colored hair and the handkerchief. Mr. Smythe-Jones.

"A little," Beatrix admitted.

"Well, then," said Mr. Smythe-Jones, fluttering his handkerchief. "Perhaps you would be so kind as to direct me to his recent acquisition. A Viking hoard, I understand." He swept the room with his gaze—an avaricious gaze, Beatrix thought, that took everything in, weighed it, measured it, and put a price tag on it.

"You shall have to ask Miss Wickstead about that," Beatrix said politely. "I'm afraid I know nothing of it."

The man stamped his foot. "Miss Wickstead claims not to know anything of it, either!" he exclaimed angrily. "No one knows anything of it—or if they do, they won't say. But it's here, I tell you! I've come all the way from London to find and buy it and I won't be turned away!"

Beatrix herself felt suddenly angry. "I can do no better than to refer you to Mr. Wickstead's solicitor," she said coldly. She turned to the open door and pointed. "He is the gentleman in the dark suit."

Smythe-Jones stormed out without so much as a thank-you, and Beatrix turned back with relief to her examination of the displays. It was a good thing that Dr. Butters had been so sure Mr. Wickstead's death was accidental. If not, the foxy gentleman might find himself under suspicion.

"Oh, here you are, Bea," Sarah Barwick said, entering the room. "Is this the old gent's collection?"

"Yes," Beatrix said, looking up. "A part of it, anyway—there was more when I was here earlier with my father, but I imagine it's locked away. It's quite remarkable, isn't it?"

"If you say so," Sarah replied. "I'm more of a modern person, myself." She glanced around. "I wonder where the treasure is. Now, that's something I'd love to get a look at."

"You and everyone else," Beatrix said with a little laugh. "Mr. Smythe-Jones was just telling me that he intended to buy it and take it back to London." She paused. "Is it quite certain that there's a treasure? P'rhaps it's only just a lot of talk. You know how people are—worse than magpies for chatter."

"Could be just gossip, I suppose," Sarah said doubtfully.

"Although Billie Stoker certainly seemed sure of himself. And of course, it could really be a Viking treasure. There were plenty of Vikings around here, I've been told, eons and eons ago. They could've buried anything anywhere, I s'pose."

"That's true," Beatrix said slowly. "There was a great hoard found some years ago at Cuerdale, on the River Ribble. I've seen it in the British Museum."

"Well, there you are, then. P'rhaps he did find something." Sarah tilted her head. "What did you think of my Savoy cake, Bea? Mrs. Stoker gave it pride of place on the table."

"I haven't had any yet," Beatrix replied. "Actually, I haven't eaten, although the table looks lovely."

"Better hurry," Sarah cautioned, "or it will all be gone. Mr. Crook and Mr. Llewellyn were on their way for second helps. The two of them could clear that table in a flash. In fact, I'd better get back to the kitchen and see if all my baked goods have been put out."

As Sarah turned to go, her brown woolen skirt caught on one of the carvings of a small three-legged table topped by a tall stack of books. The table teetered. She caught it, but too late—the books slid with a crash onto the floor.

"Oh, blast," she muttered, kneeling down to pick them up. "Skirts are such a bother, always getting caught on things. If I had my way, there'd be a law saying that all women have to wear trousers."

Beatrix had mixed feelings on the subject of trousers. They were highly appropriate for bicycling and climbing over walls, and she had no objection to others wearing them. But she herself was a bit old-fashioned on the subject, preferring skirts. She knelt beside Sarah to help, gathering up two books—*Oliver Twist* and *Vanity Fair*, both favorites of hers—with Mr. Wickstead's name written on the flyleaf. She held them in her hands, thinking how sad it was that he would never read them again.

"Oh, look, Bea," Sarah said eagerly. She had picked up a larger volume, leather-bound, with gilt embossing on a fancy cover. "It's a family album." She had opened to a title page on which was written, in a slanting copperplate:

Wickstead Family Album

"Perhaps Miss Wickstead gave it to her brother when they were reunited," Beatrix mused. She loved looking at old photos—there were such a lot of them in her family, because her father was a keen photographer who could never let an occasion go by without lining everyone up for the obligatory photographs. Sometimes you could learn a great deal about people just by looking at their pictures. Her mother kept her lips pressed tight together and never smiled at the camera or looked at any members of the family. Her brother Bertram, who was married and living on a farm in Scotland, usually stood just a little apart from the family group, stiffly, as if he were holding in a secret—as he was, of course. Their parents knew nothing of Bertram's marriage, which he had kept secret from them for some seven years.

"I wonder if there are any photos of Manchester," Sarah said. "That's where the Wicksteads are from, I understand. Like me. Maybe I'll see something I recognize." She began turning the pages, holding the album so that Beatrix could look, too. Photographs, newspaper clippings, and other things had been pasted onto the pages, some with captions written beside them in the same sloping hand that had created the title page. "Yes, it's definitely Manchester," Sarah added. "There's the Town Hall."

"And that's the cathedral tower," Beatrix said, pointing to another photo. "The year Grandmama died, Papa and I stood on the street and listened to the bell. Papa thought the sound of it very fine. After that, we went to see Grandpapa's warehouse in Mosley Street, and the house in Exmouth Terrace where Papa was born."

Beatrix half-smiled, remembering. Her father had enjoyed showing her around the city where he'd grown up. It had been an adventure, just the two of them. Her first tram ride, actually, and she'd found it great fun. Her smile faded. That was long before Norman's proposal, of course. The way her father had behaved—as if she were disgracing the entire family by marrying someone who worked for a living—had changed everything. She could never again feel the same affection she had felt for him as a girl.

"And here is Mr. Wickstead's dad and mum," Sarah said thoughtfully, turning the page.

Beatrix shook her head to clear away the memories and bent for a closer look at the captions. *Dad*, said one, under a photo of a jaunty-looking man in a bowler hat. *Mum and Dad and Louisa*, said another—a pretty, brown-haired woman seated in a chair in a garden, a year-old baby on her lap and the bowler-hatted man standing beside her. *Dad and Little Hughie*, said a third. The same man, but without his hat, held a boy of two or three in his arms. The child had blond curls and was wearing a ruffled white pinafore.

"Makes you sad, doesn't it?" asked Sarah, studying the photos. "I wonder how the family happened to get split up. The mum and dad must have died—mustn't they?—because the little boy was chucked off to an orphanage. Wonder where Miss Wickstead grew up. Was she in another orphanage, or with relatives? Maybe the relatives wanted a little girl but wouldn't take a boy. Which happens sometimes. A great pity, I'd say. No wonder the brother and sister were so glad to be reunited." She turned another page, and then another—pictures of people, pictures of houses.

"Stop, Sarah!" Beatrix exclaimed suddenly, and put her hand on Sarah's. "Turn back, please!"

"What? To this page?" Sarah asked, doing as she was bid.

"No, one more," Beatrix commanded. She was frowning, and something—surprise, disbelief, apprehension?—had suddenly knotted tight inside her. "There." She pointed at a photograph. "Look there!"

"'Wickstead Family Home,'" read Sarah, "'1865.'" She whistled between her teeth, looking at a photo of a large stone house with a Greek-Revival portico, tall windows, and a great many chimney pots. "Poor little Hughie Wickstead, turned out of a mansion like this and sent off to an orphanage. Looks like the family had quite a lot of money at some point, although I suppose they must have lost it. Maybe it happened when Mum and Dad died, and—"

"But that's not *their* family home," Beatrix said in a low, trembling voice. She was staring at it incredulously. "That's the house my mother was raised in, Sarah! That's Gorse Hall, in Stalybridge, just to the east of Manchester."

"Of course. I know where Stalybridge is." Sarah frowned. "But you can't be remembering right, Beatrix. You see what it says? Right there." She pointed. "'Wickstead Family Home.' Your mother's home might be similar, but—"

"I don't care what it says, Sarah!" Beatrix said fiercely, now beginning to feel quite angry at the idea that someone, anyone, would usurp one of her favorite houses. "I have been in Gorse Hall too many times to count. My grandparents built it in 1835 with stone from a local quarry, on property they bought from the Dukinfield family." She jabbed a finger at the photograph. "You see that window? That's the room I slept in when we visited—the old nursery. There was a music box, and a rocking horse, and engravings on the stairs. The house is on a hill, and you could look out and see Grandpapa Leech's cotton mill in the valley. And there was an orchard, and a bowling green, and Grandmama Leech's formal garden." She took a deep breath. "It's the same house, I tell you! It's Gorse Hall!"

Sarah looked uneasy. "Well, p'rhaps the Wicksteads bought it afterward," she reasoned. "After your grandmother died."

"Impossible," Beatrix said flatly. "The house sat empty for a very long time, and then it was bought by a mill own-er named Storrs. He gave it to his son as a wedding present." She stopped, her mouth suddenly dry. "In fact, his son was murdered in the house just last month. George Harry Storrs, his name was. The story has been in all the newspa-pers."

"Murdered!" Sarah scoffed, but her tone was uneasy. "You're having me on, Bea."

"Would I joke about something like that?" Beatrix de-manded impatiently. "Anyway, look at the date that's writ-ten beside the photograph: 1865. My grandfather died in 1861, and Grandmama Leech stayed on in the house. She was living there in 1865, and she went on living there until she died in 1884."

Sarah's eyes were dark, her face troubled. "But I don't un-derstand, Bea. It doesn't make any sense. Why would Miss Wickstead put a photograph of *your* family home into *her* family album? Did she make a mistake?"

"Well, I suppose it could've been a mistake," Beatrix said, trying to see both sides of the question. "I suppose she might have found the picture in an old scrapbook and just assumed—"

"Yes, that's right," Sarah said. "She saw it and jumped to conclusions."

"On the other hand," Beatrix said slowly, "she might have done it because she wanted to deceive Mr. Wickstead. And if she was using this photograph to deceive, it's possible that none of these other photographs are real, either." She began turning the pages, looking at the photos of people. "Anybody can paste photographs into an album and write anything they please about them. I could paste in photographs of King Edward and Queen Alexandra and call them 'Mama' and 'Papa' and it wouldn't make me a princess."

Sarah cleared her throat. "Really, Beatrix, you can't think—"

"Of course I can." Beatrix pointed at the page. "Just look at this, Sarah. The children in these photos are no more than two or three years apart in age, wouldn't you say? But Mr. Wickstead was older than Miss Wickstead by at least seven or eight years. When she was a year old, he would have been eight or nine."

"The photographs could have been taken at different times," Sarah objected.

"They could have, but they weren't. Look closely, Sarah. They were all taken in the same garden, in front of the same rhododendron shrub. See? There's the very same rosebush off to the right, against the brick wall. The *same* brick wall, with the same ivy creeping over it."

Sarah peered at the photo more closely. "By golly, Bea, you're right! I'd never have noticed it if you hadn't pointed it out. There's the shrub, and the rosebush, and the wall and the ivy—all the very same! If the little girl is Louisa, the boy can't be Hugh. And vice versa." She looked up, puzzled. "But why would Mr. Wickstead's sister write all these wrong captions in her photograph album?"

"Because she's not really Mr. Wickstead's sister," Beatrix replied. "She wanted to convince him that she was his sister and hoped that these photos might strengthen her case."

"What an awful thing to do," Sarah exclaimed heatedly. "Poor Mr. Wickstead is dead, God rest his soul, so it can't matter to him now. But . . ." She puffed out her breath.

"Yes, 'but,' " Beatrix said emphatically. "Miss Wickstead has inherited Mr. Wickstead's estate. But what if she's not Miss Wickstead?"

"Not Miss Wickstead! But then, who *is* she? And why did she do this?"

"There's only one way to find out." Beatrix scrambled to her feet. "We'll ask her."

Sarah stared up at her. "What? You mean, right now? With all these people here? That's not such a good idea, Bea. What if she makes a scene?"

Beatrix frowned. She had been so caught up in her discovery that she had forgotten all about the funeral luncheon. "You're right," she said. She thought for a moment. "Mr. Heelis and Captain Woodcock are in the drawing room," she said. "Mr. Heelis was Mr. Wickstead's solicitor, and Captain Woodcock is the Justice of the Peace. I'll ask them what they think."

Sarah bit her lip. "Yes, but—"

"Stay here with that album, Sarah," Beatrix commanded. "Don't let anybody take it. I'll be right back." And with that, she left the room, closing the double doors firmly behind her.

In the drawing room, Will Heelis was still in conversation with Miles Woodcock, talking over what they had just learnt from Joseph Adams, who was not, as it turned out, a well-known photographer at all. He was a government agent from the Home Office, who had come to Briar Bank at Mr. Wickstead's request, to take custody of the treasure.

"At Wickstead's request?" Captain Woodcock muttered. "Deuced odd, if you ask me. I could understand Hugh turning in his find to the government, if he did it right away. But after all this time? Are we sure this man Adams is who he claims to be?"

"He showed us his identification," Will reminded his friend. "And the letter Wickstead sent him. He's legitimate, Miles."

"And Miss Wickstead insists she knows nothing about that treasure," the captain said thoughtfully. "Which rather leaves the Crown holding the bag, doesn't it?"

For that was what Joseph Adams had told them. A fortnight before his death, Hugh Wickstead had written to the Home Office, reporting that he had discovered a valuable hoard of Viking treasure—several dozen pieces, he said, all unique and, he felt sure, very valuable. He wrote that he was not sure he could guarantee the security of the find, and hinted that he thought someone—he did not say who—might be after it. He asked rather urgently if a person from the Home Office would come and take the find in charge as soon as possible. In the meantime, he had hidden it away for safekeeping.

It was Mr. Adams' job to deal with discoveries that came within the aegis of the Treasure Trove law, so he had arranged to come to the Lake District as quickly as he could get away from his other duties. Mr. Wickstead had suggested that he book a room with the Crooks since he expected to spend at least two days in the area, taking photographs of the site where the find had occurred. Adams had done so. But when he learnt of Mr. Wickstead's death from the charabanc driver, he thought at once that the poor man must have been killed for the treasure. In the circumstance, he thought it best not to mention his real reason for coming to the Lake District. Having his camera with him, he told Mrs. Crook he was a photographer—and she took care of telling everyone else.

"I can see why Adams thought Wickstead's death was no accident," Will muttered.

"Indeed," said the captain. "Especially when he discovered that the treasure has disappeared."

For that, it seemed, was what had happened. Mr. Adams had come to Briar Bank House, identified himself as a Home Office agent, and asked to see the treasure, which he was prepared to take back to London with him, at the request of Mr. Wickstead. (Do you remember the letter that Mrs. Crook posted for him, to a Mr. Howard Peasmarsh, Queen Anne's Gate, London? It would not in the least surprise me to learn that it was written to his supervisor in the Home Office, reporting on this visit to Briar Bank.)

Miss Wickstead, however, seemed very surprised to learn that her brother intended to hand over the treasure to the Crown. She insisted she had no idea where it was. Yes, she admitted to having seen it once or twice, but now, she claimed, the treasure could not be found. She had searched the house from top to bottom. It was gone. Her brother had hidden it somewhere before he died, and that's all there was to it.

Well, now. A few things are becoming clear, aren't they? At least to us, that is—although I'm afraid that Mr. Heelis and Captain Woodcock must still be in the dark. You and I know—because we heard it from both Pickles the fox terrier and Bailey the Badger—that Mr. Wickstead was returning the treasure to the dragon's lair when he was killed by the tree, or by Thorvaald the falling dragon, if you want to see it that way. And now we can understand what Mr. Wickstead meant when he said, "She'll never think to look here." He was talking about Miss Wickstead. No doubt he had discovered that she had photographed the treasure and was afraid that she was out to steal it. So he was putting it back where he had found it, until the Home Office sent someone to take it into custody.

"And then there's Smythe-Jones," the captain added. That gentleman, steaming from the cold shoulder Beatrix had given him, had blustered up to Mr. Heelis and demanded information about the treasure.

"I don't think he's involved," Will said with a wry grin. "If he were, he wouldn't be calling attention to himself." He thought quickly through the consequences of what they had just learnt.

"Before anything else, we ought to discuss this matter with Miss Wickstead," he said. "Her brother's death does indeed seem to have been an accident, but this treasure business raises some other questions. He wrote to Adams that he thought someone might be trying to steal it. That someone might be his sister—and she might have already succeeded. What do you think, Miles?"

"I agree, Will," the captain replied gravely. "She couldn't have known that shortly she would inherit everything—including the treasure. So she might well have attempted theft. She might have brought it off, too." He frowned. "Still, I'm not sure that this is the time nor the place. So soon after—"

"What better time could there be?" Will asked. He looked around, noticing that several people were leaving. "The luncheon is almost over. I suggest that we wait until—" He felt a light hand on his sleeve and looked down into a pair of very bright blue eyes. Startled, he said, "Oh, hello, Miss Potter."

"Excuse me, Mr. Heelis." She colored and took her hand

away, hastily, as if she had not meant to put it there in the first place. "I'm sorry to interrupt you," she said in a low voice, "but it really is rather urgent. Would you and Captain Woodcock step into the library for a few moments, please?"

Will frowned. Miss Potter had a way of seeing things that other people missed. Was it possible that she—

"Do you mind telling us why?" the captain asked.

"It has to do with Miss Wickstead," Miss Potter replied uncomfortably. "I've something to show you, and I would really rather not discuss it here. You'll understand when you see it, I think."

"Well, then, come along, Woodcock," Will said, taking charge of the situation. He smiled at Miss Potter, who was looking exceptionally pretty in her neat gray silk shirtwaist. In his opinion, in fact, she was the prettiest lady in the room, bar none. "Lead on, Miss Potter."

The three of them went into the library, where they found Miss Barwick, holding what appeared to be a book of some sort and looking rather frightened. Miss Potter closed the doors behind them. She took the book—showing them that it was the Wickstead family photograph album—and placed it on a small table, turning the pages without commentary. When she got to one—a photograph labeled "Wickstead Family Home," she left the page open and stepped back, so they could look at it.

"Palatial, I'd say," remarked Miles in an appraising tone. "The family must've had money at some point."

"That's what I said when I saw it," Miss Barwick put in excitedly. "It's a very grand house."

Will frowned down at the photograph. He had the feeling he had seen it before, and recently, too.

"Yes, it is a very grand house," Miss Potter said. "But it

never belonged to the Wicksteads. It was built by my grandparents, John and Jane Leech. This is Gorse Hall." And in a few terse sentences, she told them the story. "The house never belonged to the Wickstead family," she concluded.

As she spoke, Will suddenly remembered where he had seen the house before. "Gorse Hall!" he exclaimed. "Why, that's where the Storrs' murder took place. I saw the photograph in one of the newspapers when it happened, back at the beginning of November. The police have finally arrested someone, I understand. A cousin, I believe."

The captain wheeled to look at him. "You're talking about the murder of Harry George Storrs, in Stalybridge?" he asked incredulously. "I read about it, too. This is the house where he was stabbed to death?"

"Yes," Miss Potter said unhappily. "My mother's family home. In fact, Mama and I discussed the killing just before I came down from London." She gave them a crooked smile. "She's afraid I'll be murdered in my bed, you see."

Mrs. Potter wasn't the least bit afraid of that, Will thought darkly. She only wanted to make Beatrix afraid. He frowned. "It doesn't seem likely that this business here at Briar Bank has anything to do with the murder."

"I agree," Miss Potter said. "Miss Wickstead—or whoever she is—has been here since August or so. Isn't that the case?"

"That's right," the captain said. "She came, I believe, at the end of July. It's an odd coincidence, granted. But it doesn't seem related to Storrs' death."

Will was regarding Miss Potter. "'Whoever she is,' you said. Do you have reason to believe that she's not Hugh Wickstead's sister?"

"Yes!" Miss Barwick put in excitedly. "Show them the other photos, Bea!"

Miss Potter turned the pages to photographs of a woman, a man, and two little children. In a few careful words, she made her case. "These children cannot be Hugh and Louisa Wickstead," she said. "I am sorry to say it, but I think this entire album was designed to deceive Mr. Wickstead. I do not think Miss Wickstead can be who she claims to be."

"Astonishing," Will muttered. He was not sure whether he was thinking of Miss Wickstead's clever deception or Miss Potter's cleverer discovery of it—the latter, he rather thought.

The captain rapped his knuckles on the album. "What we have here is a clear case of fraud."

"What's will happen now?" Miss Barwick asked.

"It's time to have a talk with the lady," Will said. The reading of Hugh Wickstead's last will and testament was scheduled for the next morning. If there was some sort of fraud, it would be better to sort things out now. "It may take a little while, however, since we should wait until everyone else has gone. Miss Potter, I hope you won't mind remaining here." He cleared his throat and said, as tactfully as he could, "Miss Barwick, perhaps you would prefer to leave."

"Well . . ." Miss Barwick said, with a glance at Miss Potter. "I suppose I really ought to box up the leftover baked goods." She looked back at Will. "P'rhaps I'll ask Mrs. Crook if I can ride back to the village with them."

Will nodded, painfully aware of the meaning that hung in the air. "That might be best," he said. "I don't know how long this is going to take."

Miss Potter had colored, and he wondered if she had understood, as well. "I'll wait here," she said, after Miss Barwick had gone. She glanced around at the collections with a little smile. "I shan't be bored. There is plenty to occupy me. I've already found myself wishing for a sketchpad."

Will nodded and turned to his friend. "Well, then, Captain. Let's fetch Miss Wickstead. I want to hear what the lady has to say for herself."

19

The Lady Comes Clean

It was another twenty minutes before the guests had all left, once again offering their condolences and best wishes to the sister of the deceased. Dr. Butters might have liked to linger, but he received a message saying that he was urgently required by Mrs. Knox, who was expecting the imminent arrival of a baby. With a dark look at Mr. Knutson, the good doctor left to do his duty.

Constable Braithwaite was on his way out the front door when Captain Woodcock caught him up. There was a brief consultation. The captain returned to the drawing room and the constable went outside to ask Mr. and Mrs. Llewellyn if Mrs. Braithwaite might ride back to the village with them, since he would not be coming back for a bit.

Mr. Knutson clearly intended to outlast all the other guests, but Miss Wickstead, who was very pale and drawn, said something to him privately. (Will, shamelessly eavesdropping, caught the words "so very tired.") Clearly not pleased, Knutson took his hat and coat and left, with a promise to "see you tomorrow, my dear." The phrase held, at least to Will's ear, something of a threat. As Knutson left the room, Miss Wickstead looked so enormously relieved that he almost felt sorry for her. Whatever the relationship between the two of them, he had the feeling that the association did not fill her with joy.

When the last guest had left, Will approached Miss Wickstead, with the captain close behind. "Captain Woodcock and I are sorry to trouble you," he said quietly, "but there is an important matter to be discussed."

"Can't it wait, gentlemen?" she asked wearily. She took a handkerchief out of the pocket of her black dress and touched her eyes. "It has been a long day, and I should very much like to rest."

"I wish it could," he said. "But it has to do with the inheritance. The reading of Mr. Wickstead's will is scheduled for tomorrow. I really don't think we should delay."

If Miss Wickstead wondered why the Justice of the Peace might be involved in a discussion of an inheritance, she did not ask. She put on a brave smile. "Oh, very well, then. Shall we?" She gestured to the sofa. "I'll ask Lucy to bring us some coffee. Or perhaps you'd rather have tea."

"Neither, thank you," Captain Woodcock said. "And we should prefer to speak in the library. There's something there we should like to show you."

"In the library?" She gave a half-impatient wave of her hand. "Oh, very well. I certainly hope it won't take long." Then, as she went into the library, she saw Miss Potter waiting. "Hello," she said, surprised. "I don't believe we've met."

"This is Miss Beatrix Potter, of Hill Top Farm," Mr. Heelis said. "She was acquainted with your brother."

Beatrix gave her a steady look, noticing that while Miss

Wickstead was trying to put on a show of confidence, she seemed unsure of herself. Or perhaps she was just very tired, which was certainly understandable, in the circumstance. Her face was pale and the corners of her mouth seemed to tremble.

"My father and I visited here at Briar Bank several times," Beatrix said gravely. "We were both quite fond of Mr. Wickstead. I am very sorry for his passing."

"Thank you," Miss Wickstead said. "He was a very dear man. He shall be missed." She took out her handkerchief and touched her eyes, then looked from Beatrix to Mr. Heelis. "I'm afraid I don't understand, Mr. Heelis. I thought this was to be about the inheritance."

"It is," Mr. Heelis said. "However, there is a matter that must be cleared up first. Please sit here." He seated Miss Wickstead in a chair beside the table. "Miss Potter, if you will be so kind, please?"

Beatrix stepped forward, put the album on the table, and opened it to the page with the photograph of Gorse Hall. She explained, as she had to the others, that this was her mother's home and had been in the family for over fifty years. As she spoke, Miss Wickstead's face grew even paler, and she bit her lip. But she did not try to deny the truth of what Beatrix was saying.

"I . . . I can explain how that happened," she began nervously. "You see, there were quite a number of photographs. Some of them were hard to identify. If I've made a mistake—"

Mr. Heelis raised his hand. "I believe we should keep the explanations until we have finished," he said. "Please, Miss Potter."

Beatrix turned back to the photographs of the family and pointed out the difficulties with the ages of the children.

"And as you can see," she added, "it appears that these photographs were taken at the same time. And that means—"
She hesitated. By this time, Miss Wickstead had turned her
head away, as if she could not bear to look at the pictures,
and her cheeks, no longer pale, were a dull red.

"And that means, Miss Wickstead," Mr. Heelis said,
with a quiet firmness that Beatrix very much admired, "that
these cannot be photographs of you and Mr. Wickstead as
children. Put this together with the fictitious Wickstead
family home—" He gave a little shrug. "I think you must
see the difficulty we face, Miss Wickstead. It is a question of
identity."

"But my brother didn't see any difficulty!" Miss Wickstead cried, starting out of her chair. "He was perfectly satisfied with my explanation. He recognized many family
similarities between us. Why, he even made me the benefi-
ciary of his will, which shows you how he felt about me!"

"That may be quite true," Captain Woodcock said.
"However, as a Justice of the Peace, let me try to explain the
situation from the court's perspective. Now that the question
of your identity has been raised, the Magistrate's Court—
that's where Mr. Wickstead's will must be probated—will
require you to provide documentary proof of your identity. A
certificate of birth is preferred."

Miss Wickstead made a faint mewing sound, like a kit-
ten, and twisted her handkerchief in her fingers. "But I
don't . . . I can't—"

"Really, my dear lady," the captain said in a tone of impatient disapproval. "If you are who you say you are, there
should be no difficulty in proving it. You surely cannot expect the courts to hand over a very substantial inheritance
without so much as an inquiry into your claims." He
scowled sternly. "Is that not so?"

In answer, Miss Wickstead dropped her head in her hands and began to cry.

Sensing that the tears were the beginnings of a confession, Beatrix felt a sharp pity for the woman. Putting a hand on her shoulder, she said, "I am very sorry for your trouble, Miss Wickstead. I am sure that none of this was in your mind when you came to Briar Bank. You could not have known that the pretense would go on so long. And I'm sure you never imagined that Mr. Wickstead would die and leave you his property, putting you in this horrible position. What started out as one thing has become something else altogether, hasn't it?"

At the touch of Beatrix's hand, Miss Wickstead had raised her head, the tears streaming down her face. "It's true!" she sobbed. "I never meant anything at all! It was just a job. I was only to find the treasure and tell—" She stopped.

"Tell who?" Mr. Heelis asked, leaning forward.

Miss Wickstead pressed her lips together, her glance darting from side to side as if she wished she could flee.

"Whom were you to tell, Miss Wickstead?" the captain demanded roughly. "Come on, now, come clean. Out with it! Tell us what you were aiming to steal."

"But I wasn't aiming to steal it!" she cried, her eyes widening. "No, never! Not that at all, truly!"

Beatrix saw that the captain was about to say something angry and insulting, and forestalled him with a shake of her head. "Miss Wickstead," she said, "will you tell us who employed you?"

Miss Wickstead looked at her wildly. "How did you—" She stopped, and her voice dropped. "Employed? What makes you think that?"

"I believe you were employed to learn about the treasure Mr. Wickstead is said to have found. It would be easier to do

that, of course, if you were in the house, if only for a short
time. You might have come seeking employment, but there
was none to be found here. So you came as a relative. A
long-lost sister." She paused. "Perhaps it would be easier if I
could call you by your real name. It must be painful for you
to hear yourself continually addressed as Miss Wickstead."

"It is so painful I can scarcely bear it," the lady said, in a
very low voice. There was a long silence. At last, she said,
"My name is Emily Mason."

Beatrix smiled. "Thank you, Miss Mason. There. That is
a relief for me, and it must be for you."

Miss Mason nodded wordlessly, the tears spilling over
her cheeks.

"It is true, then," Beatrix went on, "that you came to Briar
Bank posing as Mr. Wickstead's sister?"

Miss Mason's "yes" was barely audible.

"And you came in search of the treasure?"

"Yes." Miss Mason cleared her throat. "But I didn't . . .
didn't stay for that." She put out her hand to Beatrix. "I was
supposed to leave when I found it and took the picture, Miss
Potter. My work was over then. But I stayed because I began
to—" Her voice broke.

Captain Woodcock started to say something but Mr.
Heelis put a cautioning finger to his lips. It was as if the two
women had forgotten their presence and were alone together
in the room.

Beatrix took Miss Mason's hand. It was icy cold, the fingers like frozen twigs. "You stayed because you began to
care," she said.

"Mr. Wickstead was very kind to me. He accepted me
without question. He was loving, in all the ways a brother
should be." Miss Mason closed her eyes. "No one had ever
loved me in that way before, Miss Potter. He wanted me to

stay." She shook her head, her voice falling almost to a whisper. "He offered me a home. A real home, for the first time in my life."

"And yet you were concealing yourself from him," Beatrix said, still holding the hand and thinking how hard it must have been for Miss Mason to feel herself loved and wanted, but under false pretenses. "It must have been dreadfully painful for you. I imagine that you would have much preferred to tell him why you had come. Had you done so, I think he would have forgiven you."

"Oh, I'm sure he would have!" Miss Mason cried. She pulled her hand back, took out her handkerchief, and wiped her eyes. "If only I could have told him—" She stopped.

"Told him?" Beatrix prodded gently, and then hazarded a guess, based on what she had seen of the group around Miss Mason in the drawing room. "About Mr. Knutson?"

Miss Mason's eyes grew large. There was a long silence, and then a sigh. "You know?"

"Only a little."

"Well, then, I suppose you might as well know the rest." And in very simple terms, she told them the story. She had been approached by Mr. Sven Knutson, the director of a Norwegian museum, who had heard that a treasure of immense value had been found by an antiquarian in the Lake District. The antiquarian, Mr. Wickstead, had refused to discuss his find or to reveal any of the details, but Mr. Knutson was persuaded that he had truly discovered something significant and that it was a Viking treasure. In his opinion—a passionate opinion, arising out of his love of Norway's heritage—it belonged, not to a British collector nor to the British Crown, but to Norway, and should be returned there. He was prepared to do whatever was necessary to obtain it, but first of all he had to confirm its existence.

So Mr. Knutson had come to Miss Mason, who had done some investigative work for another museum in the past. He directed her to pass herself off as Mr. Wickstead's long-lost sister, in order to gain access to the house. Her task was very simple. She was to find the treasure, photograph it, and send the photographs to Mr. Knutson, who would then take care of the rest of the operation.

"What do you think he was intending to do?" Beatrix asked.

Miss Mason shook her head, her eyes dark. "I don't know—that part of it had nothing to do with me. I assumed, of course, that he would try to buy it. But whatever he intended, it didn't happen." She raised her head. "I want you to know that. It didn't happen!"

Beatrix nodded, saying nothing.

Miss Mason pulled in a deep breath. "I did what I was supposed to do. It took a while, but I finally found the treasure here in the house, where Mr. Wickstead had hidden it. I took the photographs and sent the lot to Mr. Knutson. He wrote to tell me that, indeed, it was a Viking hoard, but that he needed a closer look so that he could evaluate the pieces. He said he was coming to the village and would book a room at the Arms."

"When did he arrive?" Beatrix asked.

"Last week. He came to Briar Bank on a day when Mr. Wickstead planned to go to Kendal. I gave the servants a half-holiday and prepared to show him the treasure. But it was not where I had last seen it, and I had no idea where it was to be found. Mr. Knutson was very angry. And then Mr. Wickstead was killed, and I was afraid . . ." Her voice broke. "I was afraid . . ."

"You feared that Mr. Knutson had killed him."

"Yes." Her eyes were swimming with tears. "I could

scarcely believe it when Dr. Butters testified that the death was accidental, and the jury's finding was an enormous relief. At least I wasn't implicated in . . . in—" Her voice broke.

"In his death," Beatrix said. "Or his murder."

Miss Mason swallowed painfully. "Yes. But then I learnt that Mr. Wickstead had named me as his heiress—" She broke down completely. She could say nothing more.

Beatrix put her arms around the weeping woman and held her until she quieted. "I think," she said to Mr. Heelis, "that we've heard all we need to know, at least for the moment. You will discuss the matter with Mr. Knutson?"

"Yes, of course," Mr. Heelis said, his eyes on hers with a look she could not quite comprehend.

"Indeed we will," Captain Woodcock said, very firmly. "Constable Braithwaite and I will see to that directly. As to Miss Mason, I shall see that she is conveyed to—"

"As to Miss Mason," Beatrix said, with equal firmness, "I believe that she will be quite all right here at Briar Bank, for the present."

"Heelis!" the captain protested. "We cannot allow—"

"I agree with Miss Potter," Mr. Heelis said. "If you like, Woodcock, you might leave instructions that she is not to leave the house." He gestured toward the window, where the snow had dropped an opaque white curtain. "After all, it is not as if she will be able to leave the district."

Beatrix gave him a grateful look. "Thank you, Mr. Heelis," she murmured.

20

We Catch a Dragon by the Tale

So comes snow after fire and even dragons have their ending.

J.R.R. Tolkien

When we last saw our friend Thackeray, he was enjoying a sandwich and a bowl of Parsley's delicious potato soup and the company of the various animals who had gathered around the luncheon table at The Brockery. In addition to the two guinea pigs, there were a half-dozen badgers, a pair of hedgehogs, a trio of mice, several voles, a blind ferret, and a large tawny owl whom everyone called "Professor." They were all talking at once on a variety of subjects, and to Thackeray's ears, the hubbub was intense. But whilst there was a great deal of confusion, there was also a great spirit of camaraderie and friendliness, and Thackeray could not help feeling very much at home.

On Thackeray's left was seated a badger named Bailey,

whose right foreleg and paw were wrapped in white gauze. Somehow (afterward, Thackeray could not quite remember how it happened) the subject of books came up, and it turned out that Bailey, too, was an admirer of Mr. Gibbon, and possessed—*mirabile dictu!*—all six volumes of *The Decline and Fall of the Roman Empire,* as well as an extensive library of other notable literary works.

If Thackeray was almost beside himself with astonishment, Bailey could scarcely believe his good fortune. Fancy encountering a fellow bibliophile over soup and sandwiches! Imagine meeting someone who not only adored evenings reading before the fire, but had had experience in cataloguing a library (as had Thackeray, who had helped his dear book-collecting friend, Mr. Travers)! And when this bibliophile was as fluent and erudite a conversationalist as was this guinea pig—well! I think you can understand Bailey's delighted feeling that he had met an animal after his own heart. It will come as no surprise to you that when the badger learnt that this remarkable creature was in want of a good home and a good book, he extended an invitation forthwith.

"Come home with me to Briar Bank," said Bailey. *"You are welcome to read as much as you want and stay as long as you like. There's plenty of room. And if you are inclined to perhaps take turns in the kitchen and lend a paw in the cataloguing project—well, a bit of help is always welcome. No obligation, of course,"* he added offhandedly. *"If it doesn't work out for any reason, no hard feelings."* But deep within, he found himself wishing very much that it would work out, and that he and Thackeray could carry on discussing Gibbons and cataloguing books for a very long time.

Thackeray was so moved that he could manage only a gulp and a whispered, *"Oh, dear me, yes, thank you, I should like that very much!"* before he broke into hiccupy sobs and had to be comforted by Tuppenny, who was seated to his right. And the assembled animals greeted Bailey's announcement that Thackeray had agreed to be his roommate with a round of applause and cheers. For the most part, animals are a companionable lot and are grieved when one lives alone, without company, even when he professes to like it that way.

"*A momentous occasion,*" said Bosworth. "*I must make a note of this in the* History." He raised his glass. "*To friends.*"

"*Tooo friends!*" hooted the professor. And from all around the table came the gleeful cry, "*To friends!*"

And then, as if Bailey's cup of joy was not almost brimful, it completely spilled over the top when, a few hours later, he opened the front door at Briar Bank. The rug on the floor greeted his toes with a cozy warmth, the pictures on the wall smiled down at him, the lamp glowed with a welcoming warmth, and the whole house seemed to embrace him, whispering happily into his ear, "*There you are, old thing, home at last, after such a long time away!*" and "*Who's this you've brought with you? A new friend? Let's put another cup on the table.*"

But the dearest, happiest, most astonishing thing of all was the sight of Thorvaald the dragon, who was curled up asleep in a corner of the sitting room, his wings folded, his scaly tail tucked under his nose in the manner of a cat, the iron teakettle tucked close against a belly that glowed faintly pink with banked fire. Thackeray gave a faint cry and hid behind the badger's bulky form.

"*Thorvaald!*" Bailey cried ecstatically. "*Oh, my dear, dear, dearest Thorvaald, how wonderful to see you! Where on earth have you been keeping yourself?*"

"*Bailey?*" The dragon blinked and scrambled to his feet, nearly upsetting the kettle. "*Iszs it really you, Bailey?*" he cried incredulously. "*I thought you were drowned! You dove into the water and disappeared and—*"

"*Not drowned! Not drowned at all, but rescued!*" cried the

badger, dancing a delighted jig. *"Dragged out and dried off and well fed and home again. But I thought you had flown away forever, old chap! I imagined that you refused to spend another boring minute guarding that treasure and had gone somewhere to get away from it all—not that I could blame you, of course, not in the slightest. But here you are, back again! It's beyond belief, that's what it is. Beyond belief!"*

"I did fly away," said the dragon. *"I had an errand. I had to disposzse of the treaszsure."* He peered behind the badger. *"I say, Bailey, it appears that you are being followed by a dish mop."*

"It's not a dish mop, it's a new friend," Bailey said, pulling the guinea pig out from behind him. *"He's come to live with us."*

"It lookszs like a dish mop to me," said the dragon, but in a kindly way. *"Doeszs it have a name?"*

"Thackeray, sir," the guinea pig said in a trembling voice. He knew very well who Thorvaald was, since the badger had told him all about the dragon as they made their way to Briar Bank. He understood that the dragon was a dear friend of Bailey's. Moreover, he had frequently encountered dragons in the pages of books. But of course, it is one thing to hear or read a story about a dragon and quite another to bump into one in the flesh, especially in such tight quarters, where one inopportune breath could incinerate everything within thirty paces. And while Thackeray had always thought of himself in the largest and most important terms, he felt quite small and insignificant in the company of this creature, as I'm sure you and I would feel, if we were in the same situation.

"Delighted to meet you, Thackeray," replied the dragon, with grave politeness. *"Any friend of Badger's iszs a friend of mine."*

With that assurance, Thackeray felt a little more comfortable. It is no small compliment to be offered friendship by a dragon, even if it does come secondhand.

"The kettle's hot, I see," said Bailey to the dragon, *"many*

thanks to you. We'll have a cup of tea and Parsley's scones. Oh, and Bosworth sent along several bottles of nettle beer. There's nothing much else to eat, I'm afraid."

"Oh, yes, there is," said the dragon. *"On the way back from London, I flew over a wagon stuck in the snow, abandoned, and full of things to eat. My pockets were empty, so I filled them. It's all in the cupboard now. Tinned sardines and salmon and peaches, and boxes of biscuits, and German sausages, and pickles and plum cake and marmalade, and oh so much else."*

"*Well done!*" cried Thackeray and then quickly subsided, lest the dragon think him impertinent. As you can see, his new colleagues are having quite a salutary effect on our guinea pig's behavior.

"*Well done, indeed,*" said Bailey warmly, really quite beside himself with the unimaginable luxury of it all. *"Sardines and salmon and pickles and plum cake and even nettle beer! We shall have ourselves a feast, a right royal feast. And did you say London, old fellow? You must tell us all about it—where you've been and what you've done."* He paused and grew serious. *"And of course, what you mean by 'dispose of the treasure.'"*

So the badger got out his tin opener, while the guinea pig fetched the plates and knives and forks and spoons, and the dragon brought the kettle back to a boil. And then they gathered round the table—yes, a right royal feast indeed!— and Bailey and Thackeray ate their fill and listened raptly whilst Thorvaald told his tale, all about what happened after Mr. Wickstead died and how he came to believe that Bailey had drowned and what he did in consequence and who else was involved and what happened after that. And then, of course, he told what became of the treasure. And since it is an interesting tale and resolves some of the remaining mysteries, perhaps you will want to listen, too.

The Dragon's Tale

Dire portents appeared over Northumbria, immense whirlwinds and flashes of lightning and fiery dragons were seen flying through the air.

Anglo-Saxon Chronicle, 793 C.E.

When Thorvaald saw that the yew tree he was climbing had struck Mr. Wickstead and killed the poor man dead, he was covered filled with shame and deep remorse. He had never meant to cause such a calamity, but what was done could not be undone, so he had flown away to grieve and (as we would say in our own post-Freudian day) work through his issues.

The dragon had a lot to work through, actually, and not just his guilt over the accidental homicide that he and his tree had just committed. Thorvaald, you see, was an essentially medieval fellow who had gone to sleep when the stirrup and the crossbow were the latest technological marvels. (With the stirrup, a knight could put all his weight behind his lance and skewer a dragon without being unhorsed. With a crossbow, an uncouth peasant could put a steel-tipped bolt through a knight's Sunday best, or nail a dragon at a remarkable altitude.) But now, Thorvaald found himself wide awake in the company of railway trains, aeroplanes, telephones, and the wireless telegraph. Things had changed. He could no longer tolerate the idea of hunkering down upon two bags of treasure, like a silly goose on a nestful of eggs, for uncounted centuries into the future. What good was there in that? He was sacrificing his whole long life, and for what? For nothing, that's what!

Moreover, it was beginning to dawn on Thorvaald that

treasure brought out the worst in everyone. Yllva's stories, which she told with a dragonish relish, were all about knights who murdered other knights over odd bits of gold, and boys who killed giants for their pots of gold, and geese who were slaughtered for their golden eggs. Was there any piece of gold, anywhere, that wasn't stained with blood? He'd seen it close at hand, too. Mr. Wickstead had taken the gold, and then had been afraid that somebody was out to steal it from him. That's no way to live, the dragon thought quite sensibly.

But if he were not to guard treasure, what should be his Mission in Life? Dragons, like the rest of us, are at very loose ends if they do not have an Important Mission, and a dragon at loose ends is not something I wish to contemplate. (It is not perhaps an accident that significant numbers of adolescent dragons have been assigned to guarding hidden treasure, for it does serve to keep them occupied and off the streets.) Without a Mission, how would he organize his days? How would he spend his time? Dragons live a very long time, as you know, and the centuries ahead might look rather bleak if Thorvaald could not think of something important to do.

That was the long of it. The short of it was also vexing, especially with regard to the treasure. Mr. Wickstead and Pickles had returned the sacks to Briar Bank. Ought he to go back and sit with it, at least until the next time Yllva popped in? Unfortunately, there was no telling when that might be. She hadn't come along in the last three centuries. It was entirely possible that something had happened to her. Perhaps she was sick. Perhaps she had died!

It was that last thought that finally decided Thorvaald. He would not devote another minute of his life to guarding that treasure. He would fly back to Briar Bank (without making his presence known to Bailey, who was no doubt very angry with him, and quite right, too), pick up the treasure, and take it . . .

But where would he take it? Perhaps his cousin Thorwinn, at Money Hill, would agree to look after it. But he hated to offload his duty onto another dragon, and it had been a long time since he had seen Thorwinn, who might have given up his post centuries ago and gone off to be an explorer, which was what he had wanted to be when he was younger.

And then he thought of the British Museum, for that was what Thorvaald had heard Mr. Wickstead say to Pickles when he was putting the treasure back: "When the man from the Home Office gets here, we'll dig it up again and hand it over. It'll be better off at the British Museum." Yes, of course! If he took it there, the museum would go to the trouble of looking after it, and he could get on with his life. In fact, he thought, he might even zip over to Money Hill and suggest to old Thorwinn that—if he still had his treasure—he might drop it off at the museum, as well.

But of course things weren't all that simple. They never are, are they? Thorvaald went to Briar Bank early in the morning, which turned out to be very good timing. For he had no sooner slipped out of Briar Bank with the bags in his claws than he saw Yllva, cruising toward him in the early morning light.

Now, you may have grown comfortable with Thorvaald. He is, after all, a fairly amiable dragon who turns his fire to folks' advantage, using it to boil the kettle and make Briar Bank a cozier place for Bailey. It would not be wise, however, to feel too relaxed and easy with Yllva, for there was nothing at all amiable about her. Temperamental, possessive, obsessive, neurotic, irrational, and maniacally cunning, she had an inflammatory temper, and the slightest thing could make her fly off the handle. (As Thorvaald has said, temper is rather a liability when one has a fire in one's belly, for one has a tendency to scorch.) Her only vulnerability was her eyesight. She was nearsighted, which made it difficult for her to identify and acquire her target, let alone estimate its range. Her eyesight also gave her trouble when she was trying to judge her altitude, which made her landings a little uncertain. This vulnerability made this dragon even more dangerous, since a hungry Yllva might barbecue a whole flock of sheep when she was aiming for a single roast lamb!

Luckily, whilst Thorvaald spotted Yllva, she did not see him, or appear to suspect anything out of the ordinary, in spite of the downed yew tree that lay in front of the opening. Why should she? She would naturally expect that things would be just as she had left them some three hundred years before: she would catch her junior dragon napping on the job and chastise him severely, then make sure that the treasure was safe. Business as usual at Briar Bank.

Warily, Thorvaald hovered amongst the trees as Yllva folded her wings and crept into the opening that led to the Briar Bank dragon's lair. He was a safe distance away, but he still heard her angry shriek when she discovered that both he and the treasure were missing, and saw the smoke and lava-like fire that snaked out of the entrance. And when she burst out, she was angrier than he had ever seen her. Flame shot from her nostrils, steam belched from her mouth, her belly glowed an awful red, and she stamped on the ground so hard that the bushes and trees quaked with fear and the terrified rocks rolled away as fast as they could.

With three powerful strokes of her leathery wings, she climbed high into the sky and flew this way and then that, as though so blinded with rage she didn't know which way to go. And then, quite suddenly, she wheeled and began flying with purpose, as if she had spotted something.

"*Uh-oh,*" Thorvaald thought apprehensively. In this state, Yllva was dangerously unpredictable. There was no telling what she would do. He dropped the treasure sacks at the foot of a tall beech, rose into the air, and followed her, flying as fast as he could. Dragons have no rearview mirrors and are not likely to look over their shoulders (who in their right minds would be following them?), but he kept to the trees, anyway, and at a safe distance behind. In a moment, he saw what Yllva saw, and his heart leapt into his mouth.

What Yllva saw was Bailey. Wearing a heavy woolen coat and hat, the badger was trudging across the frozen surface of Moss Eccles Lake, a burlap sack slung over his shoulder. Thorvaald was close enough to be horrified by what he saw but too far away to do anything about it. Without a sound except for the flap-flap-flap of her wings, Yllva flew at the badger. Bailey flung up his arm to try to protect himself, but she snatched the sack from his shoulder, like an eagle seizing an unwary rabbit. Thorvaald knew exactly what she was thinking. Irrational as it may seem, she imagined that the badger had stolen the treasure—*her* treasure!—and was making off with it in that burlap sack.

Thorvaald tried to cry out, but his throat was so parched with fear that even his steam had dried up, and he could only squeak. Yllva, completely beside herself now, wheeled, and stroked her powerful wings to get up speed. She had saved the treasure, or so she thought, and now she was going to put a quick end to this meddlesome creature. She made straight for the defenseless Bailey, her dragon's mouth yawning as wide as the gaping crater of an erupting volcano, snorting fire and brimstone. But just at the last second, Bailey miraculously evaded her, leaping sideways and making a frantic headfirst dive into an open patch of water.

Now, Thorvaald had never been acquainted with badgers until he met this one, and had no idea that they could swim. In fact, water was a horrid, fearsome thing to him, for even a bucketful in the right place could quite easily put out his fire, and without a fire, he wouldn't be much of a dragon. So when Bailey sank like a stone into the black depths of Moss Eccles Lake, Thorvaald closed his eyes, convinced that his friend had drowned and feeling as if his dragon's heart would break in two. And it was all his fault, just as Mr. Wickstead and the tree had been his fault! If he had simply left the treasure where it was, Yllva would have merely taken it away and the badger, his dearest friend in all the world, would still be alive.

But there was no time for regrets or self-recrimination, for Yllva was angry beyond reason, beyond any thought, and she might do anything in her malicious spite. She might heat the water in the lake to boiling, hot enough for tea but far too hot for the poor fish. She might fly over the forests, setting the trees afire with her lava-like breath and baking all the birds on their branches. She might even shoot like a flaming arrow straight to the village and set the houses ablaze, killing all the men, women, and children. Somehow, she had to be stopped! How, Thorvaald didn't know, but he knew that he was the only one who could do it.

He beat his wings, rose up into the air, and looked around. There she was, off to the east, turning for another sweep of the area. What would she strike? Who would be her next victim? Bailey had eluded her, and she was mad with rage. That there would be another victim, he had no doubt.

Thorvaald flew toward her. When he was close enough to be heard, he reached deep inside himself and found a voice he had not known was his. It was the deep, cruel taunting voice in which dragons call to one another when they are provoked or provoking, the voice whose cadences are immortalized in *Beowulf*.

"Yllva!" he cried. *"Is that Yllva the She-Wolf? It is I, Thorvaald the Hoard-Guarder. Are you by chance looking for me?"*

Yllva turned and saw him. *"Thorvaald!"* she shrieked, and her cry licked the treetops with flame. *"Dim-witted dragon! Dunderhead! Dunce! No Hoard-Guarder, you! You allowed that wretched worm of a badger to off-snatch the treasure while you slept on unwitting. Fine keeper of rings and gold you are, Thorvaald! You shall answer for the trouble and toil I had getting it back."*

"Got it back, did you?" Thorvaald chortled ironically and clapped his wings together over his head in the insulting gesture that drives dragons mad with rage. *"Is that what you think, O Yllva the Short-Sighted? Look in that sack you clutch in your claws. You will find there no treasure, but twigs and trash!"* On that last taunt, he rose high above her, hovering while she peered into the sack.

Yllva looked. Then, with a scream of rage, she dropped the sack and turned on one wing. *"Where is it?"* she cried. *"What have you done with the treasure, Thorvaald the Unthrifty? Return it forthwith, or I shall hunt you to hell-gates, to the ends of the earth and beyond!"*

"Come then and get it," Thorvaald said. *"Follow me, old Astigmatic One, if you dare!"*

And with that, he wheeled, dipped, and flew as hard as he could, swinging and swerving and swooping just over the tops of the trees, right across Moss Eccles Lake, across Stony Lane, across the meadow and the silver thread of the frozen Wilfen Beck, toward the dark line of trees that marked the edge of Cuckoo Brow Wood. And there, just at the foot of Holly How, stood what he was looking for.

He glanced over his shoulder to see that Yllva, who was much stronger and faster than he, was gaining on him. This was going to require some challenging flying, and he wished he had put in a few more hours of practice. But he took a deep breath, climbed another hundred feet, and called out,

"Here I am, my myopic friend! Up here with the eagles!" He burped a belch of flame and waggled his wings.

"I'll eagle you, saucy whippersnapper," Yllva snarled, and climbed to catch him. *"You're nothing but a mouthful of sparks. When I'm through with you, you'll be cinders!"* She opened her mouth and blasted a flaming roar.

And then, just as Yllva was within scorching reach, Thorvaald did a very brave and, yes, a very foolish thing. He folded his wings, rolled, and dove down, down, down, straight down, faster than a plummeting falcon—the fastest-flying bird on earth—hurtles toward her prey, plunging straight for the ground. At the bottom of his dive, at the very last second before he crashed into the earth, he unfolded his wings and pulled up steeply, barely skimming the roof of a building that lay straight ahead.

And Yllva? Of course, she followed, rolling and diving and hurtling toward the earth. But she was the heavier dragon, and blinded by rage and blood-lust and her own poor eyesight. She could not at the last second pull up quite as fast as the more agile Thorvaald. She crashed into the building with all the explosive power of a fireball.

Yllva the Short-Sighted had blown up Lady Longford's haybarn.

"And then what happened?" cried Thackeray breathlessly, feeling that he had never heard such a thrilling story in his life. Not in the writings of Charles Dickens or Thomas Hardy, nor even Wilkie Collins or Lewis Carroll, although perhaps Robert Louis Stevenson—

"The barn was burning smartly," Thorvaald said, *"and it was clear that Yllva was being consumed by her own fiery rage. So I flew straight back to the lake to see if I could catch a glimpse of Bailey.*

But there was nothing, just that hole in the ice, and the black water." He looked at the badger and great dragon-tears began to run down his cheeks. "*I felt sure you were drowned, old friend.*"

"*You must have flown over during one of those times I was going under,*" Bailey said. "*There were too many of them to count. I tell you, I wouldn't have made it if young Thorn hadn't come along and pulled me out.*" Which necessitated the relating of that fortunate rescue, and of the day and a half Bailey had spent drying out and recuperating at The Brockery, and how he had met Thackeray there, over a sandwich and a bowl of potato soup, and discovered their mutual interests.

"*And you?*" Thorvaald asked Thackeray. "*Where did you come from? And how in the world did you manage to make your way to The Brockery?*"

Which required Thackeray to tell about Mr. Travers the book collector, and being sent off to the pet shop in South Kensington, where he and the incessantly chattering Nutmeg were bought by Miss Beatrix Potter, who intended to give him to a girl who lived at Tidmarsh Manor, where also lived an intrepid guinea pig named Tuppenny, who (when implored) led him over a vast glacier-like expanse of snow to The Brockery, where by the greatest good luck he was seated next to Bailey. And of course, all of this required another full pot of tea and second helps of sardines and salmon on crackers, whilst Bailey looked on, beaming and muttering, "*Dear chaps, dear, dear chaps.*"

By the time all the stories were told, it was getting past time for bed. All three friends retired and Thackeray was shown to his new quarters. With a gratefulness that shivered from the tip of his nose down to his very toes, he saw that the room was furnished with a full bookcase and even a shelf to put his candle on so that he could read in bed. Indeed, all three friends went to bed with very happy hearts that night, the dragon happiest of all, perhaps, because he had thought the badger was dead, and lo! he was alive and well and sleeping in the chamber right next door. But the badger was happy, too, for not only had he been reunited with his dear dragon, but he had discovered a new friend, one who would help him catalogue his library and with whom he could share the joy of reading every evening for the rest of their lives. And so they went on in this happy way for years and years, although it must be said that there will be some intense days ahead, when the dragon begins to seek his Mission in Life, and the badgers of the Land Between the Lakes learn about a terrible threat, not only to the health and well-being of the wild animals and the farm creatures, but to the welfare of all the Big Folk who share this beautiful land with them. But that is another story which I have not yet told, and I'm afraid that you shall have to wait for it.

What's that? I've left something out of this one? I have? Oh my goodness, I think you are right! You are wondering what has happened to the treasure, aren't you? Confess now, it's been on your mind ever since Thorvaald told us he dropped it at the foot of a large beech tree so that he could fly off in pursuit of Yllva.

Where is the treasure now? Who has it? What has become of it?

Well, then, here is the rest of the dragon's tale. After Thorvaald had given his friend up for lost, he returned sorrowfully to the beech tree, picked up the treasure, and flew off with it straight to London, through all sorts of bad weather. (Please don't ask me what map he used or how he navigated through the fog that blanketed the south of England that whole week, for I cannot tell you. Dragons take some things for granted, and don't bother telling the rest of us.)

But I do know that when Thorvaald arrived, it was nearly midnight, for the flight from Lakeland to London is quite a long one. He encountered a pea-soup fog as he flew into the city, a thick, odiferous brew of coal smoke, soot, and mist that reduced visibility to a few yards. Descending in the vicinity of Hampstead Heath and plotting his course by some remarkable built-in navigational capability that might baffle today's Royal Air Force, he made his way through the fog, flying low over Bloomsbury until he spotted the huge squarish bulk of the British Museum dead ahead. Hovering lightly over the steps that ascend from Great Russell Street, he saw a uniformed bobby dozing, propped against a lamppost. A moment later, the bobby came awake with a start as two leather sacks dropped at his feet, spilling their valuable contents across the pavement. He looked up to see where they had come from, but the fog was so thick that nothing at all was visible, except for a dim red glow that dwindled to darkness just as he caught sight of it.

And that is how the Viking hoard that Mr. Wickstead found at Briar Bank came to be delivered to the British Museum, where you can see it today.

21

Miss Potter Departs

It took several days, but things gradually got back to normal in the village of Sawrey. The snow lingered, as lovely as before, but the temperature moderated, the lanes became passable, and people began to get around with greater ease. The ferry boiler was repaired, and Henry Stubbs began his regular runs across Lake Windermere. The road was restored north and south of Hawkshead, and Jerry the charabanc driver could complete his circuit. The post was resumed, and Beatrix wrote her overdue letter to her mother, explaining that she had not been murdered in her bed. She did not relate all that had happened, but included a note to her father to let him know that Mr. Wickstead had been killed by a falling tree. "I expect to be home in time for the dinner party," she added, to reassure her mother. "I trust that all is well at Bolton Gardens."

All was certainly well at Hill Top, although her time there was flying by, happily but all too quickly, since there was so much to do. The children put on a perfectly lovely Christmas pageant at Sawrey School, the Sawrey Ladies Club gave a highly satisfactory Christmas Tea at the Sawrey Hotel, and the choir from St. Peter's came caroling through the village one magical night. Christmas trees appeared in cottage windows, topped with angels and alight with candles, holiday garlands were festooned over the entry to the Tower Bank Arms, and Lydia Dowling replenished the stock of *Ginger and Pickles* in her shop, much to Beatrix's pleasure.

There was work, too, but it was all enjoyable. She finished the drawings for *The Tale of Mrs. Tittlemouse* and readied the little book to be given as a New Year's gift to Harold Warne's little girl, Nellie. She painted several beautiful watercolors of snow scenes in the village as presents for friends. With Mr. Jennings, she drew up a plan to add several more cows and pigs to the Hill Top barnyard in the spring, and a dozen more ewes to the small flock at Castle Farm.

And she and Mr. Heelis walked several times up to Castle Cottage to look at the other work that had to be done there. Once, he came back to Hill Top with her and stayed for tea and she read him her new book and they laughed together over Mrs. Tittlemouse, much as she and Norman had used to laugh. If he were romantically interested in Miss Barwick, he gave no indication of it, and Beatrix gradually came to understand that poor Sarah's affection for Mr. Heelis was not returned. Briefly, she felt sorry—she would have liked for her friend to be happy—but only briefly. She did not ask herself why.

The day before she left for London, Mr. Heelis dropped in at Hill Top with some delightful news and a note for Beatrix. He had been to Raven Hall and brought word that Dimity Kittredge had just had her baby—a boy, a little brother for Flora. The note, from Dimity, said that the child was to be named Christopher Miles, after his father and his uncle, and that he was indisputably the strongest, handsomest, most perfect baby in the whole, entire world.

"A new baby! How wonderful!" gushed Tabitha Twitchit, who had followed Mr. Heelis into the house. She had come to visit her friend, Felicia Frummety, who often stayed with Miss Potter when she was at Hill Top. Tabitha, now retired from a long and distinguished career as a mother, was always thrilled to learn that another life had come into this world.

Felicia was lying on the hearth, enjoying the warmth of the fire. *"New babies are a great deal of work,"* she remarked critically. She was not particularly fond of infants. A vain cat, proud of her slim figure and on the whole rather lazy, she preferred to have none.

"I also have news," Mr. Heelis added, as Miss Potter got out the teapot, "about Knutson and Miss Mason."

"I was wondering what had happened to them," said Felicia. She sniffed. *"Proper villains, if you ask me."*

But not so very villainous after all, it seemed. After lengthy discussions on the matter, the magistrate at Hawkshead had determined that they would not be charged. Mr. Adams of the Home Office suspected the pair of stealing the treasure, but it now appeared that Mr. Wickstead himself had hidden it somewhere and there was no evidence to connect them with its disappearance. (The house and grounds had been searched several times, thoroughly, but nothing was found.) Captain Woodcock raised the issue of fraud and conspiracy, but there was so little evidence that the magistrate was not inclined to waste the Crown's time on prosecution.

"But they're getting off!" Felicia exclaimed indignantly. *"That's unfair. Evil should always be punished!"*

Tabitha gave a philosophical shrug. *"When you've lived as*

*long as I have, you will understand that sometimes evil is punished
in ways we don't recognize. We just have to trust that things turn
out for the best in the end."* She flicked her tail. *"If Mr. Wickstead hid the treasure, it must be somewhere nearby. Let's go find
Rascal and Crumpet and organize a search party!"*

Felicia turned over to toast her other side. *"What would
we do with a treasure if we found it?"* She yawned lazily. *"Let's
let somebody find it."*

"They've gone, then?" Beatrix asked. "Mr. Knutson and
Miss Mason?"

Yes and no. According to Mr. Heelis, Mr. Knutson had
gone back to Norway, presumably to continue his passionate
pursuit of all things Viking. Miss Mason, however, had decided that she very much liked the Lake District and, having a small income of her own, was currently in search of a
cottage, far enough away from the village so that she could
escape being recognized. Dr. Butters was using his considerable influence in the district to help her locate something
comfortable that she could afford.

"I am glad that she is not to be prosecuted," Beatrix said
thoughtfully. "There have been tragedies enough in this affair."

"And mysteries," Mr. Heelis said, handing her a copy of
the latest Kendal newspaper. "See if you can solve this one,
Miss Potter."

The paper was folded open to the second page, where
Beatrix saw a small article headlined, PTERODACTYL TEETH
FOUND IN BARN RUBBLE. It reported that the origin of the
fire that consumed Lady Longford's barn had not yet been
determined. A careful search had revealed no lump of mete-
oritic iron, although general opinion had it that the barn
had been struck by a meteorite. But the search had turned

up something rather unusual deep in the debris: several large pterodactyl teeth, like the fossilized teeth that had been found not very long before in the vicinity of Blackpool. The teeth had been sent to a noted authority on the pterodactyl fossils of the Cretaceous period. It was hoped that he would be able to shed some light on the discovery.

"How interesting," Beatrix said, handing the paper back. "But as far as a solution is concerned, I'm afraid I haven't a clue. I shall wait with interest for the report on the teeth."

"*Teeth!*" Tabitha cried. "*One shudders for the safety of the barn cats.*"

"*Oh, they're safe enough,*" Felicia replied dryly. "*They came caroling last night. Didn't you hear them?*"

As for sending the photographs of the claw marks on the yew tree to Professor Trevor Hall at Carlisle, that effort had yielded nothing. The professor could offer no suggestions at all, except to say that perhaps they were not claw marks, but marks of some tool or another that Billie Stoker and his brother might have used to drag the tree off poor Mr. Wickstead. However, since Billie Stoker swore up and down that no tools were used in the rescue effort, the matter had to rest there.

Two other things happened in the last few days that brought Beatrix a great deal of pleasure. She went up to Tidmarsh Manor when Mrs. King came to hear Caroline Longford play Mozart's "Fantasy in C-minor." Mrs. King pronounced Caroline sufficiently advanced to profit from her instruction, which pleased Lady Longford greatly, although she pursed her lips tightly together and scarcely acknowledged the fact. Caroline reported that Nutmeg had settled happily into life at Tidmarsh Manor, although the other guinea pig, the recalcitrant Thackeray, had mysteriously disappeared on the day of his arrival and nobody had the slightest idea where he had got to. Tuppence might have told, of course, but he was not asked.

And on the day before Beatrix was to return home, Deirdre Malone came over to tell her that very nearly all of the villagers had settled their overdue accounts and that the Suttons had reached a compromise with the bank. Courier Cottage was no longer in danger of being foreclosed, and Mrs. Sutton and all the little Suttons were safe.

"It's all thanks to you, Miss Potter," Deirdre said, and gave her a grateful hug.

"Not at all," Beatrix told her firmly. "You recognized the problem and came up with a solution. Mrs. Kittredge and I were glad to help you by spreading the word, but you are the one who should be thanked." She smiled. "I do hope Mr. Sutton will stop offering credit," she added practically. "It's such a temptation."

"P'rhaps he'll be more selective about it," Deirdre said. "And I heard Mrs. Sutton reading *Ginger and Pickles* to the little ones. When she got to the part where Henny Penny insists on being paid cash, she laughed so hard she cried."

Which made Beatrix smile. She wrote for children, but if grownups, too, enjoyed her books—well, all the better.

But at last, sadly, the day came when Beatrix had to return home. She packed her bags, left Hill Top in the watchful care of Mr. and Mrs. Jennings, and took the ferry back across the lake. At Windermere Station, she stopped to buy a newspaper before she boarded the train. When she was settled on the train and unfolded the newspaper to read it, a headline caught her eye:

VIKING HOARD AUTHENTICATED!
TREASURE DISCOVERED ON STEPS OF
THE BRITISH MUSEUM!

She read the article with interest, noting that the hoard, while a small one, was said to be the finest since the rich Cuerdale Hoard was discovered buried in a riverbank in Preston, Lancashire, back in 1840. But she couldn't help shaking her head at the irony of it all. Poor Mr. Wickstead was said to have discovered a great Viking treasure, but it could not be found. And now another hoard had turned up on the steps of the museum, "as if it dropped out of the sky," according to the astonished bobby who had found it.

" 'Twere magic, that's wot 'twere," said the bobby wonderingly, and it seems that nobody cared to dispute him.

Beatrix finished reading the article and made a note of the date the treasure would be put on display. She folded the paper, and gazed out the window at the wintry landscape flashing past. It was nice to live in a world where there was at least a little magic.

She would have to remember that, once she was back at Bolton Gardens.

HistorICAL Note

The Story Behind the Story

Beatrix Potter's life was never simple, but by 1909, it had become even more complicated than before, and was beset by a number of uncertainties that must have seemed to her very much like dragons. She was constantly at her mother's beck and call, and was required to arrange all the details for their holiday travels, as well as deal with the servants at home. She completed two books (*Flopsy Bunnies* and *Ginger and Pickles*) and began a third (*The Tale of Mrs. Tittlemouse*), paying her usual careful attention throughout the production process. She went to Hill Top Farm briefly in February and came back for a short time in April. In May, she purchased Castle Farm, on the northern outskirts of Near Sawrey. (Hill Top lies to the south.) During August and September, having settled her parents for the holiday at an estate near Bowness on Lake Windermere, she visited the farm frequently. She was back again in November, writing to Millie Warne that she had been tending to drains, the quarry, the fire insurance, the sale of pigs ("their appetites were fearful—five meals a day and not satisfied"), and the twenty white pullets she hoped would grow into good layers. The newly acquired farm brought her in closer contact with Willie Heelis, who had overseen its purchase and was acting as her property manager. Purchased for just £1,573, it was a good buy and, since it was already tenanted, would bring in some of the funds needed to cover improvements.

But more money was always needed, and (as I show in Chapter Nine) Beatrix had to continually ask Harold Warne—an owner with Fruing Warne of the company that published her books and a brother of Beatrix's fiancé, Norman—to pay what was owing to her. She wrote in March 1909, reminding him of a payment that was nearly thirty days past due. She wrote again in September, requesting two checks. She had to insist on having contracts prepared for books already completed and begged over and over again for a proper accounting for her royalties. Throughout this period, she grew increasingly annoyed at Harold for his carelessness in overlooking licensing possibilities, and as the years went on, she began to dread dealing with him. Later, she confessed to Millie Warne, Harold's sister, that she had long felt that there was a "great risk of ending in a smash." The smash—a calamity for both Beatrix and the Warne family—came in 1917, when Harold Warne was arrested, charged, and pled guilty to forging checks to the tune of some £20,000. Beatrix, the firm's most valuable asset, largest creditor, and a loyal supporter of Norman's family, worked to ensure its survival, creating a number of games, toys, and other merchandise, as well as developing a book of nursery rhymes and a painting book.[1]

1. Linda Lear tells the full story of this financial disaster and Beatrix's role in rescuing the firm in *Beatrix Potter: A Life in Nature*, pp. 284–89.

In Chapter Nine, I also mention the Potter piracies, one of the more interesting episodes in the long tale of Peter Rabbit. As Carol Halebian shows in her fascinating article "Peter Rabbit Piracies in America," piracies of Beatrix's work began even before the official publication of *The Tale of Peter Rabbit* and continue to this day. They range from a 1904 reproduction of the text with redrawn illustrations to "prequels, sequels, facsimiles, parodies and entire series, based wholly on the character of Peter Rabbit."[2] Beatrix herself was sadly aware of these piracies and understood that they all stemmed from Warne's omitting to register the American copyright to *Peter Rabbit*.

These elements of Beatrix's life—her property purchases, her dealings with Warne, her concern for licensing agreements—are all entirely factual. Other elements of *Briar Bank* are entirely fictional but are based in fact. For example, Mr. Sutton's veterinary business is invented: I have not seen any evidence that the Sawreys, Near and Far, had a resident veterinarian. (In earlier books, he is referred to as "Dr." I have now learned that this is incorrect, and that British vets are addressed as "Mr." I have made the correction in this book.) Beatrix Potter was a good citizen, deeply concerned for the health and well-being of the village, and organizing a drive to keep the village veterinarian is something she would have done. After Spanish influenza raged through the Lakes in 1918, she campaigned to create a district nursing association and hire a district nurse, raising the money through bake sales, jumble sales, and subscriptions. When the first nurse was hired, Beatrix gave her a rent-free cottage.

2. "Peter Rabbit Piracies in America," by Carol Halebian, in *Beatrix Potter in America: Beatrix Potter US Studies I,* edited by Libby Joy, Judy Taylor, and Ivy Trent. Published by the Beatrix Potter Society, 2007.

I must also mention the Storrs murder at Gorse Hall, a factual event that I stumbled upon when I was two-thirds of the way through the writing of this book. I had planned to have Beatrix discover the fraudulent "Miss Wickstead" by recognizing a photograph of her own Grandmother Leech's Stalybridge home pasted into the "Wickstead" family album. While I was looking for a photo of this house on the Internet, the word "murder" caught my eye. Within a few minutes, I had read several online accounts of the events of November 1, 1909. Feeling that this awful business would have troubled Mrs. Potter deeply (the murder must have seemed to her a personal insult, happening as it did in the house where she grew up), I rewrote the prologue to include a reference to it, and referred to it again in the scene where the fraud was uncovered. The Storrs murder is an interesting case with a variety of angles (some of which are explored in a recent television show).[3] But it's also distracting. I would have preferred to have left it out, except that it happened so near to the time I chose for this book that I felt it had to be included. The Gorse Hall murder, by the way, remains unsolved to this day. Although two men were tried (separately), neither was convicted. Our Miss Potter should have taken the case.

With all my fussing about reality and factuality, you may think the talking animals and the dragon—oh, yes, the dragon—a bit odd. But I confess to loving the animals, for I find that they offer dimensions of story that are simply not possible when the narrative is relayed only through human

3. The television show, produced by Julian Fellowes and available on DVD, is called "A Most Mysterious Murder." The Storrs case is featured in Series 1, Disk 2. An account of the murder may be read at http://www.gorse-hall.co.uk/murder.htm (accessed July 25, 2007).

characters. Beatrix Potter herself mingled fact and fancy in her stories, portraying her talking animals as realistically as possible. And while I have never found any evidence that Beatrix considered the possibilities of dragons, I do know that she believed in the powerful magic of nature and in a life-energy that informed even inanimate objects. In November 1909 (while at Sawrey, perhaps during a winter storm like the one in this book), she jotted down a lovely story about a penniless old lady who owns a singing kettle. Unfinished and unpolished, it begins this way:

> *Once upon a time there was a frosty night, eh but it was cold. The stars twinkled and the crisp herb crinkled, and the sheep fleeces froze to the ground.*
>
> *All across the fields was spread a sea of blue and silver moonlight, and the shadows of the trees and walls were very long and black. White gable ends and chimney stacks, and black under the eaves, and a floating whiff of peat smoke above Sally Scale's chimney. A white owl sat on the rigging and coughed.*
>
> *Then he flitted across to the roof of the inn where there is a row of pot chimneys with round smiling faces—at least there seem to be faces in them by moonlight—like five little old women in bonnets.*
>
> *The white owl made a bow to each old woman chimney. Then he flitted off the roof and over the little meadow, skimming over the white rag grass, and back across the orchard . . .* [4]

At the end of the story, when the old lady is sitting by the last of her peat, with the last of her candle sputtering beside

---

4. "The Little Black Kettle," in *A History of the Writings of Beatrix Potter,* by Leslie Linder, Frederick Warne and Company, London, 1971, pp. 330–31.

her, the magical white owl shows her a hoard of golden guineas hidden in her chimney.

I wouldn't be at all surprised to learn that Miss Potter also believed in dragons.

Resources

There are many excellent resources for a study of Beatrix Potter's life and work. Here are a few of those that I have found most useful in the research for the series as a whole. Additional resource material is listed in the previous books and on my website, www.cottagetales.com.

Denyer, Susan. *At Home with Beatrix Potter*. New York: Harry N. Abrams, Inc., 2000.

Halabian, Carol. "Peter Rabbit Piracies in America," in *Beatrix Potter in America*. Beatrix Potter US Studies I. Edited by Libby Joy, Judy Taylor, and Ivy Trent. Published by the Beatrix Potter Society, 2006.

Hervy, Canon G.A.K. and J.A.G. Barnes. *Natural History of the Lake District*. London: Frederick Warne, 1970.

Lane, Margaret. *The Tale of Beatrix Potter*, revised edition. London: Frederick Warne, 1968.

Lear, Linda. *A Life in Nature: The Story of Beatrix Potter.* London: Allen Lane (Penguin UK), and New York: St. Martin's Press, 2007.

Linder, Leslie. *A History of the Writings of Beatrix Potter.* London: Frederick Warne, 1971.

Potter, Beatrix. *Beatrix Potter's Letters.* Selected and edited by Judy Taylor. London: Frederick Warne, 1989.

Potter, Beatrix. *The Journal of Beatrix Potter, 1881–1897.* Transcribed by Leslie Linder. London: Frederick Warne, New Edition, 1966.

Potter, Beatrix. *Letters to Children from Beatrix Potter.* Selected and edited, with introductory material, by Judy Taylor. London: Frederick Warne, 1992.

Rollinson, William. *The Cumbrian Dictionary of Dialect, Tradition and Folklore.* West Yorkshire, UK: Smith Settle Ltd., 1997.

Taylor, Judy. *Beatrix Potter: Artist, Storyteller and Countrywoman,* revised edition. London: Frederick Warne, 1996.

Recipes from the
Land Between the Lakes

Raised Pie

A "Raised Pie of Poultry or Game," as served at the Wickstead funeral luncheon and described by Mrs. Beeton in her incomparable *Beeton's Book of Household Management*, was a pie baked in an embossed spring-form pan 3 to 4 inches deep. The pan was lined with a stiff pastry, which was then piled high with layers of boned cooked chicken or pheasant seasoned with mace, allspice, pepper, and salt; forcemeat (finely chopped, highly spiced meat); veal; and ham. This was covered with a decorated pastry top in a domed shape, rather like a lid, with a hole in the top. When baked, a thick gravy made from the bones was poured through the hole, and the pie was allowed to cool. The gravy, Mrs. Beeton says, "should form a firm jelly, and not be in the least degree in a liquid state."

Parsley's Savory Potato Soup

Potatoes were grown in every Lakeland garden and appeared in a variety of forms on every Lakeland table. Here's how Parsley makes the delicious potato soup she serves to a crowd of hungry animals at luncheon at The Brockery.

3 tablespoons butter

1 onion, diced

1 rib celery, diced

1 medium carrot, sliced thin

1 clove garlic, minced

2 tablespoons flour

3 cups chicken broth

¾ cup diced ham

2 medium potatoes, peeled and diced (about 2 cups)

½ teaspoon dried thyme

½ teaspoon dried ground bay leaves

1 cup half-and-half

½ teaspoon salt, or to taste

¼ teaspoon fresh ground black pepper

Heat butter in a large saucepan over medium-low heat. Add diced onion, celery, and carrot. Cook, stirring, until vegetables are tender. Add the garlic and cook for 1 minute longer. Stir in flour until well blended. Add chicken broth, ham, and potatoes. Continue cooking, stirring, until thickened. Add thyme and bay leaves. Cover and cook for about 10 minutes, or until potatoes are tender. Stir in half-and-half, add salt and pepper to taste, and reheat. Serves 4 Big Folk.

Mrs. Lester Barrow's Bread Pudding

Mrs. Barrow bakes bread pudding with apples and raisins and serves it warm, with a dollop of whipped cream, to Mr. Heelis and other appreciative patrons at the Tower Bank Arms.

> 2 cups milk
>
> 3 eggs, beaten
>
> 1/3 cup sugar
>
> 1/2 teaspoon salt
>
> 1/2 teaspoon vanilla extract
>
> 4 slices white bread, without crust, cubed
>
> 1 apple, cored and diced
>
> 1/2 cup raisins
>
> 1 teaspoon cinnamon, mixed with dash of nutmeg

Heat milk until hot, but not boiling. In a bowl, beat together eggs, sugar, and salt. Gradually stir a half-cup of the hot milk into the egg mixture. Stir in remaining milk. Add vanilla. Pour over cubed bread. Stir in apple and raisins. Pour into a 2-quart greased baking dish. Sprinkle cinnamon/nutmeg mixture over top. Bake, uncovered, at 300° for about 50 minutes, or until a knife inserted near the center comes out clean. Serves 6.

Bosworth's Nettle Beer

Nettle beer was brewed throughout the north of England. Wear thick gloves when you are gathering nettles, and avoid being stung by the plant. This traditional recipe comes from Maude Grieve's *A Modern Herbal* (1931) and is probably very similar to the one Bosworth used:

> The Nettle Beer made by cottagers is often given to their old folk as a remedy for gouty and rheumatic pains, but apart from this purpose it forms a pleasant drink. It may be made as follows: Take 2 gallons of cold water and a good pailful of washed young Nettle tops, add 3 or 4 large handsful of Dandelion, the same of Clivers (Goosegrass) and 2 ounces of bruised, whole ginger. Boil gently for 40 minutes, then strain and stir in 2 teacupsful of brown sugar. When lukewarm place on the top a slice of toasted bread, spread with 1 ounce of compressed yeast, stirred till liquid with a teaspoonful of sugar. Keep it fairly warm for 6 or 7 hours, then remove the scum and stir in a tablespoonful of cream of tartar. Bottle and tie the corks securely. The result is a specially wholesome sort of ginger beer. The juice of 2 lemons may be substituted for the Dandelion and Clivers. Other herbs are often added to Nettles in the making of Herb Beer, such as Burdock, Meadowsweet, Avens Horehound, the combination making a refreshing summer drink.

Mrs. Prickle-Pin's Comfrey Salve

Old Mrs. Prickle-Pin (*prickle-pin* is a country name for a hedgehog) had a great many recipes for various sorts of salves. Comfrey and plantain are traditional healing herbs that were much used by people who had no local pharmacy. Many relied on Nicholas Culpeper's *Complete Herbal* (published in 1653 and reissued in many editions) for information about medicinal plants.

> 2 cups olive oil
>
> 3 tablespoons fresh or 2 tablespoons dried comfrey leaves
>
> 3 tablespoons fresh or 2 tablespoons dried plantain leaves
>
> ½ cup beeswax

Put olive oil and herbs in the top of a double boiler. Simmer gently for 30 to 45 minutes, stirring frequently. (Do not allow to boil.) Strain to remove herbs; discard the herbs and set the oil aside. In the top of the double boiler, melt the beeswax, then add the strained oil and stir, blending thoroughly. Pour into jars or salve tins. When cool, label and date. (This will keep for about 12 months, longer if refrigerated.)

Sarah Barwick's Queen Cakes

For these feather-light cupcakes, Sarah uses a recipe that was developed by Elizabeth Raffeld (1733–1781), a well-known eighteenth-century Manchester confectionary, and preserved in her book *The Experienced English Housekeeper.* I wonder if Sarah had the time to beat her egg whites for "near half an hour"! However, unlike Mrs. Raffeld, our Sarah would have possessed one of the metal rotary egg beaters that came on the market after 1870, when Turner Williams of Providence, Rhode Island, patented the now-familiar hand-cranked beater with two intermeshed, counter-rotating whisks. It was an improvement on earlier rotary egg beaters that had only one whisk.

To make Queen Cakes

Take a pound of loaf sugar, beat and sift it, a pound of flour well dried, a pound of butter, eight eggs, half a pound of currants washed and picked, grate a nutmeg, the same quantity of mace and cinnamon. Work your butter to a cream, then put in your sugar, beat the whites of your eggs near half an hour, mix them with your sugar and butter. Then beat your yolks near half an hour and put them to your butter, beat them exceeding well together. Then put in your flour, spices, and the currants. When it is ready for the oven bake them in tins and dust a little sugar over them.

Glossary

Some of the words included in this glossary are dialect forms; others are sufficiently uncommon that a definition may be helpful. My main source for dialect is William Rollinson's *The Cumbrian Dictionary of Dialect, Tradition and Folklore.* For other definitions, I have consulted the *Oxford English Dictionary*, second edition (London: Oxford University Press, 1989).

Awt. Something, anything.

Auld. Old.

Betimes. Sometimes.

Bodder, boddersome. Trouble.

Charabanc. A long wagon with rows of seats facing forward.

Couldna. Could not.

Doan't. Does not.

Dust. Does.

Girt. Great.

Hasta. Have you?

How. Hill, as in "Holly How," the hill where Bosworth Badger lives.

Joinery. Carpenter's shop.

Knowsta. Do you know?

Mezzlement. Mystery, puzzlement.

Mezzling. Puzzling.

Nae. No, not.

Nawt. Nothing.

Off-comer. A stranger, someone who comes from far away.

Ownsel. Own self.

Pattens. Farm shoes with wooden soles and leather uppers.

Pickle. A person, usually a small child, who is always causing trouble.

Reet. Right.

Sae. So.

Sartain. Certain.

Sommat. Somewhat.

Tha, thi. You.

Tha'rt. You are.

Toffy, a toff. A term used to describe someone (usually wealthy) who is stylishly dressed and behaves in a superior and condescending way toward others.

Trice. Very quickly, all at once, "in a trice."

Verra. Very.

Wudsta. Would you?